Also by Cathryn Grant

Cathryn Grant

FACELESS

A Novel

DⁱC
D2C Perspectives

ISBN: 978-0-9896410-8-1

Give a man a mask and he'll tell you the truth.
— Oscar Wilde

Expose a man's face and he'll lie.

A Faceless Voice

EVERYONE THINKS I'M happy, enjoying life in the paradise called Silicon Valley. Friendly photos posted on social media define me — the good friend, always ready with funny and helpful comments, constantly available to click a pale red *favorite* star. They think they know me. They know what they see on my page, the pictures, the attempts at humor, the mundane stream of thoughts, the effort to be friendly and supportive, and nice.

They don't realize that I'll kill to get what belongs to me.

Maybe, someday, I'll post something true.

Allie

ALLIE SINCLAIR *NINE velvety red roses from Marcus on our third anniversary. A note that says: three years, squared, that's how much I love you. I think he's a keeper!*
83 favorites — 17 comments

Kristen Thomas *How extravagant!*
Kimberly Frank *Always the mathematician, isn't he?!*
Jake Ash *You're a keeper too, beautiful.*
Dave Eddington *I wonder what he'll do for your fifth?? Hard act to follow!*
Seth Porter *Congrats!*
Byron Jones *A rose by any other name . . .*
Adam Jamison *Happy Anniversary.*
Megan Miller *Lucky girl!!!*
Tiffany Jones *Have a beautiful, memorable celebration. Treasure your love :)*
[See 8 more comments]

THERE'S ONLY ONE thing I don't adore about Marcus. It's a small thing. Maybe a medium thing.

He's smart. He knows things like why Israel and Palestine don't get along and how to decide when to invest in a particular stock. It's not that I'm not intelligent, it's that I don't care about those things. I care about making the world better, and I care about my job, which is the same thing. I care about friends and parties. Not wild partying, not drinking, not pouring alcohol and squirting chocolate into someone's open mouth. Mostly I care about my friends and eating good food together and talking about everyday life.

He's good looking. His body is smooth and soft and hard in just the right way. I could lay my head on his belly for hours and never get tired of smelling his skin.

He's quiet and strong and devoted.

He has a very good job. It's a scary job for a wife to live with — a pilot for Freedom Airlines. Every eight days, he packs up his small suitcase, puts on his exquisitely-tailored uniform and heads out the door, disappearing for three or four days. Most of that time, he's either floating above the clouds, completely inaccessible, or sleeping in a hotel. His routes are domestic, but he dreams about flying all over the world. I don't dream about that. I have nightmares.

Marcus treats me like a goddess. He's always surprising me with flowers and little gifts and sometimes big gifts. On our third wedding anniversary, he gave me nine roses with a cute note about his love being squared. It was brilliant of him. To be honest, I was a little disappointed I didn't get more comments on my AboutFace post. I have 485 friends on AboutFace, and I know that lots of people miss updates, and lots of people don't know what to say, a few might be jealous.

Seventeen is more than most of my friends get for their status updates, but still . . . seventeen out of 485?

The one thing about Marcus that I don't adore is that he doesn't like AboutFace. He doesn't like any social media. How he knows he doesn't like it, I have no idea, because he's never opened an account. He hardly glances at it if I hand him my phone to show him a picture someone posted when all he's doing is watching a baseball game. He knows the names and stats for all the members of San Francisco Giants, a bunch of strangers, but he doesn't want to look at what's going on in our friends' lives. I don't get it.

We sort of fight about it. Not yelling fights, but arguing, both of us saying the same things over and over and never getting anywhere. He treats AboutFace like it's a monster — destroying society, eating us alive. He actually said that, as if AboutFace is a living entity, lurking in dark alleys where it waits to attack.

I'd die if I didn't have AboutFace. It makes me feel like my friends and I are together all the time. Some of my friends work long hours, and we can't see each other every week, or even every month. But we know what's going on, and we feel close because we update each other every day, several times a day. Tiffany and Byron just had their baby girl, and it's hard for them to get out, but we see the pictures, and all of us support her when she's awake in the middle of the night. Marcus thinks it's stupid. He thinks if we want to be supportive, we should bring them a meal or offer to babysit so she can take a nap. That's nice too, but there's not always time.

Marcus has lost touch with most of his high school friends. He emails three of them and sees two of them a few times a year. That's all! My friends and I are as close as we were in high school.

ON HIS MOST recent trip, Marcus had flown a route that went San Francisco — Chicago — New York — Dallas. He'd called when he got off the plane. I wish he'd text me the minute he lands, but I don't like to complain and spoil our reunion.

I was sitting at the kitchen table, waiting for him.

It was thirteen minutes after four when he got home. Just before he turned into the driveway, I looked at my phone, and of course, I can never hear the Prius, so I was surprised to see him getting out of the car. I liked that he was able to surprise me even when I'd been waiting for an hour. I put my phone in the back pocket of my jeans, then realized he might feel it when he hugged me, so I pulled it out and put it on the half-wall that divides the dining room from the living room.

I skipped to the front hall and turned the deadbolt before he could put his key in the lock. He looked so good. I hate, hate, hate worrying when he's up in the air, and I miss him horribly. But the upside is we appreciate each other more than most couples because when he comes home, it's like falling in love all over again. We're so excited to look at each other's faces, so anxious to touch the other's skin, to kiss, to make love. We sit across the table staring at each other, forgetting to eat for minutes at a time.

The suitcase wheels rattled on the tile as he pushed it through the door and off to the side. He nudged the door closed with his heel and wrapped his arms around my waist. His jacket smelled like warm cotton. I moved my face away from his shoulder and kissed his neck, which smelled even better, his skin, a smell that I could pick out of twenty men if I were blindfolded. He squeezed me tighter, moved his head until our mouths came together. His body, pressed against mine, was growing hard, fast. We kissed a bit longer and I pulled back, giving him little kisses on his lips and nose. "I made something new."

"Mmmm. Real food." He took off his jacket and hung it over his forearm. "I'll grab a shower first."

It was early to eat dinner, but he's always hungry when he gets home. His body clock is pretty much messed up fifty percent of the time. I wonder how that is for pilots who are international. Just the time from east coast to central to the west coast gets him slightly off balance. I can't imagine never knowing whether it was day or night, today or yesterday or tomorrow.

His suitcase clacked across the tile. He stopped, grabbed the handle, and carried it up the stairs. I watched him climb until he disappeared at the top landing. The last thing I saw was his left heel with the leg of his slacks flapping at his black wingtip shoe. Seeing him, then not seeing him, made me feel, for a moment, as if the heel of his wingtip had kicked me in the chest. It seemed as if I'd only imagined him coming home, and now he was gone, not really in the house at all. Sometimes when he's flying, I feel that he exists only in my imagination. It's a strange weaving together of terror that he's going to crash and evaporate from the earth, with a collapsing of time so that all the things we've done together live only in my head.

I turned and walked into the kitchen. My toe ring had slipped forward, and the metal clicked softly on the tile. I twisted the corkscrew into a bottle of Zinfandel and eased the cork out. I untwisted the cork from the metal spear and laid them both on the counter. I poured a few splashes into a glass for Marcus. I filled another wine glass with orange-flavored sparkling water. I carried the glasses into the dining room and placed them on the table.

For dinner, I'd made pork tenderloin with balsamic-cranberry sauce, quinoa almond pilaf, and baby green beans. The salad was arugula with pears, feta cheese, and pine nuts, drizzled with vinaigrette. I adore cooking. There is not one single food I don't love, and I could make a whole career of eating. People get annoyed that I can eat so many rich foods and stay thin, but I guess they don't see how many laps I swim every day. When I started college, I thought I'd go to culinary school, but then life happened, and I got sidetracked. I love having friends over and cooking amazing food for them. But I also love doing it just for Marcus.

When he came downstairs, his hair was wet. He hadn't shaved which looked very sexy. I kissed him, and we wrapped ourselves around each other and kissed for a while longer.

He carried the plates of salad into the dining room. I pulled out my phone and scrolled through AboutFace.

There weren't any more posts since I'd looked while he was in the shower, but there were a few more comments on Jake's mysterious post. I'd first seen it while I was making the vinaigrette. There was a picture of Jake, all blonde and surfer-like, which hides his true self as a very savvy PR guy. The picture showed him at Joya in Palo Alto with three guys I didn't know. They were holding glasses of scotch in a four-way toast, the light shining directly into the gold liquid, so it glowed like moonlight.

Jake Ash *If you know what these guys are involved with, you know my next venture.*

It was driving me crazy. Jake has a knack for changing jobs. Since college, he's had five jobs — two with global corporations, and three with start-ups. Two of the start-ups flopped in the first nine months. After one of his flops, I commented on his post that it was like a stillborn baby. Tiffany Jones was pissed about that. She said I was morbid and thoughtless and hurtful, and people should be careful what they post. It's not like she'd had a stillborn baby, so I don't know why she got all worked up about it. But she's always crusading for speaking pure, wonderful niceness on AboutFace.

Marcus came back into the kitchen and picked up the dinner plates. "Are you checking updates?"

"I wanted to see . . ."

"I just got home."

"I know, but I'm dying of curiosity. Jake got a new job." I turned my phone so he could see the photo.

"Where?"

"I don't know."

We walked into the dining room. He set the plates on the table and pulled out my chair. I sat down, and he kissed the top of my head, pressing his nose into my scalp for a minute. He lifted his wine glass, glowing with red liquid and I lifted my glistening, orange-infused sparkling water.

"To us," Marcus said.

We clicked our glasses, and I thought about Jake's photo. I was sure I'd never seen those guys before, but maybe I should look again. I took a sip of orange goodness.

Marcus sat down and took another sip of wine. "If you talked to him, he could tell you the name of the company."

"Maybe not."

"That's what's wrong with AboutFace."

"I know."

"If he honestly wanted to tell you about his new job, he'd tell you. Not post pictures like he's releasing a movie trailer."

"I know."

"He's turning it into a press release."

"Not really. If he did that, I'd know the name of the company." I smiled.

I sipped my drink. It bubbled down my throat, energizing me, making me hungry for more pork and green beans. I'd skipped lunch so I'd be ravenous for our early dinner. "He's probably going to reveal a little bit each day."

"That's weird. So self-conscious."

"It's fun. Did those guys look familiar to you?"

He shook his head.

"A few days ago, he said he had something exciting in the works."

"Said, or posted a comment?"

I sighed. "Don't be like this."

"When was the last time you had a real conversation with him? At the St. Patrick's Day party?"

"I think so."

"Three months. You haven't talked to him for three months."

"He's been busy. We've been busy."

"You can't read about someone's life and click favorite and make one-sentence comments and call that a friendship. You just can't."

"I hate it when you get all preachy."

"I saw your open page on the computer when I was putting my keys in the desk. I don't like that you told everyone about the card I gave you."

"Why not?"

"I just don't. It was private."

"It was sweet. Everyone loved it."

"Now I'm your social media cachet?"

"It's not like that."

"You took something just between us and turned it into an exhibition."

I pinched a piece of feta with my fingers and put it on my tongue. It was exhausting trying to explain why I loved AboutFace. He was so stubborn. The cheese spread like liquid around the inside of my mouth. After a minute, there wasn't anything left to chew. I swallowed it. "Why are you so anti-social?"

"Avoiding all those mindless updates doesn't make me anti-social."

"Everyone's on AboutFace."

"I'm not."

"Everyone but you. I like staying in touch with my friends."

"You aren't in touch. You have eight hundred friends, and you only talk to a handful at parties."

I laughed. Even though it wasn't true, I didn't have eight hundred, thinking about all my friends gave me a good feeling. "I don't have eight hundred friends."

"Whatever."

"If it makes you feel better, I won't post anything about you."

He smiled, but his smile looked soggy like he couldn't quite lift his lips up where they should be. Then he looked down and stabbed his fork into a piece of arugula, then another, then a third. He poked the fork into a piece of feta. It broke apart. He gave up and put the arugula in his mouth. When he finished chewing, he started talking about a movie he'd seen during his layover in New York.

While he talked, I sipped my orangey water. My mind wandered over to the cat Kristen had rescued. It was solid gray, the cutest little thing. She'd put up fifteen pictures already and she'd only had it for two days. Seeing those pictures was a relief after Kristen's other posts. For an entire week, she posted articles about human trafficking. I only read one of them, but every time I saw a headline, it reminded me of what I'd already read, and it was too upsetting to think about. I don't know why she does that. It's not like we can do anything about it. I decided to tell Marcus about the cat and show him those adorable pictures another time.

Allie Sinclair [*Uploaded 3 images*] *Pork tenderloin, quinoa, and baby greens. Pear, arugula, and feta cheese salad. I feel like the real me when I cook. LOL. [46 favorites — 15 comments]*
　　Kristen Thomas *Delicious*
　　Pam Jamison *Excellent!*
　　Megan Miller *When are you inviting me to dinner?? ;)*
　　Jake Ash *You're always real, Allie!*

Dave

DAVE EDDINGTON *CHARLIE'S wife had the twins. Babies, Dad, and Mom are doing good. Cheers, bro!*
20 favorites — 15 comments

Allie Sinclair *Congrats, "Uncle" Dave :) Is that the brother who was two years ahead of us?*

Dave Eddington *Yeah, Charlie and Deborah.*

Allie Sinclair *Post some pics, we'll see if they look like you.*

Tiffany Jones *Children are a gift!! I'll keep the new little family in my prayers.*

Byron Jones *Twins mean you're twice blessed.*

Allie Sinclair *How is Ruth doing, Tiffany?*

Byron Jones *Giving us a run for our money.*

Allie Sinclair *You must be exhausted. Hang in there.*

Tiffany Jones *:)*

Byron Jones *Tiff takes the night shift . . . Since she can sleep when the kids are napping.*

Seth Porter *They say you can sleep when you're dead.*

Byron Jones *LOL. True enough.*

Tiffany Jones *But creepy. And I want to sleep now! :) Jesus will give me strength.*

Byron Jones *One day at a time.*

Charlie Eddington *Thanks Uncle Dave. Deb says hi, and so do the new kiddos!*

IT'S STUNNING THE way people hijack my posts, anyone's posts. Especially Allie. The woman can't live without commenting on every single post. Her stream is the most active one I know, and she doesn't just favorite what other people say, she has to get her voice in there and make their news feeds her own. Sometimes I think she has the feed running straight through her head. I don't want to think bad thoughts about her — she's a good friend. I've known her since grade school, and she's always been the same — talking, asking about everyone else's life, laughing, having people over, telling stories. Everyone likes her. It's impossible no to like her.

And in the end, even though she took over my update, I was glad she asked about Byron and Tiffany's new baby. I had the idea that after six months, things got easier with kids, but it sounded like they were having a tough time. I decided I'd pull the weeds sprouting under the magnolia tree, head out to the driving range to hit a bucket of balls, and after that, make a pot of my five-bean chili. The next day, on my way to work, I'd take it over to Byron and Tiffany.

GROUND BEEF SIZZLED in the pan with browned onions and garlic. Not a lot of onion, a little goes a long way. And the beans — pinto, Great Northern, black, kidney, and garbanzo — were in the colander, rinsed and ready to throw in. Most of the time, I use the real deal — dried beans that I soak and cook myself — but I ended up hitting three buckets of balls instead of one, and I ran out of time.

I had a big tiling job at a house in the foothills starting the next day. I planned to drop the chili off before heading out there. I'm a take-action kind of guy, and I wanted Byron to know their friends were behind them all the way.

Byron and Tiffany can be a little annoying with their God-this and Jesus-that, but they're great people. I've known Byron almost as long as Allie. When Byron married Tiffany a few years ago, she fit right in with the rest of the group from high school. Their kids are the cutest things I've ever seen. The boy is talking now, and Tiffany posts some of his questions on AboutFace. The kid can kill you without any clue as to how funny he is. The other day he said, *If Jesus gives joy in our hearts, how come Ruthie screams all the time?* I'd like to have been there to hear Byron and Tiffany explain that one, but she only posted the question, not the parental response.

I dumped the meat and onions and garlic in the pot with the beef stock and started sautéing chopped red bell pepper in the juice. That's one of the secrets to my chili — red pepper gives it a hint of sweetness, along with the honey. It helps tone down the greater than usual amount of chili powder and red pepper flakes. It's not that I'm a chef who cooks all the time. A guy on his own has to learn to do some cooking. I have three standard recipes — chili, spaghetti (but who doesn't), and barbecued chicken with grilled corn on the cob. The rest of the time I pick up a burger or a sandwich. Or go out with friends. The chili's the best though.

When the peppers were limp with a touch of brown along the edges, I added them to the meat, dumped in the beans, and sprinkled in the chili powder. Usually, I add red pepper flakes, but I figured the kid wouldn't like that. I turned the gas down to simmer.

In the morning, I showered, ate some toast with jam, and drank two cups of coffee.

At seven-twenty, I pulled up in front of Byron's house. It's a cottage, built in the fifties, but updated a bit with double-pane windows and a solid front door with blue glass panels at the top. The interior is partially remodeled — I laid the kitchen and bathroom tile for them. I gave them a deal — the cost of tile and supplies with my labor for free. It was the right thing to do. Friends have to help each other out. I know they'll have an opportunity to do something for me someday. Maybe babysit when I have kids, maybe something else.

Byron's Cherokee was already gone. He keeps long hours, bookkeeping at night, getting in before dawn to make vats of potato salad and coleslaw, even though he doesn't open the deli until eleven, six days a week. It's closed on Sundays. I gotta give them credit for sticking to their principles by keeping the Sabbath and all that. The place is the whole livelihood for their family. Staying closed on Sundays works well for them, though. Probably because all their church friends are quick to support the place Monday through Saturday.

There was a slight risk that Tiffany was still asleep, but from what she posted in her status updates, it sounded like one kid or the other was pretty much awake all the time. Sure enough, as I walked up the front path, I saw the glow of the TV through the living room drapes. I put the pot, wrapped in a bath towel, on the front porch. I rang the bell and picked up the pot. Just as I thought I was going to have to put it down and ring again, Tiffany opened the door.

"Dave. Hi." Her hair was in a ponytail, and she had on a terry cloth robe over a t-shirt and exercise pants. Her feet were bare. Her toenails were longer than average. I guess a new mom doesn't have as much time for details like nail trimming. It actually looked kind of sexy for some reason that I couldn't quite explain to myself. I dismissed the thought and lifted the pot of chili.

"What's this?"

"Dinner. Hopefully for two or three nights. It's my chili. I made it mild so Paul can eat it."

"You didn't have to do that."

"I saw what you posted — that you weren't getting much sleep. Maybe you can grab a nap instead of cooking dinner."

"That is *so* sweet." She stepped back and opened the door wider. "Do you mind bringing it into the kitchen?"

"Not at all." I glanced down again at her freakishly appealing toenails as she moved away from the door. Her feet sank into the carpet, looking even whiter against the dark green fibers. I walked through the living room, saying hi to Paul, who jumped up and followed me into the kitchen. I was honored that he found the smell of the chili more interesting than the animated animals he was watching. I set the pot on the counter next to six pale blue cereal bowls with milk rings glued around the bottoms. I pulled away the towel, leaving the pot on the counter. "You can put this pot in the oven or on the stove." I wadded up the towel and held it in one hand like a misshapen football. "Or put the chili in bowls and microwave them. If you put the pot in the oven too long, it might overcook and the beans will get mushy, so be careful." I turned.

She was nodding, gripping the front edges of her robe.

Paul pointed at the pot. "What's that?"

"Dinner," I said.

"It's not dinnertime." He hopped across the tile and onto the carpet in the other room.

"He's getting big," I said.

Tiffany let go of her robe and moved out of the doorway. "Too big. They grow up so fast."

"They do."

"But he's still not toilet trained." She spoke softly, hiding her voice from Paul, or her own shame, I wasn't sure which.

"He's not even four."

"He's late."

"I don't know anything about that." I wasn't sure why she

was telling me. Maybe she told everyone. Her world consisted entirely inside that tiny house, so maybe it made events like toilet training seem bigger than they were. At least she didn't post it on AboutFace. A lot of mothers would. My mother never would have — she was as ashamed as Tiffany seemed to be. Of course, I was older — eight when I was still wetting the bed. My mother told me I was a big baby. She also said I was a filthy boy. She said she wouldn't tell my father — he'd be disgusted with me. But I think she told him after all because he always seemed disgusted. It doesn't help your life when the man who's supposed to be on your team shudders when he looks at you. I shook out the towel and folded it in a square and tucked it between my elbow and ribs. "Enjoy the chili."

"We will. Thank you so much. You sure went to a lot of trouble. Thank you."

"No trouble."

She smiled. It seemed as if she didn't want to let me go, blocking the doorway instead of moving away so I'd take a cue to walk back to the front door. But we didn't have much to say to each other. I was mostly friends with Byron. Sure, I'd spent a lot of time around her — weddings, parties, watching the NFL playoffs at their place, laying their tile. She'd said I was a real artist when she saw how I placed the pattern at the threshold, the way it all fit like puzzle pieces, the way the kitchen floor seemed to flow like a single piece of variegated stone. But even with all that, I don't think we'd ever spent more than five minutes alone. It's probably hard for women who spend all day in a small space with no adults — talking to the kids, but mostly talking to herself — to remember how to carry on a conversation with someone their own age.

"Did you see Jake has a new job?" she said.

I had no interest in discussing Jake the fake. Hotshot PR guy gliding from one cushy job to another. The guy was my age and he drove a Porsche. I'd be lucky to have a car like that when I was fifty, after a lifetime of hard work. But at least it was honest work, real work. Using my hands, not making money, off talking bullshit all day every day. I was a craftsman, not a bullshitter. "Yeah, I saw. Big mystery. It shows how our society is messed up, that some guy who does nothing but tell people what his company is up to, sends stuff out to bloggers and social media or whatever, gets paid boatloads of money. For what? All that stuff is free. Why do they *pay* someone to do that? And pay them a lot. And teachers and nurses get shit. I don't understand it. I really don't. Or mothers, for that matter. They don't pay you."

"I . . ."

"Mothers are the glue of the world, the thing that makes or breaks every human being. I can see that about my mother. She can be a pain, but really, she has my back. And she's always there for me. Mothers work hard, and then the world tells them they didn't really do anything. A minimum wage daycare provider could do what they do. Or that Dads are all-fire important and Dads are so great when they show up one day a week. It's really all unbalanced. My sister argues with my Mom all the time, and I try to tell her how she should be kinder, more grateful, but she won't listen to me. No one listens to me. I think about a lot of things, and I think I have some insights. But no one listens."

She smiled. "Did you know any of those guys in the picture? He made it sound like it was the next social media phenomenon."

"Never seen them before." I leaned against the counter, bumping the cereal bowls with my elbow. Spoons clattered against the ceramic.

"Sorry about the mess," she said.

"Doesn't bother me."

She smiled and her eyes creased up, highlighting the smudged makeup under her bottom lashes. She looked so young, hardly old enough to have two kids.

"Is the baby sleeping?"

"Yeah. Good timing. She's been up since three, and now that Paul's up and running around, she decides to sleep."

"Must be tough."

"They're a blessing. I don't mean to complain. I'm just tired."

"And now you have dinner!"

"Yes. Thank you so much. My prayer was answered."

The way she said it sounded like something much more significant than a pot of chili on her kitchen counter. I was afraid to ask what prayer, but she must have seen the question oozing off my skin.

"I asked the Lord for a sign."

"A sign of what?"

"A sign that He thinks I'm a good mother. A good wife."

"How is me bringing chili a sign of that?" She was scaring me a little. Her eyes looked wider, as if she saw me as an archangel or something, more than a guy who decided to make a pot of chili, someone manipulated by an outside force. And maybe I am. Maybe we're all controlled by outside forces. How would we even know?

"I don't always have the energy to cook. Or do the dishes. Or clean. Even to feed the baby sometimes. I feel like I'm not being a good mom, that I'm letting Byron down because I'm so tired. He needs a good dinner . . . and stuff."

I nodded. I still didn't see the connection.

"This is like a miracle. Not something I planned. And so I think God is telling me my priorities are straight. That He's taking care of our needs and I should keep doing what I'm doing. Now Byron has a good dinner and I can get the dishes done, and I don't have to go to the store today. Well, I guess I still have to do that because we're out of milk. And laundry soap." She laughed. "Don't think I'm asking you to run errands for me, I'm just explaining."

"Do you want me to run to the store?"

"Oh, no. Please. I'm so tired, I don't filter what I'm saying sometimes." She giggled and moved out of the doorway.

"You've done more than enough. I'm sure you need to get going."

"I should."

She followed me to the front door.

I turned. "I could do some errands after work."

"No. Really. I'm just babbling. I need to get out of the house anyway. And Paul likes it."

"Okay. Well, enjoy the chili."

"Byron will bring your pot back."

"No hurry." I stepped onto the front porch.

She pulled the screen closed. "Thank you so much."

"Glad I could help."

"You delivered God's love right to my kitchen."

"Okay. If you say so."

I waved and started down the path.

Before I realized it was there, my foot landed hard on a snail. Three others were crossing from one side of the lawn to the other. I felt bad, leaving the snail in a big pile of goo to die on the pavement, but I hadn't seen it. If they have so little concern for their lives that they're always crawling around underfoot, then I can't be watching out for them.

I wondered about Tiffany, carrying a baby down the path, not looking at the ground, her bare feet with those remarkable toenails stepping on the wet, broken body of a snail.

Tiffany

TIFFANY JONES PROOF, *again, that the Lord hears our prayers before we speak them. Click favorite if it's happened to you. If it hasn't, read Psalm 107:28-30 — you'll be blessed.*

24 favorites — 10 comments

Allie Sinclair *What happened?*

Tiffany Jones *Dave brought us a huge pot of delicious chili. It's enough to feed all of us for three nights and gives me a nice break from cooking :)*

Dave Eddington *Glad I could help.*

Allie Sinclair *If I pray, will I get chili, Dave?*

Kristen Thomas *What a sweetheart.*

Dave Eddington *Have a baby, Allie, and we'll see.*

[See 4 more comments]

BYRON ATE TWO bowls of chili and four pieces of the cornbread I bought to go with it. "Chili's okay," he said. "The bread is dryer than the Sahara."

"Sorry."

"No problem, Baby. The chili soaks in."

"It's delicious." I took a small bite.

"It's okay. It bugs me that he showed up with dinner."

"Why?"

"He didn't even tell us he was coming over."

"So? He saw my comment that I was tired. He's trying to be nice."

"Don't complain online. It makes me look like I'm not taking care of you."

"I was just being honest. You're doing great." I put my hand on his knee. "But the dinner is really nice. A huge help."

"It's weird. He's a weird guy."

"You think everyone is weird."

"He was weird in high school. We thought he was gay."

I took my hand off his knee. I know what the Lord says about being gay, but still, I hate it when Byron thinks every guy who isn't exactly like him is gay. "Don't say that."

"Sorry. That's what we thought. And normal guys aren't so *thoughtful*. Bringing dinner."

"Men can be thoughtful. You're thoughtful."

"Yeah?"

I stood and picked up his bowl. I took the spoon out of my bowl and nested his on top of mine. Ruth poked her tiny index finger at the peas I'd put on the tray of her high chair. She pushed a pea to the edge of the tray, squashing it against the lip. She giggled. She reached for another pea, picked it up, and put it in her mouth. I smiled. I could watch a baby eat peas for an hour. They're so methodical and so excited that they can make their fingers cooperate.

Byron pushed out his chair. "Go take a bath. I'll wash the dishes."

Washing the dishes meant taking three bowls, three bread plates, three glasses, three spoons, and standing them up in their slots in the dishwasher. Still, I smiled and kissed his cheek. I was happy about him loading the dishwasher, but I didn't like him directing me to take a bath — to get all cleaned up for him. What if I wanted to put on my sweats and watch TV, without anyone touching me? No baby sucking on my breast, no little boy patting my face and touching my hair and climbing on my lap. No husband trying to do all those same things.

I hadn't had ten minutes to myself for fifty-three hours, not that I was counting.

When Dave brought the chili over, I'd just settled Paul in front of the TV, and Ruth was finally asleep. I'd put on *Start Over* by the *Afters*, which I like to listen to almost every day. I can never sit still for that song. I was trying to dance quietly, with the music low. It isn't nearly as much fun as when it's so loud you can feel it in your bones, but I didn't want Paul to get curious and come knocking on the door.

When I was growing up, I took dance classes. I think I was pretty good. But once I accepted Jesus, my youth group leader made me realize I shouldn't be doing that in public — wearing tight, skimpy clothes and shaking myself around. The problem is, dancing never went out of my blood. When I'm in a good mood, I want to dance. I like feeling my body move. It gives me energy so I'm not as tired, and it makes me happy and glad to be alive. I know it's not what I should be doing — jazz moves to Christian songs, but the beat makes me want to dance. I don't think that's terrible, as long as I just do it in my bedroom.

Then, the doorbell rang, and Dave was standing there, and I wondered if my cheeks were red and he could tell I'd been dancing.

CHILI BURNED IN my stomach while I ran the water in the tub. Usually, I love soaking in steaming water, bubbles covering up my body so I don't see the fluffy skin left by the babies. The hot water creeps into my veins and up to my head, and everything sort of unwinds until I feel loose and warm and soft. After a bath, it's the best when I can get between clean sheets and curl up on my side and let the warmth inside my skin rock me to sleep, like a baby myself. Of course, the sheets weren't fresh and clean. It had been over a week since I washed sheets. Ruth spit up nearly every time I burped her, and her diaper leaked onto her outfit at least once a day, and Paul couldn't even play on his bedroom floor without somehow getting dirty. So every day the washing machine was running, but no sheets.

The bubbles smelled like berries, foaming up so high I couldn't see how much water there was underneath. I climbed in and settled down. The water was a little lower than I like, so it didn't feel quite as comfy. I closed my eyes. After a few minutes, I heard Byron take Paul into his room to read a story. I knew Ruth would be ready to nurse before long. The last thing I wanted was for her to start screaming while I was soaking in the tub. It was better to get out while the water was still hot and make sure I could feed her while she was still in an okay mood.

I stood up. Bubbles clung to my skin. I wiped them off with my hands. I flipped the drain open, and while the water ran out, I turned on more water and splashed it on myself to get rid of the remaining foam. I stepped out, dried myself, took the elastic band out of my hair, and put on a long nightshirt, undies, and my robe.

I stepped out of the bathroom into the cool air of the hallway. Paul's light was out. I was impressed that Byron got him settled down so quickly. I wished he could maneuver Paul into lying down that quickly every night. Sometimes it seems like a game that Paul's winning, with the cup of water, and the extra story, the Bible story after that. Then there's getting up to check on baby sister Ruth, the getting up again to say good-night to his toys in the living room . . . he's definitely winning.

After Ruth was fed and in her crib with her light out, I checked the locks, got my own glass of water, and turned out the kitchen light. I went into the bedroom. Byron was sitting up in bed like I knew he would be. He was naked. He smiled and stretched out his arms. "Come see me, Mommy."

I sipped some water and put the glass on my nightstand.

Everything in me wanted to tell him I was so tired I was ready to cry, but I knew that was not what God wanted from me. And if I can't do *every* single thing God wants, I can certainly love my husband, which is the most important of all. In some ways, it's my job to love him. It's his job to take care of our family financially, and to protect us, to guide us. It's my job to take care of his physical needs — feed him and keep the house clean and be available when he wants to make love. Thinking about being tired was just self-pity, the main point being *self* — thinking only of my *self*, putting my *self* first.

I got into bed. Byron slid down onto his back and turned toward me. He tugged on my arm to get me to lie down, just like Paul does to get me to sit on the floor and roll the police car after the dump trunk he's pushing.

"Turn out the light," I said.

"I like looking at your body."

"I'm flabby."

"I like your little belly. You look perfect."

I closed my eyes and lowered myself onto my back. He tugged on my nightshirt, but it was stuck under my hip. He pressed his face against my stomach, then wriggled lower and stuck his head up under my shirt. His stubble scratched across my skin, but not in a bad way. He pressed his head up until his face was touching my breasts. "Hi, Mommy," he said. My nightshirt muffled his voice. I knew I should take it off, that I was going to get all twisted up in it, but it was too much effort, having to wriggle around and yank it over my head while he was already getting busy.

Without any warning so that I could stop myself, I started to cry. Just silent tears at first, but after a few minutes, I was sobbing. He pulled out from under my shirt and moved up next to me. "What's wrong? Did I hurt you?"

"I'm sorry. I'm so tired."

"Didn't you take a nap today?"

"I started to, but Ruth woke up as soon as I got settled on the couch. And I was up from eleven until one a.m. She woke up again at three this morning."

"She wasn't awake when I went to work."

"Yeah, but she was sleeping on me! Remember? And when you left, I tried to put her down, and she woke up again."

He sat up. He tucked his hand under my head. "Paul wasn't awake all the time at this age."

"Every child is different."

"Maybe you shouldn't go in there right away when she wakes up."

"I can't lay here and listen to her cry. It breaks my heart."

He turned my head toward his face and kissed me, nice and slow, which made me feel a little softer, but I was still crying. "Not having you breaks my heart," he said.

"I know." I cried harder. "I'm sorry. Let me drink some water. I'll be okay."

"If we hurry, you can sleep."

He sounded so pleased with himself, I wanted to laugh, but the crying won out. I sat up and swallowed some water, taking a deep breath between each sip.

"Don't cry, Mommy. Please. I love you."

"I love you."

I wanted it to stop. But I didn't know how to make it stop. It was hard to say the words because I was so embarrassed. When he said *Mommy*, my stomach shriveled into something dead. I wanted to pull the blankets over my head and disappear. The word turned my body into stone. Holding it inside wasn't good, but I couldn't say what I was feeling. Calling me *Mommy*, as if I was his *Mommy*, was so disgusting I couldn't even say the words. It made me sick that he even thought it.

I took another sip of water. He was on his side, his elbow bent, resting his head on his hand. His eyes were wide and dripping with longing, if such a thing is possible. It's the same look I see in Ruth's eyes when she's nursing. Any woman would be thrilled to have a man look at her with those eyes, but knowing what was in his head made me want to pour my water over his face so he'd be forced to close them.

Byron's mother was nice enough. She was pretty, with natural-looking blonde hair and gray eyes. She was one of those top-heavy women with large breasts and narrow hips and a slim waist for her age. Her shape and the highlights in her hair made her look younger than she was. She and I weren't close, just polite to each other, for Byron's sake. Once every few months, his parents took Paul to the park, but they didn't offer to babysit more than that. Since I was breastfeeding Ruth, they couldn't do much more, but an offer still would have been nice. I had no idea how Byron felt about her, which I suppose is strange — for a wife to not know how her husband feels about either of his parents, but he didn't comment on them much. He didn't talk at all about emotional aspects of his childhood. He told me stories, but his parents came across like TV characters. He never complained that anything hadn't gone the way he wanted when he was a kid.

It left me wondering even more what he was thinking when he called me that. He didn't call me *Mommy* because I was the mother of his children. It had started on our wedding night. It was something that apparently turned him on while turning my stomach inside out. On our honeymoon, I was too shy to ask what he meant. I was so embarrassed, so upset at wondering if he was attracted to his mother, or some other crazy thing. And then it was too late. I let it pass, too ashamed to tell him, too afraid of upsetting him and embarrassing him, or questioning his manhood, and, I suppose, too afraid of the answer.

It keeps me awake at night, it makes me depressed and lonely when we're with our friends, and it makes me hate going to his parents' house for dinner. It makes me hate holidays — any time I have to see her, and I don't even know if it's related to her. I don't know if it's normal, I don't know if it happens to my friends, or if they have worse things. There's no one I can talk to because it would shame Byron and betray him. And any person I told would think I was a freak for listening to it all these years. Every time he starts to make love, I want to cry. Since Ruth was born, I don't do a very good job of stopping that crying. He thinks it's because I'm tired, and I am tired, and maybe that's why I cry so easily, but the tears have been there since our wedding day.

He put his hand on my leg right above my knee. He squeezed it gently and then moved his hand up higher. He stuck his fingers under the elastic of my underwear, poking around, thinking he could wake me up and pull me away from crying and exhaustion. I put my glass of water on the nightstand. "Will you turn out the light?"

"Why? I want to look at your beautiful body."

I want to like sex, I do like it. I like the idea of it. I like him stroking my skin and his gentle pressure and the feel of him inside of me. If he would only stop saying that word.

"Just do it," I said. "When it shines in my eyes, I feel like I need to get up and pick up toys, or mop the floor."

He flipped over and turned it off. I slid down and wriggled out of my nightshirt. It wasn't as if crying and drinking water and thinking about how bad I felt was going to stop the inevitable.

He put his lips close to my ear, "Mmmm. You're the best Mommy."

Allie

ALLIE SINCLAIR *JUST helped one of my students understand how an apostrophe is used in a contraction. <u>Really</u> understand. As in — she feels powerful! She walked out with a huge grin on her face!! She's ready to take on the world because she <u>gets</u> it.*

39 favorites — 9 comments

Kristen Thomas *Teaching is magical. Good for you.*
Kimberly Frank *Good, because a lot of adults don't get it.*
Amelia Loc *Hey blondie, good job!*
Jake Ash *Allie Sinclair, the Power Tutor.*
Dave Eddington *Congrats!*
Seth Porter *Too bad the school system doesn't do its job, but then, you wouldn't have a job if they did.*
Byron Jones *God couldn't be everywhere, so He created tutors.*
Megan Miller *I can feel your thrill.*
Tiffany Jones *If my kids ever needed tutoring, I'd definitely hire you, Allie. :)*

AFTER MARCUS AND I made love, I lifted the blankets away from my legs and folded them back. I climbed out of bed and stepped into the dark bathroom. I didn't need the light to put on my bathing suit. I grabbed a t-shirt with an image of Yosemite out of my top dresser drawer and pulled it over my suit. I got a large towel out of the hall closet and carried it and my phone down to the kitchen. The kitchen wasn't as dark as our bedroom, making it easy to locate the fridge. When I opened the door, light poured into the room. I squinted at the brightness while I filled a wine glass with ice and poured orange juice over the cubes. I sat at the kitchen table.

I posted a comment about my tutoring session with Julie Moran earlier that day. No matter how many times I backspaced and revised what I wrote, it didn't seem like the words explained how I felt. Watching Julie's face change shape as the tiny cells in her brain bumped up against each other, like bars from a game clicking into place and exploding into electronic bubbles of color, gave me a thrill that was almost as good as having sex. It seemed like I'd made a difference in the world. Apostrophe use was constantly marked down in her papers. When we were done, she felt confident that she'd never make those mistakes again. I made her life easier. I helped educate the next generation.

Before I could scroll through the rest of my feed, an alert popped up that three friends had marked my status a favorite. Collecting those pale red stars feels almost as good as helping my students learn things that have been hard for them to grasp. It's like re-living the experience when other people click the star, or when they click the star *and* make a comment, so maybe I did explain how great it felt. Every time there's a new comment, I'm having that same amazing feeling again. Piling up all those stars makes me feel as if the good feelings keep repeating themselves, getting bigger each time. The bad things fade away faster.

Every day Marcus gives me angry looks about it. Hating social media wasn't anything new with him, but I didn't understand why he was getting more wound up about it this time. I guess he really didn't like me telling our friends about the card he wrote. But I'd tell my friends if we were face to face, so why not put it out there? It's not like it was a secret, not like it made him look bad. It was sweet, and everyone said so. He should be happy that everyone said what a great guy he is. Instead, he was sulking and saying my friends weren't my friends.

I checked Jake's page. There wasn't anything in the feed, but I wanted to be sure it hadn't slipped through the cracks because of a timeline shift. I hadn't missed anything, just a lot of comments saying that he should stop being so secretive. I clicked on the photo to see if there was anyone else in the background I hadn't noticed earlier that would give me a clue. Of course there wasn't.

He was being annoying, but that's how Jake is. He always has to have a secret and wants to keep everyone guessing, so they're always paying attention to him. He's been that way since I met him. Before Senior Prom, he wouldn't tell anyone who his date was. Every day he dropped a new hint. *She has short blonde hair. She likes to ski.* He said we'd recognize her instantly, but for every name we threw out there, he'd laugh and say, *noooo*.

He arrived an hour late to the prom. Everyone noticed when he walked into the room, because he's the kind of guy who gets noticed. It's difficult to explain why — his tan, his smile — I don't know. He's not extraordinarily tall. He stepped to the side and bowed slightly, then held out his hand. The girl who stepped forward wore a dark green dress. Her hair was loose around her face. He was right, we recognized her instantly — his mom! Jake's dad had died the year before. His mom had never been to her own high school prom. Every single girl had tears in her eyes, watching him escort his mom onto the dance floor.

He may be a male drama queen, but he's a very sweet and clever one.

I put down my phone and went out to the backyard. I turned on the pool light, turning the water bright blue. There was no moon. The glowing water was the only light, as if it wanted to stand in for the moon. I walked down the patio steps to the pool area, dropped my towel on the chaise lounge, and pulled off my t-shirt. I walked around to the deep end and dove in. That's not as bold a move as it sounds. The pool is always at seventy-two degrees, so I can count on water that won't shock the breath out of my lungs. Because the air was cooling down, the water felt even warmer than seventy-two.

I swam to the shallow end and stood for a moment. Water

lapped against the concrete sides causing a slight echo. After a moment, I slipped under the surface and pushed my feet against the wall, gliding about a third of the way down the length of the pool. I surfaced and started swimming, trying to see how many strokes I could do before taking a breath. Keeping my face in the water dulls all the sound around me. It makes me feel like nothing exists except what's inside my skull. It's like washing my brain clean, rinsing out the clutter from hundreds of AboutFace stories and comments and all the annoying parts of the day — the gnawing irritation that fills your throat when you're in traffic or standing in line or working through a voice-activated phone tree or watching a white screen when a web page won't load. The gunk that builds up gets stripped away when I swim. Plowing through the water pulls it out of my head and leaves me feeling immaculate. Not to mention it's great for your legs. I swam twenty laps. I could have gone further.

When I stopped at the shallow end again, ready to move toward the steps to climb out, Marcus was sitting on the edge of the chaise lounge. "I hate it when you do that," he said.

"Sorry, I thought you were asleep."

"I was. I hate it when I wake up and you're not there. I think I'm in a hotel, and then I realize it's our bed. It's disorienting."

I climbed out.

He reached toward me and ran his hand up the outside of my thigh. His touch on my wet skin gave me goosebumps. I shivered. The pressure of his fingers increased. I shivered again. "Brrrr."

"I thought you were shivering for me," he said.

"I already did that." I smiled, but I'm not sure the bright blue water behind me allowed him to see my face.

He handed me the towel and stood. "Please don't do it again."

"You know I need to swim sometimes."

"Wake me up."

"I feel bad."

"Do it anyway."

I felt a little bit powerful, knowing I had an effect on him, that he needed me. He was protecting a small, hidden corner that wasn't filled with his usual absolute confidence. He knew he was a good pilot, knew it took a lot of skill and dedication and brains to become a pilot. He was absolutely sure of his views of the world and the way he wanted to live his life. But he still needed me.

"Are you going to dry your hair?" he said.

"Sure."

He put his arm around my waist, and we walked across the patio. Inside, he locked the door. While he was in the pantry setting the security alarm, I went into the kitchen and picked up my phone and what was left of my orange juice. I met him at the foot of the stairs. He waited for me to go first and followed, grabbing at my ass each step of the way. I laughed and almost spilled my drink. When we reached the top, he kissed my ear and took my phone out of my hand. "You don't need this now."

"I just need to check-in."

"What do you need to know at eleven o'clock at night?"

"I just want to see what's up with my friends."

"What's wrong with you?"

"Nothing."

"It's an illusion. All those people aren't your friends."

"Why do we have to talk about this every day?" I yanked the towel around my shoulders and took a step away from him.

He was gripping my phone so hard his fingers were squished flat around the sides.

"Every single person I know is on AboutFace. Except you."

"Maybe I'm the only sane person you know," he said.

"Don't be so impressed with yourself."

"You're addicted to it. They should start a twelve-step group — AFA." He stared at me, not smiling at his stupid joke.

"Can I have my phone?"

"You'd rather read pointless, self-absorbed comments from people you haven't seen in weeks, some of them years, than go back to bed with your husband?"

"It takes two minutes."

"I bet you checked it before you went swimming."

"So?"

"Why do you have to look at it fifty times a day?"

"I don't."

"I think you do. Maybe we should keep track."

"You're making a big deal out of nothing." Water trickled down the inside of my leg. It felt like a spider running from a predator. I wanted to look. I knew it was water. My suit was wet, my hair was wet. But I still needed to look, just to be sure. I glanced at the inside of my thigh. Sure enough, a drop of water slowed in its path by the outward curve of my kneecap. "You're like some old guy. Worse than an old guy, because almost everyone's parents, and even lots of grandparents, use social media."

"People aren't talking to each other. They just type their own thoughts. No one pays attention, they just click a smiley face."

"It's not a smiley face. It's a star. I don't want to get in a fight."

"Then put it away. Stay off it for twenty-four hours."

"Why?"

"You can't do it, can you?"

"Why would I?" I backed up toward our bedroom door. The best thing to do was shower, dry my hair, and wait for him to fall asleep. In the morning, he'd be calm again. He'd forget about his silly vendetta to turn the world back to a make-believe idyllic time when people had deep face-to-face conversations. People have always talked about stupid things. I bet if someone could translate the hieroglyphics in Egyptian tombs, they'd say, *Hey, dude, I just ate the best dessert ever* — and there'd be a little hieroglyphic ice cream sundae. Even after all the years we'd been together, I couldn't figure out why he hated it so much. How did he know it was phony? He'd never even tried it.

"You could do it for me," he said.

"Why does it matter so much?"

"So, you won't do it for me?"

"I don't know why you're making such a thing out of it."

"It's taking over your life. It's more real to you than I am."

I laughed.

He turned and walked into the office. I heard the desk drawer open. A second later, it closed. Did he really think I couldn't go in there and find it? He stepped back into the hallway. "Are you going to take a shower?"

"Yes."

He walked over and kissed me on the lips, very gently. "We're both tired."

"It's a little controlling to hide my phone, don't you think? Not that it's very well hidden."

"It would be nice to get into bed and go to sleep. I'm tired."

"I'm not."

"That's because you went swimming."

My head ached. I might as well not have taken the swim. I walked through our bedroom and into the bathroom. I shut the door and turned on the hot water.

When I was finished showering and my hair was dry, I put on the nightgown that was hanging on the hook on the back of the door and remembered I'd left my t-shirt on the chaise lounge. I opened the door. Marcus was on his side, facing the bathroom. The bathroom light hit his face. His eyes were closed and his mouth relaxed, but I doubted he was already asleep. He wasn't that tired. If I went into the office, he'd get really pissed. Checking on my friends could wait until morning. Maybe then he'd realize how it made him look, taking away my phone.

I turned off the light and got into bed. He didn't move. I slid down and moved closer to him, putting my face against his forearms that were in front of him, his hands tucked under the pillow like he was inserting them into an envelope. For several minutes I remained still, feeling his breath on my face. It was steady, and he hadn't moved. He really was asleep. I thought about getting up and looking for my phone, but if he woke . . .

When we first got married, I didn't understand what it would be like with a man who was gone half the time, spending half my life eating alone, sleeping alone. He should have realized that AboutFace was my lifeline. Being alone every night, it felt good to check in with my friends before I went to sleep or if I woke up and wondered how many miles up in the sky his plane was, wondered what he was thinking as he stared into the darkness at nothing.

I wasn't addicted at all. I'm friendly, and I have a lot of

friends. We care about each other. We keep in touch. It's not fake. It's normal people talking about their lives. It keeps us close. I don't have any friends on AboutFace that I don't know in real life. Sure some are old friends from the past, but just because our lives have gone different directions doesn't mean I don't still care about them and want to know what's going on.

Jake

JAKE ASH *WE'RE entertainers. Searching our brains for something funny, something provocative, something shocking. We're doing a striptease in our status updates.*

79 favorites — 30 comments

Allie Sinclair *Marcus would tell me to post that we're all fakes. LOL. He hates AboutFace, he thinks it's destroying society. But speaking of teasing, when do we find out about your new job?*

Pam Jamison *Marcus might be right.*

Adam Jamison *Trying to make yourself quotable for posterity, Jake?*

Tiffany Jones *People can use AF for good or evil. If we share the love of God and build each other up, how can that be bad?*

Allie Sinclair *It's not Bible study night, Tiff. Don't always be dragging God into it, K? (Said with all love and kindness *heart*)*

Byron Jones *Let me . . . En-ter-tain you, let me . . . Make you smile*

Kimberly Frank *Hey, Jake, Are you going to do a striptease for us?*

Jake Ash *I just might. After you.*

Amelia Loc *Only for me, babe.*

Tiffany Jones *I don't think he meant striptease as in something* *about sex. That should be private.*

Seth Porter *Take it offline, guys!*

Megan Miller *I take pride in being the audience. ;)*

Tiffany Jones *Sometimes I wish Jesus had His own AboutFace page.*

Seth Porter *That would change the conversation.*

Kimberly Frank *But really, a striptease?*

[See 15 more comments]

AFTER SHE'D THOROUGHLY vetted me, the VP of communications smiled. I thought I saw her wink, but the moment her eye shifted, I wasn't sure whether I'd imagined it. Her smile said we'd reached the crux of the interview.

Shelly Flynn was one of those women who looks hot — long brown and blonde-streaked hair, tight shirt unbuttoned to the max, high heels — but sends the message that you'd better not allow even a tremor in your pulse to acknowledge that fact. Even a subtle glance at the top button would stir up her disdain.

It made me wonder, not for the first time, how my fiancé came across in her professional life. Amelia is hot in a different way. She's what I'd call exotic. I think because she has such contrasts. She's extremely independent but extremely controlling, suggesting she's needy at her core. She has very dark hair and skin the shade of a bar of Ivory Soap. She plays that up with dark lipstick. The most remarkable thing about her is her eyes — such a pale blue they look like something alien. She decorates them with a lot of dark makeup. Her body is nearly perfect — healthy-sized breasts, hips that are curvy enough to be enticing without making her look like a tugboat.

Truthfully, almost all women are hot in their own way. They all have a certain appeal — the overtly sexy ones and the ones who go out of their way to look innocent.

I directed my thoughts back to the woman in front of me. Along with my complete and total enjoyment of the physical world, I'm a student of meditation. And it helps me notice when my thoughts run off the tracks.

Shelly was clearly wicked smart and not to be messed with. "What's your involvement in social media from a personal perspective?" she said.

"Unlike most of my friends, most of the world, I don't have a need to document every breath online. Sure, I post a lot, but I don't have time to read every inane comment and status update, and look through every photo album."

She smiled gently.

I couldn't tell if she thought I was well balanced or an ass. But I don't want a job if they aren't going to be pleased with who I am. "I'm too busy living real life. I know how to de-prioritize the mundane."

"What do you categorize as non-mundane?"

"I work hard, play hard, live hard. Everything that sounds like is exactly what it is. I'll be a millionaire times four by the time I'm thirty. I have extreme focus and dedication. I don't pull back when long hours are called for."

This time, I know she winked.

"Playing hard means surfing and white water rafting — all adrenaline all the time."

"I've never tried either," she said.

"I don't need a sport like golf where you discuss business while you're playing, or tennis where it's all about strategy and mind games. I do that at work. Play should be play. No thinking. Just the animal instinct for survival. Stay on the board, keep the board riding the wave, row for your life."

"Dangerous sports."

"Not if you know what you're doing."

"All male."

"Wrong — no offense. My fiancé likes the same stuff. Of course, I wouldn't be with her if she didn't."

"What draws an all-male guy like you to the PR field?"

"That's not a very politically correct question. It suggests gender bias." I grinned.

She stopped smiling. "I think we can speak frankly. I think we already have. Strict adherence to HR rules is for lower-level employees. If you're going to be on the executive team, we need to be straight."

"Completely agree," I said.

"So?"

"It's a field skewed toward women, like you implied. But I like it because it's a game — trying to get the press to say what you want without them realizing they're adhering to your talking points. Anyone can issue a press release, or manage an executive interview that comes out sounding like a press release. But I can get reporters and bloggers to tell my story as if it's their opinion, as if they did research and objectively came to the conclusions I chose. I think a lot of guys don't realize how strategic and thrilling it can be."

"But you figured it out? How clever of you."

"It wasn't that hard. The first time I saw a press release regurgitated in a blog, I recognized what little value it had. No one would do anything more than read it for data points. If you want to influence the brand, set the stage for buying decisions, PR is a critical role."

"You're very impressed with yourself."

"I believe in being honest. I know what my skills are, and I have talent. The smart ones win the game. If you don't get what you want, take what you want. No one deserves the prizes more than anyone else. It's all a game."

"I see."

She placed her hand over the smartphone lying on her desk, cupping her fingers as if she wanted to protect it from something. Maybe she was subconsciously considering texting a friend about what a piece of work I was. She glanced at her computer display. "You started an MBA program but didn't finish. How does that demonstrate commitment and drive?"

Her tone was mild. It was the question I'd expected at the start of the interview, and she knocked me slightly off guard by waiting to ask it in the midst of a more casual conversation. She sounded genuinely interested, but I also had the feeling she knew exactly how I'd answer the question.

I took a slow breath and let the silence grow for half a second longer than what was comfortable. "You can't learn what I know from a case study. If you're smart, you can learn more in the real world, and create more value. It's all about taking risks and being smarter than the rest."

"And you're smart, as you've mentioned."

It wasn't a question, although it wasn't necessarily a statement, more of an echo. I smiled.

She made the verbal offer before I left her office. *Mirage* was a start-up that was at the perfect moment in time between prepping for its IPO but still handing out stock grants by the fistful.

THE GRANT LETTER arrived two days later. I'd received the scoop on the IPO date from my VC friend, who had turned me on to the position in the first place. I'd already bought a sweet piece of property in the Los Altos foothills and was almost finished constructing a showcase house. I'd known all along that I'd be picking up a pot of gold, but I'll admit, I had a small release of pressure when I saw that things were lining up so the cash would actually be there to pay for it all.

AMELIA AND I were drinking wine, waiting for our octopus appetizer at *Profond Mer*.

"Why did you put that picture and all those comments on AboutFace?" Her skin had a faint blue tinge from the bluish lighting that seeped out from recessed lights hidden beneath seashells the size of my fist. The shells and lights were nestled in small white stones, placed in planter-type boxes that lined the walls. "What if someone at *Mirage* sees them?"

"At this point, it doesn't matter. I have the offer."

"Then why not come out and say it?" She sipped her martini and made a shivery face.

She always does that. I don't know why she drinks the things if she has to go into convulsions after every taste. Maybe she only drinks them for me. My favorite drink and she's trying to mirror my passions.

"This is more fun," I said.

"I don't want you to jeopardize it."

"I'm not jeopardizing anything. I'm not connected to anyone at *Mirage*. Yet."

"Do you have any more information on the date for the IPO?"

"Before the end of the year." Even though I knew the date, but I wasn't supposed to say anything. Sometimes, I do follow the rules.

I was fired up, knowing I'd be a multi-millionaire by the end of the month, already was, really. Before long, I'd lose the rush I'd enjoyed — hiring an architect, signing a contract with the construction company, ordering wood and tile, and designing a swimming pool for my new house — not knowing with one hundred percent certainty that the IPO would come off. Or that I'd be offered the job. There was a slight thrill lingering in my veins, knowing the stock price could plummet the day of the public offering, but no one really believed that would happen.

Amelia tugged her phone across the tablecloth. She always leaves it sitting by her knife as if it's another utensil. She pressed the home button, and it glowed with life. "You're driving Allie crazy with your hints."

I smiled.

Amelia continued to scroll through her phone. She loves *Profond Mer* because it feels like you're underwater. For the same reason, I'm not a huge fan of the place. I keep this well hidden, even from Amelia, but water terrifies me. I don't even know why. It must be some forgotten trauma. A babysitter who let me slip under the water in the bathtub, never telling my mother what she'd done. Or maybe it was my mother herself who turned away to sip her clear, icy vodka tonic while I played on the sand, and I lurched my toddler self into the lake and slipped on a mossy stone and went under. How long until she'd noticed? But that's my imagination. I don't really know.

Either way, I battle this constant fear. Showing fear provides an in-road for others to beat you, and that's the real reason I surf and whitewater raft. It's not just the adrenaline. You need to face fear, grab it by the balls. If you let it control you, life is over before it starts. Every second I'm out there in the ocean or flying through a gorge, I'm scared shitless, but I do it anyway, knowing one wrong move could plunge me ten or fifteen feet underwater, no way to breathe, disoriented and unable to make my way to the surface in time.

The other thing that gets under my skin at *Profond Mer*, and I try not to think about it, is the illusion of being underwater while eating seafood, as if you're taking slow, savory bites of your loved ones' flesh.

All the furniture is white — white leather chairs, white tablecloths, white walls — everything tinged blue. Food portions are tiny, served on oversized plates, so you know you're getting the quality you're paying for. Not that the ratio of plate to portion size indicates quality, but when it's placed on the table like a work of art in its own right, you have a pretty good idea what you're in for.

I picked up the wine bottle and poured a bit more into my glass.

"I'm not done with my drink. Please wait on the wine," Amelia said.

"I didn't start it, the server did."

"He should have let me finish my drink."

I took a sip. "Very nice."

"I wouldn't know."

"We're celebrating, don't go cold on me."

"I'll just have to catch up." She took a long swallow of the martini. More than I'd be able to handle in one go. She smiled. She swiped her finger across the phone. Updates spun by. "Nothing interesting." She took another sip of her martini.

"That's because I haven't posted anything."

She laughed. "You're awful."

"But honest."

The octopus arrived — four delicate tentacles from newborns, with suction cups the size of the dimple on Tiffany Jones' left cheek. Amelia finished her martini, caught up to me with the wine, and put one of the tentacles in her mouth. The piece slid over her burgundy red lower lip and disappeared inside her mouth. "Is that why you do it?"

"Do what?"

"Tease them about your new offer. To make Allie crazy?"

"Not really. I just think social media should be fun. Everyone's so pedestrian."

"I'm not." She worked one tine of her fork into another tentacle.

"But you hardly ever post. All you do is stalk."

"I'm a woman of mystery." She smiled over her glass. A light spot glowed at the center of the wine, like a ruby had fallen into the liquid.

"You are that," I said.

After we ate our Caesar salads, the flat dead anchovy reminding me again that I was eating my associates in their underwater world, the main course was delivered with a flourish.

We talked about our wedding for a while. Just in general

terms. Once the date was set, we'd get more specific, but I didn't want to put a stake in the ground until this other thing was finalized. I love the risk, but you can only leverage so much. I had totally pulled off a coup. I signed on three days before the cutoff for issuing stock. The IPO was scheduled for June thirtieth. Of course Shelly hadn't mentioned that, despite her insistence we be frank with each other. But I knew. Weird to have an IPO just days before a national holiday, but because of the schedule for the next-generation software release, it was the right time.

Once she found out the details, Amelia would be thrilled. Not in a greedy way. She's cool. She's excited for me. Of course, she doesn't mind that she'll be a rich woman, but we're about more than that. Play hard and live hard.

"Why do you think I'm driving Allie crazy?" I said.

She shrugged. "Very good comment about the striptease, by the way. I like that."

She lowered her eyelids and smiled without revealing her teeth. It was a perfect blend of coy and sweet and sexy. It made me want to bring our dinner to a rapid conclusion. I laughed. Not about Allie, but to clear my head and focus on the firm, sweet swordfish. There was no need to rush things. A good meal is part of good sex. It was important to maintain control. "Allie does like to be in the know," I said. "She doesn't want anything to happen to anyone without being first up to make a comment. She called to try and seduce the company name out of me."

"What did you tell her?"

"To wait."

Amelia smiled and pushed her plate to the side.

"The risotto melts in your mouth, doesn't it?"

"It does, but it's so rich."

"Well, keep your plate. You might want another bite or two."

She picked up her fork and scooped up a bit of risotto. She put it in her mouth and didn't immediately start chewing. I could almost see it dissolving across her tongue, saliva surrounding it, pulling the flavor down her throat as the liquid trailed away. She swallowed. Then she chewed slowly and swallowed again. I took a sip of wine and pushed away my plate.

"You seem hyper," she said.

"No more than usual."

"Yes you are."

"Getting excited, that's all."

The server appeared and placed the dessert menus in our hands. Another guy stepped up behind him and removed our plates. A single forkful of risotto remained near the center of Amelia's plate. The server poured the rest of the wine into our glasses and left with the empty bottle. I reached to the center of the table and turned my hand palm up. She rested her left hand inside mine. Her diamond glittered, throwing off a suggestion of blue ripped off from the light around us.

"You haven't told anyone, have you?" she said.

"What makes you say that?"

"Because you're so jittery."

"I'm not."

She let go of my hand, picked up her glass, and tipped it to the left. The wine slid up close to the lip. For being the risk taker I am, watching wine slide up near the edge when people swirl it to open the flavor, I get anxious. The wine was almost gone, there was no need to open the aroma further. My stomach clenched, ready to expel everything inside of me. I wanted her to stop. She knows it makes me anxious, and I was never sure if she did it to put me off my game. It's probably one of the few ways she thinks she can get control of me. And she does want control, I can see it in her eyes, feel it rising like heat off her skin. I love her, and it's okay. Wanting to control me shows how much power she has, and I'm good with that. I like the game of it all.

"You told someone," she said.

"What difference does it make?"

"We agreed you wouldn't tell anyone."

"It's mine to tell or not tell."

"It feels like you undermined our relationship."

I laughed. "You aren't serious."

"I am."

"Why does telling someone I have big news, telling someone I'm going to be rich before I'm thirty, have anything to do with our relationship? You're nuts."

"Who did you tell?"

"Don't worry about it."

"It was supposed to be our secret."

"It's my secret, and it doesn't have to be a secret. I can't broadcast it all over, but telling a few discreet friends is not going to destroy the IPO."

"You don't know that."

"I do."

"So, who did you tell?"

"Drink your wine or put down the glass."

She smiled, slow and lazy, the same smile she has when she's watching me watch her get undressed. It proved that she does like having power over me. I don't mind, I really don't, but there are limits.

She tipped the glass further, almost parallel to the table. Wine glided to the edge. I closed my eyes. She laughed. When I opened my eyes, she was sipping her wine. "Why won't you tell me?"

"First, I want to know why you think *my* company IPO is *your* secret. It has nothing to do with you."

Her eyes got watery before I even finished speaking, then the liquid evaporated, and they grew shiny and hard, the color of pale blue sea glass.

"I can tell who I want."

"You said you wouldn't."

The server brought our dessert — tiramisu. He set it between us and laid a fork on each side, lined up with the plate, as if he was setting out swords for a fencing bout.

Maybe we'd fight over each bite of cream and cake and fruit like we were fighting over whose fucking job we were talking about.

"Why won't you tell me who you told?"

"Because it's not important."

"Was it a guy?"

"What's wrong with you?"

"Nothing's wrong with me. We agreed it was a secret. You told me it was a secret, and I couldn't tell anyone."

"It is. But it's my secret."

"You betrayed me, that's all."

"God. I didn't betray you. I didn't tell a secret of yours. I didn't do anything."

"But you told someone. And now you won't even say who. That makes me feel like you don't trust me, that you don't want to keep our relationship private. And if it was a woman, it makes me feel like you're letting someone else get between us."

"That's a lot of irrelevant stuff to pile on a company IPO."

"You'd feel the same way, if our positions were reversed."

"No, I wouldn't."

"Did you tell Allie?"

"What would be the fun of that?"

"So you told someone you're not connected to on AboutFace?"

"Let's talk about something else." I cut off a large piece of tiramisu and put it in my mouth. Cream and sugar and strawberries coated my tongue.

"Why won't you tell me?"

"Let it go."

"You're not being fair. Married couples shouldn't have secrets."

"We're not married." I cut another, larger piece of tiramisu. Before I placed it in my mouth, I took a sip of wine. The combination of Pinot Noir and the lingering softness of the cream wiped out all other thoughts.

"So that's how it is." She put down her fork.

"That's how what is?"

"The anticipation of the money is changing things. We might not get married after all."

"Where did that come from?"

"First, you're keeping secrets, then you want to control the conversation, and now you draw this clear line that we're not married. We're engaged. It's almost the same thing. It should be the same thing."

I could feel the conversation sliding out of my control. I didn't understand why she was turning this into a battle when it didn't have to be. I was pissed at myself for suggesting I'd told someone. I hadn't, but I wasn't going to admit it now. She probably wouldn't have believed me anyway.

There had to be a way to get her, and the rest of the evening, back on course. I cut another piece of tiramisu. A small one so it wouldn't look aggressive. I lifted the fork toward her and held it a few inches from her lips. She pressed her lips into a hard line.

"Take a bite."

"Not until you tell me what's going on."

"What's going on is I need you. Right now." It was a risk. I watched her lips part, a thin piece of skin from her upper and lower lips clung to each other. Slowly her mouth opened wider. She'd either take the cake and whipped cream into her mouth or launch a tirade of words about relationships.

Her mouth stayed open. Although the room was dim, her pupils were tiny, giving her a fierce expression. My hand was steady, the fork millimeters from her lips. I thought about our eventual wedding and the cake-eating tradition. We weren't the juvenile, smash-it-in-your-face types. We had more respect for each other than that. I realized I should have used my fingers in this instance, but it was too late.

She moved forward slightly and closed her mouth around the fork. She pulled back slowly, drawing the cake off the fork. I lowered my hand and watched her eat it. Without speaking, she picked up her wine, took a sip and settled back in her chair. She licked her lips and smiled.

I waved down the server and asked for the check.

Kimberly

KIMBERLY FRANK *WAITING for my flight to NYC for business.*

14 favorites — 8 comments

Jake Ash *Love NYC. Message me if you want a restaurant recommendation, or five. ;)*
Allie Sinclair *Fantastic! Post some pictures.*
Tiffany Jones *Don't worry! God will keep you safe.*
Kimberly Frank *No fear, Tiff. I love flying.*
Byron Jones *"Start spreading the news, I'm leaving today . . ."*
Kimberly Frank *There is no "news" right now.*
Byron Jones *New York, New York!*
Allie Sinclair *We get it, Byron. LOL.*

NEW YORK CITY is the center of the universe. You can say all you want about Silicon Valley and innovation and the next great thing and the California sunshine, but New York just smiles and gives a pat on the head to the excited little child called Silicon Valley. New York is the financial center of the universe, the cultural center, the tiny island that rules the world. There are quite a few countries and experts who would argue that point, but it's what I think. It's funny that Silicon

Valley is so full of itself, but the minute my company has a big product launch, everyone starts talking about whether there's budget to hold the event in New York, where over twenty-five percent of our customers have their headquarters.

Packing my bag was easy, I have it down to a science — one pair of heels, wear my flats on the plane, two pairs of slacks, four tops, wear my jeans and jacket, pack a nicer jacket, lingerie, a nightshirt, flat iron, deodorant, face lotion, mascara, and I'm done. Whenever I'm packing, I start wondering whether I need a lot less than I think I do to get by. Of course, I ignore the fact the hotel is supplying half my needs.

I love flying. The roaring engines drown out my thoughts, along with chattering people and whimpering babies. The feel of that huge hunk of ingenious engineering tearing down a runway, nothing in its way, feeling it accelerate to a hundred and fifty miles an hour, yet the sensation is the same as a car doing eighty or ninety. The best is that surreal moment when the wheels lift off the ground. It's beautiful and magical and makes me feel good to be alive, excited about where I'm headed.

I glided through security with my company provided perks that skip the ridiculous shoe removal and laptop strip down. I headed down the concourse to a Starbucks and ordered a non-fat latte. I found a seat at a tiny table near a window. I looked out at the tarmac at the fat metal bullets that look far too heavy to move with any grace, much less lift into the sky and drift through the clouds. I propped up my iPad and scrolled through the world news headlines. I checked email and responded to a few messages, relieved there were no manufactured crises surrounding the event scheduled for Wednesday. I clicked back to the news, sweeping mindlessly through tragedies and salacious gossip.

I tapped over to my personal email, answered a note from my mom, and then went to AboutFace. No matter how stupid some of the interaction is, I have this need to check it several times a day. It's addictive. There's no requirement for any effort beyond clicking a star to favorite something. You can tweak your brain with funny videos and outrageous political screw-ups without having to actually socialize or take action. It's a weird, vaporous world that I find strangely appealing and simultaneously irritating.

It's definitely good for networking. Although sometimes I think that's more theory than reality. I've never used my social media connections to find a job, and it certainly hasn't helped me advance my career, yet the promise is there. Because I'm connected to nearly everyone I ever worked with, as well as friends from high school and college, there's a whole world of people poised to ask for and receive favors. And yet, how often does that actually happen? A lot of my friends would argue that you aren't supposed to network there. You're just supposed to stay connected to your friends. But that's what networking *is* — staying connected.

Jake's teasers for some new deal he had in the works were

starting to get irritating. He's such an attention whore. I wished he'd shut up until he had something concrete, rather than whipping up a frenzy of speculation. I guess that's what a PR guy does, but he seemed to have rubbed out the line between personal and business. Maybe I have too. Maybe that's why I was annoyed. Maybe there isn't a line, we just wish there was. And then his comment about social media being a striptease. I wasn't sure what he was trying to say. It seemed like he wanted everyone to talk about sex, or maybe make us look needy, everyone trying too hard, which we were. But the implication was that he, with his profound and witty comments, was above it. That he was not needy and *his* striptease with his new secret company was superior and more artistic. We were all ratty pole dancers, and he was Gypsy Rose Lee.

I knew I was reading too much into it, but I couldn't stop myself. I didn't like him acting as if life was so easy if you were as smart as he was. And therefore, if life wasn't easy, if you weren't racing your way to the top of the food chain, you were inferior. A failure.

I took a sip of my latte. It was slightly cool, but I didn't have time for another one. Boarding was scheduled to start at seven-twenty. I scrolled through the posts and tried to think of something to say about my trip. There wasn't much I could say about the launch without revealing proprietary information. Posting SFO > NYC, like some of my friends do every week, was lame. Nothing clever about drinking a latte came to mind, or anything about the tedium of a five-hour flight. I'm lucky enough to fly business class, thanks to logging tens of thousands of miles around the world, so I always have an easy upgrade. But trying to be self-effacing and funny about luxury while others are crammed into doubtfully sanitized seats, bones and flesh pressing against strangers, caught in silent struggles over armrests, sitting on each other's laps if the plane lurches while they're getting up for a stretch, seems tacky.

Over-thinking is a flaw of mine, and it rises to the surface when I'm on social media. I knew I should just type out a few words and let it go. Other people obviously don't think much before they post, but I can never get that networking thing out of my head. I don't want to make myself look like a mindless moron. I finally posted: *Waiting for my flight to NYC for business.* The ultimate in boring and predictable. Maybe others were doing a striptease, but I was so worried about posting the wrong thing, I was wrapping myself in a burka.

Words on the Internet live forever. It amazes me how many people don't seem to remember that fact when they click the post button. There's some sort of numbing effect from writing on your little phone, not noticing anything around you, tapping out your thoughts, trying so hard to be smart, funny, interesting — worth the click of a favorite or a comment, a string of comments — that you forget it's so much more than a casual conversation. Of course, no one goes back and reads ancient posts from last month or even last week, but somewhere, it's out there floating around. Discoverable at the worst point in time. It's supposedly controlled, but if you have several hundred friends, it's impossible to control what happens. Even if it's never seen again, casual conversation in public takes on an entirely different tone, can be easily misinterpreted, and more easily remembered if you post something stupid.

The latte was cold and sour. I unwrapped a stick of spearmint gum, folded it into my mouth, and pushed back my chair. I picked up my bag and grabbed the suitcase handle. I walked to the exit and dropped the coffee container in the trash.

People waddled along the concourse, making it appear as if everyone but me was headed out for vacation. Once I passed the rows of eateries and bars, it got better — flip-flops replaced by serious shoes and a rapid pace and efficiency of movement. I felt like I'd re-entered a space with my own species. Walking fast felt good, it filled me with new energy and burned off adrenaline and caffeine.

When we started taxiing, I got rid of my stale gum and inserted a fresh piece. The sugar flowed around my tongue, and the chewing sucked up more of my adrenaline, which helped me settle down.

The guy next to me wore noise-canceling headphones. I pulled out my earbuds, opened a playlist, and went to work making the final changes to the slides my boss would be presenting at the customer event. Exchanging one word for another, changing it back in some cases, creating new images, re-drawing graphs. It was a soothing way to spend time until food arrived.

After I ate, I popped in a new piece of gum and tried to continue working, but like a fly that refuses to land in a place where you can actually smack it flat, the words I'd posted on AboutFace circled in my head. The comment was pointless. I wasn't sure who I was networking with, why I even cared whether I was witty, but I did care. And that post was the furthest thing from witty I could imagine.

The words crawled around inside me. After a minute, my mind wandered back to Jake's post. I wanted to pull sociological observations like that out of my ear. My problem was, I was thinking about work most of the time, and posting about work requires all kinds of analysis to be sure I'm not breaking company policy. Jake seems to be able to stand outside of things and talk about the world in general without being specific to his company, whatever that is at any given time. He changes so often, it's like he works for *every-company* — a composite of start-ups and struggling firms and global corporations.

It wasn't as if my lack of wit mattered. I'm not connected to people above me in the org who can impact my career. And even if I was, how would an astute observation of life change anything? But it made Jake come across like a more well-rounded person. A guy with something important to say. It raised his status, no pun intended, to a leader. Someone people looked up to, waiting to see what he had to say.

Everything comes easily to Jake. It's baffling how he keeps changing jobs, getting more money every time. Sure it's good to move around, but every eighteen months, sometimes less, is a bit much. Any recruiter or mentor will tell you that. Jake's already got everything. He's gorgeous, engaged to an equally gorgeous, intelligent woman.

Obviously, something amazing had fallen into his lap. His hints were like flirting, whispering suggestive words. And he knew what he was doing, or he wouldn't have made that entertainment comment. It seemed as if he had a secret insight into the human psyche, a magician that could make people like him even if they didn't want to. It bugged me that he and I were the same age, essentially the same education, although he didn't even bother to finish his MBA, and he was way ahead of me, title-wise, prestige-wise, and income-wise.

I became aware of the guy seated next to me. He was fifty-something, with a slight belly. He did a good job covering it with his suit jacket, but it was an uncomfortable piece of clothing for a cross-country flight. He was studying the slide on my laptop screen. I closed the cover. He removed his headphones. He'd worn them all through lunch. My jaw ached from thinking about trying to chew with padded hunks of plastic pressed against the sides of my head.

"What's taking you to New York?"

"Work."

"That's seventy percent of the people on this flight."

"Maybe," I spit my gum into the wrapper and pulled out a new stick.

"You chew a lot of gum," he said.

"It relaxes me."

"Are you tense?"

"No more than anyone else." I didn't really want to talk to him, but I was tired of working. The slides were done, and all I was doing was moving things around.

"I'm not tense," he said.

I glanced at his grinning face. "Thanks for the update."

"I practice yoga." He lifted his headphones. "These are great for listening to mantras or nature sounds. You should try it."

"I'm not tense."

"Did I say you were?" He smiled, but there was a condescending shape to his lips, curving around his teeth, leaving the rest of his face untouched.

"You implied it."

"I don't think I did. I think you're projecting."

I re-opened my laptop and waited for the screen to wake.

"Escaping into work?"

I was not going to allow him to see how annoyed I was. I had to sit five and a half inches from the guy for two more hours. I wanted to send him scurrying back into the cave of his giant earphone pads with his mantras and crickets. "I have some things I still need to get done."

"And they can't wait until you're in your hotel? This is your life, a moment, an hour that will never come your way again. I'm a person you'll never meet again."

God, I hoped not.

"You can think I'm ridiculous and too personal, but you know I'm right."

"Of course you're right. In terms of the likelihood of meeting you again. But you're wrong that my work can wait. I'm under pressure to have this ready to go when I land."

"Pressure? So you are tense about it?"

I looked at my screen. I angled the laptop a few inches toward the window to keep my slides outside his line of sight, but the glare made it impossible to see what was on the screen. I pulled the shade.

"Don't you see how sad that is? You have a chance to glimpse the vastness of the heavens. You're flying! Clouds so close you could touch them surround you. And you shut it out and stare at a screen filled with bits and bytes and electrical impulses that aren't real."

"I spent time looking out the window earlier." I didn't like the defensive tone in my voice. I do need to spend more time looking at what's right beside me, not including the pudgy, Zen corporate priest, or whatever he considered himself. But there's a practical side of life. "We can't all spend our days contemplating nature. I have to earn a living."

"There's a difference between earning a living and chasing money and status."

"I love my job."

"Love? That's a strong word."

"It's true."

"You love your job?"

"Yes, I do."

"Not just the money and the status and the power."

I laughed. "I don't have any power."

He stared at me with a blank expression. I looked away. The roar of the engines was as loud as ever, but his voice had pushed the comforting sound to the background. His tone was low but penetrating as if it was on a different frequency that crept right inside my head. "I really should get some work done," I said.

"Your choice. One day you'll wake up, and you'll be middle-aged, and what will you have to show for it? Your life will have passed you by, and all the people you've met will be a blur. You need to step out of the box."

"I don't think so."

"You're a kid. You don't know anything. Fifteen minutes after you get off the plane, you won't remember me or what we talked about."

I laughed. He was too full of himself. I wouldn't remember him five minutes after I got off the plane. I wasn't sure if he was hitting on me or proselytizing for an obscure religion. Maybe he was crazy. The ability to pay for seats in business class isn't reserved for normal people. Despite the name, half the people in those seats are anything but businessmen or women.

"If you want to live life, really live it, you have to let go of striving for success, let go of your agenda, let go of . . ."

"I get your point."

Again, he stared at me with an utter lack of expression.

"Nice talking to you." I reached into my purse and pulled out my earbuds. I plugged the jack into my laptop and stuffed the buds in my ears. He continued staring at me, but I didn't look to my right. I popped up a new playlist, ironically, sounds of a thunderstorm. He'd be pleased.

He pretended to be peaceful and Zen-like, but he was working overtime to upset me. Still, I found myself thinking back over my life and wondering what the hell my overall plan was. Maybe I *was* tense. I was always pushing ahead, always wanting more. I wanted a new relationship, but once I had that, I'd want to be engaged. I know when I'm married, I'll want a baby. I wanted to go to grad school, and then I wanted to have my degree and be out working. I wanted to get into a global corporation, and then I wanted more opportunity for advancement. I wondered when the wanting stops. Maybe never.

I've given up a lot in my life pursuing what I want, and I suppose that exudes a certain amount of anxiety. Along the way, I've lost a few things too. When I left for college on the east coast, I left my mother alone. Her only child moving pretty much as far away as she could get without leaving the country. My father was long departed for more fertile women. I reassured my mother I'd be back in four short years.

She cupped my face in her hands and looked hard into my eyes. "When you're older, Kimmy, you'll find out how short life is. Four years is a long time."

"I'll be home at the holidays. In the summer." I was not going to let a false sense of obligation to take care of her stop me from what I wanted.

She let go of my face and smiled. As if she knew. Only two years later, I lied to her, via email. *I can't afford to come home. Dad didn't come through with the plane ticket he promised.* But I went to the Bahamas for spring break and then I moved to Manhattan during the summer. Maybe that's where I started being so paranoid about what I posted online. I wasn't worried about the world finding my careless remarks, but my mother. Not that she had an account, but in case she ran into one of my high school friends. I think it was good for her that I went away. She seemed stronger, but we were never as close. I had to go far away for college, had to get away from the high school crowd. I wanted to be sure I had the best school possible listed on my resume.

I gave up Alex too. Maybe I gave up all love. First my mother, then him. I was with Alex for seven years. Then, one morning, he kissed the tip of my nose and walked out of our condo with nothing but his backpack and a duffel bag. *There's more to life than chasing career success*, he said. The soft, pitying look of his mouth made me want to smack him and kiss him. It felt like he yanked out my heart and stuffed it in the outside pocket of his backpack. I didn't see how he could say he loved me but not want to be with me. How does that work? I still don't understand. Maybe he didn't really love me enough. Maybe no one ever loves anyone enough.

I still thought about him more than I should have. I hunted for him on AboutFace. He was married. Since I'd discovered that, I'd thought about him even more, and I hated myself for that. Striptease my ass, I didn't reveal anything on social media.

I shoved my earbuds further into my ears as if the ache of plastic pressing against cartilage would push the thoughts aside. The same thoughts swarmed below the surface, like mosquito larvae in a mountain pond, rippling the water just a bit, making the thought of diving in very unappetizing. All those insects, brushing against your skin, irritating you and making you anxious. Tense.

When the plane landed, I turned on my phone and opened AboutFace. The Zen priest was wrong about letting go. If everyone did that, the world would collapse in a puddle of inertia. Now I had my own philosophical post to rival Jake's. I put a fresh piece of gum in my mouth and felt calmer than I had since the plane took off.

Kimberly Frank *Life is short. Figure out what you want before it's too late and never let go of it.*

37 favorites — 9 comments

Jake Ash *Absolutely!*

Allie Sinclair *That sounds mysterious. What's going on?*

Dave Eddington *You make it sound easy.*

Jake Ash *It is easy. Everything's easy if you practice Jujitsu.*

Dave Eddington *You have all the answers, Jake. Pass some of that brilliance my way.*

Byron Jones *Greed kills.*

Tiffany Jones *I suppose that's true in a way, but you need to make sure it's God's will for you. Blessings :)*

Kimberly Frank *Nothing's going on. Just lots of time to think on the loooong flight to NYC.*

Jake Ash *It's not THAT long.*

Marcus

THE SUN WAS well above the horizon when my consciousness poked its way to the surface. I must have been dreaming about Allie swimming, because it seemed as if my brain was underwater, then, racing up from the bottom of the pool, frantic for oxygen. The room was so bright, at first, I thought I might have slept through lunch. I sat up. Allie wasn't there, of course, and it was only seven-fifteen.

Flying messes with my body clock. It's like the whole mechanism is shot to hell anyway, and I no longer have a natural rhythm of night and day. I live in a separate world from everyone else. Since my internal clock is unreliable, I follow Allie's when I'm home. Air traffic control dictates my life when I'm flying.

The problem is, Allie can be sneaky and quiet. I'll wake up, not one hundred percent sure where I am, and she's gotten out of bed to go for a swim. Does she really need to swim in order to relax in the middle of the night? Isn't making love supposed to relax her? When I wake up and the bed is empty, I think I'm in a hotel. Then I realize I'd be in the center of the bed if that were the case. Sometimes I think that I had the flu and went to bed before dinner. It's the same thing in the morning. The alarm goes off, and she slaps it silent before I hear it, and then she's up and downstairs pouring orange juice. When I come down, she's on her second glass, fiddling with her phone, checking in with all her friends.

I got up, pulled on my jeans, splashed water on my face, and went downstairs. I found her sitting on the living room couch, facing the sliding glass doors. She was wearing white shorts and a white top with thin straps. Her legs were tucked to the side, so her shorts pulled up exposing her hipbone. Her toes were slightly pointed, and her toe ring had slipped close to the tip of her second toe. Hair fell across her face and around her shoulders. Her body curved around her hand, holding her phone as if it was an egg, and she wanted to protect the fragile shell.

"Why didn't you wake me up?"

Without looking at me, she said, "You seemed tired."

"How can you know how I feel when I'm asleep?"

"It was obvious. You were asleep." She giggled and stroked her thumb across the screen, leaned forward, and picked up her glass of juice with the other hand. She took a sip and still didn't look at me.

"I missed you." I thought that sounded better than telling her for the thousandth time that I hated her leaving me alone. I didn't want to seem needy. It's a normal thing, wanting your wife to stay in bed with you, waking up together. I shouldn't have to explain that, but appealing to her love instead of criticizing her seemed like a better move.

She looked up at me and smiled. "That's nice. Do you want eggs for breakfast?"

"Sure."

"I only have one student today. At four. So we could go somewhere, if you want."

"Let's eat first. Then we can decide."

"Okay." She ran her index finger down the phone again. She tapped it, then put down her juice. She started typing a message, thumbs tap-dancing across the screen.

Something tightened inside my chest as if a screw had been turned too far, stripping the threads as the pressure increased, determined to drive a piece of metal through concrete. "What are you typing?"

"Relax, this will just take a second."

"I asked you what you're writing? I don't want my whole life posted to your eight hundred and forty-two best friends."

She laughed. Typical Allie. She's so positive about life, so easy-going, which I love . . . I do. She balances me, she makes me happy. She's fun, but she is absolutely clueless at times. She thought I was teasing. I was not teasing. I don't like people spying on my private life, and I can't even accuse them of spying when my wife is out there trying to be cute or witty or whatever the hell it is she's trying to be, what they're all trying to be, barfing up their thoughts like the world is waiting to hear their mindless observations every hour of the day.

I'd spent a lot of time and put a lot of thought into that anniversary note. I tried to describe my indescribable feelings for her. I didn't like the fact that my feelings were quoted and then picked apart like I was some sort of high school biology project. I didn't care if they deemed me *sweet* and thought I was a *keeper*. It was private, and I felt like she'd taken a picture of me naked and posted it online for her friends to comment on my physical imperfections. I spoke louder — "I'm not kidding."

"I don't have eight hundred friends." She laughed again, talking and tapping on her phone at the same time, as if she had a miniature speech to make right then and there.

"What are you writing?"

"I'm commenting on Jake's post."

"And what's that about? How much money he made this week?"

"Be nice," she said.

She still didn't look at me. Tapping, tapping. I wanted to grab the phone, walk to the back door, and throw it into the swimming pool. Throw it so hard it would plunge to the bottom and shatter on the concrete.

"Why won't you tell me what you're writing?"

"I did."

"No, you didn't."

"It's nothing important. If you were on AboutFace, you'd be able to read it the minute I click post."

"It's too late."

She put the phone on the table and looked up at me. "What's too late?"

I was starting to think everything was too late. That it was too late to have a real relationship. I was born in some weird bubble, six years ahead of Allie and most of our friends. A phone wasn't shoved into my hand the day I graduated from high school. I didn't have an AboutFace account before I knew what was what.

As far as I could see, half the planet was atrophying into a pair of thumbs. It was frightening. I can lift a seventy-five-ton plane off the ground, and it's not nearly as scary as what I see in my own living room, in restaurants, at the mall. Even when Allie and I go hiking in the foothills or hang out at the beach. When I stand in the door of the cockpit and watch the passengers disembark, seventy percent of them don't even notice I'm there, heads bent over their phones, frantic because they've been disconnected for three or four hours.

Allie stood and took a few steps toward me. She wrapped her arms around my waist and leaned her head on my chest. "What's too late?"

A perverse part of me wanted to make it into something bigger, to try to explain the thing inside me that feared for the human race, but I was too tired. Ten minutes out of bed, and I was exhausted. "Once you post something, it's out there in the world. Something you might regret saying, captured forever. It's too late to censor yourself."

"Why would I want to censor myself? That's crazy."

She'd never understand. That's what was scariest of all. She disappeared inside her smartphone as if pictures of people she hadn't seen in weeks or months, sometimes years, were more relevant than the person standing right in front of her. It was terrifying to feel like my life was lived in a different world entirely. "Every conversation has an element of self-censorship. You start to say something, you read the other person's expression, and you adjust your words. It's almost unconscious. But it's how we interact, reading cues that don't get transmitted through a wireless connection onto a screen."

"Don't be so serious. It's just chatting."

"It's not chatting. It's talking at each other. Everyone is commenting, and no one is listening."

She let go of my waist, tipped her head back, and kissed my chin. "That's not true."

"I'm not explaining it very well."

"Actually, you are," she said. "Because you *explain* it every time you come home, until you remember how the world is, outside of the cockpit."

"I keep explaining it because I'm not getting through to you."

"If you'd try it, you'd see how great it is. We could stay more connected when you're gone."

"We are connected. I text you. I don't need your eight hundred friends to hear me say I'm thinking about you."

"Stop saying that, I don't have eight hundred friends." She giggled.

"But you wish you did."

"I don't know if I can keep up with that many friends."

"You can't. You can't have a real friendship with more than

a handful of people. And if you think all those people are your friends, I'm a little worried about your connection to reality."

"Don't be dramatic." She moved away from me. "I'll make breakfast." She picked up her glass and swallowed the rest of the orange juice in one long gulp.

"Will you make coffee?"

"Sure."

"And leave your phone in here?"

"Why are you all of a sudden trying to take away my phone?"

"I'm not taking it. I just suggested you leave it in here." That was another thing she didn't get. It wasn't all of a sudden. It was something that had been piling up, like leaves blowing across the pool in the winter, first just a few and it doesn't matter, then suddenly a big mass of them, floating toward the filter, ready to clog the whole thing and shut it down.

"I won't look at AboutFace." She picked up the phone and tucked it behind the waistband of her shorts.

She does that a lot. It stirs up this weird combination of desire to put my hand there, and fear that the phone will slide down her leg and break into a hundred pieces. Although that could be a good thing. "If you aren't going to check in, leave it here."

"Don't make it into a thing. It's just friends talking to each other. Why is that bad?"

"Because you're not talking, you're bragging and advertising and preaching."

"Preaching?" She laughed and patted her phone as if she wanted to glue it to her hip.

"Telling people how things are, posting in-your-face political opinions or going on about your religious views as if everyone wants to read them."

"I don't do that."

"Are you sure?"

She walked into the kitchen. "How do you even know what I post? You're not there! You're the only person I know, my best friend in the world, and you're missing in action."

Already, I was tired of talking about it. I'm not the only one who has these views. A lot of people do. It seems like the world is splintering into two groups — people who are addicted to social media and think it's real life, and people who recognize the dark side and see the societal breakdown.

"Why don't you just try it?" she said.

"I prefer to interact with real human beings, not avatars."

"They aren't avatars."

"They might as well be. All the pictures are flattering."

"So. What's wrong with that?"

"It's fake."

"We don't put ugly pictures of ourselves on our walls either. We didn't save any of the bad shots from our wedding, or our vacations. So what's the difference?"

"The difference is those are for us to look at. They're for

people who come over and interact with us as human beings with all our flaws. On AboutFace, everything is good, and it gives a false perspective."

"That's how all social things are. No one fights with their spouse in front of other people."

"But you talk to your friends about it. And you leave it off AboutFace. Over the years, you build this entirely phony construct of your life."

"You want me to post the stupid things you say about social media?"

"No."

"Do you want me to record this argument and post that?"

"You're missing the point."

"Then what is the point?" She walked around the center island. The sound of her feet on the tile was like lips kissing each other. It made me want her again. I walked to the center island and put my hands on the edge. I couldn't read her mood. I'd started the argument, but it wasn't going anywhere, and I couldn't seem to stop it. I really did not want to be thinking about it. I wanted to figure out if she could be persuaded back upstairs to bed.

She yanked open the fridge. "Fried eggs or omelet?"

"Omelet." I pulled out a stool and sat at the opposite side of the island. "Are you hungry? We don't have to eat right now."

"I'm starving." She pulled a carton of eggs out of the fridge and put it on the counter. She opened the drawer and began lifting out plastic bags filled with mushrooms and tomatoes and green onions. She kept talking, but the rustling plastic and the fact that her head was buried inside the fridge made it impossible to hear what she was saying. All I could see was her butt and her legs and the bumps of her spine, pressing against her top, making me admire the engineering of the human body, especially *her* body. The way her spine curved as perfectly as a suspension bridge. I stood and went to the coffee machine. I filled the pot with water, drowning out her rustling plastic bags with the spray of water against glass. I turned off the faucet and heard her phone vibrate loud against her hipbone. She pulled it out, checked the message, and set it on the island.

"My point is, there's a dark side to it."

"But a dark side means there's a light side. And that's true with everything in life, so why not enjoy the good parts and stop focusing on the flaws? There's a dark side to air travel too. Several dark sides."

"Dark side was the wrong way to put it. It has the potential to destroy your relationships. You're addicted to the constant reinforcement of trivial updates, and you don't even realize it. You can't go ten minutes without looking at your stupid phone."

This time, the bottoms of her feet smacked the tile as she walked to the rack over the island and yanked off a frying pan. She turned around and put it on the stove. She didn't slam it, but the metal on metal was quite loud, and it slid a quarter of an inch making a squeak that ran up the back of my neck and entered my brain like a needle. She poured a bit of olive oil in the pan and slid a knife out of the block more quickly than necessary. The knife was also larger than necessary for slicing mushrooms and onions. She set to work, her head bent forward, hair covering her face.

I wanted to start the morning over. But even with that desire at the front of my mind, I couldn't stop myself from driving home my point. "Look at what's going on with the Jake drama. He obviously has some fantastic gig in his hand, and he's basically bragging about how smart he is, how his career is accelerating, probably about how much money he's going to rake in. How are guys like Byron and Dave and Seth going to feel? They've probably maxed out their earning potential. Having it shoved in your face in a never-ending news feed makes a guy feel like a failure."

"That's how life is. And he's not bragging." Her voice was quiet. The more upset she gets, the softer her voice is.

"He might not intend it as bragging, but that's how it comes across."

"How do you even know? You aren't there!"

"You tell me."

"It's different when you're involved in the conversation. And you're not. So you don't get to say anything else about it."

"Is that right?"

"Yes. That's right."

"I think if you would put your phone away for a few days and think about it, you'd see my point."

"I'll never see your point. I like my friends. I'm not going to cut them out of my life." She turned on the gas and shoved the onions and mushrooms into a big pile.

"Would you consider trying it? Giving up your phone until I fly again?"

"No."

She didn't even hesitate. It was like she knew what I was going to ask, and she already had her answer ready.

Allie

ALLIE SINCLAIR *CLEANING the pantry and the refrigerator. Boring, but needs to be done.*
  27 favorites — 13 comments

  Jake Ash *Your life is truly glamorous.*
  Allie Sinclair *"Breakfast at Tiffany's" every day.*
  Tiffany Jones *LOL. No breakfast at my place. Unless you're satisfied with coffee and toast. I wish I had time to clean my refrigerator. I'm embarrassed to say how long it's been.*
  Allie Sinclair *Ewww!*
  Tiffany Jones *Just wait 'til you have kids. :)*
  Byron Jones *They're little vampires. They suck up every ounce of energy.*
  Tiffany Jones *They're not! They're a blessing. The greatest blessing.*
  Kimberly Frank *You're a domestic goddess, Allie.*
  Megan Miller *You clean your fridge and everyone comments, amazing. I could win a fridge and not get this many comments.*
  [See 4 more comments]

  Allie Sinclair *[Uploaded 2 images] Eggs Benedict I made last week and forgot to upload. [32 favorites — 18 comments]*

Kristen Thomas *Makes me hungry.*
Megan Miller *Not a fan of eggs, but they look beautiful.*
Amelia Loc *Gorgeous.*
[*See 15 more comments*]

I WIPED UP spilled rice and broken pieces of dried pasta on the pantry shelves. I re-arranged the cans and boxes of food, so they were grouped logically and lined up neatly. I took the drawers out of the refrigerator, wiped down the insides with warm, soapy water, and cleaned the shelves. I emptied a few bottles of salad dressing that were past their sell-by dates, rinsed the bottles, and took them out to the recycling bin.

Every ten minutes or so, I looked out the front window. I watched Marcus move from pruning the lemon tree to digging up the dandelions that keep sprouting on the lawn. Those poor flowers try so hard to make the lawn beautiful, not realizing we've classified them as weeds. After the dandelions were gone, he mowed the lawn and trimmed the edge until it looked like a smooth green carpet. Not that anyone would buy a carpet the color of a lawn, but it was rich and soft, inviting me to walk across it with bare feet.

Each time I looked, he had his back to me. Marcus has a beautiful back — all muscle and bone and smooth skin. His solid shoulders and arms moved without hesitation, lifting the pruning shears above his head, the muscles tensing and shifting as he opened them to clip one branch after the other.

Those shears terrify me — the blades so sharp, leading to a deadly point, made to cut through wood and, I imagine, flesh and bone.

He seemed so far away, even though he was only outside the house and across the yard. I wondered what expression he had on his face, whether it reflected what was inside his head. Was he thinking about the shape and thickness of the branch he was pinching between the blades, watching to see where it would fall, or was he thinking about me, hating me for spending time in a world he refused to visit?

When we argued, my rib cage felt like it was stuffed full of rocks. The minute he left the room, I regretted the things I'd said. But I wasn't going to stop following my friends' lives and telling them about mine. I love feeling like I'm with all my friends all the time. I wake in the middle of the night and take my phone under the covers so I can see what they're up to.

One of my greatest accomplishments so far has been acquiring so many friends. That sounds bad, like I treat them as objects, but I don't. I've worked hard to make friends, and *keep* friends. Mostly to keep them. Finding friends is easy, if you're friendly, but keeping them requires effort. I invite them over to swim, I meet up for coffee, and I connect on AboutFace. That's why it's so very important. It allows me to support them, cheer them on, and comment about the things they're doing. I praise their success and cry when they're hurt. I'm a good friend, and I value my friends. They're the essence of life. It's very upsetting that Marcus refuses to understand that.

I laughed out loud and hooked the vegetable drawer back on the track.

It's just a website. A place for people to share their thoughts and photos. There's nothing fake about it. Only fake people make something fake.

After I finished cleaning, I poured a glass of orange juice and went into the living room. If Marcus looked inside the house, like I'd been looking out at him, he wouldn't see me checking AboutFace. Although, I'm sure he was out there thinking that was what I was doing. He made it seem like I checked it every two minutes.

I drank half the juice in a few gulps while I scrolled through the updates. There wasn't anything that interesting — a bunch of pictures of Tiffany's kids, a comment from Dave about a movie he hated, and then another comment from him about Bumgarner pitching a great game for the Giants the weekend before. I wasn't sure why Dave was posting that now. It was ancient history. Maybe it took him a while to figure out what he wanted to say, although if that was the case, what he ended up saying wasn't very interesting, and it seemed even duller because the game was so long ago.

I took another sip of juice, and while I was doing that, a new story popped up.

Jake Ash *It's a done deal: IPO extravaganza! It looks like I'm a* *millionaire, at least on paper. For now. And then some. Lucky day, lucky me. But my friends are worth more, which makes me even luckier.*

0 favorites — 0 comments

I wasn't surprised. He'd dropped enough hints. I was excited for him, not at all jealous, although my second thought was how some of our friends would be raging with jealousy. They wouldn't admit it on AboutFace, but I knew already their envious feelings would be a solid thing, hiding behind the stars clicked, the words — the minimalist comments, and the longer comments.

Marcus makes a good income, and we have everything we want, and I have a nice amount of extra cash from tutoring. Jake was right that friends are worth a lot more than a ton of money, but somehow his comment sounded contrived. At the back of my mind, there was a voice, whispering that this was the phoniness Marcus was talking about. I shoved the voice out of my head. Jake didn't mean to sound phony, he really felt that way. I was sure of it. I don't know why I thought it sounded forced. Maybe all of the suspicious, negative comments from Marcus were clogging up my brain.

I tapped in the comment box, wrote a few words, and hit post.

Allie Sinclair *That's terrific news! You earned it. I'm so happy for you. What's your first new toy?*

I clicked the favorite star. It felt good to be first. Within a few seconds, a favorite star from Jake appeared under my comment. I waited to see how he'd answer my question. I tugged the screen image to force it to reload, but nothing popped up. I took another sip of juice. The front door opened and closed.

"Allie?"

"I'm in the living room." I put my phone on the table. I picked it up again and put down my juice glass. He wasn't going to make me feel like I wasn't allowed to check in with my friends. The screen had gone dark. I woke it up and saw there were two new comments.

Jake Ash *Not really a toy. My first house — I guess I'm officially an adult. The house has been in the works for a while. Look for a housewarming invite coming soon via snail mail.*

Amelia Loc *For richer, for poorer. Either way, I love you.*

I laughed when I read what Amelia wrote, but immediately thought it was a little too planned. Her comment sounded like a line from a movie. Marcus was infecting me with his negative attitude, painting my friends as phony, posturing, narcissists. And now he stood in front of me, staring at me like I was back in high school and just got caught texting in class.

"I thought you were cleaning the fridge."

"All done."

He stared at my phone. It seemed to grow hot in my hand, glowing like it was radioactive, burning my fingers as he held his gaze steady.

I grabbed my foot with my other hand and slid the ring back and forth on my toe, pressing it first against the round, fleshy part at the tip, and then down toward the joint where it dug into the bone. My head ached from the lack of sound, straining to hear even his breathing. My muscles twitched gently, urging me to get up and move. A tickle ran along the back of my neck, but I didn't want to scratch it. He seemed disappointed in me, angry. He wasn't just poisoning my chats with my friends, he was poisoning our marriage. It seemed as if he was constructing a wall between us, smearing mortar on one brick after another, and shoving it into place with each disagreement. Soon, I wouldn't be able to see him over the wall, and after that, I wouldn't be able to hear him.

My phone vibrated. I held it more loosely, hoping he wouldn't notice if it vibrated again. I felt each vibration travel across the floor and up into his body, making him more upset. It vibrated again.

"Aren't you going to check? It might be something important."

"Probably more comments about Jake's IPO."

"IPO?"

"The new company he just joined had their IPO yesterday."

"What's the name of the company?"

"I'm not sure."

"Not sure, or you don't know? Because you never actually talk to someone, so there's no actual conversation."

"Please don't spoil things."

"Spoil what things?"

"The good news."

"If it was good news, if he was such a good friend, wouldn't he call you?"

"That's not how it is. Why do you keep pretending it's 1995?" I stood and picked up my juice glass. I went into the kitchen, but he didn't follow me. I rinsed my glass and put it in the dishwasher. The minute I pushed the rack inside, I wanted more juice. I took a clean glass out of the cabinet and filled it halfway. I stood near the sink and looked out at the front yard. The grass and trees were fresh and clean.

My phone had vibrated two more times in quick succession. If I pulled it out and checked the updates and Marcus came into the room, the fight would keep going. But I had to know what was happening, and it seemed like he was planning to stand in the living room and sulk until I returned. I took three gulps of juice, rinsed that glass, and put it next to the other one in the dishwasher. I swept my finger across the phone.

Jake Ash *I love you too, babe.*
Amelia Loc *Kiss. Kiss.*
Dave Eddington *Get a room, guys!*
Kimberly Frank *LOL.*

Seth Porter *Capitalism rocks!! What's the name of the company?*

I waited for Jake to respond. If he put the name, I could tell Marcus, and he'd see how this was the same thing as a real conversation. In some ways, it was more efficient. I went into the living room. "What you don't seem to understand is that with AboutFace, we can socialize as a group. If Jake called me, it would only be a two-way conversation. Instead, it's a small party. We can all talk to each other. Do you want to see what everyone is saying?"

"No."

I slapped my phone against my thigh. "Come on, Marcus. Why are you like this?"

"Like what?"

"So stubborn."

"I'm not stubborn. I'm just telling you what I think. Why do you assume you're right and I'm wrong?"

"Because everyone loves AboutFace."

"Really? How do you know?"

"I just know. They use it all the time. It's fun! It's how friends stay connected."

"Disconnected."

My phone vibrated three times in a row. I lifted it in front of me and swiped the screen.

"Don't."

"What?"

"Don't look at it right now. We're talking."

"We are not. You're lecturing me. You're trying to spoil all my fun. Do you ever think about how it is for me when you're gone? All alone in this house?"

"Don't change the subject."

"I'm not. I like my friends. *Our* friends. I like talking to them whenever I can."

"You'd rather type messages to people who aren't even here than talk to me."

"But when you're not here, I like that I can tell them what's in my head when I can't sleep. I don't have to be alone."

"Why can't you see you aren't talking to them? It's not a conversation." He gestured back and forth in the space between us. "This is a conversation. Two people feeling each other's body heat, looking in each other's eyes, hearing voices, and saying what we really think, not what we think looks cute to a thousand other people. Not LOL and all that crap."

I looked past his shoulder. Our wedding picture was facing me. It was a five by seven in a maple frame, sitting on the mantel. The photograph was smallish, so it wouldn't look like it was taking over the room, but it was the only object on the mantel, which made it look important. A lot of our friends put their wedding pictures away after a few years, maybe because some of them had kids, and they put all those pictures out instead. But I think, *we* think, it's important to keep the memory of that moment alive, keep it in a spot where we notice it every day.

When Marcus and I first got together, when we were first

married, we never discussed AboutFace, although I was sad that Marcus didn't want to be on there. Lately, it seemed like we talked about it all the time. "Why are we fighting?" I said.

"Because I'm concerned."

"About what?"

"About your addiction to play-by-play updates. Your constant distraction."

"These are my friends!" My phone vibrated.

"I think you're losing your friends. I think you have an audience of eight hundred people you knew at one time or another, and now they're just faces on a screen, and you don't really know anything about them except one-liners and pictures of their kids and vacations and how successful they are."

"You're twisting it into something bad. I'm tired of talking about it."

"I'm tired of you choosing everyone else over me."

He looked so sad, part of me wanted to cry. But he was being stupid. I put my phone on the table, even though I was dying to know the name of the company, and I thought he wanted to know it too. The phone vibrated. I picked it up and moved it to the couch so it wouldn't make so much noise, rattling on the hard surface. I walked over to Marcus and put my arms around his neck. He put his arms around my waist, but they weren't as tight as usual. I wriggled closer and kissed his neck. He didn't move. "I love you," I said.

"I know."

It scared me a little that he didn't say I love you back, but I wasn't going to ask him. Eventually, he'd calm down. I needed to stop looking at my phone when we were talking, as hard as that was. After he went into the backyard to check the chlorine level in the pool, I'd be able to catch up with Jake's new job and all the other things going on. And later, I could tell Marcus about the housewarming party. A real-life party. That would make him happy.

A few minutes later, when I was getting out bread and turkey to make sandwiches for lunch, I looked at my phone.

Jake Ash *Mirage.*

Kimberly Frank *What do they do?*

Jake Ash *Aggregate social networking sites.*

Seth Porter *No wonder the stock took off right out of the gate.*

Tiffany Jones *Congrats on your new house, we can't wait to see it. "Then my people will live in a peaceful habitation, and in secure dwellings and in undisturbed resting places." Isaiah 32.18*

Byron Jones *Congrats. Home is where the heart is.*

Megan Miller *God, Tiffany, it sounds like a grave — undisturbed resting place.*

Dave Eddington *That's morbid.*

Tiffany Jones *We all bring our own filters to the Word of God.*

Dave Eddington *Where's the house?*

Jake Ash *You'll see when you get the invite.*

Dave Eddington *Fair enough.*

Adam Jamison *It couldn't happen to a nicer guy.*

Amelia Loc *I know. He's a sweetie. And so smart.*

Megan Miller *We're in need of a party! Let me know if I can bring something.*

Adam

ADAM JAMISON [*UPLOADED 1 video*] *Archie: when he was three months old*
   32 favorites — 5 comments

Kimberly Frank *He won't be a puppy much longer. I can't believe how big he is.*
   Megan Miller *He's so cute! And so well behaved! I should get a dog. I can't really afford one right now. I can hardly afford to feed myself. JK, but it will be a while before I get a dog. I'll come visit yours.*
   Seth Porter *Dogs validate the Republican platform. They know they have to earn their keep.*
   Allie Sinclair *Really, Seth? You have to turn Adam's dog into a political statement?*
   Pam Jamison *LOL. We taught Archie to sit, and he's only fifteen weeks old!*

THE DATE FOR Jake's housewarming was the same day Pam and the kids and I were heading out to go camping in Death Valley for three days. After that, we were driving to the Grand Canyon for a week. We'd been planning it for five months. Pam had put in her vacation request, and the kiddos were really looking forward to it. Pam was disappointed because she wanted to see whatever exotic, expensive, non-kid-friendly palace Jake had constructed. She loves extravagant things, even if she doesn't own them.

I like to look at fancy houses too, hang out at lavish parties, and consider the whole Gatsby phenomenon — maybe it makes me feel like I'm a more successful novelist than I am, at least so far. But I wasn't keen on a party where I'd be face to face with Allie Sinclair. As much as possible, I avoid parties with the high school crowd for just that reason.

Allie's and my breakup was over eight years ago, but it was so abrupt and so silent, it haunts me. The silence made it oddly profound, as if it was a kind of death experience, something so awful it couldn't be spoken about. There was no stilted and shameful conversation, eyes shifting away from the other's face. There wasn't any clichéd *it's not you, it's me* comments. There were no words of regret, no humiliating text messages exchanged, no public exhibition on social media. AboutFace was pretty new when we broke up, so it wasn't a deliberate move to keep it out of the news feed, we just didn't think about it. There weren't any tears, at least not any observed by Allie. Just a sudden absence of the other person.

Now, we're polite, if self-conscious, when we see each other. Or maybe that's only me. She never seems self-conscious, doesn't even seem aware that we were a couple, that we gave our virginity to each other. We're friends on AboutFace, but even after all these years, I don't want the awkwardness of seeing her. You'd think I would have outgrown a teenage rejection by the age of twenty-eight, almost twenty-nine.

"It wouldn't be that big of a deal to change the dates," Pam said. She stood behind me, staring at the invitation I was holding. It was printed with gold script on stiff cream-colored paper, like a wedding invitation. Although I couldn't see Pam's face, I could feel her lift her arms as she pushed her hair behind her shoulders so the strands were no longer touching the back of my neck.

"The kids are looking forward to it," I said.

"The kids won't even remember it. We'll have to go back when they're older."

"We have reservations, we'll never get different dates this late in the year."

"We could go to the Grand Canyon first and then to Death Valley. We should be able to change the reservation there."

"Why are you so anxious to go to Jake's? Looky-loo fever? You want to drool over his cash, fantasize about having a rich husband?"

She poked my spine. She ran her finger up my back. She leaned over and kissed the side of my neck. "You know better than that."

I smiled, but I was somewhat queasy.

After six years of marriage, she still hasn't figured out that I prefer to avoid Allie. Whenever these parties come up, Pam is hot to go, wanting to get to know my high school friends better. I'd just as soon move on. I don't mind the social media connection, but I have friends from college, why dredge up all that high school stuff? I guess I'm a coward for not telling Pam I was dumped. She'd probably laugh, and I'm not sure I'd like that. It's not that I still have feelings for Allie. Those withered a long time ago, before I even met Pam, I think. But the humiliation of knowing she had the upper hand lingers — the last word, even though it wasn't a concrete word. Being the one who's spurned leaves a sick feeling in your stomach. It eats at you. I should let it go. Not telling Pam makes me a bit of a coward. When we do go to the occasional party and Allie's there, once I become aware of her proximity, I'm on stage — trying too hard to be funny or smart or interesting.

"We should go." Pam stroked my ponytail, arranging it down the center of my spine. She does that as a sign of affection, I know. And it feels good, but at the same time, it feels a little like she's trying to rearrange me.

I folded the stiff paper and dropped it in the trashcan under my desk. "I don't want to go. I'm looking forward to being outside, escaping the frenzy. And we planned this. The kids . . ."

"It's not the kids, you're excited about it."

"So what if I am?" I turned the chair around and grabbed her hips. "I get you all to myself."

"You already have that. We'd only lose one day."

I didn't get why she was pushing. I mean, she pushes a lot,

so it wasn't unusual in that sense, but it was just a housewarming party. She hardly knows Jake and the others. "I don't want to go. And I don't want to talk about it anymore. We planned this trip. We're going. I hope you're more interested in the desert and one of the wonders of the natural world than a flashy symbol of Silicon Valley one-upmanship."

"I just don't think it would be that big of a deal."

"It's not. That's why we're not going."

"Okay." She tugged away, turned, and walked out of the room. I swiveled the chair back around and launched AboutFace. I went to Allie's page. Her profile picture was a shot of her riding a black horse on a beach somewhere. Because of its color, the horse looked monstrous, its dark eyes indistinguishable from the rest of its face, which gave it the suggestion of a supernatural creature. The ocean was frozen into several lines of breaking waves. Her hair was blowing behind her. With her perfectly erect back and the way her chin was lifted slightly to keep the hair off her face, she looked regal. In many ways, she looked like a stranger. If her name wasn't right below the picture, I wouldn't feel anything. There was nothing inside me in terms of wanting her or anything like that, but still, I couldn't stop looking. I couldn't let go. Maybe it was the awareness of *what could have been* or maybe simply the rejection fermenting inside all these years. I wasn't even sure what I'd done to cause things to end, whether there was a secret agenda I'd failed to meet. Almost every day, I went to her page. It's a good thing AboutFace doesn't give updates on who's looking at your profile like some sites do.

Allie's a dominating, powerful person. She's one of those women, and she was one of those girls who always gets what she wants. Everyone likes her. Even if they don't want to like her, they can't help themselves. I guess it's called charisma. Maybe that's why having her dump me had such a big impact. There's this need to make her regret saying goodbye to me, a need to have her realize what she lost and to notice that maybe she made a mistake. Kind of pathetic, all these thoughts, but I can't stop them.

There's no doubt I love Pam, but I cannot break the habit of stalking Allie. And if I'm honest, that's what it is. AboutFace provides the perfect tool for keeping tabs on a person without being a freak. You're only a freak in your own mind. You can hide it from everyone else. You can even hide it from the woman you love so much you wanted her to be the mother of your children. The woman you need. And if that was true, I couldn't figure out why I had this compulsion to review Allie's photographs, to check her status and see what other people were saying to her, even to follow, as best I could, what she wrote on the comment threads of our mutual friends. Eventually, I'm going to have to get a grip on this because when the kiddos get older and start noticing social media and hover around everything I do, I can't let them see me obsessing over a woman from high school. It's been fairly easy to hide it from Pam. Not that I'm hiding it, just making sure I look when she's not in the room. No, that's not right. It's just a daily habit that I don't feel I need to highlight to her. A mindless habit. When I'm sweating it out over my novel, I need a break. Something that doesn't require thinking, a harmless distraction.

Allie has hundreds of pictures on AboutFace. Every single time she cooks an elaborate meal, eats in a restaurant, goes to a party, has a family event, or celebrates a holiday, she uploads three or four pictures. Some people, me for example, like to upload scenery shots or animals. It's not that she's self-absorbed, she's just a people person, and it shows in her profile. It's littered with people. The most recent photo upload was from Tiffany Jones' baby shower. They didn't have it until Tiffany & Byron's kiddo was about three months old. Fifteen or twenty women were sitting in Allie's living room, and from the number of pictures on Allie's and Tiffany's pages, it looked as though Allie spent the entire party snapping and uploading photos. There were several shots of Allie — cutting cake, handing gifts to Tiffany, lifting a champagne glass full of orange juice. There was a shot of her touching the edge of the glass to her friends' glasses, which more than likely had champagne mixed with the OJ. She was smiling as if she was the happiest woman on earth. Maybe she is.

I heard the toilet flush, so I closed the page. I went to my photo app and scrolled through a few albums, looking for more pictures to put up. I don't make a lot of status updates.

I prefer pictures — one is worth a thousand words, as they say. Posting something I'd taken weeks or months earlier was lame, but I kept looking, certain I'd find something interesting, something that might entice Allie to comment. She *favorites* my posts a lot, but she rarely makes a comment. Obviously, the dog lured her in. It wasn't a comment to me directly, but it struck me that she'd briefly come out from behind the curtain. It probably meant nothing, since all she did was complain about Seth's politics. Still, it was something. It meant she looked at my page.

I couldn't come up with a single image to post. The most interesting ones were already up there. In another few weeks, I'd have hundreds of shots from Death Valley and the Grand Canyon. Those would spread out for quite a while, hopefully not boring my friends. As long as I mixed it up.

I looked out the sliding glass doors. Archie was curled up like a fur footstool, napping in the center of the patio, not realizing it would be more comfortable on the lawn, or inside the house in his bed. I could go out and take a few pictures, think of something crazy or weird to post. But who takes pictures just to have something to post? Especially something to post to attract the interest of a high school crush, a woman he supposedly doesn't have any feelings for?

The screen had gone dark while I was staring out the door, planning how to live my life on AboutFace, as if I didn't exist without it. As if it decided how I'd spend my time and what I chose to document in photographs. The waves of nausea increased like an incoming tide. I stood and pushed the chair as close to the desk as it would go. The padded armrests prevent it from tucking into the opening where it belongs.

Pam was nowhere in sight. My writing was completely derailed for the day. Maybe I'd tell Pam I was going to a coffee shop, or a bar, to absorb the atmosphere and let all the noise provide a cocoon so I could write. Not that I'm Hemingway, drinking my prose into existence, but sometimes a beer or a shot, sitting in a public place, gets the juices flowing.

I went outside and scratched between Archie's ears, massaging his scalp. He made snuffling sounds, but didn't open his eyes, or make any move to lift his head. I rubbed harder. He opened one eye and looked at me as if to ask — *What the hell is wrong with you?* I wondered that myself.

Kimberly

KIMBERLY FRANK *HEADING out to Jake's housewarming in the hills. He knows how to do events. Maybe he's an event planner at heart, not a PR savant.*

14 favorites — 29 comments

Allie Sinclair *See you there.*

Pam Jamison *We'll have to miss this one too. We need to get better timing for parties.*

Megan Miller *@Allie. Glad to hear you're going. See you in a few.*

Dave Eddington *Just saw this update, and I can see you standing by the pool right now.*

Kimberly Frank *Hey, Dave. I'll find you. Or you find me.*

Byron Jones *A midsummer night's dream.*

Allie Sinclair *It's not midsummer yet. ;)*

[See 22 more comments]

TWICE, THE GPS told me I'd reached my destination, but all I saw were pine trees, dark and dense with clusters of dry brown needles at the center, not yet fallen, adding to the pile of dead needles carpeting the ground by the side of the road. Through the trees, I glimpsed iron and brick fences and more trees and shrubbery designed to hide palatial homes from curious drivers.

Inside those homes, lives seemed more significant than mine, the staging of custom furniture and professionally designed window coverings and curated paintings and sculpture. People inside those homes ate meals prepared by expert chefs, or maybe I just imagined they did. At what point was there enough money to hire someone to cook your meals and clean your kitchen on a daily basis? All the while, the occupants probably ignored each other the same way I'd ignored Alex when we were together, clutching their phones, tapping out directions to underlings in the constant, never-ending flow of emails and text messages. There are more emails in the world than human beings. It could be there are more emails and electronic files than there are pine trees, possibly even pine *needles*.

I pulled over, the tires whispering across the soft, dry needles. I kicked off my right sandal and pressed gently on the brake to keep from skidding. I unlocked my phone and studied the map that told me Jake's house was off a side road I'd evidently passed without noticing.

The sky had been light blue when I left home, but now, the sun was slipping toward the trees, leaving it pale and colorless. It would be another hour or so until dusk. I felt like an idiot — even though I was equipped with a constantly updated app, I was lost. You'd think with the entire planet mapped online, with crowd-sourced street and traffic updates, it would be impossible to get lost. Getting lost seemed the thing of horror movies from the last century. Was it really possible any more? Even I wasn't entirely lost. A satellite was informing the pulsing dot on my map precisely where I was.

Jake's property was one of several new parcels broken off from an estate that used to cover ten acres of land tucked into the foothills, so perhaps it wasn't entirely mapped out yet.

I put a piece of gum in my mouth to give my head something more tangible to chew on. I turned onto a road that was wide enough for a single car. After a few hundred yards, the road bent sharply, and I saw Jake's house. It was something from a mythical world, gleaming white stucco, and glass that gave off a gentle green shimmer. I couldn't tell if the green was reflecting trees in the windows as the sun sank below the horizon, or if the glass was actually tinted. Either way, it looked magical — the Emerald City. Unlike the Emerald City, the semi-circular driveway was lined with palm trees. The double front doors stood open, the frame lined with a string of fairy lights.

A valet, complete with a navy blue uniform, waited for the guests. He opened car doors and extended his hand to assist them out of their vehicles before handing the cars off to three additional valets who took turns disappearing with each car back out of the driveway, up a slight hill, and around a bend in the road.

I pulled up behind a Range Rover and got out of my car

before the valet could open the door. The kid looked disappointed, but I didn't feel like pretending I have a life surrounded by staff that assists me in and out of the car.

The foyer was actually a large hallway, open to the second floor. It ran from the front door to the back wall, which was constructed of glass panels that had been opened up, so the hallway and the patio blended into a single space. Twenty or thirty people were scattered in small groups, talking and laughing.

I walked the length of the hall, nodding to a few people I knew. Most of them I'd never seen before. Outside, steps on either side of the patio led down to another level where there was an oval swimming pool. Bouquets of gardenias and some other white flowers I couldn't identify floated on the surface of the water. All around the pool were iron tables and chairs, some of them occupied by people eating appetizers and drinking cocktails. Others stood in groups talking, holding drinks and small plates piled with skewered shrimp and chicken satay.

As I stepped onto the patio, my networking instinct took over. It's programmed into my muscles to enter a venue and immediately get a read on the top dog and identify the trouble spots. The trouble spots being groups of people whose faces advertise the stagnant conversation, one individual dominating, talking loudly and gesturing just as flamboyantly, the eyes of the listeners quivering visibly as they seek escape routes.

I ticked off the three most important people I needed to connect within the first hour. In this case, the lead dog was obviously Jake. He was at the far side of the patio, the small of his back pressed against the sculpted concrete railing. Periodically, he glanced out over his swimming pool, smiling and talking a mile a minute to the people standing nearby. In his case, the listeners appeared interested in what he had to say.

Allie, Marcus, Dave Eddington, and Tiffany and Byron Jones were clustered around him. Byron wore a black San Francisco Giants cap pressed down so hard it forced his hair into a bristle at the base of his skull, his ears protruding more than usual.

Even standing immobile next to his wife, Byron looked like he was swaggering. He wasn't a guy who deserved to swagger. He'd never struck me as all that bright. He was nice enough, but couldn't carry on a conversation beyond sports and clichés. He was a walking refrigerator door, covered with magnets displaying pithy statements. Tiffany held their baby on her hip. I assumed the boy was with a sitter because I didn't see him wandering around. It was completely stupid of her not to recognize she should have hired someone to watch both kids.

Dave wore cargo shorts and flip-flops and a saggy brown t-shirt. He looked as if he was there to tile Jake's foyer rather than to offer admiration to a newly minted millionaire.

I wasn't seriously planning to network. There was no one

there who could have done anything for my career, but I couldn't stop myself from thinking in those terms. I crossed the patio. Amelia joined the group at the same moment I did, taking her position on Jake's right.

Jake grinned at me.

I wriggled past Tiffany and company and hugged him. "What an amazing place. How did you keep this quiet for all this time?"

"I know how and when to make a splash," Jake said.

Amelia giggled and took a sip of her martini. The stir stick with a single olive bobbed toward her cheek. She moved the glass away from her mouth.

"I thought the IPO just happened. And suddenly you appear with a fully formed house, like Athena?"

Jake smiled. Amelia giggled again and said, "I'll go get you a drink, Kim. What do you want?"

"White wine would be perfect."

Amelia handed her martini to Jake, who wasn't holding a drink. She wandered slowly down the stairs, glancing across the yard to see who was watching, behaving as if she'd already forgotten where she was headed.

Allie gave me a hug. "Cute dress," she said. Marcus stepped up and kissed my ear. When he moved away, Byron kissed the other ear. Dave stuck his beer bottle in his mouth and nodded in my direction. His teeth clicked against the top of the bottle. Tiffany lifted the baby up as if she were toasting me with her kid. The baby looked startled and leaned back toward her mother.

I turned back to Jake. "So, how did you manage all this when you just went public?"

"Kind of a ballsy question, don't you think?" Jake said.

"Just curious."

He laughed. "Obviously, I knew the IPO was in the works before I interviewed. I assumed success and went for it. I had enough leverage to get this off the ground a year ago."

"Well, it's spectacular. Well done."

"I'll give everyone a tour when Amelia gets back with your drink."

Dave splashed beer into his mouth as if he planned to gargle it. He dragged the back of his hand across his lips. "I'd ballpark this place at five mil. Which means you raked in about three or four right out of the gate? Or was it more?"

"Dave!" Tiffany giggled. She shifted the baby to the other hip. "You shouldn't be asking questions like that."

"It's not a secret. The cost of everyone's house is plastered all over the Internet. We know what the stock started at and where it closed. It's not like it's hard to guess."

"But you shouldn't talk about it," Tiffany said.

"Why not?" Byron tugged on his ball cap, forcing his ears out even further.

Tiffany reached over and pushed the bill up his forehead, returning his ears to a semi-normal position. "It's crude."

"It's public information," Byron said.

"It sounds greedy."

"I don't see how." Byron grabbed the baby's foot and jiggled it. The baby laughed, but the musical tone of her voice did nothing to ease the film of tension that formed on their faces.

"It doesn't bother me," Jake said. "It *is* public. Everything's public."

"It's still tacky," Tiffany said.

"Just making conversation," Dave said.

Amelia walked up the steps carrying two glasses of wine so pale it looked like water. She handed one to me and held out the other to Tiffany. "I noticed you didn't have a drink."

"I'm not drinking," Tiffany said. "I'm nursing Ruth."

"The alcohol goes right into Mommy's milk," Byron said. He touched her upper arm and stroked it gently.

"Eww." Amelia reached for the martini in Jake's hand. In turn, she passed the rejected glass of wine to him.

"It's God's plan for babies," Tiffany said. "There's nothing *eww* about it."

"It's not about the milk. He called you Mommy . . . like you're his mother." Amelia sipped her martini.

"No he didn't," Tiffany said.

"Yes he did." Amelia shivered dramatically.

"I think it's time for the tour," Allie said.

Jake put his hand on the back of Amelia's head. "I'll let Amelia show you. A lot of the best features were her ideas." He buried his fingers in her hair.

The gesture was so firm, so intimate, it felt as if he was

reaching into my belly, twining his fingers around my intestines. It's bad enough seeing relationships on AboutFace — vicariously watching the thrill of a first meeting, observing the evolution into joint selfies, if that's a word, and then weekends spent together. Watching it in the flesh is worse. Sometimes I felt I'd made the worst mistake of my life. I wasn't sure I'd ever find anyone I loved like Alex. Or find anyone at all. But he didn't love me as I really am, so what did it matter? I need a man who's equally driven, who doesn't view my business trips as a personal rejection. I looked into my glass. The wine was gone. I hardly remembered drinking it.

"I'll catch up with the tour." I held up my glass. "I need a refill." I turned and walked quickly down the steps before anyone could argue. I pulled my phone out of my pocket while I waited for the bartender to get to me. I walked over to the edge of the pool and snapped a picture of the flowers floating near the flagstone steps leading into the water. The blossoms were so beautiful, so extravagant, so alluring. I'm not sure why. Maybe because it was an unusual way to display flowers. There was something about them that advised the guests not to use the pool, it was there for decoration only. I posted the picture with a comment.

Kimberly Frank *Gorgeous. Intoxicating scent. Most pools smell like chlorine — not Jake's.*

It wasn't what I really wanted to say. I don't even know what I was trying to communicate. Deep inside, where I couldn't look without cringing, I saw a ghost of jealousy. I didn't want to be that way, didn't want to feel something so weak and helpless, but there it was, nagging at me like a barking dog or a car alarm that's far away, and at first you don't even know what it is, you just know something is making your skin crawl.

Once my glass was full of wine, a very generous pouring, I carried it toward one of the lounge chairs at the side of the pool. I kicked off my high-heeled sandals. The concrete was cool on my feet, and I was instantly calmer. I settled in the lounge chair and crossed my ankles. I was wearing a black and white dress with straps that cross in the back. Reclining pulled it up to the fleshier part of my thighs, only a few inches below my hipbones at the sides, but I wasn't in the mood to wriggle around trying to get it tugged down a few inches. I was in the mood to feel a bit exhibitionist. Everyone else did — Jake and his money, his massaging of Amelia's head, Byron and his apparent lust for his wife's breast milk, Dave and his thinly veiled envy. At least it diverted my mind from the envy worming its way up from my subconscious.

It's not that I thought my career was all about money, but money certainly says something about the status of a career. Knowing Jake was so far past me burned in my stomach like I'd eaten a fistful of tortilla chips dripping with flaming salsa. He made it look so easy. I wanted to be one of those people who rode the waves of life and enjoyed every minute. Someone who could say whatever came into my mind and do as I pleased and have it all work out, have people drawn to me like they clustered around Jake, admiring and liking me at the same time, while all I had to do was be myself. But it hadn't been like that for me, and I had no idea why. Why did he have a woman who adored him, and the man I loved gave me the choice of being another person entirely or saying goodbye? What did Jake have that I didn't?

All that pale blue water, and despite the hot, sultry air, not a single person had dipped their toes in. Surely, someone wanted to dive in and let the silky water stroke their hot, swollen skin. Only the undulating flowers were taking advantage of the soothing temperature.

Even without my shoes, my feet were puffy and red. I spread my toes. There was a chip in the polish on my right big toe. The pedicure was only two days old. Irrational fury burned inside my stomach, stirring up more self-loathing. I couldn't even manage to maintain a lovely pedicure for a few days. As I studied the chipped polish, it became a metaphor, illustrating my life, my career. All the mistakes I'd made at work, my superficial friendships, the bubbling memories of Alex, clogged my thoughts.

I glanced around the pool. The others seemed to be genuinely caring about each other, enjoying the party, not sulking alone over a drink. They were laughing, relaxed, never even starting to consider how they might turn the event into an opportunity to enable their careers.

As I closed my eyes for a moment, the wine glass tipped to the side in my hand. I tightened my grip and opened my eyes. The glass was empty again. I stood and went to the bar and asked for a refill. It seemed that all I wanted to do was drink wine, watch the others have a good time, and hopefully turn my back on the vast emptiness inside of me.

After my glass was refilled, I drank half of it and asked the bartender to top it off. Without bothering to put on my shoes, I went up the stairs, wove my way through the people on the patio, and went into the main hallway. Amelia's tour was surely over. I drifted toward the darkened dining room, sipping wine as I walked, luxuriating in the buffed hardwood floor.

Kristen

KRISTEN THOMAS *STANDING around at Jake's "housewarming" party. I say "housewarming" because this place is more like a palace than a house. Wait that's not right . . . a compound for a small city of people. Conspicuous consumption at its finest. Love ya' Jake, but wow. Just wow.*

8 favorites — 4 comments

Dave Eddington *It's stunning, isn't it?*
Kristen Thomas *It is. I don't even know what to say.*
Allie Sinclair *Be nice. We're all happy for him.*
Tiffany Jones *Definitely. It's gorgeous.*

BY EIGHT-THIRTY I wasn't sure why I'd gone to Jake's party. The amount of resources consumed by two human beings sickened me. Although I'm as hypocritical as the next person, my disgust didn't stop me from enjoying his fresh, hand-made spring rolls, plates of sushi, and tissue-thin seaweed with wasabi. He'd obviously spent thousands of dollars to feed his friends top shelf appetizers. There were seven or eight varieties of wine, buckets of beer, martinis, mixers for vodka, and all kinds of soda pop and flavored waters. But I couldn't find a tea bag anywhere in his ten thousand square feet of glass and plaster and wood.

It was bitchy of me to stand next to his swimming pool, looking up at that massive house, take a bite from one of his egg rolls, and post a comment calling him the poster child for conspicuous consumption. I didn't actually call him the poster child, but pretty close. What was he thinking? Did he have a shred of concern over the living conditions for the other 99.9% of the world? He could have created an ocean of goodness with all that money.

I settled for a bottle of plain water, hating myself for using plastic. My friends deluded themselves that the plastic wasn't destroying the planet because it was recycled. They'd stuff their fingers in their ears if I attempted to remind them of all the resources required to execute the transformation from crumpled plastic into something usable. No one wants to think about what they're doing. Would they pour a gallon of turpentine on their garden every day and hope to harvest a crop of vegetables?

I carried my water bottle into the house and headed toward the kitchen. I passed through the dining room and stopped to look out through the floor to ceiling windows. The pool glowed in the semi-darkness. Light from torches flickered across the water. The clusters of white flowers absorbed the color of the flames, looking as if they'd been soaked in blood.

At the far side of the pool, Kimberly was stretched out on a chaise lounge drinking wine. No one was talking to her, which wasn't a surprise. She always seems to have an agenda, talking about her job, where she's traveling, how important she is, how she's going to get promoted in the next year, and arguing with no one in particular that she's right on track. It's like she thinks she has to advertise herself, as if her friends are there to help advance her career, when most of us don't even understand what she does. Technical Marketing. What does that even mean? Not much different from whatever Jake does, I suppose.

I don't understand the high-tech field at all. I may not earn as much money, working outside of the gold mine, but at least I feel good, knowing I'm making the world a better place. I like knowing I impact people's lives, educating the next generation. Helping them to see how we need to work together to save the earth. Sometimes I wish I'd taught middle school so I could get kids when their brains were fresher, more open to new ideas. Getting through to high school kids is like trying to shatter bulletproof glass. All they care about is parties and sports and sex. A decent portion of them are also focused on getting into a good college, but they want the college degree for a big paycheck, not the joy of learning.

Jake's kitchen was larger than my entire apartment. Except for a track of small, dimmed stage lights over the center island, it was dark. I was pretty sure I wasn't supposed to be in the kitchen, or any room in the house where the lights were off, without Jake or Amelia as a personal tour guide. I guess when you have a new multi-million dollar house, you don't want your friends wandering around unsupervised. But all I needed was a bag of tea and a kettle.

The center island was the size of a small car. One end was a butcher block, and the rest was white granite streaked with gold. Miles of granite countertop surrounded the island. Below all of that were cabinets and drawers to hold every pot, pan, and appliance you'd ever need. Above the counters, some of the shelves were open, stacked with dishes and glassware that sparkled as if someone came through daily and polished every piece.

I opened the cabinet under the six-burner cooktop and found a kettle. There was an open shelf filled with mugs that looked as if they'd been made of sand — beige with raised granules that looked gritty but were smooth when I ran my finger over them. I put one of the mugs on the counter next to the kettle. After opening every single cabinet and drawer, I still hadn't located any tea. I was sure I'd seen Amelia drink tea and couldn't believe there wouldn't be a few bags tucked into an easily accessible crevice. After circling the kitchen twice, I realized there must be a pantry, but at one end, there were double glass doors in wood frames that led to the dining room, and at the opposite end, a door into a bathroom. There were no other doors.

A simple cup of tea was not too much to ask for, and I was starting to resent their assumption that everyone wanted alcohol or soda pop. I'd known Jake since we were ten. He knows I drink tea. It's not like I thought his party menu should be geared to me, but it should have flickered at the edge of his mind. I walked around the island again and opened the door into the empty dining room.

As I stood there trying to keep my breath calm and quiet, letting my resentment dissolve, I heard voices near the arched entrance on the other side of the dining room, about ten feet from where I was standing.

Two women were speaking. One was definitely Amelia, but I couldn't make out the other. Amelia has one of those voices that you can hear on the opposite side of a restaurant. It's not that she's loud, but the pitch carries like it's on a different frequency from every other voice in the room. "To be honest, you're too meek," she said.

The other voice murmured for several seconds.

"Jake doesn't try," Amelia said. "He's like a Jujitsu master. He releases everything, and as a result, he gets everything. And then some." She laughed. Her laugh sounded immensely proud of Jake, and herself, for some reason. I can't say why she gave that impression, but that was my first thought. She went on, "He doesn't give a shit what anyone thinks of him, and there's a lot of power in that kind of approach, don't you think?"

"That's dangerous."

Now I recognized the voice — Kimberly. Her words were blurry, the *g* in dangerous was more like a *y* — *dane-yer-ous*. A few minutes earlier she'd been in the lounge chair drinking wine, staring at the pool. She must have moved while I was looking for the tea. I took a drink of water.

"Why is it dangerous?"

"People don't recognize how capricious executives are. Not giving a shit might work as long as you're in their favor, but it can change like that."

I imagined Kimberly snapping her fingers, but I couldn't hear it.

"That doesn't matter for Jake now."

"'Cuz he has more money than he'll ever need?"

"That's right."

"It should be about doin' a good job, in working hard for wha' you want instead of just tripping over it . . . getting the respect of your peers, and management." Kimberly coughed, as if she meant to get rid of the blurry words.

"Jake gets tons of respect."

"For now."

"Don't be trying to bring him down."

"I'm not."

"I think you're jealous." Now, Amelia's voice was slightly louder than usual and definitely louder than necessary.

"Not at all."

"Jake worked hard. But part of his success is not caring. Following his instinct. You could learn from that."

"What's that suppose' to mean?"

"You're too serious, so busy following all the rules. You're obsessed with minutia and taking the right steps, you're probably missing opportunities."

"How would you know? You don't know anything about my job or my company."

"Instinct. I have great instincts."

"Well aren't you special," Kimberly said. Now her voice was perfectly clear, the words sharp.

"You asked me how Jake got where he is. I'm telling you. Don't bite my head off."

"I didn't ask you anything. I sure didn't ask for your advice. You know nothing about business."

"Excuse me," Amelia said.

"Jake lucked out, that's all."

"I think you're wrong. I think there's power in not trying so hard, in saying what you think and doing what you want and truly not caring."

"Power in not trying? What kind of new age blah blah is that?"

"This house says it all."

"Does it?"

"Maybe we should join the others," Amelia said.

"After you apologize."

"For what?"

"For implying I'm not as successful as Jake."

Amelia laughed, for several seconds longer than she should have. "You're not."

"My career is completely different. It requires a lot more knowledge and strategic thinking."

Amelia laughed again.

"Stop laughing."

"I think you should let go. Try a different approach. It can't hurt."

"What a bunch of clichés."

"They're clichés because they're true. Be bold. Do something crazy."

The room was silent, and I couldn't tell if they'd suddenly walked out or were staring at each other, wild-eyed and angry. For a second, I thought about moving closer so I could see what was going on, but I hadn't meant to eavesdrop. They intruded on me, not the other way around. I didn't want them to misinterpret and think I was deliberately spying on them. Of course, Amelia wouldn't care. But Kimberly might. She's a very proud person. Very determined and very, very proud.

Allie

ALLIE SINCLAIR [*UPLOADED 2 new photos*] *Marcus and me, Jake and Marcus and me.*
19 favorites — 7 comments

Kristen Thomas *You look like you're having more fun than anyone.*
Allie Sinclair *I doubt that, but it's a great night. Love this house!*
Pam Jamison *Sorry we aren't there, but the Grand Canyon trumped Jake's showcase.*
Tiffany Jones *God's creation always trumps man's.*
Byron Jones *A picture's worth a thousand words.*
Megan Miller *Marcus looks super handsome.*
Allie Sinclair *Always.*

Allie Sinclair [*Uploaded 8 new photos*]

BY NINE-THIRTY I'd managed to get pictures with almost everyone. Most of them with Marcus and me, but some with just my friends and me. I was standing by the side of the pool, uploading two shots when Megan walked around past some potted plants clustered near the deep end. She came up next to me and leaned close. She smelled like almonds. "Let me see the ones you didn't post."

I handed my phone to her.

She scrolled through them. "I need to catch up." She handed the phone back.

"It's not a race."

"I know, but I always forget. Let's do one of you and me, with our feet in the water."

We kicked off our sandals and sat on the edge of the pool.

"Feels good. Jake should have told us to bring swimsuits," Megan said.

"It's not that kind of party."

"But such a waste. All this nice, cool water, and he's turned it into a giant flower pot."

I laughed and held my phone out over the water. We tipped our heads toward each other, and I took three shots. "One of these should be good."

"You always look good," she said.

"Not really."

She held up her phone and snapped a picture.

After a few minutes, we pulled our feet out of the water and stood. The wind picked up as if removing our feet from the water had signaled the weather gods. It rippled the water, and the flowers began circling faster. A glass blew off the bar and shattered on the concrete. After a few minutes, they started disassembling the bar and food tables, servers appearing out of nowhere to carry things into the house.

I looked at Megan. "Have you seen Marcus?"

"He was with Seth."

We picked up our sandals. "I have to pee," Megan said. "Sticking my feet in the water after three glasses of wine wasn't a good idea." She giggled.

"You better slow down since you have to drive home."

"I'll worry about that later." She giggled again and poked me. "You should lighten up. A few glasses of wine don't mean you can't drive. Why don't you have one?"

"You know why."

"Getting ripped, and enjoying a few glasses of wine, are different things."

"Sorry, no. If I drink, I'm no different from the asshole who crashed into my mother."

She patted my arm. "A glass of wine might make you feel better."

"It won't."

"Okay. Sorry. I just thought . . ." She pulled her phone out of her pocket and opened AboutFace.

It seems like people are only happy if everyone is drinking. Maybe deep down they know they shouldn't, and they feel less guilty if everyone else does it. Or maybe they just think it's so wonderful they have to share the love. I have no idea, but I wasn't ever going to take the chance that I'd be that guy who walked away with a bruise on his forehead while my mother ended up under the ground at Chapel Hill Cemetery. I don't cry anymore when I think about it, but the pain isn't much different than it was when I curled up in my bed and cried until I felt like my stomach might slide up my throat and out of my mouth.

Megan put her phone back in her pocket. She dropped her sandals on the ground and stepped into them. "Now I really have to pee. See you later." She walked around the pool and up the stairs. She looked very determined, not at all drunk, but still . . .

Losing my mother to a drunk driver didn't make me an activist, although I suppose it should have. It did make me hate people who drink too much. Marcus never has more than one glass of wine or a mixed drink, sometimes a beer. Most of my friends drink a lot. It's not that I hate them, but there's an inexplicable mixture of anger and sadness when I watch them slam down drink after drink. When they do that, they tend to not even remember the party, except for the pictures, so what's the point? If you can't remember what you did, how do you know for sure you had a good time? Or do they just think it's fun that they lost their minds for a few hours, went to some other place they'll never remember? I really have no idea. I don't see the appeal, and I get sick thinking about the horrible things that can happen.

I looked at the comments on my pictures and clicked favorite for all of them. I put my phone away and went inside the house. I found Marcus in the living room, sitting on a black leather chair. Seth was sitting in an identical chair that he'd pulled around so he could face Marcus. At least Marcus wasn't alone in the room. I will finally be perfectly happy when I get Marcus to be more social, to not go out of his way to find an empty room at parties and sit there reading a magazine, or rolling dice on a game table, or staring at nothing. He says he's just relaxing, but I don't believe him. It seems like he's hiding.

Marcus and Seth were leaning toward each other. Marcus looked intense like he was making a physical effort to open his ears wider, to listen harder, as if that might help him understand Seth's views on the world. I couldn't hear, but I imagined Seth was giving a lecture on the decay of American society, with an emphasis on how the liberal media controlled the national conversation and treated the average man like he was stupid and didn't know enough to manage his own life. I was sure that's what he was talking about because that's what he talks about ninety percent of the time.

Marcus can shut out the entire world to focus on one person, one conversation. Even at a party, everything else and everyone else is a distraction as far as he's concerned. He doesn't really know how to mingle at all. It's annoying when I want to move from group to group so I can talk to everyone, laugh, and not have a life and death conversation. But when I don't find him in a room by himself, I find him in some corner, ignoring everyone but the person sitting nearby. He'll listen to anyone's views, even if he totally disagrees, even if it's borderline crazy talk. People love him for that, though. He pays attention, and he manages to disagree without setting off a temper tantrum. I don't know how he does it. Still, that's not what a party is for.

I walked toward the opposite end of the room from where they were sitting. Two enormous windows joined at the corner looking out over the backyard. The flowers that had been floating so gracefully were pushed up against the edges of the pool, partially submerged, bruised from banging against concrete. I stood there for a moment, inexplicably lonely. Marcus didn't seem to notice I was even in the room. After another minute or two, hearing the drone of Seth's voice, I turned and walked back toward the main hallway.

A small sunroom opened off the side of the living room, although it was more of a moon room at that point in time. Amelia and Jake were standing in the center of the room, their heads bathed in moonlight. Their arms were wrapped around each other so tightly they had the appearance of vines creeping up a trellis, four limbs, difficult to tell which belonged to which person. Watching them felt voyeuristic, but I couldn't stop. They each gulped down the other in a seeming effort to swallow the other whole. Amelia's hair swung out from her back as she reached up. Her feet were bare. She kept her feet flat on the floor, not rising on her toes to meet him, but pulling him down to her height. The inside of me turned warm and soft, like melted cheese. Not that I'd kiss Marcus like that in front of all my friends. I guess it was the alcohol, making them forget anyone might be watching.

Jake flattened his hands against the back of her waist and slid them into her pants. He gripped her butt, his knuckles protruding through the fabric as if there were giant spiders inside her jeans. Tired of feeling like a wannabe in a ménage à trois, I turned and walked into the main hallway and over to the bar for another glass of orange juice.

The bartender informed me without an ounce of sympathy that they only kept orange juice on hand for the occasional mimosa and I'd managed to suck down the entire supply. He used those words — *sucked down*. I suppose he was getting tired. He was the only guy pouring, and he'd been on his feet, uncorking bottles, twisting off caps, and shaking drinks for almost three hours.

I took the orange soda he managed to find at the back of his stand. It was too warm, but he also gave me a glass of ice. I poured half the soda into the cup of ice. I smiled and thanked him. "Do you work at parties full time or are you a bartender at a club too?"

"This is it."

"You must see a lot of crazy things."

"I'm too busy serving drinks to spy on people."

After the excessive amount of time I'd spent watching Jake and Amelia, his comment made me feel even more freakish. The back of my neck felt sticky. I was suddenly hyper-aware of the sweat on the bottoms of my feet, despite their soak in the pool.

I moved away from the temporary bar. I took a sip of my drink and watched people drift up and down the hallway. The ceiling was open all the way past the second floor, making everyone look small and somewhat lost. It was as if Jake's house was too big for a good party. He didn't invite enough people, and now that some guests had left, the echoing hallway and all those enormous rooms swallowed our core group of high school friends. Part of a good party is forcing everyone close together, so the sheer physical presence of each person makes you feed off each other's energy.

I went to one of the buffet tables where a woman was preparing sushi rolls. I took a small square plate and put three spicy tuna rolls wrapped in seaweed near the edge. I sprinkled soy sauce in the center of the plate. I added a dab of wasabi. The sushi maker smiled at me. "Fresh as you can get it."

I popped one in my mouth. I talked around the seaweed clinging to my teeth. "It's delicious."

She lifted the top off a bamboo container, revealing piles of potstickers. I sprinkled chili oil in the center of the soy sauce, took a potsticker, and dragged it through the oil. I took a bite. "Amazing. I've always wanted to try making potstickers."

"It's not that hard," she said. "Just takes practice." Her fingers, thin and bony as chopsticks, moved like hungry mice over the pieces of fish as she placed them on rice and wrapped them snugly in sheets of seaweed.

"I love trying new things, but I haven't done much Asian food."

"Amateur chef?" she said.

"No. Not really. Actually, I wish . . . I was thinking of . . .

when I started college, I was going for a degree in hospitality management. I thought I'd apply to a culinary arts program after."

"Changed your mind?" She laid out another piece of seaweed.

"I guess. Things happened. I ended up just getting a general degree."

She nodded.

Tiffany and Byron and Dave approached the table. Dave was talking, hardly breathing between words as he finished a story about why Byron should take up golf. He launched into his thoughts on the recent defeat of the Giants. I took a few steps back, but they didn't seem to notice I was planning an escape. I put my plate and empty glass on a stand set up to hold dirty dishes. I sat on a bench and opened my browser. I found a link to the culinary school I'd thought about applying to all those years ago. I pasted it on AboutFace.

Allie Sinclair *Where do dreams go when you're not paying attention?*

Two minutes later, I had three favorites, but no comments. Maybe it was a bit too revealing, too personal, too sad. I put my phone away and walked back down the hallway and out to the patio. The wind had eased off, but there was still a strong breeze. The torches sputtered, running out of oil the same way the party was running out of energy. I walked to the railing and leaned my arms on the concrete balustrade. It hurt my bones, but at the same time, the cold felt good on my skin. I closed my eyes and breathed in the scent of jasmine and a suggestion of eucalyptus from the trees bordering one side of the property. Then the smell of chlorine rose up from the pool and overpowered all of it. I opened my eyes.

The water was smooth, the flowers were still pressed up against the sides, more waterlogged than ever. There was a flash of white about a foot under the surface as something floated past the underwater light at the deep end of the pool. The object moved closer to the surface, and something dark and fine wavered near the top, then drifted lower. The water undulated, and the flash of white rose to the surface — a woman's breasts covered by a sheer white bra. I screamed.

The shoulders sank, and her hips rose, showing a matching white thong.

I kicked off my sandals and ran across the patio and down the stairs at the left side. I screamed again, not entirely sure what I was saying. My voice sounded unnatural as if it was coming from someone else, someone standing right next to me and far away at the same time. "Help me! Someone help! Now!" I ran to the side of the pool wondering why I hadn't chosen the patio stairs leading to the deep end, not that it would matter. I knew in a deep, instinctive part of my body that screaming and running in the correct direction wasn't going to change what had already happened. But I couldn't stop.

I ran along the side, and when I reached the section where it was about five or six feet deep, I did a long dive, feeling the drag of my dress changing my movement through the water. I wished I'd taken it off, but it seemed too time-consuming. It would definitely be time-consuming trying to extract my self from all that sopping wet fabric. I couldn't believe I was thinking these things as I took a few quick strokes and approached where she was floating, I dove under and saw her face, eyes open but not seeing me. Kimberly.

I surfaced and took a huge gulp of oxygen. I rolled her onto her back and wrapped my arm around her chest, tucking my hand in her armpit. I began swimming to the side.

People were shouting, but my neck and chin were submerged, so I couldn't hear what they were saying. My whole body was pushed down by her weight and the effort of pulling her through the water. My dress, now clinging to my legs, made it difficult to kick.

When I reached the side, four or five pairs of hands reached out to grab Kimberly. Her body made a sickening sound as they dragged her up over the lip of the pool. Her torso smacked the concrete, but there was no sound coming from inside of her.

I sobbed, trying to pull myself out. The edging ground its way into my ribs, tearing at my bones like it wanted to shred me. So many voices were talking, someone crying, but I couldn't tell who it was or even what anyone was saying because there was a rushing sound in my ears, and the noise of the water slapping into the filter opening.

Marcus reached out and pulled me up. He knelt beside me and wrapped his arms around me, pressing his face into my neck, breathing with loud gasps.

Behind me, Jake's voice became clear. "Amelia's calling 9-1-1, but I guess it's . . ."

"No," I said, my voice still sounding as if it belonged to another being.

"She's not moving."

"That doesn't mean anything."

"Do something."

I opened my eyes. Byron was bent over Kimberly, pinching her nose, blowing air into her, but it sounded like grunting as if the air couldn't find its way into her lungs.

Marcus squeezed me harder, and I curled into a ball inside the circle of his arms. I started to cry. I heard their voices, still talking all at once.

"What happened?"

"Did anyone see her?"

"Last I talked to her, she sounded loaded."

"Did she trip and fall?"

"Why'd she take off her clothes?"

"Do you think someone pushed her?"

"She knows how to swim."

"How much did she drink?"

"She's a good swimmer, I think."

"How do you know?"

"She had at least four glasses of wine, that I saw."

"Why did she take off her clothes?"

Further away, I heard Tiffany's daughter screaming. I cried harder, and one by one they stopped talking, stopped asking questions that only Kimberly could answer.

Silence surrounded the pool and spread across the yard. Even Marcus's breath in my ear was softer, fading to nothing as he moved his head. Then a siren, two sirens, split the air. Raw fish, and seaweed, and orange juice roiled in my stomach. I sat up and tried to take light, shallow breaths. I thought about my mother and how she loved her life and wondered if Kimberly felt the same. I knew all the things Kimberly posted sounded happy and confident, but who knows for sure.

Dave

DAVE EDDINGTON *I spent three years remodeling, and Jake throws up glass and concrete in two weeks and wows the world. Well done, dude. ;)*

19 favorites — 6 comments

Jake Ash *It's been in the works for more than two weeks. Stealth mode. Your place is awesome — a work of art.*

Kristen Thomas *I love your house Dave, it shows love.*

Allie Sinclair *I agree. It's a work of art. You need to have a house-warming party, Dave. Whatever happened to that?*

Tiffany Jones *What they said. :)*

Dave Eddington *I feel like a creep, posting this when Kimberly was probably already gone, and we didn't know it.*

Tiffany Jones *It's okay. You didn't know. None of us knew. Only God.*

AFTER KIMBERLY DROWNED, her AboutFace page was flooded with comments. There were hundreds of photographs added, going all the way back to kindergarten — Kimberly holding one of her pigtails with one hand, her arm extended with a lizard on her radius bone, staring straight into the camera, Kimberly and her cat. Kimberly playing the flute in a school talent show. Her family posted baby pictures and videos of her learning to walk, high school graduation, college graduation. Even her ex popped up and shared photographs of her laughing, tastefully leaving himself out of the shots he chose.

If she'd ever had a moment of craving popularity when she was alive, she should have seen this. Every time I checked, there were updates. It was sickening and unsettling to see her name coming up in my feed, as if she were making the posts herself. I wondered when someone would get around to changing her account to a static page. I also wondered who had her password and was keeping it alive. Did the AboutFace technical staff read obituaries to see if they needed to change someone's status, so to speak? Or was that all done by the person's family?

For the time being, it seemed as if she was still alive, living a ghostly, shadowy existence. There was this weird cutoff from when she'd been alive and posted the normal, slightly tedious thoughts all of us do, except possibly Jake, to this dramatic fantasy where suddenly she was the most amazing woman who had ever walked the earth. I guess it's always that way. A person's flaws die with them or are transformed into lovable qualities. If she was a bitch, she became someone who was honest and didn't pull her punches, someone to respect and admire. If she was a whiner, she turned into a person who felt her emotions strongly, sensitive to the world, too tender to deal with reality.

It made me wonder what they'd say about me if I died before my time, or even at my time. You never know what people *really* think of you, and then the one time they speak those thoughts out loud or post them on your wall, you're not around to hear it or read it. But if you could, you still wouldn't know because they'd all be polished, buffed up versions of you.

I scrolled through pages of pictures and comments, pausing the longest on the high school shots of our group, amazed by how different I looked. It had been years since I'd opened my yearbook. You don't notice how you're changing every day, every year. In a lot of ways, I didn't feel any different inside than I had back then. I knew more stuff about life now, but I thought I knew a lot about life then. In the older me, my face was harder, my skin thinner, the bones of my skull more visible. My hair still hadn't pulled back as far from my forehead as it had for some guys — Seth, for example. My neck looked thicker now. I had more muscle than fat all over — that's what working with your hands does for you. I realized that now, I might be able to succeed at football. Now that it was too late.

After a while, it was too depressing looking at all those smiling kids, oblivious to how life would kick us in the balls. I scrolled further, back to the things Kimberly had posted when she was alive. I read all the after-the-fact comments on her final post announcing that she was headed to Jake's party. Some were creepy, posted before she drowned, or before we knew she'd drowned, saying great to see you. Looking good, and shit like that.

I went back more, scrolling up to the post she made a few weeks ago from New York — *Figure out what you want before it's too late.*

Whatever she meant, whatever made her post that, was a mystery forever. It was a little creepy because you could interpret it that she prophesied her own death — *life is short.*

She had thirty-seven favorites on that one. It was probably one of those comments where people didn't know how to respond. Clicking favorite is easy. *Easy!* Some people get fifty favorites by saying the lamest shit, and other people, even when their updates are more interesting, get half that. I can never figure it out. Is AboutFace just one big popularity contest? It could be a percentage thing — some people have more friends, so they get more comments. Who knows. It pisses me off, sometimes. It's like walking into a party and getting ignored.

THE MINUTE I'D arrived at the housewarming, part of me had wanted to leave. Maybe my gut knew something bad was going to happen.

Jake's house was like no house I'd ever been inside. Sure, I'd driven past its type, blocked from the view of peasants, nothing but flickering glimpses of stucco and brick and wood from behind dense shrubs and mature trees, surrounded by thick, walled gardens or iron fences wrapped with vegetation.

With all the homes where I'd tiled everything from kitchen counters to foyer floors and bathroom walls, in quiet, wealthy communities, none had been as extravagant as this. It was enormous — twelve thousand square feet — and so finely decorated, I had a very hard time believing he hadn't had a lot more money before the IPO than he'd let on.

I followed along on the house tour, listening to Amelia babble on as if the house was her design. Jake was always staring at her with a sappy look that said she was a heavenly creature who had appeared on his doorstep — special delivery from the gods. She's attractive enough, but not my style.

Byron and Allie and Marcus were dogging Amelia's steps. Tiffany held herself back slightly, whispering and cooing at the baby, shushing her every few minutes. She acted as if we were on a museum tour instead of wandering around a house designed in every detail to highlight the excellent taste and bottomless bank account of the owner. We walked through sparsely furnished room after sparsely furnished room. Plaster walls and vaulted ceilings echoed our footsteps off the buttery hardwood floors. There wasn't a dust bunny or a pile of loose change or an unwashed coffee mug anywhere in all those twelve thousand — *twelve thousand!* — square feet of perfectly laid out space. The rooms flowed into each other as if a psychologist had designed them to appeal to human desires and habits. The furniture was all gleaming wood and leather, metal and glass. The house gave off the impression that no human beings inhabited the place. No hairs, no sloughed-off skin cells or bits of broken toenail.

Thinking about broken nails reminded me of Tiffany's weird toenails. I inched to my left so I could get a better view of them. Although it had been weeks since I'd delivered my chili, her nails were still longish, somewhat pointed, as if she'd filed them. She must have deliberately trimmed them longer than average. Or they were slow growers. I wanted to ask, but it would probably be one of those questions that made me sound like a freak. I couldn't take my eyes or my mind off of them. There was something both unclean and sexy about it that I couldn't explain. Maybe they gave the impression she had a secret side because they didn't fit with the rest of her. She has a round face, the kind they call cherubic. She has a sweet smile and very round, dark brown eyes. Her hair is cut a bit like a little kid's — with straight bangs. The rest hangs just below her jaw. Her skin is so smooth she could be four years old. The toenails definitely suggested there was something else going on inside of her. Something she never unveiled to anyone, maybe not even to Byron. They suggested a wilder, bohemian side. They suggested she wasn't as clean and pure as her face wanted you to believe. She was all over the baby, kissing it and smelling its head like she wanted to eat it. I turned away.

Suddenly, we were in the master bedroom. Amelia showed us how the lights were all independent and could be adjusted to make the room go from broad daylight, even at night, to a ceiling that seemed to be open to the sky, filled with stars. There was a huge picture window behind their bed. I imagined them having sex in front of that window, hoping someone would drive by and admire their perfection. I'm sure it wasn't like that, but the way she lowered her voice to a husky whisper made me wonder. The floor was bleached the color of sand, and the bedding and the frame were black. There was a couch and coffee table. A large rock sat in the center of the table. The closet had built-in drawers, no need for a dresser. So there was this vast room with three pieces of furniture and a mirror big enough to reflect a tour twice the size of the group following her around, all their mouths partially open in gasps of astonishment. Except mine.

I moved up next to Tiffany and asked her in a quiet voice if I could hold the baby.

She looked at me with her eyes wide, circled with feathery lashes. She didn't blink. "I don't think that's a good idea. She gets fussy at this time of day."

"I'm pretty good with kids," I said.

"But you don't have any."

I don't think she said it to be cruel, she's not a cruel person, just the opposite. A lot of religious people can be extremely cruel, and completely oblivious to how vicious they sound, but not Tiffany. From her round face and dark eyes to the sound of her voice, she was a big pot of honey.

"I'm around kids a lot. My brother's sons . . ."

"They were just born! A six-month-old is a lot different.

Anyway, Ruth is already on the edge and handing her off will tip her past the boiling point. Now shhh. We should listen to Amelia so we can be done with this." She giggled.

I agreed with that. Forty minutes to show off your house to your friends is beyond excessive. "Why are we even listening?"

Tiffany shrugged. "It's polite."

"Is bragging polite? Is rubbing your money in your friends' faces polite?"

"Shhh." She gave me a look that said she thought I was funny but I should do as she said.

"The baby looks heavy," I said.

"She is."

"Do you want to go sit in the media room? There's a rug. She could crawl around."

"Oh. I don't think so. It would be terrible if she did anything to that carpet. It's better if I hold her."

"I'm tired of listening to this blah, blah, blah . . . me, me, me."

"We asked for it."

"Did we?"

"By saying yes when Jake asked if we wanted to see the place."

"And now I've seen it."

"Are you jealous?" She smiled as if she'd figured out a secret I was trying to keep.

"No."

"You sound like you are."

"I'm not. I don't like people who brag. I think Amelia is being a bit of an asshole. It's not even her house."

"Don't say that. I don't want Ruth to hear words like that."

"She's too young to understand."

"You're wrong. Their brains absorb everything. I'm molding her brain into what God wants. It's an unformed lump of clay. And even if she can't understand the word and would never know what it meant, it's ugly, and the hatred becomes part of her."

"Do you really believe that?"

She nodded.

"So I'm one big mass of everything my parents pounded into me?"

"It's more than that, but everything we become starts building when we aren't even aware — babies in our parents' arms. That's why the job of mother is the most important in the whole world."

"What about the job of father?"

"That too. But let's face it, in most cases, mothers are there all the time. So I said mother. They have more influence."

The conversation was boring me. Her toes no longer looked alluring, they were disturbing, as bizarre as her views on life. Still, I couldn't stop looking at them, wanting to touch them for some morbid reason. But I'd only offered to hold the baby because Tiffany looked tired from lugging all that weight around on her hip. I didn't want a lecture on parenting, or to be told to watch my language. I moved away from her. "Sorry to offend."

She put her hand on my arm. "Just be careful, that's all." For some reason, the touch of her hand made me angrier.

"I do know what you mean, though," she whispered

"What's that?"

"About people bragging. It makes some people feel bad. Even though I have everything, sometimes I feel kind of bad when I look on AboutFace and see vacation pictures of places I wish I could go to. I don't know if we'll ever be able to afford anything except camping."

I wasn't sure what to say to that. I took a few more steps away from the group, then looped around the outside of the cluster of people to where Allie was staring out the window. "Wishing it was yours?" I said.

She smiled. "Not really. It's kind of cold. And much too big. Are you wishing it belonged to you?"

"Not at all," I said.

"Liar." She laughed and punched my arm.

"I'm not a liar."

"I think you are." She looped her arm through mine and led me further away from the group.

"Done with the tour?" I said. I pulled slightly, hoping she'd drop my arm, but liking it at the same time. Allie has the ability to make everyone feel like they're her best friend. I liked that about her. I liked that by pulling me away from the others, she changed my mood. At the same time, she seemed a little flirty, and it bugged me. If I flirted back, she'd get pissed. It was okay for her, but I had to just go along, let her be the party time lead while I was turned into some kind of toy. I pulled again, and she let go of my arm.

"What's wrong?"

"Nothing. I think I'll go get another beer. Want anything?"

"I'll go with you," she said.

"I'm not lying. I couldn't live in a house like this. It'd be like living in an office building."

"Your house is cool. I guess you and Jake have different tastes."

"In many ways."

"What does that mean?"

"Nothing. It means nothing, I don't know why I said it."

She took my arm again and led me outside where she asked for a glass of orange juice, and I got a microbrew that I'd never tried before. The beer was cold. It put me back in party mode.

Megan

MEGAN MILLER *GOD! I can't believe one of my friends is dead!!! She was the exact same age as me!! It's so sad. So awful.*
   0 favorites — 6 comments

   Allie Sinclair *I didn't favorite this, calling it favorite makes no sense for something like this. It's too horrible.*
   Megan Miller *I know what you mean. I can hardly get out of bed. I'm devastated. Beyond devastated. No words.*
   Allie Sinclair *Let's have tea or coffee. I'll message you.*
   Tiffany Jones *I'll pray for you, sweetie. It's so hard. Your first word is the one that matters. Only God can help with something as terrible as this.*
   Dave Eddington *It sucks.*
   Byron Jones *^This^*

MOST OF MY life I've been expecting bad things to happen. And now something has. Kimberly is dead. The best they can piece together is that she had a lot of wine, too much wine, took off her clothes — although how she did that without anyone noticing is a mystery — dove into the shallow end of the pool, and whacked her head on the concrete step because her aim was sloppy.

It makes me feel sick every time I think about it, which is almost all the time. I don't know why anyone would do something so crazy, especially someone like Kimberly. She was the most methodical person I knew. I want to scream and pound my fists against the sky, although, of course that's not possible. How can such terrible things happen? Why did it have to happen to us, to me? At Jake's party where we were all having a fantastic time? I can't bear to think of her in a coffin, going into the ground. I can't bear to think of her rotting away. She was my age. Was. Was. *Was.*

I posted how I felt on AboutFace, and everyone ignored me for five or six hours. Finally, Allie commented. She comments on everything, so big deal. I wouldn't tell her that, but she always has something to say. It seemed like she didn't get what I was feeling, and it seemed like no one felt as bad as I did. So bad, so scared. Sometimes I hate AboutFace. All these people chatting and posting pictures and clicking favorite, and it feels like I'm locked in a room alone, cut off from the human race, no one to hear what I have to say and no one really noticing me, just noticing themselves. Maybe I'm that way too.

Two days after she drowned, I was standing in my bedroom brushing my hair, wondering if I should put a white or red streak of dye in it. I felt the need to do *something* to make it more interesting. I felt like I was back in high school. Not because I was thinking about how Kimberly disappeared from our lives after high school — how she found new friends in college and business school and kind of forgot about the rest of us for a few years. It felt like I was in high school because I was in the bedroom where I'd grown up. I couldn't forget that for a single minute because my twin bed was reflected in the mirror. The bed was covered with the same fluffy white thing I'd had since I was twelve. Back then, I liked all the pictures of birds stamped on it. As I got older, I grew to hate it. I moved out and covered my bed with an antique quilt I'd picked up at a yard sale. Now, here I was, back home like a kid. And the quilt is in the closet because my mother said it doesn't match the decor of the room. She doesn't say it, but she makes it clear that if I'm going to live here rent-free, I'm not allowed to turn this into my own funky place that doesn't fit the rest of her house.

The bedroom door was closed, but I could hear her in the kitchen, banging the dishes into the dishwasher like she always does when she wants my help, and I'm not taking any initiative. But I didn't eat breakfast, she didn't cook eggs for me, that was all for my stepfather and my half brothers, who live here too, by the way. But somehow I'm the one who failed. They never moved out at all, so I guess it doesn't count as failure.

She's so tense, my mother. And passive-aggressive. I studied that a lot in my healing and therapy classes. She should get therapy, or at least take up yoga, or get massages. Something to chill out, but all she does is bang dishes and vacuum and go to her aerobics class. And that doesn't seem to provide any mood-altering endorphins whatsoever. She's a bigger grouch when she comes home than when she left. I guess the people in the class get on her nerves. They spend too much time chatting and are always trying to get the teacher to start late so they can talk, and my mother wants to get down to business and get her fitness fix.

When I told my mother that Kimberly drowned, she pressed her lips together and murmured something about drinking and wild parties. After that, she looked at me for a minute, and then she was more sympathetic. She told me about a girl who died when my mother was a senior in high school. But that girl had Leukemia, so it's not at all the same. I don't mean to undermine the sadness of it, but it wasn't shocking. I suppose the unfairness of the world was the same, but she kept talking about that girl, and I didn't get to say much about how I felt. Still, she was trying. I could see that.

I'd been sitting at the table, holding my mug of tea with both hands. It had been forty-five minutes since I brewed it, and the icy chill had now penetrated the ceramic. Every time I took a sip, I felt queasy. There's nothing as unappetizing as cold tea. Iced tea is fine, but not herbal tea that's made to drink hot.

My mother put her hand on my wrist. "It wouldn't have hit you so hard if you had some purpose in your life."

My bones tightened beneath my skin, but she didn't seem to notice that my arm was trying to make its own effort to break free of her grip. Her fingers were light and cool, she wasn't squeezing hard, but it felt as if she had me locked in shackles. The room was silent except for the sound of my bones, grinding against each other, crunching and squeaking with the effort of resisting her touch and the pressure of her mental space shoving up against mine.

"Did you hear me, honey?"

"I have purpose." I hated myself for speaking. I shouldn't have to defend my purpose. She's my mother! The fact that I exist should be purpose enough. My friends' mothers worship the ground they walk on, but mine is never happy. I wonder if she cherished me even as a baby, like Tiffany does with Ruth. Kissing her face, touching her skin as if she's the most precious gem on the planet. A goddess in human form. My mother, on the other hand, wants to tear me apart, peel off my skin, dismantle my bones, and re-build me into something acceptable.

"Rubbing your hands all over the filthy skin of strangers is not a purpose."

I was not going to have this conversation again. If I didn't speak, she would run out of fuel and wind herself down. All I had to do was listen to her assault and deflect the words so the pain couldn't penetrate.

"I found my greatest purpose in my family. In raising my children," she said, oblivious to my thick skin.

"And now that we're all raised, what's your purpose? I guess that didn't work out so well." It was a mistake to respond. She would win. Every time. Her will was stronger than mine. It had taken root on the earth twenty-seven years before I came into existence. I would never beat her. Never.

"When I was not that much younger than you, I was searching also."

"Stop."

"I'm trying to help, sweetie." Her face looked kind enough as if she'd organized her features to be sure I believed she was trying to help. Her dark brown hair, not a single strand of gray, straight cut bangs, was tucked behind her ears. It was a very contemporary haircut for a very old-fashioned woman. She had the values of Mrs. Cleaver but the hairstyle of Uma Thurmond in *Pulp Fiction*. Except for the wrapping it behind her ears. Uma let it brush across her face, looking chic and resisting the urge to tame it.

"Giving people back rubs is not a meaningful life."

"They aren't back rubs. I release stress from the body's memory system. I help people heal. Not only physically, but mentally."

"Stress is an over-used word. It was invented by people who don't have their priorities straight."

I closed my eyes. I smelled the crispy cheese topping from the lasagna we'd had for dinner, the cleanser she uses on the sink, and a hint of ripening oranges. "I hate it when you trivialize what I do."

"I'm not trivializing. I think you've realized you can't make a living at it."

"It takes time to build a client list."

"It's a little disgusting, I'm sorry. Thinking of your hands all over total strangers. How do you know they don't have diseases?"

I yanked my arm out of her grasp. It was surprisingly easy.

"I'm really concerned about you. I want to help."

"I don't need help. Being a masseuse is a gift. People need touch, they die without it."

"You're telling me you're one step above a prostitute."

I shoved my chair away from the table. As I stood, the chair wobbled. I grabbed it to keep it from falling.

"Careful."

"Did you just call me a prostitute?"

"Surely, you see the connection. That's why your choices are such a concern."

"I can't believe you said that."

"Sit down."

"I'm not a child."

"You're my child. And I'm worried about you."

"My friend just died! And now you're calling me a hooker? My profession is part of the healing arts."

"You're not a doctor."

"It's proven that touch releases oxytocin and improves the sense of well-being. Touching isn't always about sex. It's insulting that you'd even think of making that kind of connection."

"Calm down."

"Why can't you support me?"

"Because I'm worried about you."

I wanted her to scream, to tell me all the horrid things she thought about me. Instead, her voice remained even, deliberately calm, trying to make me look hysterical, overreacting. She was calm, she was caring. I was crazy and unstable. Giving truth to her statement because she was proving by my outrage that she'd struck a nerve. I pulled my phone out of my pocket, clicked it awake, and scrolled through AboutFace.

"What are you reading?"

Without looking at her, I said, "Just checking Kimberly's memorial page."

"Were you really that close?" She looked at me, not afraid of my rage, or maybe she didn't even know it was there.

"It doesn't matter that my friend died, since we weren't as close as you think we should have been?"

"That's not what I meant."

"Oh."

"Just don't fixate on it."

"That sounds easy. I'll pretend she never existed. I'll pretend we were just casual acquaintances."

"Megan, please." "Mother, please."

She closed her eyes as if she was searching inside her head for some way to control me, to get me to be the kind of woman she envisioned, not someone who blurted out words as ugly as hers. Of course, when she said things, she was just being truthful. When I was blunt, it was cruel or hysterical.

"Can you put the phone away so we can finish talking about how to handle your feelings of sadness?"

"I think we're finished." I walked to the doorway. "I'll be fine. Like you said, how close were we, really?" I shoved the phone in my pocket and went down the hall to my bedroom. Like an angry teenager, I slammed the door closed.

I WAS AT Peet's Coffee, waiting for Allie to show up. The line went past the food display and looped around a rack of mugs with the coffee shop logo in chocolate brown on a white background. Every table was occupied. I'd been lucky to see a guy leaving just as I finished paying for my coffee.

I tapped my AboutFace page to see who had commented on my post about Kimberly's death. My friends must have been thinking the same things as me, but if they were, they weren't saying much. Still only five comments, not counting my own. And Byron's was hardly a comment. All he posted was "this", pointing to Dave's brief comment. I couldn't think of a comment requiring less effort than that.

I hit the page refresh, knowing it was just going to make me feel worse when it came up empty.

I'll be honest, because no one else is. It hurts when most of my friends ignore my posts. Sometimes no one comments at all. Or it's the same old someones. Allie remarks on anything to anyone, so when she makes a comment, it hardly means anything. It feels like she's just being nice because she's such a nice person. I hate that she's so nice, so easy to get along with. Which I suppose makes me a terrible person. I do all this stuff — meditate, practice yoga, study how to remove emotional gunk through touch and pressure, drawing in the other senses with instrumental music and scented oils — but then I have these bad thoughts. I worry a little bit if that's why I haven't built a solid client list and a business that can support me consistently. It's because I'm full of all this emotional baggage and resentment. Instead of healing my clients, I'm infecting them with my own poison.

I guess Tiffany almost always has something to say, but she acts like she's shoving a religious tract into your hand. She's never really commenting on what I'm thinking. Instead, she looks for a way to twist it into what she wants to spout out as if her canned messages are going to make people believe in god.

I looked at other pages, and they were filled with comments. People wrote about what it was like seeing Kimberly's body floating among the cut flowers. Some pages had fifteen, twenty comments. Amelia's had even more, and she didn't even go to high school with us. She probably hadn't spoken more than a hundred words to Kimberly the entire time she'd known her. The comments were genuine, supportive. I looked at my page and saw those five replies, and it made me feel like a loser, like no one cared about me. I couldn't make them respond. I could post more things I suppose, and comment on their pages more. But I do. I write notes all the time, and only a few people do the same for me. I start to wonder if they even like me, if I have any friends at all.

Sometimes I study their words. I try to decipher what it is that gets other people to respond. I can't tell if they're more vulnerable, or they're funnier, or wittier. I don't understand why I'm ignored, if I post at the wrong time of day or if I make people uncomfortable. I worry there's something wrong with me that I can't figure out. Maybe I'm just not that likable. I mentioned it to Allie, and she said, *well, the feed is always jacked up*, so who knows what appears and what doesn't. It made me feel better when she was saying it, but later, I realized her feed never seems to be "jacked up".

Crowded around the tiny round table to my left were two guys and a girl. The girl was thinness personified, thigh gap and all. Even though that's supposed to be a very anti-feminist, unnatural and unhealthy thing to aspire to, I can't help my aspirations. The desire is there as if it's some freaking pot of gold that having thin thighs will make my life perfect. This girl also had long silky hair, the kind that makes you wonder what the hell kind of shampoo and conditioner she used because I've tried more than I can count and my hair still has a fuzzy halo. I don't have curly hair, I don't have waves, just a permanent buzz of tiny strands of fluffed up hair.

I unlocked my phone again and started looking for something, anything, to distract me from that perfect girl and the two guys who were bleeding devotion all over her. They listened, looking straight into her eyes. The nodded like some caricature of guys, not real guys, who usually only look at you when you're telling a story because they know they're supposed to, but really they're thinking about World of Warcraft or the Giants or their next trip to Europe where they can drink beer on the company credit card.

Candy Crush was one possible distraction, but as I launched the game, I kept missing the target because my attention drifted to the table next to me, as if it was covered in Karo syrup and I'd placed my hands on the surface and couldn't pull them away. I wanted to be that girl with the friends who drank every word like it was crystal clear, slightly cooler than room temperature water. The kind of water that feels like silk as it goes down your throat. I wanted to be that girl with perfect hair, perfect legs, looking cute in whatever piece of crap outfit I yanked off the rack at a discount store, and equally fantastic in designer clothes. Instead, my clothes look like they don't quite fit. Sort of the way I don't quite fit in the world. And surely those guys weren't devoted to her because of her hair or her thigh gap.

I dragged my attention back to my phone. I closed the game and checked the time. Allie was seven minutes late. I checked email. I deleted text messages. I listened to the girl tell the guys about her job interview and how she was scared she wasn't going to get this job either. They made encouraging sounds, told her how talented she was. I felt like

I couldn't breathe. I looked at the door. Still no Allie.

At twenty minutes after three, the girl and two guys stood. At the same time, Allie walked through the door. She waved at me and went to order her tea. My cup was half empty. I couldn't afford to buy a second drink, and I didn't need the caffeine anyway. Part of me no longer wanted to talk to Allie. I wanted to go home and slide into bed and pull the spread up over my fuzzy hair, close my eyes, and disappear into a world of dreams. Even if they weren't good dreams, they'd be better than this.

Allie sat down. She smiled, managing to look grief-stricken and happy at the same time. "I'm so glad you had time to get together. We need to stick closer than ever, all of us. Life is so, so short."

I nodded and took a sip of my cappuccino, which I shouldn't have because, at this rate, I wouldn't be able to stretch it out through a thirty-minute conversation.

"Your post upset me," she said.

"Why?"

"It sounded so, I don't know, despairing."

"Isn't that how you feel?"

"Yes. But yours seemed more like a cry for help. I was worried."

I swallowed more of my cappuccino. I realized she hadn't invited me for coffee because she felt the same loss, the same emptiness. She didn't understand my feelings at all. She wanted to fix me. Within two minutes, she managed to make me feel like even more of a failure as a healer, and a slightly disturbed individual.

"She had everything. Why would she do that?" I said.

"She didn't kill herself," Allie said.

"She took off her clothes and dove into the pool when she was drunk. Even if she didn't plan to kill herself . . ."

"I guess you never really know what's going on inside people," Allie said. "They look fine on the outside . . . People need to speak up and let their friends know how they're feeling." She smiled and blew on her tea.

She didn't want to know how I felt at all. First, she patronized me with her worries, and then she wanted to gloss over it like it was too much trouble to really understand me. Suddenly, I hated her. "Everyone knows what's going on inside you, right?"

She smiled. "I'm an open book."

"What if no one wants to read?"

She laughed. "What's wrong, Megan? You sound really depressed."

"Aren't you?"

"I'm sad. Devastated, actually."

"You don't sound like it."

"We're all having a hard time. Our group will never be the same."

"The same as what?"

"As it was. Everyone in their places."

"So you only miss her because of how it affects our group?

If we even have a group."

"Why do you always have to be like this?" she said.

"Like what?"

"Acting like everything that happens in the world happens only to you?"

I sucked on the tiny hole in the lid of my drink, knowing nothing was inside my cup, but needing to do something besides look at her condescending smile. The voices around me all seemed to grow softer as if they were waiting to hear me speak. Her question echoed in my head. Had the voices around us been lower for several minutes? Had they all heard her accusation, followed by a question that set me up for sounding selfish?

"That didn't sound very nice," she said. "I'm sorry."

"Is that what you think of me?"

She met my gaze, dark blue eyes like the sky at dusk, without a hint of malice. "Everyone is upset about Kimberly. Have you seen her AboutFace page?"

I nodded.

"You sort of make it sound as if she was your best friend." She pressed her left ring finger into the outer corner of her eye and rubbed it gently. She took it away and studied the smear of mascara and shadow on the tip of her finger. She wiped it on her napkin. The diamonds on her wedding rings glittered like fallen stars.

"I can't believe someone my age, our age, is dead. I can't believe we were all there, and she died right in front of us, and we didn't see. I can't stop thinking about how she looked. I wake up and see all of us standing around, staring at her not breathing, knowing it was too late, but thinking maybe she was just passed out, and she'd sit up and start talking any minute."

Allie nodded. She took a sip of tea. After a short pause, she started talking about how she hoped Jake didn't feel his beautiful home was damaged now that someone had died there, that he wouldn't be averse to using the pool.

I didn't give a shit about Jake and his pool.

Jake

JAKE ASH *MAYBE we're all drowning.*
67 favorites — 3 comments

Allie Sinclair *what does that mean?*
Jake Ash *It's a mystery.*
Tiffany Jones *God knows all things.*

AMELIA WOULDN'T LEAVE me alone.

She put her glass on the table and stood. "Let me get you some water with lemon, babe." The light behind her made her look like a shadow despite the fact she was dressed all in white except for gold, Greek goddess-looking sandals. Her dress had an uneven hem and a loose top that fell off one shoulder. Her bare shoulder was sliced in half by a white bra strap. At another time and in another place, that uncovered skin, that interfering bra strap, would have been the center of my attention.

I shook my head and took a sip of my martini. My second, and it was only four-thirty on a Saturday afternoon.

"I haven't even finished my first drink," she said.

"Is it a contest?"

"No. But you're getting so morose."

"My friend died in my swimming pool."

"It was an accident."

"Was it?"

"Of course it was."

"I'm not so sure about that," I said.

"That's absurd."

Keeping my eyes on her lips, I fingered the giant olive out of my drink and sucked on it.

"Why are you looking at me like that?" she said.

I rotated the olive with my tongue, sucked out the pimento, and swallowed it. I bit the olive in half and chewed one piece, continuing to suck the gin and vermouth out of the other section, enjoying the combination of salt and alcohol. It was the only pleasure I'd found during the past few days — salt and numbness. But it wasn't enough. It wore off fast, and the questions bullied their way through the fog of gin.

"I don't know how to help you out of this masochistic mood," Amelia said.

I looked across the expanse of the living room that until seven days ago had given me extreme satisfaction and now felt like a waste of space. My eyes re-focused beyond the window, the roof of the lower patio opposite the pool. From my slumped position on the couch, I couldn't see the water, but I knew it was there, inviting the inebriated, the suicidal, the murderous. I'd worked so hard to face down all those thoughts of water, how it washes over you without warning, shoves its way into your nostrils, fills your lungs, and snuffs out your life. You can't grab it or push it away or escape those liquid arms, dragging you down and swallowing you like a piece of chum. When I rode a wave on top of my surfboard or propelled a raft through a gorge, it felt like I was the master. But it was an illusion. Water dominates the earth, and we're helpless against its force.

A swimming pool and alcohol weren't any different from an automobile and alcohol — a seemingly innocuous entity with the power of death. Allie knew all about that.

A woman's life ended in my fucking swimming pool. No matter what Amelia said, I was responsible. Somehow, in some way, Kimberly's blood, or rather her lack of blood, was on my hands. I felt that deep inside my gut. It was irrational but true.

"I can see you're thinking morbid thoughts again," Amelia said.

I sipped my drink. The second olive bobbed against my upper lip. "How can you see that? You're Superman now?"

"Huh?"

"X-ray vision. Except even Superman couldn't read thoughts."

"I don't understand why you're doing this."

Other women would start crying at this point. I'd been with enough of them to know. But Amelia was on her way to getting pissed off. She didn't like having her good-time, revenue-generating lover snatched out of her hands by something beyond her control. "What am I doing?"

"Blaming yourself for an accident. Letting it destroy our life."

"We only have one life?"

"What?"

"You said our life. It's *lives*. We have two lives. Your life. My life. And Kimberly had a life. Now it's gone."

She folded her arms across her chest. Usually, when she did that she was careful to place her arms gently across her ribs, pushing up her breasts so they bulged slightly out of her top, inviting me at the same time she was chastising me. Now, she pressed down hard, flattening them against her body, mostly covering them as if a stranger had caught her naked. It didn't matter. The only desire right now was the thought of pouring more gin into the metal shaker, hearing the ice rattle as it chilled the alcohol within an inch of its life.

"Please stop doing this. You've turned into a total stranger."

"How is that?"

"I don't recognize you. Guilt is a manufactured emotion. It's the product of conditioning. You do something contrary to how you were socialized, and voilà — guilt!" She lifted her chin a few inches to force her hair away from the sides of her brow, not wanting to uncross her arms to brush it out of her face.

"There's no such thing as guilt. Hmmm." I swallowed the rest of my drink, tapped the olive into my mouth, and stood. I gave the olive a few chews and swallowed. "All of the religions and most philosophical views in the history of the human race might disagree with the opinion of Amelia Loc."

"No one can make you feel guilty except yourself."

"You've never felt guilty?" I wondered, suddenly, how we could be engaged to be married without ever discussing a topic like this. Was the woman a sociopath? As far as I knew, they were the only types who'd never encountered guilt.

"I don't allow other people to tell me how I feel. I can say what I think, and if others choose to act, that doesn't mean my views or suggestions are at fault."

"That sounds very specific. Is someone trying to make you feel guilty even though guilt doesn't exist?"

"No."

"Then what are you referring to?" I crossed the room, turning my head to look at her, mostly so I wouldn't look out the window and see that glistening blue water. I went into the dining room and through the doors into the kitchen. Amelia followed, her sandals clicking on the tile when she passed through the swinging doors.

She folded her arms again and leaned against the counter. I unscrewed the cap from the bottle of gin.

"Really? Another drink? You're just going to drink yourself into a stupor and stop living because some girl you knew in high school went over the edge?"

"She wasn't some girl. She had ambitions, a great career, tons of friends. I don't understand what happened."

"How does that make it your fault?"

"I didn't say it's my fault, but I feel responsible."

"Same thing."

"It's not. It's a normal human reaction. And it changes everything."

"What's changed?"

I opened the freezer and got out some pristine ice cubes, put them in the shaker, and poured two shots of gin over them. They crackled like I was stepping on glass. The outside of the metal container grew frosty. I splashed in vermouth, pressed the lid into place, and began shaking.

"Can you stop doing that?"

"What?"

"Shaking that thing. It's hard to talk."

"It only takes a second."

"You don't need another drink."

She clicked toward me. She put her hand on my forearm. I lifted my arm out of her reach. She grabbed my wrist. I shook harder, moving her arm with my own. The motion made her breasts shake. I still felt nothing. The clean fire of gin was my only desire. Gin kept all other thoughts outside of my brain where I could study them and wonder if my life would ever be the same. It was a form of meditation — observing my thoughts. It was just that now, I preferred observing them through a numbing cloud, instead of their razor-sharp reality. I never expected to be responsible for a human being's life. That kind of trauma belonged to doctors and pilots. It belonged to drunk drivers, but I wasn't planning on driving anywhere.

"I do need another drink," I said. "I need another martini more than I need you."

"Stop it! I hate it when you're drunk. You turn into an asshole."

I laughed.

"Don't."

"Why? I need to sound like the asshole I am."

"When did you become such a jerk?"

"When my friend drank my wine and drowned in my swimming pool."

"Don't keep saying that."

I removed the lid from the shaker. I poured the crisp-looking liquid into a clean glass and shoved two olives onto a stir stick.

"Ouch," Amelia said.

"What?"

"You look like you're trying to murder those olives."

I laughed harder. Somewhat deliberately, I made myself sound more sinister, more unbalanced. She was right, I was drunk, and tormenting her was quite entertaining. It pissed me off that she felt nothing.

Then, in the time it took for me to lift the glass to my mouth, maybe less, I felt a great hollowness inside. I thought about Tiffany and Byron and their religion. Was there some kind of comfort in all the stuff they subscribed to? Of course, no one died on their property, but still, I wondered.

Until that moment, I'd thought both of them were a pain in the ass. I'd always considered Tiffany's vague, never-changing smile, slightly moronic. But maybe she really was at peace, assured that god had everything under control. Maybe they had some spiritual light that none of us saw, allowing them to live in a different realm.

Byron worked in his deli, and they loved each other and their kids. It was entirely possible that vacuous look hid an utter lack of inhibition. Didn't her comments, her constant quotes from the Bible indicate she didn't have a shred of self-consciousness? Maybe she was wild beneath all those conservative tops and skirts. Those dopey looks she shot at Byron might be whispering *take me home and take off my clothes*. It didn't matter that they had a dumpy little tract house. What pleasure was I getting out of this palace? And Amelia. Gorgeous and cold as the metal container still bleeding an icy film on the counter. Very sexy and as driven as I was. Except now, the parts of me that had conceived aggressive PR campaigns, kept me riding the various waves of social media, and lusted after Amelia, had drained out of me in the time it took to lift Kimberly's body out of the pool.

"I don't want to be with a drunk," she said.

"Then don't."

"Wait, I didn't . . ."

I smiled with one side of my mouth, some might call it a sneer, and carried my glass back to the living room. Once again, I carefully avoided looking at the picture window and the pale blue chasm of death lying below. I parked my ass on the couch and took a sip of my drink. So chilling, so tasty without really tasting like anything. Martinis are perfect in their simplicity. I wish I could write a press release for the drink, persuade the world to give up all other cocktails. And I don't mean martinis with fruit juice or chocolate. The genuine, classic martini. There's a reason it symbolizes an entire era and class of people. I took another sip.

Amelia was still in the dining room, just beyond the arched opening, her hair absorbed by the darkness of the room, all the shades pulled tight. The effect was to make her face glow like a pale moon. I put my drink on the coffee table. "I don't mean to be an ass. I feel responsible, and the world seems very fucked up right now."

"People die every hour. People are killed by disease and slaughtered in illegal wars and starved by corrupt political regimes every single day. One girl drowns in your pool, and now you have a conscience?"

"And you don't have one?" I picked up my drink and took a long, cooling sip. I held it out from me and admired the clarity of the alcohol.

"Of course I do."

"Then why haven't you shown a shred of feeling that someone dove into my pool and died?"

"It's not my fault she wanted attention."

"I didn't say it was. But there should be some sort of feeling over the fact that it was on our watch. Some sadness for a life that ended way before her time. And yeah, she was trying to attract attention in some fucked up way. I posted that comment about a striptease and then she goes and takes off her clothes. Doesn't that bother you?"

She walked into the room and sat on the arm of the chair across from me. "Your comment was funny, and metaphorical. Besides, she didn't do a striptease because no one saw her take off her clothes."

"It's still disturbing."

She spread out her fingers and tilted her hand slightly, studying her diamond. "I'm sad that she's dead."

"Are you? You seem more . . . I don't know, defensive. Like you want to make sure I don't put any blame on you."

"Because it's not my fault!"

"Why do you keep saying that?"

"It was an accident."

"Maybe you think it was your fault. Did you tell her to do a strip tease?" I laughed, inappropriately, I know, but I wanted to see her react. I wanted that composed face to show some of what tore at my insides as if I'd swallowed barbed wire.

Her face hardened, transforming from the soft glow of a moon into a glacier. Even her features shifted, becoming sharper. "I'm not responsible for anyone's bad decision."

"Did you talk to her at the party?"

"A little."

"What did you say?"

"I don't really remember the details."

"You must remember something."

"She was jealous."

I could tell she was holding back. Amelia was very good with details. I'd heard her recall conversations verbatim. I sipped my drink. It didn't really matter what she'd said, I was still responsible. My question was more curiosity, still hoping to see evidence of a conscience.

The world around me had definitely changed. I wondered about my single-minded pursuit of success. I don't just mean the satisfaction of being admired, but the satisfaction of the outrageous rewards that surrounded me and mocked me with their lifeless perfection. I had no idea who this woman was, living in my house, sleeping in my bed. Our bed, she would say. Did I love her? Did I even know what it meant to love another human being?

My phone chimed and vibrated against my thigh. Without letting go of my drink, I maneuvered it out of my pocket. I felt Amelia watching me. I sensed her irritation that I was going to dismiss her by walking out of the room and into a virtual conversation, via text or AboutFace or one of many ways the human race has devised to find a more interesting or less stressful or more entertaining conversation.

Like a mad juggler, I pulled one of the olives off the stick with my teeth, chewed it, and clicked on my message box. A direct message from Allie.

Allie Sinclair *I hope you're doing okay. Kind of worried about you*

— your last status update made me sad. Message me.

I wanted to let loose the same phony laugh I had a few minutes earlier — more phony messages from a world of phony people. Maybe Marcus had been right to cut himself off from digital society. Why hadn't Allie called? How was I supposed to explain in a tiny little box with letters smaller than my fingertips, how I was doing, which was definitely not okay? She claimed to be worried, but it sounded flip, like part of a checklist. That she was performing her due diligence.

"I'm talking to you," Amelia said.

"Not really. You're talking at me. Trying to beat the humanity out of me."

"If you feel so damn bad, take some of your cash and start a benefit, or do some work in third world countries. Kristen can point you to her human trafficking campaign. All the stuff you didn't give a shit about until some depressive decided to be an exhibitionist."

I swallowed my drink and ate an olive. The sun had moved low, and the sky was shedding the pale blue that made me think of nothing but swimming pools. Miles of water. Endlessly deep. I took another swallow of the drink. I didn't feel that great, drinking it too fast. I put the glass on the table.

"What are you going to do?" she said.

"I don't know."

I pressed my thumb in the message window to start my reply to Allie. I started typing.

"Stop texting!"

I didn't look at her. Maybe she was going to turn into another person entirely. Right before my eyes. Like I was apparently doing before hers.

Jake Ash *I have no status.*
Allie Sinclair *Call me.*
Jake Ash *Trying not to see that damn pool, but it's right there.*
Allie Sinclair *Don't blame yourself.*
Jake Ash *Who else is there?*
Allie Sinclair *It was an accident.*
Jake Ash *What makes you so sure?*

"Jake! You are not going to check out and start chatting with someone else. I'm your fiancé."

"I'm aware."

She walked to the table and picked up my glass, balancing the bowl between two fingers as if she'd contract a disease if she held it properly. She turned and carried it out of the room. I was too shit-faced to stand up and follow. Not shit-faced exactly, but my mood had made the alcohol more potent or something. I was being ridiculous. Wallowing in the drama of it all, but I felt bad. Really, really bad. All this time I'd thought I was golden. I couldn't do anything wrong, and everyone thought I was hot shit. And now, I felt like Kimberly had chosen my pool to end her life, trying to destroy the pleasure of my new house. She was smart. Her career was rising, maybe not as fast as mine. I didn't know why she'd done it, but I was responsible. No matter what Amelia said.

Allie

ALLIE SINCLAIR *GOOD-bye Kimberly Frank. We will never, ever forget you.*

135 favorites — 8 comments

Megan Miller *Every light that goes out leaves the world darker.*

Tiffany Jones *You can't give in to despair. THAT'S what makes the world darker.*

Allie Sinclair *I know, Megan. That's how it was when my Mom died — the world was so dark. But after a while, you see that their light is still inside you. Tiffany is right — don't give in to the darkness, girl.*

Dave Eddington *You want to make someone pay.*

Tiffany Jones *Revenge belongs to God.*

Byron Jones *Anger does more damage to the vessel in which it is held than the object on which it is poured.*

Seth Porter *Don't turn a woman's death into a cliché, man.*

Amelia Loc *A tragic accident.*

I STARED AT my phone and tried to think about what I could say to make Jake stop blaming himself, but my mind was blank. It was horrifying to think that Kimberly killed herself. If the stripping and swimming was a demand for attention, how pathetic was that?

It was his pool, and his alcohol, that made her do it. His gorgeous new home was tarnished now. He'd never look at the pool without thinking about her body floating among the flowers.

I stood up and slid my phone between the waistband of my skirt and my belly. I walked to the mantle and picked up our wedding photograph. My hair was shorter then, but you couldn't tell because it was piled up on my head with curls hanging around my face, which somehow made me look younger. It was three years ago. I *was* younger. Marcus was looking at me, not at the camera, so his eyes weren't visible, but the way he held his head, his hand on my waist, made it seem as if he didn't even know the camera was there. I think it was a posed shot, but he didn't act like it. Neither of us did. It was the best picture of all because it gave the impression we were the only two people in the world. I set it back on the mantle, turning it slightly, so it faced the couch more than it had earlier. I went outside.

The sun was a pale ball of yellow in a cloudless sky. A seagull floated above the pine trees bordering our neighbor's yard, its white feathers so bright against the blue, my eyes filled with tears. It was unusual to see a gull inland on a cloudless day, usually, their presence meant a storm on the coast. Maybe the gull had come to Silicon Valley looking for discarded fast food, tired of fighting the others for tiny sand crabs. The endless, perfect sky felt like a shard of glass in my throat. I couldn't believe that a girl I'd known since elementary school was dead. No warning, no reason, just a lifeless, soggy body dragged out of the pool.

Her hair had been plastered to her head, as if her skull was forcing its way out from beneath her skin, the hair clinging more tightly than it did after a simple swim. Seeing her so exposed, not just because she was mostly naked, but her gaping lips, like a dead fish, and her staring eyes, and the way her legs were spread, nothing hidden from view or imagination, everyone staring — and she couldn't do a thing to hide herself from their shocked and sickened eyes. Every stray pubic hair and scabbed zit and the chipped polish on her toenail was exposed. Strange men, and the female paramedic, touching her, letting her breasts flop around so they looked gross, was too much. I hated myself for it, but I cried as much over how it would feel to be her as I did over knowing she was dead.

When my mother died, I felt those same things a thousand times more — hating that all those strangers were touching her, that men she didn't know would be taking off her clothes, seeing her body. That she couldn't cover herself or arrange her face in a pleasant expression. I wanted to take her body and cover her in a shroud and put her in the coffin myself so no one would see that birthmark she hated on the back of her neck. It was hidden all her life, but she hated it. She refused to cut her hair short or ever put it up on the top of her head.

It was so unfair that two people in my life had died before

they were supposed to. I wasn't even thirty. A lot of people get to live into middle age before things like this happen. And it isn't fair to have people ripped off the earth before they get to do all the things they planned. Before Kimberly could find her soul mate, before my mother could watch me grow up and find my own soul mate, or figure out my career. Or have children.

Marcus could die without warning. He had a greater chance than most. I know that statistically, you're more likely to die in a car accident, but when you die in a plane, it's so dramatic. And flying itself seems to thumb our collective noses at gravity, so it's scarier. I didn't want any more holes in my life. Holes that will never be filled.

The pool glittered at my feet. It was hard to think about diving in, knowing the slightest miscalculation of the angle could kill me! I'd been diving into my pool, into lots of pools, for most of my life, and I'd never thought that one twist of my arms or slip of my foot meant I'd wind up dead. Of course, Kimberly had quite a lot of wine, so her dive would have been sloppy. Who knows. No one will ever know.

I kicked off my flip-flops. I sat down and dangled my legs in the water. It was warm and soothing and reminded me of how I love the water. It reminded me of sitting on the side of Jake's pool with Megan, so blind to what was coming in just a few hours.

"What are you doing?" At the sound of Marcus's voice, I glanced over my shoulder. He stood just under the patio roof.

"Cooling my feet. Thinking." I turned back to the pool. On concrete, you can't tell if someone is walking or standing still. So when he sat beside me, I was startled for the second time.

He didn't put his feet in the water. His body isn't drawn to the water like mine is, needing it to feel alive.

"I traded routes with Ted so I can be here for Kimberly's funeral." He looped his arm around my waist.

I leaned my head on his shoulder and fingered my waistband to be sure my phone wasn't going to slip out and jump into the pool. He moved his arm lower, passing his hand over the hard bulge of my phone. The muscles in his shoulder tightened against my back.

"I'm worried about Jake," I said.

He didn't answer. I felt his thoughts, wanting to ask me if I actually talked to Jake, and knowing I hadn't. That I was worrying over a status update.

Is that why couples don't talk to each other as they get older? I see older couples in restaurants, shoveling food into their mouths, eyes fixed on their plates, the air around them silent but for clinking utensils. I guess after a while, you know everything about the person you chose to spend your life with, and you know every word they're going to speak, so there's no need to do so. Losing Marcus to silence depressed me more than the death of someone I loved.

After my mom died, my father and I spoke only when necessary. I'd come home for the weekend and cook spaghetti or lasagna, not asking what he wanted, because I already knew his favorite comfort foods. He'd watch TV, as if the news or a game had any importance now that my mother was dead. Yet, when he looked away from the TV screen, his eyes were so empty I couldn't bear to face him. Occasionally he'd say things like, *your mother would have . . .* or *your mother used to . . .* But never once did he say he missed her, or speak any other word about how he felt. I followed his lead. I never saw him cry. It seemed as if his entire being had been frozen under a thick sheet of ice, and he was terrified that if he let out one tear or a single word, his skin would crack open and all his organs would spill out.

I pressed my head more firmly against Marcus's shoulder. I straightened my legs until my toes popped out of the water, then lowered my feet a few inches. If I held my toes just below the surface, my pinkish flesh and bright yellow polish made them look like tropical fish bobbing in the water. "What are you thinking about?" I said.

"Nothing."

"That's not true."

"Just watching your feet."

I smiled. I wondered if he felt my face change shape. He didn't hold me closer or shift his position, so maybe not. "Thanks for trading flights. I couldn't manage the memorial service without you."

"No big deal."

"I haven't been to a funeral since my mom died."

He squeezed my arm, then took it away from my waist.

My phone buzzed against my hip. I pulled it out of my waistband.

He stood up. "Are you kidding me?"

I unlocked my phone.

Jake Ash *Do you two want to come over for a drink?*

"Jake wants to know if we want to come over for a drink," I said.

"Why?"

"Does there have to be a reason?"

"No."

Allie Sinclair *Maybe.*
Jake Ash *Six-thirty?*
Allie Sinclair *Sure, see you then.*

I tucked my phone under my thigh.

"Do you think we can hang out with them without everyone checking their phones and wishing they were somewhere else?" Marcus said.

"I don't wish I was somewhere else."

He walked a few steps toward the diving board.

"What are you doing?"

"The pump doesn't sound right."

He knelt and lifted the lid off the filter. He stuck his hand in the water. I pulled my phone out from under my leg and scrolled through AboutFace. Lots of updates, but if I started looking at them, he'd finish with the filter and see what I was doing. I put the phone back.

"I'm kind of sick of seeing your hand glued around that phone."

He was still peering into the filter trap. He scooped out three large black feathers, joined at the tips as if they'd been ripped in a single piece from a crow's back. He walked around the side of the house to where the trashcans are stored. When he returned, he was holding his hands in front of himself at an awkward angle, clearly afraid of getting any trace of crow flesh on his body. "I'm tempted to throw your phone in the pool. Or flush it down the toilet."

He replaced the filter cover and walked back to where I was sitting. He stood over me, his shadow covering everything but my legs. My skin was so acclimated to the water temperature, it felt like my legs had become disconnected from the rest of me. He folded his arms.

"Stop turning it into a thing," I said.

He moved away, and the sun hit me full on the face. It hadn't bothered me a moment earlier, but after the comfort of his shadow, it felt like a spotlight in my eyes. I squinted. I pulled my feet out of the water and stood. "I don't want to fight. I'm going to change into jeans."

"How about leaving the phone here when we go to Jake's."

I swallowed. He was serious. If I said no, he'd say that proved I was addicted to social media, but I couldn't imagine not having it with me. It wasn't an addiction, just a habit. And the security of knowing you're connected. AboutFace is bringing the world closer together, connecting everyone on the planet. That was a good thing, no matter what Marcus tried to make it into.

WHILE MARCUS AND I were driving to Jake's, a bank of thick, white clouds had moved across the sky, just above the foothills, covering the sun. The cooler air was welcome, but seeing his house with the shadows across it, darkening the windows, turning the white stucco a dull gray, made it look stained. And it was.

The last time I'd walked up Jake's front path, the door had been circled in fairy lights, and the enormous foyer was filled with people laughing and talking. Then, before we'd even absorbed what had happened, we were all walking away in the darkness. We were trying to shake our minds free of the image of the blue paramedic truck in the center of the sweeping driveway, two guys loading Kimberly's body in the back like it was a UPS pick-up. Seeing her with a heavy plastic bag over her was the worst. I couldn't stop thinking she was suffocating inside. The silence among the rest of us had been as thick as the bag settling over her face.

Marcus rang the bell. I held onto my purse with both hands, pulling it against my hip. The missing weight of my phone wasn't truly noticeable, but somehow I felt it anyway. My phone was sitting on our kitchen table, just as Marcus had asked. I wasn't going to destroy my marriage over immediate access to social media. I didn't really think my marriage was at risk, but I wanted to show him I was trying.

People react differently to grief. I know that better than anyone, and you can't see what's going on inside another person, even when you're married to him. Marcus hadn't known Kimberly as long as I had, but all of us were in shock.

Until she died, we'd blissfully assumed all of us would pass life's milestones and carry on until old age, even though we didn't precisely think of ourselves growing old. No one considered that all the things we took for granted might never happen.

I really didn't know if Marcus was having those thoughts, but no matter what, he felt some sort of grief. After we made it past her memorial service, things would be more normal. I could do this one thing for him.

I felt a little anxious not checking in. And I was completely dependent on Marcus if I needed to make a phone call. Not that such an occasion comes up that often, but the phone is part of me. It's hard to go anywhere without it.

I was completely cut off from my friends. Updates were scrolling through my newsfeed, but I wasn't there to join the conversation. The only thing saving me was knowing how Jake had a way of consuming all the particles in a room. He would distract me.

As if Marcus was suddenly aware that I'd lost my tether, he reached across and pulled my left hand away from my purse strap. He wove his fingers around mine and held my hand with a firm grip.

Amelia opened the door. She was wearing a white dress with a wide neck that exposed her left shoulder. The tiny diamond in her nose glittered. "Hi." She let go of the door and stepped back a few feet.

Inside, the house was chilly. I wasn't aware of the air conditioning blasting icy breath, but maybe it was so well-designed there was no sound of air blowing, just a steady, creeping cold. Goosebumps ran up my legs and traveled along my spine. Even my scalp felt cold.

Amelia turned and walked down the hallway. The white fabric rippled around her body while her dark hair remained motionless. The hallway seemed to swallow her, making her even more diminutive. She disappeared into the living room without looking back to check whether we were following. Except for my sandals tapping the tile and the thud of Marcus's shoes echoing my steps, the house was silent. Because of its size and distance from any major roads, there wasn't even a whisper of traffic, and no sound of birds or any neighborhood activity drifted inside.

We stepped into the living room. Jake was seated at the center of the couch. Amelia stood just inside the doorway. Without speaking, she waited for us to choose a place to sit. By the time we'd settled on the leather love seat facing Jake, I felt there was something very wrong. It's not like I'm one of those people with a sixth sense or always tuned into the things that are unspoken — the buried, simmering emotions. I'm actually the opposite. I take things at face value. I think that's best, rather than interpreting motives and moods. If people want to reveal what's beneath the surface, that's their choice. Otherwise, why interpret? I would just be making it up based on some weird blend of my own feelings and views and my selective experience of the human race. But something wasn't right, more than what Jake had let on in his messages.

Amelia seated herself in one of the twin chairs that was set slightly apart from the arrangement of the couch and love seat as if she wanted to remove herself from the room altogether.

"It's nice you could come by," Jake said.

"How are you doing?" Marcus leaned forward. He pressed his palms against his knees, so it looked as though he planned to stand up again the minute he got his answer.

"Fine. Fine," Jake said. Then, after a moment, he said, "Not really." He waved his arm over his head, sweeping in the room and angling his fingers toward the window behind Marcus and me. "What can Amelia get you to drink?"

Amelia kept her eyes focused on Jake. She didn't look at us and smile or give any encouragement that she was interested in what we wanted to drink. Despite my desire to take things at face value, she seemed deeply unhappy.

"Vodka and OJ would be good," Marcus said.

"I'll just have the OJ," I said.

"Or you could have a mimosa. To get your orange juice fix."

Her words sounded kind as if she really wanted to be sure I had the beverage I preferred, but her face was so bland, it was unnerving. I wasn't sure if she was pretending ignorance of my dislike for alcohol, or had honestly forgotten.

"Plain OJ is fine." I smiled.

She stood and went into the dining room, disappearing through the kitchen doors.

"So . . . did she kill herself on purpose?" Jake said.

I glanced at Marcus, then back at Jake. "I don't think so."

"Why?"

"I just don't."

"That's not an explanation."

"Her friends. Her career. She was a very positive, forward-looking person."

"Why'd she take off her clothes?"

"It was hot out. Maybe she just wanted to go for a swim," Marcus said.

Jake laughed. It was a quick sharp sound, almost metallic.

"What did the police say?" I asked

"They don't say anything. They had all those questions when you were here, but I haven't heard anything since then."

"Maybe she was drunk, or maybe she just wanted to show off. But I know she didn't plan to kill herself," I said.

Jake shrugged.

Amelia returned carrying two bright orange drinks. She

handed the short glass with ice to Marcus and the champagne glass to me. The stem was as long as the length of my hand, tinged with green, and twisted into a knot below the start of the flute. The top edge was flared like a trumpet flower. The green tinge looked a little sickening next to the orange. I'm sure with champagne, it was gorgeous. I took a sip. The table was too far away to put the glass down without half standing, so I held onto it.

"You don't know for sure," Jake said.

Amelia left the room again.

"It was an accident," Marcus said. "Things happen that we can't explain."

"Is that what you'd expect Allie to think if your plane fell out of the sky? Or disappeared into a black hole like that Malaysian flight?"

"Don't say that," I said.

Amelia returned with two glasses of white wine.

"I wanted a martini," Jake said.

"Have this for now."

He folded his arms. "A martini."

"Please." Her voice sounded like a sharp piece of glass. Her mouth formed the words without smiling, yet there were no lines of anger or any other emotion.

Jake took the drink and finished half the wine in one swallow. Amelia sat down next to him, leaving two feet of space between them. Jake drank the rest of the wine and put the glass on the table. "Now, I'd like a martini."

"Whoa," Marcus said. "Slow down."

Jake leaned back. "I think she killed herself in my pool. To fuck with my head — since I posted that joke about a striptease."

"She wouldn't do that," I said.

"Well, she sure as hell did something. Diving into the pool naked."

"She wasn't naked. And it was an accident." Marcus spoke softly.

For several moments, we were silent.

"That's what I keep telling him," Amelia said.

"Where's the martini?"

"Let me drink my wine," she said.

Jake stood. He left the wine glass on the table, part of the base was just over the edge, as if he wanted to force Amelia to move it. He walked out of the room, and a moment later the sound of ice rattling against metal came through the kitchen doors. He returned more quickly than I thought possible for mixing a drink. He sat on the couch, raised his glass, and took a sip.

"It's my fault." His tone was flat, his eyes staring past us.

After a few minutes, I put my hand on the base of my glass to hold it steady and turned to see what had his attention. Nothing was behind me but the large picture window that went almost to the floor, and in front of that, a long, low dark wood table with two round beige stones placed in the center. I turned back.

"It's no one's fault. It was an accident," Marcus said.

"You haven't answered my question about the missing plane. Was that an accident? There are random events — *accidents* — and we're supposed to sit back and shake our heads and then go on as if nothing happened?"

"He's been like this." Amelia put her wine glass on the table. She pushed Jake's empty glass toward the center. She stood and walked to the window. I turned again so I could see her. She spread her arms as if she thought she could block the window. "Why don't we all go for a swim."

"You're sick," Jake said.

"It's like riding a bicycle." Amelia lowered her arms.

"It's nothing like riding a bicycle," Jake said. "I'm going to sell this place. I'm thinking of buying a motor home and traveling around the country. Or maybe go to Africa and help a village develop better farming techniques."

"What do you know about farming?" Amelia said.

"Please don't talk like that," I said.

"He's crazy," Amelia said. "He has everything, and he wants to throw it away. How will that help Kimberly? How will that change anything?"

"Life isn't what I thought it was."

"The world has always been full of bad shit. Every day there are three or four or fifteen or a million tragedies, he just never paid attention. I told him . . ."

He interrupted her. "If it weren't for me, she'd still be alive."

"You are fucking nuts," Amelia said. She returned to the couch and drank half the wine in her glass, almost as fast as Jake had swallowed his.

They were scaring me. Had they invited us over to act out their bizarre drama in front of us? In some ways, it felt like we weren't even there. I wanted to see how my other friends were feeling. I reached for my purse and remembered my phone was sitting alone in the center of the kitchen table, buzzing its little heart out, but I wasn't there to keep up. I'd have a hundred messages and posts when we got home. I took a long sip of OJ.

"Do you think you should talk to someone?" Marcus said.

"I'm talking to you."

"I mean a professional."

"A professional listener?" Jake laughed. "Done with friends, headed toward a professional friend."

Marcus smiled, but there was a sagging quality in his upper lip, giving the impression he was going to vomit. "Are you okay? You sound really upset."

"Upset?" Jake laughed. He lifted his drink and swallowed most of it. "Drinking with friends. Good times."

"Everything you say sounds like a status update." I tried to laugh, but it didn't work out. I gave him a warm smile, hoping he'd see I was trying to lighten things up, hoping he'd follow my lead, hoping that things were going to turn out okay. Amelia sat like she was carved out of marble. I half wondered whether she was breathing.

Marcus finished his vodka and orange juice and stood. He walked toward the dining room.

"I'll get you a refill," Amelia said, but she remained seated, legs crossed, her blue-painted toenails adding to the pallor of her skin so I felt I was looking at the feet of a corpse. I shivered and turned to look at the huge abstract painting hung on the adjacent wall, hoping it would layer itself over the images of Kimberly's body lying on the concrete, the bluish color of her lips.

Marcus went into the kitchen and returned without his glass. "It was good to catch up. I didn't get to talk to you very much at the party." A wave of panic crossed over his face as he recalled the dreadful conclusion of the party, the reason he hadn't talked much to Amelia or Jake that evening. "Anyway. We should head out."

"You just got here," Jake said.

"I was going to get you another drink," Amelia re-crossed her legs and spread her toes. Her tendons rose along the tops of her feet.

"I can't have two drinks that quickly and then drive."

"Allie can drive," Jake said.

"No, we should leave." Marcus walked to the couch and put his hand out for Jake to grab it in a manly handshake.

Jake took the hint, but I could tell even from where I was seated that his hand was limp. He didn't move his arm, letting Marcus do all the work. I stood and carried my glass, still half full, into the kitchen.

When I returned, Marcus had his hand on Jake's shoulder. "Take care of yourself. There's no shame in talking to a therapist. Most everyone does at some point in their life."

Jake stared at the picture window and said nothing.

Amelia walked us to the door. When we stepped outside, she said, "Thanks for stopping by. Have a great evening." She closed the door before we could say anything.

"THAT WAS BIZARRE," Marcus said when we were settled in the car. "Why did they even have us over?"

"Why did you rush out of there? I thought you were all about face to face connections?"

"They were scaring me. I don't think they really wanted us there. And I'm not going to sit and get drunk while they put on a drama for us."

I couldn't argue. It had seemed as if they were staging a fight for our benefit, waiting for us to play our parts.

I folded my hands in my lap, pressing them hard against each other. They ached without my phone to hold. I squeezed them tighter, trying to force the thought out of my head, trying not to think Marcus was noticing I was anxious. I didn't need him commenting about my *addiction*. Even if it was an addiction, it was an addiction to my friends. There's nothing wrong with that.

When we went inside the house, my phone was not on the kitchen table. I checked the living room couch and coffee table. I climbed the stairs and went into the office. I opened the center desk drawer. It was empty except for a few charging cords and three pens. I opened the two drawers at the side, but it wasn't there. The bottom drawer was designed to hold hanging folders, but I opened it anyway and checked inside the cardboard folders. I slammed the drawer and went into our bedroom. I flopped on the bed, feeling the soft, feather-filled comforter billow around me. I closed my eyes and tried to picture what had happened when we left for Jake's. I knew I'd put my phone in the center of the table, right next to the vase of pink roses Marcus bought me the day after he'd come home from his last flight. The memory was clear because I'd noticed one of the petals coming loose and I pulled it off so it wouldn't fall on my phone.

What I couldn't remember was actually walking out of the house. Usually, I go first. Marcus is right behind me, and he locks the door. Surely I would have noticed if he'd gone back inside. And if he'd hidden it, how had he done it so quickly, without it crossing my awareness that he was inside longer than expected?

I sat up. Where the hell was my phone? Even though we hadn't been gone more than an hour, I had no idea what was going on with my friends. I needed to see if Jake or Amelia had posted that we got together for drinks.

I slid off the bed. If Marcus didn't see me hunting around, he'd put the phone back where I could find it. It scared me a little because I didn't like to think of him as a controlling person. If I read that list where it talks about the ten signs of a controlling relationship, hiding your wife's phone, cutting off access to her friends, is definitely on the list. I know I've seen it on the list.

My black tank suit was still damp from the night before, and I couldn't bear that clammy feel of wet spandex. I pulled my hot pink suit out of the drawer. I changed in the bathroom and dropped all of my clothes into the laundry basket. There was something about being in Jake's house, Amelia's stony face and odd silence, Jake's bizarre comments, that left me with a clammy feeling even without my wet swimsuit. Maybe I'd been sweating the whole time Jake was talking, and their cold house turned my sweat into something sticky and uncomfortable. He was nothing like the Jake I'd known most of my life. He'd always been strong, unaffected by what other people did. I didn't think he and Kimberly were all that close, but maybe I'd called that wrong.

I braided my hair, trying not to look in the mirror. Normally, I don't mind admiring myself a bit. The pink suit with high cut legs and straps that crisscross the back is hell to put on but looks very chic when it's finally fitted in place. It looked great on me, but I was hyper-aware of my skin and my breath and my heartbeat. I tugged the straps to fit them more smoothly and went downstairs. I didn't see or hear Marcus anywhere. Maybe he'd gone into the office while I was changing my clothes, even now, sitting there waiting for me to come looking for my phone. I didn't like what was happening between us, but I didn't know how to fix it.

I stood on the edge of the pool beside the diving board, put my palms together, and arched my arms overhead. I rose up on the balls of my feet and gave myself a lower arc than normal as I dove into the pool. During the nanoseconds when my body was in the air, and as I broke the surface of the water, my head was filled with Kimberly. I wondered if she'd plowed in without putting her arms above her, or if somehow they'd wobbled because she was tipsy. Of course, she'd been at the wrong end of the pool, slamming her head on the concrete steps. Was that the only problem, not being clear which was the deep end? How could you miss that? Even though the sky was dark, the pool was lit. It seemed to me it was impossible to confuse the two ends.

When I'd finished twenty laps, I climbed out. Marcus was sitting on one of the patio chairs with a glass of wine on the table next to him. I went over to him and sat on his lap.

"You're all wet."

"Do you want me to move?"

He put one hand on my waist and his other hand on my thigh. He grabbed the strap of my suit with his teeth and pulled it over my shoulder. The wet spandex stuck to me like another layer of skin, but desire swelled inside me as if it had the power to melt the suit off my body. He kissed my neck, and I relaxed into him. He kissed me gently, and his mouth tasted like wine. I wondered if mine tasted of chlorine. After a few minutes, he slipped the other strap off my shoulders and pulled the top of my suit down to my ribs. He put his hands on my breasts, and my whole body swam toward him except a tiny part of my mind, trying to figure out where my phone was, longing to post an update about how many laps I'd done and wanting to see what Jake and Amelia posted. The evening had been unsettling, and I wasn't sure if Jake was having some kind of breakdown, or being typical Jake and trying to get a reaction out of people.

After a while, Marcus nudged me off his lap. He stood, keeping his arms around me, and walked toward the house, pulling me alongside him. We went inside, and he spread out the quilt hanging over the back of the couch. He pulled me down on top of him, and we made love and fell asleep wrapped around each other.

I woke up at twelve-thirty in the morning. The patio light was still on, like a spotlight surrounding his wine glass. I unwound my body from Marcus and slid to the floor. I crept forward and found his t-shirt. I pulled it over my head and went outside. I shoved my hand between the back and seat cushion on the chaise lounge, feeling for my phone. I picked up the glass and carried it inside, locked the door, and turned out the light. I went into the kitchen and poured the wine down the drain.

Starting at the end near the pantry, I opened every drawer. In the drawer with towels, I felt underneath each layer. The towels were jumbled looking, but I didn't have time to straighten them. Any minute, Marcus would wake and come looking for me.

I went upstairs and searched the desk again. It was possible he'd put it somewhere and moved it while I was swimming. All the calming effects of swimming and sex had run out of my body as fast as the water poured off me when I climbed out of the pool.

I sat at the desk and woke up the computer. I opened AboutFace. It was clear he didn't want me to find the phone. He was treating me like a little kid. He thought he was so superior, not needing social media. He acted as if he didn't need friends at all.

Tiffany

TIFFANY JONES [*UPLOADED 14 images*] *A few new photos of my beautiful children. #feelingblessed #Godisgood*
37 favorites — 9 comments

Jake Ash *Cute kids, Tiff. They take after their Mom. ;)*

Allie Sinclair *They're adorable!! Like I always say, you and Byron did good!!!*

Seth Porter *Fascinating how they look so much alike, yet so different.*

Kristen Thomas *They are so precious.*

Byron Jones *Doesn't my wife look great?*

Dave Eddington *Very cute pics.*

Tiffany Jones *God is so good to me. I hope Kimberly found Him in time.*

Allie Sinclair *Don't be so preachy, Tiff. It's supposed to be "social" media. LOL.*

Tiffany Jones *Sometimes I think the Lord wants to use technology to save the human race.*

AFTER KIMBERLY DROWNED, I couldn't concentrate on praying. I realized I'd been asking God for all the wrong things. The thing I should have been asking for — that my friends not die — hadn't even crossed my mind. I prayed every day for blessings on my friends, protection for my family, and blessings on them as well, but I never asked for protection for my *friends*! I worried about something happening to my children, about losing Byron, so naturally, protection for them came to the front of my mind.

I don't think Kimberly cared much for God, but that didn't mean He'd let her die. He lets people die every day, and I never thought much about that, but after *she* died, I thought about it a lot. All day long. Giving in to despair was not pleasing to God. He wanted me to focus my mind on beautiful things, lovely things, but I couldn't forget that picture of her pale body and her white underwear, so much whiter than her skin, floating in Jake's pool. Jake had probably already pushed it out of his mind. He never lets bad things upset him. He's super confident about life and the world and the way things work. God was supposed to make me feel at peace. I was supposed to be confident that He had a plan for me, but I didn't feel peaceful at all.

Paul and Ruthie were both asleep, a miracle really. So God was absolutely looking out for me in that respect. Of course, I had no idea when Paul might wake again. He was going through a period of bad dreams. I was very sympathetic to him because I know how dreams can seem so real. Byron was not as sympathetic. He wanted Paul to be a big boy. Byron gets very upset when Paul cries, especially after a dream. Byron couldn't seem to grasp that if a dream seems real to adults, imagine how terrifying it is for an almost-four-year-old? *Almost* four! It's perfectly fine and normal for a toddler to cry, but he acted like it was shameful. It's healthy to cry, and maybe he would feel better if he cried once in a while. Crying doesn't make you unmanly. It doesn't turn you into a female, which is what he believes — *crying is for girls.*

Even though I could see from the living room that all the bedroom lights were out, I knew Byron was sitting up in bed, watching the doorway, waiting for me. Without seeing, I could see. His hair was sticking out on one side as it always does after he wrestles with Paul on the living room carpet, getting it filled with static and turning him into a wild man. I could see the sheet pulled up to his knees, the rest of him exposed and eager for me. That should make me happy. And he does make me happy. I adore him. I'm the most blessed woman there is with my two healthy, gorgeous children and my devoted husband.

But more than anything in the world, I wanted to sleep. I wanted to go into the bedroom, slip beneath the weight of the blankets, let my head sink deep into the pillow, and not feel any skin but my own.

I'm trying so hard to be a good mom, but I'm so tired, I feel like crying. I'm covered in spit-up and baby poop, sweaty and unglamorous and unlovable. I used to have a habit of not going to sleep until I read my Bible. No matter how tired I was, I had to read it. At least a chapter. It made me know God was speaking to me, even if I couldn't quite hear Him.

But since Ruth was born, I forget to do that most of the time.

Sometimes, when I'm feeding Ruth, I draw a picture in my mind of a tiny one-bedroom apartment. I never had an apartment of my own. I can see the clean kitchen counters, nothing but a coffee pot and a set of canisters to mar the surface. I can see my little table with a plant in the center and my tiny bedroom with a hand-made quilt over clean sheets, and an antique dresser with a silk scarf draped across the top.

And besides all of that, it seemed wrong to think about sex when our friend was dead. I felt we should be praying, but God was so far away. In my dreams, I was trapped in a place I didn't recognize. I felt things clawing at me. So I understood Paul's screams. Sometimes I wondered if I screamed in terror during my dreams, and Byron, who could sleep through three fire trucks arriving at the front door, didn't notice, and my screams were what woke Ruth. Maybe my screams transferred themselves into Paul's soft little brain and stirred up things he shouldn't have to face when he wasn't even four years old.

"Mommy." His voice was soft. I took a few steps out of the living room, hoping to listen outside Paul's door. Sometimes he calls out even though he's sleeping and doesn't really need me.

"Mommy."

My stomach and lungs, my uterus and my heart, turned into granite. The voice wasn't Paul's. It was Byron. I wanted to turn and walk out the front door, even though I was barefoot and wearing yoga pants without undies because they were all in the dirty clothes, and a sweatshirt that probably wasn't all that clean because it had been too hot for a sweatshirt that day, but I'd never had time to change into something cooler.

Most people would call me stupid for not dealing with my feelings on our honeymoon, or on any of the hundreds of nights since then. For letting it go on so long, turning me into a woman who, at night, hated her husband. When I looked at him across the dinner table or saw him playing with our children, or sat in church and listened to his gorgeous voice in my ears, I adored him. I thanked God for him with my whole being. But in the dark, when the nightmares are waiting behind the curtains, I hated him. I wasn't even sure why it bothered me so very much. What was the big deal? It didn't mean anything. It was a pet name. I wouldn't get upset if he called me bunny rabbit. I wouldn't start thinking I was actually a rabbit and he wanted to have sex with an animal. It would sound cute. It would be a name that was only between the two of us. Our private place where no one else in the universe could intrude. Except God. I wondered what God thought of his pet name.

"Hurry up." His voice was no longer soft. There was no mistaking it was a man, not a little boy, calling out to me. And not a man playfully teasing me with a pet name. A man who wanted me right now. That was a good thing, right? Having your man wanting you? That's the way God designed things.

I went into the kitchen and turned on the light over the sink. I took the sponge and wiped out the peas and bits of rice that hadn't made it down the drain when Byron cleaned up the dinner dishes. I rinsed the sponge and wiped the table, which never seems to look clean. It was permanently discolored, and we should have been saving for a new one. The deli was doing well, but all our savings were for the future, and we couldn't quite manage saving for closer future things. Only for college for the kids, and our old age.

I wrung out the sponge and put it in the plastic tray. I opened the drawer where I keep my Bible. The drawer had a few pictures that I wanted to frame and the small jars where I kept Paul's and Ruth's fingernails after I trimmed them. I wasn't exactly sure why I saved their nails, it just seemed important to not let parts of them wind up in the trash. When their teeth started to fall out, I'd collect them as well. A mother's job is to preserve her children's childhood. Their whole lives should be cataloged. I'm the only one, well Byron too, but mostly me, who will have known them their entire lives. I'm the one who brought them into the world. I needed to do these things so they'd grow up always knowing how precious they were. How every part of them was important. It would help them recognize how God cherishes them.

Even in the kitchen, I could hear Byron's voice, but luckily I couldn't make out his words. He was getting insistent. I closed the drawer.

This wasn't the way it was supposed to be. I needed to talk

to him. This was just as much my responsibility. If I kept hating how he was, it would eat away at the foundation of our marriage. I had to get the courage to tell him how disgusted I was. I wasn't criticizing him or rejecting him, just explaining my feelings. And he would accept that and apologize. He'd stop saying it, and everything would be fine. I never should have let it go on so long. It was my fault, in a way, for not speaking up.

I turned off the light and walked down the hall. Because of the brightness in the kitchen, our bedroom looked even darker. I couldn't make out Byron's form, but I could feel the shape of his body, still sitting up.

"There you are," he said. "What have you been doing?"

"Cleaning the kitchen."

"I cleaned the kitchen so you could get the kids to bed."

"I just gave it an extra wipe down."

The covers rustled. "Come here."

His voice was warm and caring, but chills ran across the back of my head. I wove my fingers through my hair and grabbed my skull, holding it steady. "I should take a shower."

"No need. I love you the way you are."

"Really, I . . ."

"I have to get up early. I need some sleep."

"Then maybe . . ."

"Hurry. Daddy can't wait to hold you."

Peas and rice and the chicken that Byron had barbecued, but maybe hadn't cooked absolutely as well as he should have, swam around my stomach and pushed their way up my esophagus. I put my hand on my belly.

"Can I talk to you?" I walked closer to my side of the bed.

"The time for talking is over, Babe."

"We can cuddle and talk."

He laughed. "We talked all through dinner."

"We didn't talk just you and me."

"Yes we did."

"Not really."

"I talk to people all day."

"I know." I climbed into bed and tucked the sheet and blanket around my ribs. The window was open. Outside, dogs barked at each other as if they were having a conversation. It didn't sound like a very friendly conversation.

Byron turned on the light. "Why are you all dressed?"

"I just want to tell you something."

He put his hands behind him and grabbed the rail at the top of our bed. His fingers squeaked slightly on the brass finish. I shivered.

"What do you need to tell me?"

"I love you and . . ."

"I know. I love you."

"Can I finish?"

He gripped the railing harder, tightening his hands like he was making fists, the skin pulling until his knuckles looked like the bone was going to break through. I shivered again. Another shiver followed that. I turned on my side and grabbed my upper arms and bent my legs. "I want you to know I love you and I'd do anything for you. I love being with you." I closed my eyes. "But I don't like it when you call me Mommy. And I don't like you calling yourself Daddy. I feel sick when you say that." The last words came out in a shriek and even as I was saying them, I wished I wasn't. Nothing was ever going to be the same between us. I'd assaulted some part of his soul, I was sure of it. But I couldn't hear him call me that one more time. I might hit him. Or worse.

"Why not?"

It wasn't what I expected him to say. I don't know what I'd expected. My head was so full of how much I hated it, I couldn't think past the shameful feelings poking at every part of my body. I wondered if God was trying to give me a message, to point out that I was completely full of myself and not caring for Byron at all as a wife is supposed to care for her husband. I could feel I was going to start crying. In the same breath, I felt bad that I wasn't submitting and sick that he kept calling me that. I didn't want to have to explain why it disgusted me. I wanted him to listen to how it sounded coming from my lips and immediately realize it was not how things between us should be. I wanted him to sense how I felt and change how he was. It seemed like I wanted everything, except him the way he really was — my husband and the man I married for better or for worse. But I didn't want to submit. I didn't want to just take that and accept it every night for the rest of my life. I shouldn't have to explain why it gave me a creepy, dirty feeling. I shouldn't have to live like this.

"What's wrong? You look upset," he said.

I bit my lip. I pressed my teeth over the skin beneath my lower lip, trying not to gnaw at my skin, turning it red and raw, but needing to do something to keep my lips from trembling, to stop from crying like a helpless, hopeless child. "Yes. I'm upset." My voice was hoarse. I coughed. "I don't like it when you call me that."

"But why? It's cute. You're a cute Mommy."

"I'm not your Mommy." I held my breath for a second. I let it out and whispered, "It makes me sick."

He let go of the headboard and slid down next to me. He lifted my shirt and wriggled his head up against my belly.

I closed my eyes. I prayed silently, blessing God, blessing Byron. My thoughts raced through all the things I should be thankful for. I'd been given so much, everything really — healthy children, an adoring husband. *Remember that*, I whispered inside my head where Byron couldn't hear me. *This man, this godly man, adores you! He has one flaw, one tiny little flaw and you've looked at it so hard your eyes have turned to magnifying glasses, and you've made it huge, let it become an enormous, insurmountable wall between the two of you.* I recognized that my own mind had retreated into the background and this was God speaking to me. I knew He was speaking directly to me. There was a vast, empty feeling inside my skull, as if the space around my brain was expanding, leaving my brain a tiny lump of flesh at the center. It glowed with life, turning soft and pliable the way God wanted it, the way a woman is supposed to be for her husband.

Then I remembered what I'd read during my quiet time that morning. A quiet time that's supposed to be part of my waking routine, but didn't actually happen until nap time. While I was reading my Bible, my eyes had begun to drift, seeing double. My lids turned into thick drapes, falling over my eyes, and then I'd jerked awake. This happened several times, and I finally fell asleep for ten solid minutes while I was supposed to be reading in Deuteronomy. When I woke, I told the Lord I was sorry for not being attentive. He rewarded me by bringing my attention to a place further down the page. It was one of my favorite passages — *Every place where you set your foot will be yours.*

I knew that applied to taking the land, taking what God had given you. I just needed to figure out what He'd given me, and take it. If I figured it out, then things would be okay with Byron and me.

Tiffany Jones *Isn't this sunrise perfect? With Jesus, there is always light everywhere. I believe this.*
39 favorites — 0 comments

Tiffany Jones [*Added 8 new photos to the album Gifts of God*]

Paul holding his baby sister.

Paul in the wading pool.
Paul helping Daddy wash the car.
Mommy holding baby Ruth.
Ruth eating cheerios.
Daddy and his baby girl.
The amazing father of my children. How can I not adore this man?
Mommy and Daddy.

Tiffany Jones *"Every place where you set your foot will be yours."*
Deuteronomy 11:24
   1 favorites — 0 comments

Dave

DAVE EDDINGTON *HARD to return to normal life, whatever normal is.*

39 favorites — 4 comments

Kristen Thomas *Agreed.*
Byron Jones *Time keeps marching.*
Seth Porter *It's a shock, still can't believe it.*
Allie Sinclair *It's hard to focus on anything.*

LOOKING AT THE pictures of my friends' kids on AboutFace was a knife in my heart, I'll admit it. A guy shouldn't admit he's weak, shouldn't admit he isn't in control of everything, but I can admit it to myself. I want kids. Realistically, there's plenty of time. I'm not even thirty. But more of my friends are popping them out, and they never let me forget about those kids — plastering their photos all over social media until you can't open the app without a long stream of happy toddlers. I love kids. They're cute, they're fun, they blow your mind with the stuff they say that seems to come right out of the universal intelligence or something. It's like they're speaking truth because there's no filter and no bullshit clogging their view of reality. Seeing all those happy, laughing kids, knowing they'll grow up together and my future kids won't be in that group, hurts. Not very macho of me, saying I'm hurt, but it's an ache that won't go away.

Since Kimberly killed herself — on purpose, or through stupidity, whichever it was, no one really knew — she occupied my mind more than all those kids. Taking her clothes off was weird. She definitely wanted to make a statement. I suppose killing yourself is the ultimate statement.

All of us had stood around the pool that night, her body plastered to the pavement in front of us as if her dive had been onto concrete. Her thong was so wet it was transparent. I couldn't stop looking at her ass. It was so beautiful. I felt like a pervert, looking at a dead woman's ass and thinking how nice it was. It made me sick, but the need to look at it wouldn't go away. I almost didn't want them to take her out of the water until they covered her up. Lately, it seems like the only way I get to see a naked woman is on the Internet, and seeing a live one was exciting. I'm sorry. I can't help my body, can't help nature. I'm not a pervert, just a normal guy who was in an unusual situation, with a friend dying right in front of my eyes.

I thought about diving into the pool and lifting her out myself. I knew I could lift her, no problem. I'm bigger than most guys. Not tall, but my shoulders and back make up for that. The bulk gives the impression of being bigger than I am. But before I even completed the thought, Allie beat me to it. And maybe that was a good thing, because what if my body reacted to holding Kimberly? And what if I touched her wrong, nudged her bra to the side? Or worse?

I tried to look away, but I couldn't. The girls were crying, and the guys were all saying *Shit. Fuck.* Over and over like some weird chant, their voices low, humming until it sounded as if the pool was surrounded by cursing monks. Then everything got quiet. Not a sound. All of us feeling like complete morons that our friend was dead and we had no idea what to do. Her hair was glued to the concrete like seaweed. I can't even describe her face.

I knew I should turn away, we all should have. She was so exposed, but wasn't that what she wanted, for us all to look at her, notice her? We all want that. Look at me. We never grow past being kids shouting for mom and dad to watch us. I see kids do that all the time. *Look at me, look at me. Look. At. Me!* They sound frantic as if they'll die if these super-beings called mom and dad, the people who are so powerful they appear to be gods, don't pay attention. You need them to look at you and notice what you're up to. If they don't look, maybe you don't exist.

My dad noticed me all right, but not in a good way. He noticed I sat on the bench during most of my high school football career. Now that I've learned to swing a golf club fairly well, I wonder why I let him bully me into football. Just because I was big. But I wasn't big in the right way. You need height as well as girth. I guess he thought I'd keep growing, not stop short at five feet, nine inches. Football was too brutal for me, and I shouldn't have pretended I was okay with it. I don't know why I didn't go for golf. I would have liked it better because winning would have been all on me, not this teamwork crap. I would have gotten more respect, not lost in the crowd. Second-string. How can you work at football and improve your game? With golf, you can do drills on your own — hit balls, practice putting. Not so with football. But my dad wanted a football player — a man's man.

That attitude got planted in me early. I was the weakling of the crowd, and being weak is not cool. The pack turns on weaklings and removes them from the group. I tried too hard to make myself the predator, not the victim. In middle school, I picked on a gay kid, tormented him for weeks. I guess a little bit of why I did it was because I didn't want anyone to think I was gay. I didn't hurt him, didn't beat him up or anything, but I called him queer and flipped my hand around and walked on my tiptoes so the other guys would laugh. Getting them to laugh was a thrill, but even when I was doing it, I was disgusted with myself. I wonder where that kid is now — Jim. Jim Fitzsimmons. I can still see his face, looking like he might start crying.

I guess we all want people to think well of us. We want them to notice us so bad we invented AboutFace. We can make sure they're seeing everything we do and think, viewing all our pictures, commenting on how clever and amazing we are. What some people don't seem to notice, is that it's all one big fucking lie. A billion people lying through their teeth every minute of every day.

No one wants to talk about why Kimberly took off her clothes. They want to think about the tragedy of it all. The *accidental* smashing of her head against concrete. There are all kinds of tributes to her online. Tributes that make me wonder who the hell they're talking about. I guess that happens when someone dies. All their flaws slip off like she slipped out of that dress. She left it on the lounge chair in a puddle of silky fabric, the heels of her shoes poking out beneath, like bones poking out of a body, tearing through the flesh.

Finally, the paramedics arrived. They lifted her onto a gurney. Her head started to loll before they grabbed it and held it in place. Suddenly, all my desire evaporated. It was a sight no one should have to see. And the looks on everyone else's faces said they felt the same. I was no longer a pervert at all, I was sick to my stomach, and I wondered where those earlier thoughts had come from. They weren't me. I'm a decent, normal guy. I don't want to have sex with a dead woman. Her body just looked good, at first, that's all.

Then the cops came.

The tributes to Kimberly are wild. You'd think she was the most brilliant businesswoman who ever walked into a high-flying Silicon Valley company. You'd think she had one hundred and seventy-five BFFs.

I didn't post much. Not at all for the first few days after she died. I read what others wrote. I couldn't stop checking it. Even while I was on my knees laying tile, I was thinking about the phony bullshit. And every time I stood and took a break, I drank a can of Coke and looked through the latest string of lies. That's what it started to sound like. You'd think the woman never said a bitchy word or did something shitty to anyone.

No one posted comments about how hot she looked in her thong and see-through bra. And there wasn't a single word about that time right after high school graduation when she took those pictures of her friends at a slumber party. All those girls who showed up at school every day — gliding and strutting, wiggling and prancing across the quad. Their hair was long and shiny, their faces perfect, their skin soft and smooth. It was like a field of girls blossoming out of the grass like wildflowers. I'm surprised any guy could manage to graduate from high school with all of that swirling around him every day, lingering on the backs of his eyes so that even when he was home playing video games or trying to eke out a bit of homework — there they were, smiling, holding themselves at arms' length after flinging themselves all over you.

But those pictures from Kimberly. Shit. What a combination of exposed body, humiliating positions, and facial expressions. Even Allie, who is prettier than most, looked like crap. Her head was back, and her mouth was open, her lips kind of sagging sideways, drool puddling in the corners of her lips, her eyelids partially raised, showing the whites of her eyes, which made it look like she was having a seizure. The strap of her top was down her arm on one side, most of her boob hanging out, but it didn't look that great. It was flattened out, so she almost looked like an overweight boy with man-boobs.

A few girls had retainers over their teeth and white scum forming around their lips from breathing through their mouths. The pictures were extreme close-ups. She got right in their faces, pointing the camera up their noses in some cases. One girl had her hand down her pants, her knuckles bulging so she looked like a guy.

They were not the field of flowers we saw every day.

I never figured out why she did that. I guess some of the girls who were there called her on it, but the guys never got to hear the inside scoop. At least I didn't. Maybe guys who had girlfriends heard all the gory details and told a few people. But I heard nothing. I was left trying to imagine why she would do that to her friends. Did she hate them all? It wasn't as if she was ugly and wanted to make them look bad. Nothing like that. And she put them right out there, so it wasn't some kind of leverage for a threat. It was just mean. They were the kind of pictures you didn't want to look at but couldn't stop yourself.

What she did had faded over time. Surprisingly, they all stayed friends with her. But it made me wonder what the hell was going on inside her head. Now we'll never know.

I poured a cup of coffee and went out on my back porch. Four snails had made their way onto the bottom step. No matter what I do, they keep coming back. The things are indestructible, unless you step on them, which I hate because it's just so pathetic and disgusting. But they eat holes in the plants and they breed like fruit flies. I could see them taking over the entire back porch if I didn't stay on top of it.

Except for putting out snail bait, the whole Saturday stretched in front of me with nothing much to do. Well, there was one thing I needed to do — visit my mom. She was going into the hospital the following Monday for hip surgery. My sister was driving her. My mom knew I'd be working on the Monday, but she kept mentioning it. *Please come see me. I want to see you before I go under the knife.* She's dramatic like that.

I wasn't looking forward to the visit. It would be the same hide and seek activity it always was with her. She'd try to pry into my private business, ask questions, trying to sound casual. She'd never come out and be nosey. She'd pretend she was being friendly. Still, I had to do it. I'm a good son. My mom is great, she really is, except for this nosiness and eagerness to find out stuff so she can fix it. As if she can fix her kids' lives now that we're adults. It's crazy.

Dave Eddington *Saturday in the suburbs — where did all these snails come from?*
19 favorites — 8 comments

Kristen Thomas *If you're going to get rid of them, think of the ecosystem and make sure you use natural exterminates.*

Allie Sinclair *I've never seen a snail in my yard. Marcus takes care of them. They give me the creeps.*

Dave Eddington *There are "natural" ways to kill things?*

Kristen Thomas *Absolutely. Cinnamon is one. At least for ants, not sure about snails. Maybe salt?*

Adam Jamison *Natural killing is an oxymoron.*

Byron Jones *First world problem.*

Seth Porter *Kill the bastards. Man over nature.*

Allie Sinclair *I agree, Seth.*

PARKED CARS BLOCKED the entire curb in front of my mom's house and all her neighbors' on both sides of the street. The people two doors down looked to be having a kid's birthday party. Yellow helium balloons were tied to their white fence, and Mylar balloons with Disney characters were attached to one of the porch posts. Most of the cars were minivans and mini SUVs, half of them badly parked. I couldn't pull my truck into my mom's driveway because her car sat right in the middle, even though there was plenty of room for her to pull to the side.

Since my sister's car was nowhere in sight, my shoulders relaxed a bit, and my neck didn't feel like it had an iron rod inside. It's never a surprise when my mom invites me over and springs my sister on me as if that's a pleasant surprise and we're just dying to see each other. My sister is okay, she's nice enough, but she talks incessantly, and I really don't have the energy to listen to her more than once a month.

My mother had the door open before I stepped onto the porch.

"Hi, honey." She held up her chin, where I was supposed to place a kiss, which I did. I know the drill. She really is a great lady. She did a terrific job raising me, despite my father, but interacting with her can be a little like playing golf — lots of obscure rules that catch you by surprise.

"Hi, Mom." I walked inside, and she stepped around me to close the door.

"I'm making fried chicken."

"Sounds good."

"Why don't you sit at the table while I finish up. Do you want a beer?"

I agreed to both and squeezed into the bench that runs under her front window and takes the place of three chairs.

She took a bottle of beer out of the fridge. She put the beer and a glass on the table in front of me. I popped off the cap and took a sip. That's one of my preferences she's finally learned. No canned beer. The fact that I don't want a glass hasn't quite sunk in even though I've been drinking beer in front of her for seven years now.

Oil spit in the pan, and she hurried over. I was surprised the oil wasn't smoking since it looked like she'd left the burner on while she answered the door. Quite the risk-taker, my mother.

"How are you doing?" She flopped a boneless chicken breast into a bowl of egg and milk, pulled it out, and rolled it around on a plate of breadcrumbs.

I had to look out the window at the line of cars baking in the sun. I couldn't watch that pink flesh getting slapped around and covered in crumbs. It took away my appetite. Once it started cooking and I smelled sizzling fat, I'd be good, but the sight of dead, pale skin and the hint of pink flesh splashing in the bowl of milk took me right back to the image of Kimberly's body flopping around as they dragged her out of the water.

I took a long swallow of beer. "I'm okay."

"It's so awful about your friend, Kimberly. What a tragedy."

It felt like a tragedy until my mom said it. Then I wanted to argue with her. Explain that it wasn't like the world had ended. It wasn't like I was that close to her, it wasn't like Kimberly didn't ask for it. She's the one who slammed down four or five glasses of wine. She's the one who took off her clothes. Maybe she wasn't getting enough attention in her career, jealous of Jake's house and all his success.

"Yeah, it's a bummer." I took another sip of beer.

"I'm sorry I can't go to the funeral. I'll still be in the hospital. I get discharged Thursday."

"I know, Mom."

"I really feel bad about that, although it's not my fault."

"No one said it was."

"The surgery's been scheduled for months."

"It's okay. You didn't even really know her."

"She's your friend. She was at your twelfth birthday party.

Such a pretty girl. Very mature for her age."

I nodded. I drank some more beer and pulled my phone out of my pocket.

"Are you expecting a call?"

"No."

"If a girl calls, it's okay to take it while you're here. I won't listen."

"I'm not expecting a call, just checking AboutFace."

She didn't sigh, but I could feel the sigh coming out of her pores anyway. The oil spit again, and she yanked her hand away from the frying pan. She rubbed her knuckles.

"Did you get burned?"

"I'm fine." She grabbed the tongs and turned the chicken over.

"What else are we having?"

"Macaroni and cheese."

I scrolled through the posts on Kimberly's tribute page. Then I clicked over to Allie's page. She had a string of info about how many laps she'd swum that day. I looked at Seth's page, read his usual diatribe about the government trying to steal his guns and the liberal media being nothing but one big pity party, and then looked at Tiffany's page — scrolling past the pictures of her kids. Her latest post was a Bible verse. That girl loves to quote the Bible. So does Byron, but not as much as she does. So does Seth for that matter, but his quotes sound like threats. Like God is threatening all of us via AboutFace. It's almost funny. I should hide the guy's updates, but sometimes I think I like the anger I feel reading all his shit. I get angry, but then I can't stop reading. He's such a stubborn, mean SOB.

I read Tiffany's quote again. I had no idea what it meant. Obviously, no one else did either because there were no comments. And only one favorite — from Allie, of course.

"What are you reading?"

"This weird Bible verse from Byron's wife. Tiffany?"

"Oh, yes. I think I met her once at . . ."

"Yeah." I gave myself a silent pat on the head for being so quick even though I was getting dopey with the smell of that fried chicken and the beer filling me up.

"What does it say?"

"Every place where you set your foot will be yours," I said.

My mom laughed. "I wish."

"I don't even know what it means."

"It's obvious. You can get whatever you want just by taking it."

"Really?"

"That's what it sounds like to me," she said.

"That's bullshit."

"Watch your language. Although, I agree with you."

I grinned and took a sip of beer. She really is a great lady. "Why would she post that?"

"How would I know?"

"Tiffany has everything she wants," I said.

"No one has everything they want."

"It sounds like she wants to take over the city or something." I laughed.

"Religious people can be strange," my mom said.

"No stranger than un-religious people."

"Non-religious."

Every place where you set your foot will be yours. It was worth more thought. She put it there for a reason. And if stuff in the Bible is true, and sometimes I think — what if it is? — it had a lot of possibilities. It made me feel more optimistic about my life than I had in a while. I'd give it more thought later. After another beer and some fried chicken and my mom's equally great mac and cheese.

Seth

SETH PORTER *DON'T get slaughtered like a sheep. This is a long article, but you need to read it. dayofreckoning.com/when-they-come-for-your-guns-you-will-turn-them-over/*

17 favorites — 4 comments

Kevin Scalla *Scary. I'll pass it on. People gotta get their heads out of the sand ;)*

Allie Sinclair *Calm down, Seth. You're scaring me.*

Seth Porter *Wake up, Allie.*

Allie Sinclair *Love ya'! Even if we don't see eye to eye. ;)*

LORI WAS IN the kitchen, fixing ham sandwiches for lunch. I was in the backyard watching Michael climb. For his fifth birthday, we'd bought him a thick rope with a large knot on the end. I tied it into the oak tree that more or less consumes our backyard.

Before Michael could walk, he spent more time pulling himself up onto furniture, trying to scale the legs of the kitchen table, even trying to grab my pants and make his way up my leg, than he did trying to walk. Of course, he went nuts over the rope. It had been three weeks already, and every minute of daylight he wanted to be outside scaling that rope.

Unlike most kids, he wasn't that interested in maneuvering across the tree branches, looking for footholds. Just up and down the rope.

Sundays are the best day of the week. I can hang out with my kid and enjoy my wife. That particular Sunday was a bit of a downer, knowing the memorial service was coming in a few days, thinking about a dead girl that I'd known since I was ten. Everyone acted like it was such a tragedy, that somehow it wasn't her fault she was dead. I was keeping my thoughts to myself because I thought it was obvious she wanted to make a scene, and she didn't plan very well. Or maybe the scene she wanted was a gorgeous dead body. The point is, yes, her death was unpleasant, you hate to see anyone lose her life. But it was her choice. What decent woman strips down to her underwear and flashes her body around? Dead or not? Drunk or not? She wasn't that drunk. All she had was a few glasses of wine. But people jump on me enough for my views, and I didn't need a dead-girl, supposed *victim-blaming*, lynching-party, so I wasn't making any comments. Just enjoying the day and the family.

My phone was next to me on the bench, but I was trying not to look at it. I'd broken my rule to leave it inside when I'm with Michael. Electronics are going to destroy what's left of the family, after the federal government gets done picking it apart like the vultures they are, pecking out our eyeballs, eating our guts. Another view I don't share is my opinion of social media since I try to focus on the things that will really make a difference. If I over-share the less important stories, people will stop reading my posts. I know that because I've done the same to more than a few people whose spouting got tiresome.

I can't help but think the government likes America's devotion to their digital devices. It numbs the average person. They spend their days passing around jokes and funny videos and cute comments about the meaning of life. It's like the frog in the boiling water — they don't see what's happening as the heat gets turned up and they lose their privacy and rights, app by app.

When I consider my relationship with AboutFace, I feel like a bit of a masochist. I don't think that's an extreme statement. I'm not given to extreme statements, I'm a very easy-going, logical guy. AboutFace is a viral infection on this planet, yet I can't seem to break its grip on me. Marcus has the right idea — avoid it. The problem is, like anything, it has its benefits. One of which is all this online interaction helps me connect with people who recognize the truth. Living in the San Francisco Bay Area, where liberals grow like crabgrass, can be isolating. With AboutFace, I have reinforcements. I have compadres. It's not that I need others to bolster my views. I know who I am, and I know how the world should work, but a guy needs friends and a place to hang out where he doesn't get ripped a new one for speaking the truth. The other good thing with AboutFace is that, if you're casual about it like I am, the site can be a great tool for helping some of these morons realize they're being brainwashed. I can post stuff they'd never see on their liberal news sites and their left-wing blogs.

Lori kicked open the screen door with her bare foot. It's easy to open without using the handle because it doesn't latch right. She stuck out her hip to hold it open and rotated herself out of the house and onto the patio carrying a plate of sandwiches and a bowl of barbecue-flavored potato chips. She smiled, set them on the table, and went back inside. Michael didn't even glance at the food. He continued twirling like a stir stick in a drink. Watching him spin shoved my equilibrium off-center. I got up and repositioned myself on the bench, so I was facing the picnic table. I couldn't imagine what the spinning was doing to Michael's head. Maybe nothing. Kids have a different experience of the world. Watching him made me see what was lost over the years. I wonder when all that happiness and excitement evaporates and you become a dried out, trapped adult. It's probably the education system. In some ways, that's their job — pound you into an uncomplaining corporate citizen.

The screen door banged open again. With any other woman, all that banging and crashing would be interpreted as a pissed off wife. But that's not how Lori is, she's forceful, and she gets shit out of her way and makes her presence known in the world. I respect her for that. It's one of the reasons I married her. She's a great woman, wife, mother, and I couldn't ask for any more in terms of how she stands by me. I feel bad that I can't do better by her. I work hard, but construction is hit and miss, even with a supposedly recovered economy. She never complains, never even gives me a look that indicates she's disappointed with our lot in life. She stands by me like a heroine in a movie. I'm pretty lucky.

She was carrying two cans of coke attached to their plastic straps. She had one of the circles looped around her wrist. She put the cans on the table along with two glasses filled with ice and a plastic cup of milk that she'd managed to wrap her delicate, beautiful hands around in a triangular formation, avoiding a third trip into the house.

Michael abandoned the rope when he saw that cup of milk. He might not come running for food, but he's right there when a glass of milk is available. Before Lori could sit down, he drank all the milk, pulled the meat out from between the slices of bread, ate that, and raced back to the rope.

She sat beside me on the bench. "Relaxing day so far."

"I guess."

"What's wrong?"

"Nothing."

"Are you thinking about Kimberly?"

"It sucks. No one should die young. Although I still think it was her fault, any way you look at it."

"I wish you'd stop saying that. It's not very nice." She tucked her hair behind her ear.

I wanted so badly to touch the lobe, the skin was so pure — no holes stabbed through her flesh just to hold earrings that no guy on earth really cared about — but she was just beyond reach. I love that pillowy skin. It's like silk. It feels like it's some type of delicious piece of human flesh that makes you think women were specially crafted in heaven, made to look unearthly. I ate some chips instead. "I don't care if it's not nice, it's the truth. Taking off her clothes? What's that supposed to be? Anyway, that's not entirely why I'm bummed out."

"Why?"

"Just sick of the bullshit on AboutFace."

"Again? Then why do you go on there all the time?"

"I dunno. It sucks you in, don't you think?"

"No."

"Sometimes, it feels like a high school clique. Everyone piling around the popular kids and ignoring everyone else."

"Then don't look at it."

I grabbed another half of a sandwich and took a bite.

Lori picked up a large chip and broke it in half. It crumbled along the break line and dribbled a dusting of red spices on her finger. She stuck both pieces in her mouth. I don't get why she's always breaking chips and crackers in half and then eating both halves at once. I suppose I could ask her, but it seems overly fixated on trivia, and maybe a little critical. I don't like to criticize her. She just ignores me anyway, and I end up feeling small-minded. Not the way a guy likes to feel.

"I like to see what's going on," I said.

"Half the time you're pissed off at someone's point of view."

"I'd be pissed at that anyway."

"Well, it riles you up."

"No it doesn't."

She smiled. She leaned over and put her hand on my leg. "Don't be so serious."

"I'm not."

"You are. And I love you for that, but you need to lighten up once in a while."

I ate some more chips and washed them down with coke. Michael was sitting on the knot at the end of the rope, leaning back, so his torso was parallel to the ground. A rock formed in my gut, picturing his little hands slipping off the fat rope, his body plummeting into hard-packed dirt covered by a wispy layer of grass. I closed my eyes for a moment. We're lucky to have a kid like him. Most kids whine every ten minutes that they're bored, but our kid has more persistence than most adults. He'll master a project if it kills him. I credit Lori for that. She doesn't give in to every whim, and she doesn't let him spend a lot of time watching TV. She's strict about meals too, no snacking, refusing to eat lunch, then saying you're hungry two hours later.

She wants another kid, and I do too. We should do it before Michael gets too much older, but I worry about money. That's another thing that pisses me off on AboutFace. It's one big keeping up with the neighbors. *Look at the great party I went to, look at my awesome vacation, look at the construction progress on my new house, look at graduation from a pricey school, look at my new car, haha, I got promoted again.* I know that's not how people mean it, but it can make you feel like a loser when you look at the bills popping into your inbox like a spray of semi-automatic bullets.

We're doing better than most, it's not like we're drowning in debt. We're very conservative. But it's not right that we can't afford a brother or sister for Michael, and we have to watch someone throw their new house or their half a million dollar remodel in our faces.

"I can almost see the clouds gathering over your head," Lori said.

I smiled, but I knew it was a stiff, angry smile and she wasn't going to buy it.

She took her hand off my leg and put it on my forearm. "Maybe you should take a vacation from AboutFace."

I laughed. "You're kidding."

"It makes you so angry."

"It doesn't. I like keeping up with the real news and . . ."

"There are other ways to do that."

"You can't interact though. I want to hear what my friends are thinking, get their take on situations."

"Yeah, but you look at your high school friends and get all jealous and pissed off."

"Not really."

She pulled her hand away. She took a potato chip out of

the bowl and broke it in half. She put one half in her mouth and sucked on it. "Maybe you should unfriend them all."

Watching her suck on the chip, I wondered if we should just say what the hell and start making a baby. It wasn't like my income was going to change dramatically.

"Do you want another coke?"

I nodded. She went back in the house, and I picked up my phone. I opened AboutFace and looked at the comments on the article I'd shared. Typical. Minimal reaction from the people who really needed to read it. I looked through the updates. There was a Bible quote from Tiffany — *Every place where you set your foot will be yours.* I tried to think of a comment, but nothing came to mind. I want stuff like that to be true. I want all the stuff in the Bible to be true, but sometimes, I'm not sure. Maybe if I were more convinced, it would be true for me. If I threw my self all in, would we stop living paycheck to paycheck? Would that needle-thin crease of worry disappear from Lori's forehead? She never acted worried, but there was something there, hidden behind her confident smile. I could feel it.

Byron and Tiffany sure seemed to be doing okay, two kids, maybe more in the plans. Why did she post that? Was the deli not doing so great after all? Was she trying to convince herself, or convince her friends? Usually, she posted things about getting right with God, thinking about the good things in life. This seemed, I don't know, like she was wanting something but wasn't going to say what it was.

Lori returned and put the coke cans on the table. She snapped open the top and filled my glass. Caramel-colored foam rose up near the edge, receding just in time.

"Look at this." I held out my phone.

The metal tab snapped on her can, she took a sip and reached for the phone. She read it and handed it back. "What does that mean?"

"That you can get what you want?"

"Sounds greedy."

"I think that's what it means. Maybe it means we should have a kid and the money to support it will be there."

"Sounds delusional to me." She sat down and put her hand on my leg.

Michael needed a sibling, maybe two. If the government wasn't taking all my cash to give free healthcare to a bunch of losers who don't give a shit about their health — people who smoke and drink too much and eat fast food for three meals a day — I could afford another kid. It's not right that they can breed and expect Uncle Sam to help them out and we watch every dollar and can't afford a baby brother for Michael.

One minute I was pissed at Tiffany for all her gooey pictures of her kids, like it's free to just keep popping them out and the next minute, kind of appreciating her weird, almost magical promise. But it did give me a strange, hopeful feeling in the pit of my stomach. I don't think it was completely delusional.

Marcus

TAKING ALLIE'S PHONE had turned out better than I ever thought it would. Watching her sneak around, pretending she wasn't looking for it, was entertaining. There was something perverted about being entertained at my wife's expense, but I couldn't help it. There was also a controlling, threatening aspect to what I'd done, but hell, you'd think she had a screen embedded in the palm of her hand. Sometimes it seems as if she doesn't have a single thought in her head, she had to adopt thoughts from other people. On that level, it wasn't entertaining, seeing her so bereft.

I don't know when things got so bad. It's not like she wasn't on social media all the time when we first got together or during the first year or two of our marriage. Maybe I was different then, so it didn't bother me. We were in the honeymoon phase, and she couldn't do anything to irritate me. I thought she was exquisitely beautiful, and she is. I also thought she was charming and clever and friendly, and she is all of those things, still. But I didn't see her tendency toward superficiality. I didn't recognize her obsession. And it is definitely that. An obsession. Does someone really have to look at a dog video right this *minute*?

I hadn't decided how long I was going to keep the phone hidden. I knew I was being a creep, but I couldn't stop myself. That inability to control my actions should have given me a glimmer of insight into my wife — the not wanting to do something but doing it anyway. Although it wasn't exactly the same. She didn't recognize that she was bordering on a sick fixation — wanting to peer inside her friends' lives twenty-four-seven, talking non-stop about her own life, never considering how she came across or how crass some of her posts appeared, shoving her good fortune in the faces of 483 people.

Yes, I did know how many friends she had. I knew her password. She used the same password for everything, never thinking about how that could come back to bite her. I occasionally looked at her AboutFace feed, and I recognized in myself a ghoulish fascination with the unfiltered thoughts of hundreds of people. For a few moments, I felt I was god, seeing what they were all thinking. Although I guess unfiltered is relative. It was unfiltered in that they didn't pause to consider whether it was interesting or relevant to other people or have any conversational quality to it or TMI, but it was bleached with disinfectant as far as actual honest dialog. All trying too hard to be funny and witty. Ninety percent of what I read had a self-conscious ring to it. As if everyone was vomiting out fortune cookie statements or yearbook inscriptions.

While I had Allie's phone in my possession, Tiffany had posted an obscure line from the Old Testament. No one commented on it, which made me laugh. Okay, maybe

AboutFace can be entertaining. Either no one understood what the hell Tiffany was talking about, or they were too uncomfortable with the blatant religious tone infused with a strong element of magical thinking.

I put the phone back inside the cereal box and walked to the patio doors. The pool sweeper was madly circling, its arms stretching out, trying to grab every broken piece of leaf and every drowned bug. Allie had been taking her daily swims the same as always. She seemed unfazed by Kimberly's drowning. Of course, Allie's a great swimmer, and she doesn't drink, so she probably figured there was no relationship between swimming laps and Kimberly's death. The water was placid despite the hungry machine prowling the surface. There's something about the pale blue of a swimming pool that makes it look innocent, friendly, incapable of hurting anyone when it's as deadly as a handgun. As impartial as a plane that randomly disappears from the sky, as Jake had helpfully pointed out. I opened the sliding glass door and walked to the edge of the pool.

A part of me had wanted to toss Allie's phone into the water, be done with it for good, but I'm not a total asshole. Just a frustrated guy who's losing his wife to mindless entertainment and pseudo-friends. Maybe I was jealous. Maybe I wanted to shake things up.

I took off my shoes and socks and tugged up the legs of my jeans until they stuck at my calf muscles. I sat on the edge of the pool and lowered my feet onto the surface of the water, keeping my legs angled so water didn't touch my jeans.

I felt sorry for Kimberly. She appeared to be aiming for shock, but you can't shock people anymore. Everything's been said and done and posted on AboutFace and recorded on a smartphone, photographed and blogged about. It's insane. I know I sound like an old man, but when I'm flying, and we can't use mobile phones, the crew and I talk. And it's great. Sometimes when we're waiting to taxi, we can look each other in the eye, and there's a genuine human connection. I don't think Kimberly planned to die. Maybe she didn't want to be reduced to digital marks on a glass screen that are swept away in the tsunami of chatter.

I had no idea how I would shake things up. It's not the kind of guy I am, but taking Allie's phone had given me a certain satisfaction. It put me back in control of my life. I wanted that feeling to last.

The water lapped at my ankles, making the hairs darker. Below the surface, my feet were ghostly white. So white, they reminded me of Kimberly's waterlogged skin.

"What are you doing?"

I turned. Allie was wearing a very short skirt and a tight t-shirt, all pale pink, which made her hair look like rays of sun falling around her shoulders. She was barefoot, and her toenails were painted the same color as her clothes. She stepped out from beneath the overhang and took a few steps toward me.

"Cooling my feet."

"Oh."

She squinted and moved back under the overhang, and the shade concealed her face so I couldn't read her expression or even tell if she was still squinting.

"How long is this going to continue?" she said.

"I don't know." It was the truth. Until then, everything in my life was pre-ordained. I knew when my paycheck was going into my account and I knew what day I needed to mail our property tax payment. Every moment of every flight was meticulously planned. I couldn't remember the last time I hadn't known what was going to happen. When I came home from a trip, Allie cooked one of my favorite meals the first night, and we made love. It's not that I didn't want all those things. I felt good about my accomplishments. Part of being successful is building security and part of security is sameness — the income, the savings, the group of friends, the great marriage. Eventually, the kids. Hiding her phone had turned into a game, and I felt powerful and petty at the same time. I smiled, but she didn't notice because I'd turned back to face the pool.

Behind me, she was silent. If she'd gone back inside the house, I would have heard the door sliding on the track, but I wasn't sure, couldn't remember, whether she'd left it standing open. I hoped not. We didn't need a bird darting into the house, confused and lost as Allie without her phone.

When they were digging the hole for our pool, a Finch got into the house. It was disoriented because we ripped out a lot of vegetation in our backyard — the lemon tree, and the shrubs where the bird had presumably gathered construction material for its nest. Allie invited one of the workmen inside for a glass of water. He left the door open. The bird raced into the house, desperate for security.

Allie didn't squeal, but her eyelids were wide open, her eyeballs as motionless as two balls of glass. Her voice took on a childlike quality, and she seemed to be trying to calm herself, but failing. She repeated useless phrases as she followed me around, offering unhelpful hints on how to snare the bird. *It's okay little thing. Don't fly. It's okay. Everything will be okay. Sit still.* After a few minutes, I knew it would be easier to catch the bird without her assistance.

Now that I thought about it more, her reaction to her missing phone was exactly the same as that bird. She was frightened, manic. Without her usual habits, she was darting into windows.

I felt her hands on my shoulders, gripping harder than necessary, then loosening until her palms were pressing lightly against my trapezius muscle. For half a second, I thought she was going to shove me into the pool.

"I need my phone."

"Why?"

"To stay in touch."

"I'm right here. You're in touch with me."

"Not with my friends."

"You'd rather be with your friends than me?" I knew she

didn't, and I knew I had the sulky attitude of a pre-teen kid, but I truly wondered about her answer.

"I don't understand why you're doing this," she said.

I didn't either, but I wasn't going to back down now. "Why don't you just give it a rest for a few days. See how it goes."

"My students need to reach me."

"Only if they cancel."

"How would I know?"

"If someone doesn't show up, you'll know. We can go for a hike, catch a movie and eat out. And then there's the memorial service."

"You're not giving it back until after the memorial?" Her hands left my shoulders, and I pictured them fluttering in the air over my head. "You're being a total control freak. It scares me."

"You should be scared." I pulled my feet out of the water. The smell of chlorine was sharp. It felt as if my feet had been simmering in a vat of chemicals. My legs almost looked whiter, as if they'd had the skin burned off, revealing the bone.

"What's that supposed to mean?" she said.

I turned. Allie stood with her arms folded. She looked as terrified as that Finch but furious at the same time.

I stood and picked up my socks and shoes and went into the house. I felt like I'd lobbed a stick of dynamite into our relationship, but I didn't really care.

Allie

ALLIE SINCLAIR *THIS picture of my mom and me was taken on my tenth birthday at Disneyland. [112 favorites — 43 comments]*

Dave Eddington *You look exactly like your Mother.*

Allie Sinclair *It makes me happy to know that, Dave. Thanks. *Sniff**

Tiffany Jones *Such a beautiful soul, you can see it in her eyes. I'm sorry I never knew her.*

Megan Miller *How sweet. Your mom was pretty. I never went to Disneyland. Can you believe that? Almost thirty years old. It's probably too late to get matching mouse ears with my mother, but I should go. I really should. Who else is up for it?*

Tiffany Jones *I am. When Ruth is two.*

Megan Miller *I'll be thirty then, too late! LOL*

Allie Sinclair *We should plan a trip.*

[See 36 more comments]

WHEN MY MOTHER was killed in the cute silver Mercedes coupe that she loved, all my friends ostracized me. They didn't intend to do that, and I would never tell them how I felt, but that's what happened. I still remember exactly what I posted on AboutFace.

Allie Carson *The most amazing and beautiful and kindest woman who ever lived has been erased from the earth. Without my mom, I'm an orphan.*

People clicked favorite, and they made statements of sorrow. AboutFace was new back then, but everyone was on it already. I thought my post would make them write things that would make me feel better — even if there were nothing to be said — they would say *something*. They would say how awful it must be and how they couldn't imagine what I was going through. But mostly they just clicked the favorite and said I'm so sorry for you. They came to her funeral. They hugged me, but their arms felt like plastic because all I could see was their pathetic pale red star and as few words as possible. I needed my friends more than ever, but they lived in a parallel universe. I could see them and hear them, but I couldn't touch them. When they looked at me, I didn't think they saw me.

I was a freshman in college when she was killed. Adam and I were still together. We'd been together since junior year of high school, and we'd picked the same college. I thought he was my forever one and only, but my mother dying killed everything we had.

It was March. She'd been dead for five weeks, and I still hadn't gone back to school. Adam was home for the weekend. It was pouring rain, great huge buckets of it, like someone turned an apple-bobbing tub of water upside down. I stood on the front porch waiting for him to come over, watching water cascade off the roof, too much water for the gutters to manage. My father was out talking to the District Attorney about the drunk who murdered my mother.

When Adam got there, he hugged me and asked how I was doing. I didn't answer. We went into the living room and sat down. I put my hand flat on the couch, palm down. He put his hand over mine, each of his fingers placed in the spaces between my fingers. I wanted him to hold me close, so tight I wouldn't be able to breathe. I wanted him to take me upstairs and make love to me so that his skin and the pressure of him all over me and inside of me would blot out my thoughts. I wanted him to do something crazy to show that he understood how ripped apart I felt, but he just sat there. I wanted to punch his face.

"Are you coming back to school at all this year?" he said after a while.

"It depends on the trial."

"That could take months."

"I know." His hand felt like a piece of meat on top of mine. I thought my fingers were twitching, but when I looked at my hand, the twitching wasn't visible.

"You're not going to do anything until it's over?"

"I guess so."

"Missing school won't change how it turns out."

"Really?" I yanked my hand out from under his. I thought

he'd reach over and take it back, put it on his lap, hold it with both of his hands, but he just left his piece-of-meat hand resting on the couch. "I thought if I were there, it would transform the asshole into a repentant saint. I thought my mother might rise from the dead."

"Don't be like that."

"Like what?" I knew then — Adam couldn't handle it. He only liked the friendly social me. The cheerful me. The party girl me. He liked what he wanted me to be, not what I really was — a human being with bad thoughts and feelings, as well as good. "I'm not going back to school until that guy gets put in prison for the rest of his useless life. Or worse."

"I don't think drunk drivers get sentences like that."

I stared at him, waiting for him to wake up and absorb my sarcasm. After a few minutes, I stood. "It doesn't matter what you think. It matters that there's justice."

"Life isn't always *Just* with a capital *J*."

"Aren't you the wise man." Even then, I hoped he'd stand up, do something shocking, something to equal the shock echoing through each one of my cells. I was mildly disgusted with myself because my body was reaching out to him, wanting him to make me forget my mother and death and being an orphan and how terrible she looked when I saw her. I wanted to feel alive and loved and needed. It seemed, right then, that no one needed me anymore. My mother had needed me. I was the center of her life. She was a rare mother who managed to have a life of her own and still make me feel like she existed solely for me. None of my friends' mothers were like her. They were either completely selfish and ignored their daughters, or they were neurotically attached to them as if they didn't exist without their offspring.

"I don't know what you want from me," Adam said. "I just think it would be healthier if you came back to school. A distraction."

He wanted everything to go back to the way it was before. He wanted me to be the same girl I was before. That girl died with my mother.

Still, he could have done something wild. Picked me up and carried me to my bedroom. Or he could've undressed me right there. He could've grabbed my hand and taken me out to the car and put down the top, even in the pounding rain. We could have driven to the ocean and let the storm consume us.

"I'm not going back to school until I see that guy punished. So stop asking."

"But we won't graduate together."

"So what."

"I thought we planned to . . . I thought you wanted . . ."

"There aren't any plans. There's Justice."

"Come sit next to me."

That was the worst thing he could have said. I walked out of the room and down the hall, past the pictures of my parents, the school pictures of me, past the large photograph of me in my high school graduation gown with the red tassel covering part of my face, like a huge, bloody gash. I walked past the portrait my mother had painted of me. It was on a wall by itself, on the opposite side of the hallway from the photographs. It looked like me, but not. She'd painted it when I was ten, and she was just starting to take painting classes. There was another portrait of me that she'd started the summer after high school. It sat on an easel in her art room, half-finished, a painting with no mouth and only the faint suggestion of my nose. I wondered if I should hang it in my room — forever an unfinished woman.

I went into my bedroom. I took off my clothes and laid on top of my bed and waited for Adam to come in, but he never did. When he texted me later that night and asked if I wanted to see a movie, I didn't text back. The next day, I texted him and said he should go back to school and that he'd always be my friend and have a place in my heart. He didn't respond to that text, which also said a lot.

I took off the rest of the school year to be with my Dad, although it turned out he didn't really need me. The drunk was given five years in prison. My Dad took the sudden change in his life as a signal to change everything. He flipped his entire existence upside down. He retired early, if you can even call it retirement at the age of fifty-one. After I went back to school, he sold our house and bought a one-bedroom condo. He got rid of the unfinished painting, so all I have are some paintings of trees and the one of ten-year-old me. He started traveling all over the world, dropping by his condo once every few months so I could come for a visit. He never stops moving, even now. He changed all the scenery of his life so he wouldn't notice that empty space. Sometimes I wonder if he realizes how much of his life is missing.

Three years and seven months, and that's how Adam and I ended. Sometimes we see each other at parties, and we're always friendly. There's no animosity, no hurt, no unfinished business. We've never talked about it. We've never talked alone at all since that day.

The closest I ever came to wanting to kill someone, or torture someone, was when I saw that guy get a shitty five-year sentence for killing my mother. He's a murderer, out walking the streets now. It's so unfair, so sick. There is no justice. Maybe my justice came with a happy life with Marcus and getting to help kids be successful in school. All I can do is hope that killer lies awake every night of his life thinking about what he did. That he took a human life. That he destroyed a beautiful, loving woman. That he gutted a man and mangled a teenaged girl. That he doesn't deserve a moment of peace. He ripped her out of our lives, and he gets to be all — *oh so sorry. I'll never do it again.*

Nine years from tomorrow is the anniversary of her death. I wonder if Marcus remembers. I wonder if I should put something on AboutFace. Of course, without my phone, I'll have to do that on the computer, sitting at the desk like I'm doing an office job.

If I post something about the anniversary of my mother's

death, will Adam comment? He never comments on my posts, just clicks *favorite*. On the fifth anniversary of her death, I wrote something, and he was MIA. Of course, not as many people made that a favorite because it's awkward. They might have thought they were saying they liked that she was dead. Everyone knows that's not what it means, but it's still awkward. Maybe I'll wait until the tenth anniversary.

AFTER OUR FIGHT by the side of the pool, Marcus went for a bike ride. I ran upstairs and yanked open the drawer in his nightstand, knowing my phone wasn't there, but I had to look anyway. It was hard to breathe. Instead, little squeaks came out of my throat.

Inside the drawer was a magazine from the airline and a thriller he's reading, although he's only been reading it when he's home, so I'm not sure how thrilling it is. I stuck my hand under his pillow and felt around. I shoved both hands up to my elbows between the mattress and box spring and ran them from the headboard to the foot. The eighteen-inch deep mattress weighed on my bones as if I was groping under a slab of concrete.

I pulled my arms out, stood, and looked around our room, trying to get inside his head. I'd already checked the drawers on his side of the dresser, gone through the boxes on his side of the closet, and even looked through every drawer in the bathroom. There was no place to hide it on the balcony. I sat down on the love seat in the corner. Maybe he moved the phone every few hours. I could turn the house upside down, and I'd never find it because it had been under the mattress when I was searching the office, and under the couch cushion when I was searching the pantry.

I went into the office, sat at the desk, and woke the computer from sleep. I opened a new window and loaded AboutFace.

Before we got married, I knew he liked to be alone, and I wasn't sure if he'd grown to want that even more, or if I'd become more social. If we only saw our friends once or twice a month, it was fine by him.

Everyone has an AboutFace account. Everyone. And he was going to find himself cut out of life if he didn't stop acting so superior like he was more intelligent, more aware of the world because he shunned all of that.

He's a pilot, for god's sake. His whole life is surrounded by computers and high-tech communication, and he acts like he wants to live on Walden Pond.

There were so many updates from my friends, it took me fifteen minutes just to favorite everything.

I posted a comment on the article Seth had shared about how we all need to arm ourselves and hunker down before the government turns us into slaves. I try not to read the articles he posts, but I felt I should at least skim the opening so I could respond authentically. Even skimming it made me worry about who lived next door, how many people were stockpiling guns.

I was lucky to be married to such a reasonable man.

I tried to think of something clever to post about Marcus. Of course, he'd never see it, so it wasn't really worth the effort. If I showed it to him, it wouldn't be the same as him reading it on his own. I get jealous when Tiffany and Byron, and Adam and Pam, and Seth and Lori, and *Every. Other. Couple. In the Whole. Entire. World* . . . comments back and forth on each other's posts. It makes me feel very alone. I hate that feeling.

Allie Sinclair *Feeling lost. [37 favorites — 19 comments]*

Dave Eddington *Cheer up, life will get better.*
Tiffany Jones *You're in my prayers. More than ever. More than you know.*
Byron Jones *You are so sweet, Tiff. That's why I love you!*
Jake Ash *We're all lost right now.*
Megan Miller *I know the feeling.*
Amelia Loc *It'll pass. Life goes on.*
Kristen Thomas *That's kind of shallow.*
Amelia Loc *But true.*
Byron Jones *Life is for the living.*
[See 10 more comments]

WHEN I SAW Byron's comment on what Tiffany said, I felt worse. I closed AboutFace and read two emails from parents of my tutoring students.

Marcus came home from his bike ride remarkably un-sweaty, but he took a shower anyway. The minute I heard the water stop, I decided to go for a swim. I didn't want to talk to him. He couldn't cut me off from my friends. They say that's one of the signs of an abuser. I wondered if that meant he had the potential to be abusive. I hated myself for thinking of him that way. But our marriage was turning into something I didn't recognize. Is that what happens after only three years? And how did it get so messed up so fast? We'd never had a fight like this. I wasn't sure how to patch things up with him, but until he gave me my phone, nothing was going to get fixed. I couldn't post about not having my phone, although part of me wanted to ask my married friends if this had ever happened to them. But I didn't want to make Marcus look bad, or make it look like we weren't happy, that we were in trouble, headed for the big D.

I went to the downstairs bathroom and put on my black swimsuit, which I know he really likes because even though it's a one-piece, it's more low cut on top and high cut on the bottom than my bikinis. Maybe that would change his stupid controlling behavior. Or maybe not.

Diving into the pool didn't give me the clean, slicing away of my thoughts that it usually did. I swam an entire length without taking a breath. I did a racing turn, pushing off from the end with an adrenaline burst that seemed like it wanted to propel me out of the pool and onto the small grassy area.

Thinking that Marcus had the potential to be abusive made

me sick to my stomach. The thought locked into my head, and I tried to remember the rest of the warning signs I'd read. They're always shoving those lists down your throat during domestic violence awareness week, in magazine articles, in the answers of advice columns. No woman can avoid seeing them, and they seem vague enough that you could call anything a warning sign. What's the difference between a guy calling you when you're with your friends to tell you how much he loves you, making you feel great, and a guy controlling you by calling when you're with your friends? It seems like half of the signs could be all in your interpretation of things, how you're feeling about him and whether you want him to call and touch base. It's very confusing.

He acted like he was in charge and smarter than me, and absolutely right about how life should be lived. He was the one with a problem, not me. Who avoids social media? It's anti-social. The whole world is connected, and unless you want to go live in a secluded shack in the mountains and shower once a week and eat beans out of a can and hoard guns, that's how people live.

By the fifteenth lap, my breath sounded so loud in my ears I felt like my head had swollen to twice its size and the air was echoing between my brain and my skull. He was not only controlling, maybe he was a little unbalanced. And if that was true, should I be expressing my concerns to his boss? Does the flying public want a pilot who has such a bizarre view of the world he tries to disconnect his wife from her friends and refuses to socialize online? What's he afraid of? My arms felt so weak I was having trouble lifting them out of the water. I switched to breaststroke, but even that was difficult. I stopped moving and turned onto my back, floating and staring up at the sky. I closed my eyes and tried to think about what to do, but nothing came to me.

I let myself drift to the side of the pool. I reached out for the rail on the ladder, but my body was too limp to hoist myself up onto the bottom rung. I pushed my feet against the side and swam to the shallow end. Climbing out on the concrete steps was an enormous effort. I collapsed on the chaise lounge and spread my towel over me like a blanket. I closed my eyes and tried to breathe, but my heart was pounding as if I'd just finished swimming five miles. Water from my sopping hair and bathing suit was spreading across the lounge cushion. It was gross, but I couldn't move. I heard the screen door open.

"What are you doing?" Marcus sounded calm and casual as if everything was super fine. As if he wasn't trying to imprison me.

"Resting."

"How was your swim?" The cushion shifted, and my body collapsed toward him as he sat on the end of the chair. He put his hand on my ankle.

"Exhausting."

"Exhausting? Why?"

"I don't like being controlled. I don't like that you think you're the normal one and there's something wrong with me."

"I never said that."

I sat up. The towel fell onto my legs. I felt him looking at my breasts, although I can't imagine they looked that great, all squashed by wet spandex. "Either you're controlling, or you're treating me like a four-year-old. Maybe it's the same thing."

"No I'm not."

"Then give me back my phone."

"I think it will help our relationship. I'm not trying to control you, and I'm sorry if you think I am." He stood and moved toward the patio.

"There's nothing wrong with our relationship. We have a great marriage."

"Is that right?" He slid open the door and went into the house.

What was he talking about? Our marriage was awesome. We were soul mates, until this. And once he saw how annoying and controlling and stupid he was being, it would all be perfect again.

The greatest thrill of my life was falling in love with Marcus. It made me feel complete. It made me feel I'd have a good life. Before that, I knew I had friends and the potential for a good future, but I didn't know if I'd find the *one*. There was this scary feeling that maybe I'd be alone and never have what everyone else had. I realize that not everyone does, but once I knew that I was going to be one of the lucky ones in love, it was thrilling and exciting.

Now, suddenly, I was scared. How could he think something was wrong in our marriage? How could I think everything was so perfect, until this, and he didn't? He'd never said anything before.

I looked across the pool. The water darkened as the sun lowered itself behind the trees. Maybe I didn't know him at all. I really had no idea what he was thinking. I had no idea what he talked about, thought about, what he even did when he was flying. He was in a different world during those times, and I think I was so aware of my own thoughts and what I was up to, I never stopped to consider his life apart from me. I didn't really know who he ate dinner with, not specifically, or what he did in the evenings. I had no idea what his thoughts were when he was flying 120 human beings and all their suitcases stuffed with crap. I didn't know if he thought about me, about our life, about our future, about death. Nothing. He was a complete blank to me.

Adam

ADAM JAMISON [*UPLOADED 30 images*] *The Grand Canyon, dawn to dusk. And a few shots of my gorgeous wife and children!*

6 favorites — 3 comments

Dave Eddington *"A few"? You look like you're vying for having the most photographed wife on AboutFace. LOL.*

Tiffany Jones *Gorgeous — God's creation and your wife. And she's God's creation too!*

Megan Miller *Awesome. I hope I can see it someday.*

CLICKING THROUGH THE photographs I'd uploaded so far was like living through the day again. We'd spent most of it walking a trail along part of the south rim. Jared was in a pack strapped to Pam's shoulders, and Claire gripped my hand as if she wanted to squeeze the blood out.

Or, rather, I gripped her hand, feeling the gaping hole a few yards away, the sheer drop into a seemingly bottomless canyon that's pulled so many careless hikers into its soul-less mouth over the decades.

Because I'd been so focused on a squirming four-year-old — too nervous to stop and drink in the majesty of carved rock and shifting colors — I felt as if I was seeing the canyon for the first time in the photographs. After all the planning for the trip, it seemed as if I hadn't really been there. We had two more days, and I vowed I'd manage my fears better. But Claire was unpredictable. A squirrel racing along a low stone wall could yank her away from me before I even blinked.

During our hike, I'd had grandiose thoughts about a short story I wanted to get started on once the kids were settled in their beds, but now, I couldn't stop staring at the documentation of the day while the story shriveled to nothing inside my head.

Pam was sipping a glass of red wine and checking her work email, which I wasn't happy about, but when your wife earns enough to support the family and allows you to be a full-time fiction writer, you don't complain about how she spends her time. Still, she was supposed to be on vacation. She'd promised to disconnect from work, but she couldn't seem to let go. I suppose she felt pressure to ensure her value didn't fade while she was out of sight, knowing she had a husband and two kids depending on her. What hope did I have, what kind of writer was I that I'd rather review my photographs than write the first page of a story?

Fifteen minutes ticked past. Pam came over to the desk where I sat staring at the screen saver. It was made of repeatedly dissolving photographs of Jared's face as a newborn, then at three months, and six months, layered with Claire at the same milestones, continuing on through the first years of her life, aging right before my eyes.

"How's it going?" Pam said.

I shrugged.

She kissed the top of my head. "Isn't it awful about Kimberly?"

"What?"

"I thought you were on AboutFace."

"I just uploaded some pictures. Want to see them?"

"You didn't read any updates?"

I shook my head.

"Kimberly drowned — at Jake's housewarming party."

I stabbed the return key. The kids disappeared as if they'd been shot. "What?"

"She dove into the pool, a little drunk if you read between the lines. She hit her head on the concrete and died."

"That makes no sense." I clicked in the search bar and typed the first four letters of her name. The rest of her name and Santa Clara University — her MBA alma mater — appeared. I clicked on it. Streams of posts and pictures spun past as I scrolled down. "Shit."

"I know."

I clicked back over to my page, knowing what I was going to see before it came up on the screen.

Adam Jamison [*Uploaded 30 images*] *The Grand Canyon dawn to dusk. And a few of my gorgeous wife and children!*
  7 favorites — 4 comments

Dave Eddington *"A few"? You look like you're vying for the most photographed wife on AboutFace. LOL.*

Tiffany Jones *Gorgeous — God's creation and your wife. And she's God's creation too! Cool shots, but kinda hard to enjoy right now.*

Megan Miller *Awesome. I hope to go there someday.*

Byron Jones *Really? Not quite the right time for this.*

There were now seven favorites, none of them from Allie. I thought Byron's comment was unduly harsh. They must know I wasn't aware of what had happened. I wasn't there, and I hadn't been in direct touch. No one sent me a text or called. I clicked back to Kimberly's page — a digital roadside memorial. But in this case, it wouldn't deteriorate to a bunch of dead flowers and soggy stuffed animals in three months. The traffic would decrease to a trickle and then it would live on in cyberspace for eternity. I guess the everlasting life we all hope for, but most of us doubt, exists after all.

I bit the cuticle on my left thumb and scrolled down again. Allie, predictably, had posted the most pictures on Kimberly's page. I tried to remember Allie and Kimberly in high school, but I couldn't bring up a clear image of how close they were. This might be a good reason to get in touch with Allie in a more concrete way. I could send her a condolence text right now. Or I could wait until we got home and call her. I wondered if that would be too weird, after so many years. But I felt if I talked to her alone, maybe she'd stop worming her way into my head all the time. Once and for all, I needed to eradicate my unhealthy need to secretly observe her life.

Pam took hold of my wrist and pulled my hand away from my mouth.

"It bugs me when you grab me like that," I said. "You act like you're my mother."

"Just trying to help you break the habit."

I think she wanted me to break the nail biting habit more than I did, but I did it long before I met her and I'd done it the entire time we'd been together. I don't know what she thinks she's going to accomplish.

She never gives up. At least she doesn't do it in front of our friends anymore, although I'm just waiting for her to do it in front of the kids, because she's so worried they'll adopt my bad habit.

Once my hand was back on the keyboard, she wrapped her fingers around my ponytail. She held it, tugging gently to let me know she was there, loving me. I leaned into her.

"It's so awful. I can't believe it," I said.

"It's terrible. So sad." She let go of my ponytail. "Did you get anything done on your story?"

I shook my head.

She sighed. "You need to stay off AboutFace."

"I was just uploading the pictures. Should I take them down? I guess it looks insensitive."

"I don't think so. They were already there. Life keeps moving. I guess you won't get very many comments. But maybe after a while, when the memorial is over, people will see them."

"The service is Thursday."

"Mmm-hmmm." As she moved away, her feet were heavy on the wood floor of the faux-rustic cabin.

The sound reminded me where we were — thirty yards from one of the wonders of the world, yet I was staring at a computer screen, and my emotions were stronger than they'd been when I was looking out over the vast sweep of the canyon. "I guess we could make it home in time."

"No way. Like you said when I wanted to change it, we planned this all year. We're not going home early."

"Yeah, but . . ."

"There's no need for us to go. You weren't that close."

"But everyone will be there."

"No one will even notice you're not there."

"Thanks."

"You know what I mean."

"Shunning someone's memorial service is cold. What does that say about the human race?"

Once again, she was standing right behind me. I could feel her warmth, even though she wasn't touching me. "Don't turn it into a sociological analysis. As *you* pointed out to *me*, this is our vacation. Our family takes priority."

"It feels wrong."

"Only in your head." She tugged on my ponytail. She's constantly playing with it, but I always read some sort of message into the gesture. I pulled away from her. I jiggled the chair around the spot where she was standing and got up. I tipped the laptop screen forward. The screen went dark — like Kimberly's life. If I expressed that idea to Pam, she'd say I was trying too hard to think of a literary turn of phrase, but the image stayed with me as I walked to the bathroom and turned on the water.

"You're taking a shower?"

"Yes."

"Let's just go to sleep."

"I need to think."

"You can think in bed."

"It'll be quick."

"If you're planning to think about how to convince me to cut short our vacation, you're wasting energy. And water." She laughed.

I closed the door and stripped off my t-shirt and jeans. I could hear her on the other side, talking to me, arguing her case. She seemed to have forgotten how easily she was willing to let go of our "only" family vacation when she wanted to go look at Jake's new house.

Sometimes I imagined her getting out PowerPoint slides and showing me charts and bullet points and other imagery to try to sell me on her point of view, like she did all day at work. I shouldn't mock her job, not even in my head. I'm lucky to earn ten grand a year. But it'll get better. It takes time to build a career in the arts. I ducked under the stream of water and adjusted the mix of hot to cold, so it delivered a slight burn to my sweaty skin.

Of course, I couldn't tell Pam that part of the reason I wanted to go to the memorial service was because I was worried what Allie would think if I was a no-show. Not that I had the remotest clue what she thought of me at all. Not that I'd ever know. It was like that part of me, and her, had been written on a whiteboard, and someone took a large, soft eraser, and wiped it clean, not even the shadow of a line remaining. Yet, it was still there. Part of me, and part of her. I wished I could view her in the same light I saw all my friends. I didn't like having her in a special category.

The soap had rinsed off my skin several minutes earlier, but I continued to let water stream over my face and across my shoulders, splashing the tops of my feet. My hair needed washing even less than I'd needed a shower. Nevertheless, I squirted shampoo into my palm and lathered up. I stood for several more minutes under the flow, but couldn't settle on what I needed to do. The reality was I had no choice in the matter. I just wished I could get a grip on how I felt about Allie, and understand why she haunted me after all this time. My life on the outside had moved on, but inside, I couldn't stop circling like a crow waiting for access to a half-eaten hamburger tossed in the gutter.

Jake

JAKE ASH [*UPLOADED one image*] *I've found martinis are as enlightening as meditation.*

37 favorites — 6 comments

Dave Eddington *Pricey looking bottle. Are you aiming for ad revenue from Tanqueray Ten?*

Tiffany Jones *Only the Lord gives true enlightenment.*

Megan Miller *Maybe you haven't given meditation enough time. I suggest a silent retreat.*

Adam Jamison *I'm fond of martinis myself. Let's meet up when I'm back in the Bay Area.*

Allie Sinclair *Be careful!*

Kristen Thomas *Cheers!*

THE DAY BEFORE Kimberly's memorial, I knew I'd show up, assuming I could manage to go an hour without a drink. It seemed wrong for the person who supplied the venue for her death to mourn her, but not going would make me the most callous guy on earth. I am a callous guy, always have been. People should take responsibility for their own lives, their own mistakes. If you don't like your job, if you're in a bad relationship, then do something about it. That's my view.

Seeing her empty body dragged out of my pool rubbed off that shell around my head. It wasn't as if I could have saved her, I wasn't anywhere near the pool when she went in. I just wanted to go back in time and change how things played out. I didn't want someone dying on my property. I couldn't figure out why she'd done it, and I couldn't imagine the horror of being under all that water and not being able to rise to the surface.

Maybe I was still callous. Maybe, what was really bugging me, was seeing her suffer my worst fear. Maybe I didn't care about her at all, I was just scared out of my head.

I couldn't stop thinking about Tiffany's one-liner sermon about taking what you wanted. It echoed my philosophy, and it surprised me that god apparently agreed with me. The problem was, I wasn't sure I wanted the same things anymore. I wanted to take everything life has to offer, but I'd thought those things were admiration and money and thrills. Was that what Tiffany meant? It didn't sound like her at all. It didn't sound like anything I'd heard from the Bible before.

Amelia was getting on my nerves more every day. Every so often, I wondered whether I wanted to kill her. I really did. Her appearance, which I used to find exotic, now gave the impression of a vampire — her too-white skin, made whiter by the makeup she spent forty-three minutes applying every morning, and her dark hair and freakishly light blue eyes, her lips with too *much* color, undeniably the shade of blood. She wanted to suck all my thoughts out of my head. She wanted the old me, the party me, the cavalier guy spouting off when he knew nothing, proclaiming that we all do what we do and we can't wallow in regrets. Those are the words of an ignorant man who hasn't experienced death.

I was sitting on the couch, looking out the window at the sky, considering the nature of the universe. Is that such a bad thing? I think it's a good thing. I had a transformed perspective on the world, on the brevity of life. I'd been so busy moving to the next step, doing the next thing, failing to pay attention to what was around me. Now, I felt like I didn't know anyone at all. What was inside all of these people I considered friends? Kimberly hid her entire existence behind a facade, and I'd never know what was in her mind. Considering the nature of the universe is something we should all be doing. Every day. Why else are we here? Just to go out to bars and play games and eat and drink and have sex? Earn gobs of money so we can do more of the same? That's it? We might as well be rabbits.

Amelia appeared just inside the entrance to the living room. I hadn't heard her approach and wondered if she'd been standing there for a long time. I took a sip of my drink.

"What are you doing?" she said.

"Thinking."

"About what?"

I shrugged, more dramatically than I should have. "The usual."

"Morbid thoughts about death?"

"Death is an important part of life. We ignore it to our peril."

"Who talks like that?" She folded her arms and took another step into the room, as if she didn't want to get too close, holding herself back from whatever was wrong with me. Protecting herself from infection.

"I do." I sipped my drink.

"You sound like a preacher."

"You want to pretend nothing happened and that it can't happen to you. That it won't happen to you."

She laughed. Laughing is everyone's answer when they don't want to admit you're right, or don't know what to say — laugh, as if they're sure you're crazy or screwing around. I've always been an outspoken guy, a grab-life-by-the-balls kind of guy. Even though I was contemplating the idea of turning from a life focused on earning more and more money, toward figuring out what the hell life is supposed to be about, my basic nature didn't change — tell it like it is, throw the provocative ideas out there and see what shakes loose. I half smiled, wondering where this would go. I picked up my phone.

She walked toward the love seat and turned to face me. "I hate it when you pick up your phone when I'm trying to talk to you."

"So talk."

"Quit looking at your phone."

I scrolled back to Tiffany's post again. No one had

commented. There was one favorite from her husband. I was stunned. I couldn't remember the last time I'd seen a post with no comments and only a single favorite. It looked as though Tiffany had won the AboutFace award for silencing the world. No one knew what the hell she was talking about, so they said nothing. If Kimberly hadn't died, they would have asked Tiffany what she meant. But in this new world, where your friends got themselves killed, unusual sayings were creepy.

As Amelia glared at me, I thought more about Tiffany's devotion to her religion. Maybe she was deeper than I'd realized. She posted things that people couldn't figure out and wasn't afraid to not be understood. Her little girl voice had made it hard to take her seriously. Now, her childlike simplicity suggested she knew the secrets of the universe. Or *the* secret. Maybe there's only one. I wanted to talk to her. I wanted to find out what she knew. I had the sudden feeling that she would understand exactly what I was going through. She'd want to discuss all the unanswered questions, and she could hold the lack of answers and the assurance of deeper meaning simultaneously in her hands.

The only time I'd had a one-to-one conversation with Tiffany that was longer than ten words, was at my engagement party. It was held at Amelia's parents' golf club in the foothills. The club was very old school with lots of dried-out people wandering around in LL Bean clothes looking not very sophisticated but not needing to because they had a lot more money than any of us rising tech stars. They had a lot more money than most of us would ever have — the kind of money that's passed down through generations, and people outside can't even tell how much there is because it's not flashed around. They wear common, moderately priced clothes, they drive Mercedes, not Maseratis, and they eat at the club, not over-priced restaurants.

The party room opened onto a large semi-circle patio that looked out over palm trees and grass. I was sitting in the main hallway just outside the room. Tiffany came walking out, looking as if she was searching for someone, but I don't think it was me. She sat in the armchair next to me.

"How do you know Amelia's the one?" she said. Just like that. No preamble. No, *I don't really know you that well, or we've never talked much about anything serious, but I was wondering* . . . she charged right in. Like a little kid.

"There's only one?"

She sipped her coke. "That's what I believe."

"Why?"

"Marriage is a big commitment. It better be the person God designed for you."

"I'm ambivalent about god," I said.

"I know. But most people still think they have a one and only. A soul mate. I think that's because God's looking out for them, directing them to that person who will help them find God at some point in their life."

"Sounds complicated." I sipped my champagne, letting it

swirl around in my mouth and tickle the back of my throat before I swallowed. "I have no idea if she's the one. We're a good fit. I can't see myself with anyone else."

Tiffany nodded. "You don't want to take it seriously. You're afraid of your feelings."

"Not me."

She didn't argue. And I had the sense it was because she was certain she was right and didn't feel the need to change my point of view.

She stood. "I wish you and Amelia the best. I really do. You deserve someone who's a hundred percent devoted to you."

"I do? Like Byron has with you?"

She smiled. The curve of her mouth was very mysterious. For a moment, she lost the round-cheeked, wide-eyed, peaches-and-cream baby girl appearance she usually has. Instead of looking not very bright, she looked wise, ancient. An old soul, as they say. I felt I'd misjudged her and wanted to know her better. And yet, I never followed up on that. Never had a serious conversation with her again, and our engagement party was more than a year ago. I'd returned to my opinion that there wasn't anything all that interesting inside her head. I'd forgotten all about that conversation, until now.

Reading her Bible verse, the sensation returned. Her demeanor wasn't an accurate indication whatsoever of the person inside. She was a woman of mystery.

"What do you think this means?" I stood and walked toward Amelia. I held out the phone.

She looked like she was going to knock it out of my hand, but after a small hesitation, she took it and studied it. She handed it back.

"What does it mean?" I said.

"Religious BS. Who cares? You need to get a grip. Let's go to a club tonight."

"It's Monday."

"When did that ever stop us?"

"I'm not in the mood."

"It'll be good for you. Once we're there, you'll be in the mood."

"I don't feel like it."

"Even more reason to do it."

"No. End of discussion."

"Don't tell me when a conversation is over. We need to work this out, and you're acting like a child."

"Why aren't you being supportive of how I'm feeling? Isn't that the female's role? To nurture and comfort?"

"God, Jake. What's wrong with you? I don't recognize you or anything coming out of your mouth."

"I'm the same me. Just a wiser me who realizes I'm living a superficial life."

"Cut the bullshit."

"You really have no idea what this means? It sounds like she's saying take whatever you want, but that's not really like her, is it? I mean, isn't religion all about giving up the shirt on your back?"

"I have no idea." She lifted her chin, the better to look down her nose at me.

"I can't stop thinking about it."

"That's because you're obsessing about one thing after another."

"There's more to Tiffany than meets the eye. It makes me think you could learn a few things from her. You should be more like her."

"No fucking thanks."

"Come sit down with me. Rub my neck."

"I want to go out."

"I don't."

"You're trying to upset me."

"I wouldn't do that."

She laughed. She moved slightly to her left. Now the sunlight was behind her, making her look like a film negative. The light was too bright, the rays slicing through the glass, making it look splintered.

"Can we please go out?" she said.

"We always do what you want."

"That's not true."

"Tonight, I think it's time for you to submit to me."

She smiled carefully. "That's more like it." She stepped closer. "Tell me what you have in mind, baby."

"Not what you're thinking. Not that at all. I want you to

grill some burgers for dinner and then give me a back rub, so I can unwind."

She made a face and walked out of the room. I wasn't sure if she was planning to look for ground beef or go out to a club by herself.

Tiffany

TIFFANY JONES *PAUL asked me why I was crying, and when I said our friend died, he said, "Did she got stepped on like the snail?"*
15 favorites — 5 comments

> **Dave Eddington** *I can't imagine explaining that to a kid.*
> **Tiffany Jones** *I told him the snail didn't go to heaven, but hopefully Kimberly did.*
> **Byron Jones** *Either she believed or she didn't. There's no "hopefully" about it.*
> **Allie Sinclair** *That's harsh.*
> **Byron Jones** *God's plan, not mine.*

KIMBERLY'S FUNERAL WASN'T actually a funeral because her body was already gone. Burned into nothing and set to be scattered somewhere privately, without all of us watching.

The chairs were arranged on a patio facing a lake on the ninth hole of the golf course. It was a weird choice because Kimberly didn't play golf. And the idea of staring at water while all of her family and friends talked about her life, carefully avoiding the subject of drowning, made me anxious before we even sat down.

Paul and Ruth were with a babysitter. I figured I had about three hours before my breasts started to feel heavy with milk, and maybe five hours before any leaking started. I couldn't imagine the service and lunch would last longer than that.

It was such a pagan atmosphere. Where was God? Most of Byron's friends from high school were unbelievers. Since Paul was born, Byron and I had tried to spend less time with those people and more time with friends from church, but Byron felt we couldn't miss the funeral, especially since we'd been there when she drowned. And he thought it was a good opportunity to talk to people about the Lord, although in my experience, that was a fruitless mission. They changed the subject faster than I could change Ruth's diaper. No one wants to think about how they're messing up their lives, and no one wants to think about their lives being over, even at a funeral. And it *was* a funeral, even if there was no coffin. No one wants a coffin because it forces you to realize the person is actually dead. And I guess that was the reason for the golf course. Pretend it wasn't real. Inside a church, the quiet and the sense of awe turn your thoughts to God. Out on the golf course, half of the guests were probably wondering if they were too young to take up golf.

We sat at the end of the fifth row. The family took up the first two rows. I'd never met any of them.

It was breezy and my hair stuck to my lip-gloss. When I pulled the strands away, they felt greasy. But the breeze also made it bearable to sit out in full sunlight. It *was* beautiful.

The lake was such a soothing dark blue. Acres of grass stretched out like a soft blanket inviting you to lie down and look up at the sky. Songbirds twittered and chirped and peeped from trees that were sixty or seventy years old, maybe older. The breeze ruffled the leaves, branches bowing down every so often. It started to make me think a golf course wasn't such a bad idea after all, because God's creation was wrapped around us. We couldn't escape. We can never escape from His loving presence, His hand on everything. If people would just open their eyes.

Of course, no one's eyes were visible. Everyone wore sunglasses. No one wanted to be caught crying or worse, looking scared and uncertain.

Byron took my hand and held it inside both of his. The sense of him next to me, his shoulder higher than mine, the hardness of his legs compared to mine, made me feel safe. We were exactly where God wanted us to be. Even if no one else in all the chairs around us believed, we were a community of two, bringing His presence into an ungodly atmosphere. Still, it was sad not to see a cross or a minister to guide us to the truth.

I slid my hand out of Byron's grip and opened the program. There weren't any Scripture readings and no hymns or spiritual songs. A harpist sat near the podium, stroking the strings of her instrument. It sounded lovely, but there was no tune, really, no words to turn our thoughts in the right direction.

A man stood and introduced himself as Kimberly's brother-in-law. He was a lawyer, which he mentioned right away, and three or four more times after that. I guess being a lawyer meant he was good at speaking in front of a crowd, but it sure didn't mean anything to me. A lawyer? I couldn't understand why anyone would think that qualified him to lead a memorial service.

After that, it was a long parade of people talking and saying nothing. It made me want to go back to the wordlessness of the harp. This is why songs about faith and Scripture would have been so much better. People that lived long before us said important things that bring real comfort. Talking about what sports Kimberly liked, her travels, and her career was not only boring, it was depressing. And completely meaningless. So what if she liked hiking? What did that have to do with anything important? Wasn't anyone concerned whether she was in torment, separated forever from God and just now realizing it? Maybe they deliberately didn't want to think about that. I finally decided that was the whole purpose, just like the missing coffin — numb themselves with nonsense so they didn't have to think about where she really was.

When it was over, everyone stood and wandered away from their chairs. There was no orderly procession out, no line of family members where we could talk to them easily. We were left to go by memory for what they looked like, hunting down each one to express condolences. The harpist began playing again, but after a few minutes, it was almost impossible to hear over the voices.

We ended up at a table with Allie and Jake and Amelia. Allie had her purse on a chair, saving it for Marcus. I'd seen him earlier, but he'd wandered off, as he often does. I wished I had the courage to wander away. I was tired of everyone saying over and over how terrible it was, then shutting me down if I even mentioned the name of God.

Allie took a bite of potato salad, if you could call it a bite. She cut an already small chunk of potato in half and put that in her mouth. After she'd chewed it thoroughly, she said, "This is quite good for golf course food. I wonder where the chef was trained."

No one said anything. Amelia looked bored, and Jake looked slightly drunk.

Allie chewed some more and said, "I love this music. It makes me want to learn to play the harp."

Amelia nodded, although it wasn't clear if she was agreeing she wanted to play the harp, or just liked the soothing music. It was never clear what Amelia was thinking. I always felt she was looking at me with disdain, and today I felt it more than ever. I smiled at her, and she twisted up the corner of her mouth as if anything more was too much effort. She managed to make me feel I was inappropriate for smiling at a memorial service.

"I'm so used to every song having so many words crammed against the notes," said Allie. "My mom used to listen to instrumental music all the time. I think our generation forgot how important that is, don't you?"

"Maybe our generation forgot everything," Jake said.

"The harp is just the right mood." Amelia took a sip of wine. Her eyes were unfocused, which made me feel she wasn't really talking to me.

We all chewed in silence for a moment. The chords drifted through the air as if they'd attached themselves to the breeze.

"The music is pretty, but the words are the important part," I said.

"Music is the universal language," Byron said.

Allie laughed. "Cliché man!"

Byron made a face at her. Everyone laughed.

"Yes, but for something like this," I said, "we need words. We need to communicate with each other. That's what puts us all in the same frame of mind. It draws us together. It makes us a community." Byron put his hand on my leg and squeezed it.

"You can't control what people think," Amelia said.

"That's not what I meant."

Byron moved his hand to the back of my neck and squeezed less gently. I tried to duck out from under his arm. He gripped harder.

"Words direct your mind to comforting thoughts," I said.

"You mean to religion," Amelia said.

"Yes. In the end, that's the only thing that helps us."

"No offense, sweetie, but it's paternalistic and archaic,"

Amelia said. "Around the world, you'll find that mostly uneducated, dare I say stupid, people are the ones who still believe in myths."

"Okay," Jake said. "That's enough."

"Don't talk to me like that." Amelia spoke softly but not softly enough to cover the rage in her voice.

In fact, speaking so quietly almost made the words sound angrier, like the wrath of God.

Byron's hand was so tight on my neck I thought he was going to fracture my vertebrae. He hates conflict, but this was too important. Everyone was busy marching down the road to eternal separation from God, pain they couldn't begin to imagine out on a golf course with the breeze and the birds and the silky surface of the lake.

I thought about my post from a few days earlier, the one that everyone ignored. It seemed like it was okay to say whatever you wanted, post whatever you wanted, constantly talking about yourself, saying, *look at me, listen to me*, but the minute God comes into it, suddenly it's all inappropriate, and you don't get to say what's on your mind.

I wrenched away from Byron and bumped the table. I felt like crying.

Maybe God wasn't going to give me every piece of earth where I placed my foot. Maybe I didn't have enough faith, or there was something else wrong with me.

Byron should be supporting me, standing up for me, telling these unbelievers it was time to wake up before it was too late. I pushed back my chair. The wooden legs squeaked on the concrete.

"Don't be a child," Amelia said.

"I need to be alone with the Lord."

Amelia laughed, her bright red lips, vicious looking against her teeth, curled into a sneer. She was exactly what we were warned against — caring about nothing but money and image. She had no soul, I could feel the hollowness. And I think Jake could feel it because he was looking at her with such horror I wanted to kiss him and try to ease his pain. I don't know where that thought came from, and I didn't necessarily mean kiss him sexually, but touch my lips to his, erase that look, that seemed to be saying his whole world had collapsed. At the same time, I wanted to punch Byron. He was grabbing my arm, trying to force me to sit down.

"Don't be upset," Byron said. He gripped my forearm harder.

I tugged, but he didn't let up.

"Please, Tiff. Be a good Mommy."

Amelia laughed.

My face was hot and sweaty, the sun beating hard as if it was focusing all its energy on me, everyone staring at me, knowing what Byron was like in bed, how sick he was. Amelia was grinning, and her eyes had a knowing look. I felt like she could see right through my clothes — my lumpy, milk-filled breasts with the nipples all stretched and my flabby belly. I'd thought if I believed, the Lord would make me powerful, give me the husband I wanted, a husband who didn't want disgusting things from me.

Why was the Lord humiliating me in front of everyone when He'd promised the opposite?

I peeled Byron's fingers off my skin and walked past the other tables and down the steps to a path that wound toward a grove of trees. I had no idea where I was headed or what I was looking for.

Byron

BYRON JONES *LET the dead bury their dead. I don't mean to be cold, but the funeral for Kimberly makes me want nothing more than to throw myself on the living room floor and roll around with my son, tickling him and listening to him giggle.*

9 favorites — 3 comments

Dave Eddington *Our friend is dead, show a little respect.*
Allie Sinclair *Yeah, Byron. I thought Christians were supposed to be compassionate.*
Byron Jones *Missing the point, Dave. Life is for the living.*

A HEAPING PILE of potato salad, a rolled-up slice of turkey, and the nubs from a bunch of radishes sat on Tiffany's plate. I don't know how she eats those things, it's like eating water with a taste of dirt followed by a mean kick to your tongue. I batted at a fly circling over the potato salad. I pulled out my phone and looked to see if there were any more comments on my status update.

I wanted out of there, but Tiffany was nowhere to be seen. All the other plates at the table were empty, or at least as empty as they were going to get. Glasses were clustering in the center as Jake and Amelia switched from white wine to red wine. Soon, coffee cups joined the cloudy glasses. Tiffany's potato salad had a yellow tinge.

I was tired of thinking about Kimberly dying without the Lord. It was too late to change her destination. She'd never said she wasn't a believer, but she never said she was. Knowing her life and her fixation on moving up the corporate ladder, I assumed she ignored Him all her adult life, never thinking she might die so young. Only the good die young, they say. But that's not true.

It depressed me. I don't want to see anyone wind up in eternal torment. But it also got me thinking about how I'm on autopilot. My thoughts are consumed by the deli and maintaining the house, and most of all, the business of raising kids, the grunt work, instead of the joy and the blessing — children are a gift from the Lord. I forget that sometimes, because Tiff and I had kids too quick. I should have realized kids would interfere in our marriage. We should have had more time alone, and now I feel it's a little bit my fault that she's burned out. She'd never admit it, but she is. I should help more, but I'm tired too. I need my wife, and I don't think the kids need quite as much attention as she seems to think they do. But I guess I feel a little guilty about it too.

Watching Tiffany give birth the first time made me realize we were getting shoved into adulthood as hard and fast as Paul was getting shoved through that birth canal. God, that was awful. The worst experience of my life, listening to her whimper, and then scream. She really wanted me there, and I mean right there in the thick of things. I'm not squeamish, but I didn't think I needed to see her split nearly in half. I didn't let on how disgusted I was, but I don't think that's meant to be seen, especially by a woman's husband. Why couldn't they put up a screen, or keep a sheet over most of it?

I swatted the fly. I picked up my glass and took a sip of lemonade. The ice was melted, leaving a taste of water with too much lemon. I stood and looked around the patio. Finally, I saw her — dark hair brushing the base of her neck, her hips slimmer than they looked up close. She put her hand on Seth's arm, and her hair swung as she laughed. I hadn't known he was such a funny guy.

I said goodbye to the others, pushed my chair under the table, and started across the patio. I felt in my pocket for my keys and kept my hand on them.

The woman turned. It wasn't Tiffany. I looked at the thin face, the non-existent breasts, and became aware of her narrow shoulders and wondered how I'd mistaken her for Tiffany. I turned in the opposite direction. The glare of the sun made every table look like nothing but a bunch of glasses, smeared with greasy handprints, filled with the residue of wine and champagne and lemonade. On the table to my left, two flies were exploring the insides of the glasses. I cupped my hands around my eyes and turned back the other way. I thought she'd walked toward the golf course, but it stretched out in a long, empty green expanse, except for three guys in neon shirts. I couldn't believe she'd decided to explore the entire eighteen holes.

I walked around the tables, making my way to the edge of the patio. I leaned on the low brick wall that circled it. Near the base of the steps was a pair of sandals — flip-flops, but with spiky little heels. I have no idea how they walk with shoes like that. The shoes looked like something I'd seen on Tiffany.

I walked down the steps, trying to picture the sandals on her feet. At the bottom, I bent down and picked up the shoes by the heels. Almost every woman I knew wore shoes like those. I had no identifying feature to tell me whether they were Tiffany's. I dropped the shoes and headed along the path. After a few yards, I glanced back. Everyone was talking and drinking, voices getting louder as if they'd forgotten why they were there. No one seemed to notice I was leaving, and they certainly hadn't noticed Tiffany had been gone for a long time. Half an hour. Maybe more. By now, her potato salad was probably covered with flies. That seemed like an irrelevant thought, but lots of thoughts are irrelevant.

The path wound through a grove of trees and out past the tee box, shaved into a perfectly flat platform. Beyond that was the edge of the lake. The water was like dark blue glass, thick and opaque. I tried not to think about Tiffany following Kimberly's lead. If a woman had gone in, it would have covered her up, and the ripples would have faded minutes after she entered. I walked close to the edge. Nothing. Not that I could see beneath that beautiful blue. It looked darker now that I stood so close, almost black.

I waited for the guy in a pink shirt to tee off. The other two cheered his shot. I walked closer to the tee box.

"Have you seen a woman . . . she's barefoot, maybe, with dark hair and a . . . a, uh, wearing a dress? Maybe crying a little bit?"

"Nope."

"Not me."

The pink shirt shook his head. They turned and went to their cart.

I walked back toward the lake and followed the edge of the shore for fifteen or twenty feet. The water was so dark. The bottom wasn't visible except in the few inches very close to the edge where there were small stones covered with moss. As I studied the water, my heart beat faster, and my fingers trembled slightly. A breeze rippled the surface, then it quieted again. I closed my eyes and pictured Tiffany's feet buried in the muck, slipping as she tried to walk across the half-buried stones. She was a good swimmer, and there was no way she was suicidal. She wasn't a drinker.

I turned away from the water and followed the path down the length of the fairway, past the golfers, and around one of several large pockets of sparkling white sand surrounding the green. I did not want to go walking around the entire 200 acres looking for her. For all I knew, she was back with the others. She'd have to feed Ruth soon. She'd be as anxious as I was to head home.

I pulled out my phone and texted her. I should have done that before I got all worried and started thinking about women drowning. I stared at the screen. Nothing. I tapped my frequently called list and pressed her number. It went immediately to voice mail. I sent another text, this one more terse — *Where are you?*

After a few minutes, I sent a third text. I walked quickly back to the stairs, picked up the sandals, and jogged up the steps. "Hey!" I put my hand next to my mouth in a pathetic attempt to mimic a megaphone. "Anyone seen Tiffany?"

A few people glanced at me. Amelia looked blank. Allie scrunched up her face as if she couldn't hear me. Marcus, Kristen, and Megan all shook their heads. I dropped the shoes near the brick wall and walked to the first table. "Seen Tiffany?"

"I said no," Megan took a sip of her coffee.

"Can you go look in the restroom?"

"Text her," Kristen said.

"I did. Several times."

"Oh."

"And I called her."

"Maybe she went home," Megan said.

"She wouldn't leave without telling me and making sure I had a ride." My voice sounded high-pitched. I cleared my throat and concentrated on relaxing my forehead and keeping my lips from twisting in a funny, awkward shape. I turned so the sun was behind me.

Megan stood. "You're right. She's too sweet to do something like that. I'll check the restroom."

She started toward the building. I followed so close I was in danger of stepping on the backs of her sandals. I dropped back and moved to her side. She reached over and patted my arm. "I'm sure she's fine. Maybe she's expressing milk."

There was no way she was expressing milk. She wouldn't do that right before feeding time. She rarely did it, period. She hated expressing it. She would have found me and dragged me out of there.

I felt I was watching myself from an increasing distance — a man diligently searching for his wife, carefully avoiding panic. Something bad had happened. It wasn't just fear stirred up by a friend who had died suddenly and obscenely. I knew how crazed I would look if I started shouting at them to drain the lake, but I couldn't wait for Megan. There was no way Tiffany was in the women's restroom, milk or no milk.

I turned and hurried back to the table where we'd been sitting, moving too fast. There was something alive clutching my throat from the inside — like a tapeworm wiggling up along my esophagus, trying to escape my body.

"It's okay." Allie smiled, bold and confident as if it really was okay.

"She's been gone for at least forty-five minutes."

"It's a big golf course."

"I need someone to seriously look for her."

"Okay." She took my elbow and steered me in the direction of the pro shop.

When she opened the door to let me go in, I glanced back at the table. Amelia hadn't budged. She lifted the wine glass to her mouth.

"Where's Jake?" I said.

"I don't know," Allie said. "People are starting to head out. I guess it's over. You hate to leave, but there's nothing else to say. It's not like a party where you want to stand around and talk about whatever."

"Amelia's still here."

"I know," Allie said. "I don't think those two are doing so great."

We stepped inside and let the door fall closed behind us. A kid with a buzz cut stood at the counter. "Can I help you?"

"My wife's missing. I need you guys to search the course."

"Uh, missing?"

"We were here for the funeral, and after we ate, she went for a walk, and she . . ."

"Did you text her?" the kid said.

"Yes."

"Well, we don't really have people who can do that."

"There's no one else working here but you?"

"The pro, but he's giving a lesson."

"Look," Allie said. "Just let us use some carts so we can drive around ourselves."

"I don't know . . ."

"My wife is missing!"

"Okay. But you don't know that for sure."

The door opened. I turned. Kimberly's brother stepped inside. He stood near the rack of clubs for sale.

"We need two or three carts," Allie said. "She's a nursing mom."

The clerk looked at her as if he either didn't know what that meant, or it had nothing to do with anything, which it really didn't. He went into the office behind the counter, picked up the phone, and called someone. After a few minutes, during which my stomach let go of the nausea and turned into something hard and shriveled, he came back out. "Okay, sure, you can have three carts. But I need your driver's license."

Kimberly's brother went out, letting the door slam behind him.

I yanked out my wallet and slapped my license on the counter. Allie dug in her purse and did the same.

"I only need one."

Allie rode in the cart with me. Megan took a cart, and Marcus took the third one. Allie and I bounced over unseen bumps as I pushed hard on the weak accelerator, slamming it to the floor.

"Careful, these things tip easily," she said.

I eased off the gas. We drove around the lake, following the sign pointing to the tenth hole. We rode all the way to the eighteenth, seeing nothing but golfers, two deer, and a rabbit.

Allie texted Megan and Marcus, who were covering the first nine holes.

After twenty minutes, no one believed she was strolling around enjoying the park-like quiet. We returned to the pro shop, and the kid called the police who were damn slow about getting there, convinced she was indeed, enjoying the golf course.

The cops took a bunch of info but didn't seem too keen on launching a search, when a woman simply went for a longish walk less than two hours earlier. They dismissed the lake, even after they heard why we were all there. They walked the circumference and concluded there was no sign whatsoever that anyone had gone into that lake. That was what I wanted to hear, so I accepted their word, but I couldn't take my eyes off that gorgeous, blackish blue, silky smooth surface of death.

Allie

ALLIE SINCLAIR *THE greatest thrill of my life was falling in love. It made me feel complete. It made me feel I'd have a good life. Before that, I knew I had friends — all of you — but I didn't know if I'd find the ONE. There was this scary feeling that maybe I'd be alone and never have what everyone else has. Now I realize that not everyone does, but I do and when I knew that I was going to be one of the lucky ones in love, it was thrilling and exciting. I wish that for all of my single friends. Sorry for gushing — losing one friend, seeing another go missing, is making me think about what's important in life.*

87 favorites — 14 comments

Dave Eddington *Everyone loves you Allie.*
Allie Sinclair *Awww, *sniff**
Megan Miller *So happy for you and Marcus.*
Jake Ash *Is there only one?*
[See 10 more comments]

IT WAS ALMOST eleven p.m. I was upstairs in the office with the lights off, staring at the computer, thinking about Tiffany. When the sun was out, and we were driving around the golf course, soothed by all that grass and water, watching herons glide in and stop near the edge of the lake with their long legs, thin as straws so you wonder how they hold themselves up, not being able to find her was unsettling. We were worried, scared, but now . . . there were still a few possibilities as to where she might be, but they were starting to seem like nothing more than excuses, all of us trying to remain positive and not show how scared we were. Someone had found her purse under the table she'd been sitting at for lunch. She'd shoved it to the center of the big round table, and no one noticed it at first. Her cell phone was tucked in the side pocket, dutifully turned off so it wouldn't disrupt the memorial service.

I was thinking about starting a *Help Find Tiffany* AboutFace page. I wasn't sure how useful it would be, but I had to do something. I couldn't just sit and wait for her to reappear. There were hundreds of posts on her regular page, but it seemed like we needed more than strings of comments about how scared we were, and comments meant to reassure her — *If you're depressed, know that we all love you.* Not that she could read them without her phone. Quite a few people thought her disappearance was related to postpartum depression. Byron didn't seem to even know what the term referred to.

I wanted to do something proactive.

I glanced up. Marcus was standing in the doorway. He wore sweatpants. I could see he didn't have anything on underneath them, and his chest was bare.

"Busy discussing Tiffany on AboutFace? The digital river

has moved away from Kimberly. She didn't even get to own her entire funeral."

I turned my gaze back to the computer screen. I clicked over to what I'd just posted and looked at all the *favorites*. Everyone knew he was the center of my life. Everyone except him, because he refused to be part of my life on AboutFace.

A small part of me could see that he was right, in some ways. I didn't post everything. Only the good stuff. I didn't post that I missed what I had when we were first married, that I wanted to have those same feelings every day. There's a sameness now. Not just a sameness, a gap between us, gradually splitting wider. We talked to each other, we made love, we said we loved each other, but we each lived separate lives inside our heads.

I felt so far away from him, and he didn't even realize it. As far as he was concerned, if I would stop interacting with my friends online, everything would be great. But it was more than that. He wanted things his way. He didn't even try to see how I felt, he didn't want to try. His opinion was the right one.

"How are status updates going to help find her?" he said.

"Not now. I'm not going to fight about that. This is the way to get the word out fast."

He walked into the room and came around the desk. He leaned against my back. It felt nice. The weight of him softened the hard shell around my heart into something so thin I hardly noticed it. Or maybe it was fear for Tiffany washing over everything else, filling the chasm between Marcus and me.

It would have been a perfect moment for him to pull my phone out of his pocket and return it to me. He could have considered how it would be if I was missing and my phone was left behind. Cut off from the world. Not that having a phone would help her if she was unconscious or . . . maybe she'd run away. Maybe all her blessings that she posted on AboutFace weren't making her feel particularly blessed after all. And maybe she didn't trust god with her whole heart and believe that wherever she put her foot, that place belonged to her. It was such an inscrutable post. She'd been quoting Bible verses for years, but they were usually obvious in their meaning. It made me wonder if there was something wrong with her mentally. If she wanted to disappear, a phone wouldn't help anyone get in touch with her.

I clicked the link to set up a new page.

"What's that for?" Marcus said.

"I'm putting up a different page to help people find her."

"What's the point of that? If it helped anything, wouldn't the police do that? If she wants to be found."

His words were sharp, cold splinters digging into the back of my neck. If he and I both wondered the same thing, did that mean our instinct was telling us it was true? "It's something to do."

"Why don't you do something real?"

"This is real."

He put his hand on the back of my neck. I wanted to lean into him, I wanted everything to be okay, but I was not going to choose between him and my friends. Of course, he was more to me. But why did I have to make a choice? No one else had a husband who tried to cut her off from social media. Sometimes I thought I wouldn't exist if it weren't for AboutFace.

His hand tightened on the back of my neck while I searched Tiffany's profile for a picture of her that I could put up. There were so many. There was one of her holding Ruth, gazing into the baby's face with Paul next to her, touching the tip of his finger to Ruth's lips. Or her wedding picture with Byron, or the one of her standing on the shore of Lake Tahoe, looking across the water, unaware that someone was taking her picture. The indecision made me want to check my feed, to distract myself. Then, I'd return to Tiffany's page and grab one without too much thought, but I couldn't go to my page with Marcus looking over my shoulder.

It seemed as though time had stopped moving forward. We would sit there forever, his hand slowly tightening around my neck. Me, afraid to make a move. The computer hummed. Outside the open window, the wind was picking up, rattling the palm fronds and causing the tarp over the neighbor's woodpile to flap against the wood. I never understood why they couldn't build a proper cover for their firewood. It was delivered every October, an enormous pile stacked in a pyramid. The tarp didn't really keep it dry, so I wondered all winter how they actually got it to burn with any consistency. But there was always smoke coming from their chimney when it wasn't a spare the air day, so I guess they figured it out.

The computer screen dimmed, preparing to go to sleep. Marcus's fingers crept up the back of my head, burrowing into my hair. It felt so good, I wanted to let go. The whole world, except for that snapping tarp, seemed so far away. There might be news of Tiffany, and I wouldn't know about it. They might have figured out where she'd gone or found something on her phone that hinted at a secret life. Did people really have secret lives? I suppose so, or it wouldn't be acted out all the time in TV shows and movies and books. Tiffany seemed so innocent, like a little girl with her glossy and slightly too-short bangs, her soft skin with such round, rosy cheeks. She grinned more than she smiled. Sometimes it was hard to think of her as a mother. Her eyes always looked like she was asking whether you liked her.

The pressure of Marcus's hand was more comforting now. I took my fingers off the keyboard, and immediately he put his other hand on my shoulder, then moved it down slowly and wrapped it around my breast. I sighed. The computer screen went dark. I put my hand on the mouse and moved it to the side.

Marcus stepped back and took his hands off my body.

"Where'd you go?" I said.

"I'll let you finish." He moved around the desk and walked out of the room. For a few minutes, I thought he was coming back with my phone. That he'd realized how important it was to do whatever we could, use social media tools to try to spread the news that Tiffany had disappeared.

By the time I had her page set up, I knew Marcus wasn't coming back. I sent an invite to all my friends from high school and clicked to my news feed. There were updates to Kimberly's page, mostly by people I didn't know. Everyone that I knew had already posted, and most of them had gone to her memorial service, and most of those had now moved on to worrying about Tiffany. A notice popped up that a few people marked my Tiffany page a favorite.

I saw the favorite star through Marcus's eyes. Calling a page that announced a woman had disappeared a favorite seemed almost sick. And it was pointless. Tiffany wouldn't see it. But that can't stop you from trying. How did I know she wouldn't see it? Wherever she was.

I looked through all my updates and then wheeled the chair away from the desk. I went out and stood at the top of the stairs. There was a single light turned on downstairs, but I couldn't tell where it was coming from. I walked down slowly, quietly. The kitchen was dark, and I could see it was the light in the living room near the doors to the patio. I went into the living room. It was empty. I turned out the light and went back to the kitchen. He'd already armed the security system. I poured half a glass of orange juice and drank it quickly. I rinsed the glass, turned out the light, and went back upstairs.

In the darkness of our bedroom, I could barely make out

the shape of his body, his back to the door. I took off my clothes and let them fall on the floor. I climbed into bed and wrapped myself around him. He was wearing his boxer shorts. I slid my hand beneath the waistband. He didn't move. As I held onto him, I kissed his back. I pressed myself against him as hard as I could. Part of me didn't want to go to sleep. People were disappearing from my life. It felt wrong to hold onto him and fall into a peaceful sleep when Kimberly and Tiffany were out there. For each in her own way, no one had any idea where she was.

After a long time, Marcus turned over and wrapped his arm around my shoulders. I let myself relax into him, but the feeling that I was betraying Tiffany grew stronger. At the same time, I hated that I was enjoying the warmth and texture of his skin, yet not thinking only about him. I hated that she was interfering with my life and I felt guilty that I wasn't doing something useful to help find her.

Marcus lifted my camisole and kissed my breasts, barely touching them so that his lips felt like flower petals. That doesn't sound very masculine, but men can be tender, I think, and still be very strong. Stealing my phone was proving how strong he was. There's a strange, very powerful attraction in a man taking authority, being decisive.

Yet part of me hated him. I absolutely hated him for severing my connection and making me feel so helpless. Instead of a desire to touch him, I suddenly wanted to bite him, hard. I wanted to gnaw on his nipples until he bled. Or maybe just that soft skin at the edge of his armpit.

What would it be like to post that on AboutFace? Maybe he was right, it was a contrived world. If it were real life, I'd type — *Hating Marcus right now. What would he do if I bit off his nipple?*

But I would never do that. None of us post thoughts like that. Still, the desire was there, growing more intense. Like the desire you have when you're on the balcony of a fifteen- or twenty-story hotel, wanting to climb over the side and let yourself fall because you need to know what it feels like.

Marcus

THE DAY AFTER Tiffany went missing, I got up at three-thirty in the morning. I got dressed and went out for a run. The air was a moderate sixty-six, even at that hour, promising a day in the 90s, but I wouldn't be there. I'd be locked in a climate-controlled cockpit until evening. I had to be at the airport by six to prep for my flight to O'Hare. From there, I was continuing to Newark, then back to O'Hare, Miami, Atlanta, and home.

I grabbed my right foot and pulled it until the heel touched my butt. After a few seconds, I did the same with my left foot. I stepped off the porch, pressed the ball of my foot against the edge and stretched my calf muscles for a minute or so on each leg. I jogged down the front path, dodging snails that survived despite the poisonous treats I left for them and turned right. I jogged to the corner, then started a full sprint.

My feet pounded the sidewalk, the only sound, except for the occasional siren. I tried to listen to my breathing going in and out, refusing to allow missing women or dead women or my socially obsessed wife to intrude. I ran hard. The two-mile route I'd mapped through our neighborhood avoided all streets with traffic lights. When I had more time, I followed a five-mile course. By the time I passed the one-mile mark, the sky wasn't as dark, and the doves and finches were already cooing and chirping.

Back at the house, I pried off my shoes in the front hall and tossed them in the closet. Once the shower water was hot, I tugged off my socks and shorts. Steam fogged the mirror and clung to the window, desperate to escape. As desperate as I was to get away from Allie's bitter coldness for a few days. I climbed in and let the water sear my skin. The pain felt good. Kind of twisted, but I need intense heat or snow-pack cold to wake me up, get me in shape for the non-stop flow of adrenaline overload that accompanies flying a plane. Every nerve cell has to be in tune with the aircraft, the rest of the crew, the instruments, the weather conditions, air traffic control. Every brain cell has to be on fire. Running so hard I think I'll drop on the sidewalk or bench-pressing a hundred and fifty pounds, and having extreme water temperature are required. Not all pilots feel that need, but for me, it's essential.

Water poured over my face, steaming droplets stinging my raw nipples. When'd we'd made love, Allie had made me feel excellent as always, but there was a rage burning beneath her skin. When she pinched me or bit me a little harder than necessary, she didn't apologize and back off like she usually did. It felt like she wanted to hurt me. And maybe she did. Maybe she wanted my nipples cracked and rubbing against my shirt all day.

She didn't know it yet, but I was taking her phone with me.

If she thought I'd relent, she didn't know me very well. I was sick of that virtual world she lived in. It seemed as if she wasn't a real person anymore.

I walk through the airport, and I'm surprised people don't run into each other. Every single one of them is hunched over their damn phone. Everyone laughs at that cartoon that shows the ape evolving into so-called modern man, each creature in the evolutionary step has a straighter spine, chin lifting higher, looking toward the future, which is what separates man from the animal kingdom. But the last man in the series has reverted to the ape with his curved spine, his head thrust forward and down, staring at the thing in his hand.

I don't fit in with my generation. I should be a fifty-year-old man, as Allie accuses me of. She's wrong. People in their fifties and sixties are hunched over their phones too. Maybe I'm just more aware than most. I can see what this is doing to the human race. People in restaurants can't have a conversation without their fork in one hand and their phone in the other. They think they're being social because they pass the phone around, sharing pictures, watching videos. It's insane.

I turned off the water and yanked the towel across my back until my skin burned even more than it had under the steaming water. I dropped the towel on the floor. I wasn't in the mood to be sensitive and considerate. I was in the mood to make my position clear. Real life or her virtual world. She couldn't have both. I was going to force her to choose. I didn't think I was being an asshole. I loved her.

When we're sitting in the family room at night, watching a movie, my hand on her leg, I can feel her muscle tense like she's on a timer. Every thirty minutes or so, her body pulses. Her eyes jitter in their sockets, glancing at her phone. She refuses to set it so there aren't alerts for every brain fart from one of her seven thousand friends. She's wanting that phone, wanting to see what's going on, wanting to look at all the lame pictures and stupid comments, everyone trying so hard to be clever. Shakespeare claimed the world's a stage, but he had no idea what was coming. Everyone thinks they're an entertainer, a philosopher, a teacher, a preacher. Everyone shouting at each other and no one listening. Maybe in the past, people faked their interest in others while they were just as self-absorbed as they are now. Who knows, I wasn't there. But now, why is it even called social media? There's nothing social about it. There's bragging and complaining and shouting. *LOOK. AT. ME. Aren't I all that?*

I knotted my tie and put on my jacket. I patted the wings and straightened the shoulders. I ran the comb through my hair again and winked at my reflection.

Too bad a pilot's rarely seen in his uniform. I walk to the boarding area, crawl into my tiny space, the cockpit is locked, and I'm strapped in that seat, wrinkles forming before the engines are fired up.

The bedroom was dark. Allie was on her side, facing the

bathroom. She'd slept all night with her back to me. Not that I'd been awake to notice. My sleep was deep and dream-free. It always is after sex — best sleeping pill there is. Too bad I can't have it when I'm between flights in one hotel or another. I could take her with me. But she'd hate that. Sitting on planes half her life. Her life would be nothing but a shadow of mine. I bent over and ran my thumb along her cheekbone. She didn't flinch or change her breathing.

I never leave without waking her. Usually, she gets out of bed, and we have a long kiss goodbye. A real kiss. Not a peck on the cheek or the lips. She says we aren't going to be one of those couples who starts drifting past each other, saying the same words over and over, barely touching, not really noticing each other. But isn't that what we were already becoming? AboutFace was more real to her than I was.

It was time to walk out the door. Taking her phone meant I'd cut off her communication with me, at least easy communication. She could still email me, or text from the desktop computer.

I took my hand away from her cheek. If she woke and saw me standing over her, she wouldn't like it. She'd be worried her face looked ugly — her word, not mine — when it was collapsed into unconsciousness. She doesn't realize she looks absolutely perfect whether she's asleep or eating or breaking the surface of the water in the pool. I wonder sometimes what she sees when she looks in the mirror. It's like all that reflects back are her flaws, because that's what she's always pointing out. There's a never-ending fussing over the frizz factor of her hair, a microscopic zit or two on her chin, the shape of her toes, the soft parts of her thighs. I don't know why she can't get her head around the fact I like the soft parts.

There's a flight attendant I know who's maybe twenty-five. She doesn't have a single mark on her face, that I can see. But she covers her skin with this thick make-up, paints on her eyebrows so I can't tell if there's actual hair under there. She draws dark lines around her eyes and has mahogany shadows brushed into perfectly symmetrical patches on her eyelids. It's hard not to stare at her when she's talking to you because she looks like something from a horror movie. A giant porcelain doll come to life. Blemish-free is not really a good thing. It can give you nightmares.

I touched Allie's nose. It twitched. Sneaking out with her phone was a shitty thing to do. But that phone was going to destroy our marriage. The only way to make her see that she was in need of rehab in order to break her addiction was to force her into it. They call it tough love.

EVEN THOUGH MY father disappeared from the scene before I was old enough to recognize the guy's face, I was luckier than a lot of kids. I had my Uncle Pete.

While I sat on a weirdly low branch in an oak tree in our backyard, he sat on a plastic chaise lounge drinking Ginger Ale, telling stories about flying during the Viet Nam war.

Stories that made me want to be a pilot, to have the power to lift a giant machine above the clouds, hang out with the birds, look down on the earth and see it in proper perspective. He told me stories that made the war seem glamorous, none of the ugly stuff that I found out later when I studied it in high school.

When my mom went to work, Uncle Pete was there. When my mom fell asleep on the couch watching TV, Uncle Pete ushered me up the stairs and made sure I brushed my teeth before bed. He taught me to fish and climb trees. For my thirteenth birthday, he got me a PlayStation. It was all I wanted. He told me video games were stupid and brainless, but I knew he was out of date. Board games were nothing compared to live action on the screen. I played those games over and over. I felt like I was in the game. Digital men and women raced across the screen, drove fast cars, defended their people. I felt powerful. I got so good, I beat all my friends. Uncle Pete finally caved and tried it once. He lost the game on the first round and said it wasn't for him.

Still, he was so excited when I advanced to a new level. He looked me right in the eye as if he was gobbling up my words when I described the characters or told him about my thirteen-year-old strategy. Even though he didn't like the games, he never acted like I was stupid for being consumed by them. He loved hearing about them because he loved me.

It was a hot July morning, and the sun was just coming up. We'd slept all night with the windows open, so the house smelled sweet. I remember that, thinking it smelled like a bowl of Captain Crunch cereal. I was playing Air Combat. The night before, Uncle Pete suggested we go outside, and he'd have a beer while I climbed the tree. I told him I was too old for climbing trees and he said you're never too old to climb a tree. I said why don't you climb the tree, and he said his back wouldn't let him. I told him I wanted to play Air Combat because it was too hot to be moving around. He shrugged and got a beer out of the fridge and went outside. When I went to bed, he was still sitting out there.

I'd won four rounds and wanted to tell Uncle Pete, but he and my mom were still sleeping. They'd been up late. I'd heard the TV when a siren woke me up in the middle of the night, piercing my ears so that I had to put my hands over them.

When I beat level six, I couldn't stand it. My mom was cranky if she got woken up before she was ready, especially on a Sunday. On weekdays, she was up before me and appreciated it if she happened to oversleep, and I went into her room and touched her shoulder, moving it slightly. Uncle Pete never minded being woken. Maybe because he napped a bit in the afternoons. Mom said it was the pain that made him need a nap. I realized when I was older, it wasn't the pain in his back, it was the pills he had to take when the pain got really bad that made him sleep in the middle of the day.

I climbed the stairs, making sure not to run so I wouldn't create a racket. The upstairs was hotter and didn't smell as sweet as the downstairs, even though all those windows were open too. The hallway was dim, all the doors closed, but mine. I walked past my bedroom and the hall bathroom and my mom's room. Uncle Pete had the master bedroom. My mom said she didn't need it, and it was good for Pete to have his own bathroom and a little more privacy. After all, I wasn't his kid, and maybe sometimes he needed to get away from me. Although he never acted like he did.

I knocked on his door. There was no answer. It was after nine in the morning at that point. He'd never slept that late. I knocked louder and whispered his name. I was dancing from foot to foot, so excited to tell him. My sweaty feet squeaked on the wood floor.

I knocked harder. The latch slipped out of the socket, and the door opened. It was hard to close all the doors in the house, especially in the summer. You had to yank them several times, almost slamming them shut, which made my mom crazy. She hated the banging doors. I pushed gently, so it opened a bit more.

Pete was on top of the covers in dark blue boxer shorts and a black Madonna t-shirt. His mouth was open, and a fly was sitting on his lip. I waited for him to brush it away, but he didn't. I went into the room to wake him up, to make that fly leave him alone. When I got near his bed, I said, "Uncle Pete?" I brushed my fingers across his mouth, and his lips were cool, much cooler than the over-heated room. I didn't need my mom to explain what was wrong.

The fly moved quickly to the window and started buzzing in the mini blinds. I rushed to the blinds and grabbed Uncle Pete's flip-flop off the floor and smacked the blinds. They rattled and crashed, and three of them bent. The fly buzzed over my head and went up to the ceiling light. I threw the flip-flop at the light, and the fly just sat there. I started crying. "Get out, get out of here!"

The fly darted to the dresser and sat on Uncle Pete's hairbrush, washing its foot. I grabbed the flip-flop and charged at the dresser. I slammed the flip-flop on the hairbrush, impaling the fly on a bristle. I kept hitting it. The brush crashed to the floor. I heard my mom's bedroom door open.

"What's going on?"

I slumped onto the floor and threw the flip-flop at the window. When my mom came into the room, she started crying and sat down next to me.

Five years later I joined the Navy. It was my ticket to college and a career as a pilot. But most of all, wearing the same uniform he wore made me feel connected to Uncle Pete.

I SQUEEZED MY eyes tightly to wipe out the memory, for now.

I put my hand on Allie's shoulder and shook her gently. "I'm leaving."

She opened her eyes. I leaned down and kissed her.

"Don't forget to leave my phone on the dresser." Her words dragged and her voice was rough. I wasn't sure she was entirely awake.

There was no need for me to respond. Her phone was in my bag. I wouldn't be gone long. She'd be fine.

Megan

MEGAN MILLER [*UPLOADED 1 video*] *You have to watch these little kids discovering their shadows for the first time. So cute!*
15 favorites — 6 comments

    Allie Sinclair *Amazing! That's adorable. It's funny how you don't remember those parts of your life.*
    Megan Miller *I wonder what other stuff we forget?*
    Kristen Thomas *It's fun watching kids finding anything for the first time.*
    Seth Porter *Sad to say, I don't remember Michael doing that.*
    [*See 2 more comments*]

TWO DAYS AFTER Kimberly's memorial, two days after Tiffany disappeared, Allie called. I didn't answer because I didn't recognize the number. I should have because it could have been a new client. What kind of business owner ignores calls? But I figured if they wanted to book a massage, they'd leave a message. I wasn't in the mood to be grilled about pricing.

Allie left a message to call her when I had a minute. I hit callback, and she picked up right away. She said she'd used her landline because she couldn't find her phone and she'd never activated the *find me* feature.

I'd die without my phone, which is a terrible way to think when one friend is dead and another might be dead. But I would. Allie was kind of casual about losing hers, but she's more easy-going than I am.

"I was wondering if you want to come over," she said. "We could go for a swim."

"Okay." It wasn't what I'd expected, although I'm not sure what I'd expected. The last thing she and I had talked about was her fear that Jake wouldn't want to use his pool anymore. So asking me to come for a swim seemed significant, but maybe not. Maybe she'd forgotten all about our conversation.

"Marcus is flying," she said.

"Oh, okay." Maybe all her going on about Jake's pool was because she was afraid to swim in her own pool. Maybe she didn't really want to hang out with me, she just wanted someone to make sure she didn't drown or take her mind off drowning.

"I have a client this morning, and then I can come over. A little after one?"

"That's great." She sounded way too excited. It was hard to think of Allie being scared, but I guess everyone gets scared, they just don't always show it.

My massage appointment was with an older gentleman who played soccer every weekend and was constantly tweaking one muscle or another. He winced every time I touched him, and it never seemed as if the massages made him feel all that much better, which was discouraging. He asked me to give the massage on his screened back porch. It must have been ninety degrees in there. I didn't need as much lotion because the sweat on my palms, mingled with the sweat on his skin, made my hands slide across his back like I'd hit an oil slick. I didn't mention that to him.

After I was finished, I was definitely up for a swim.

The minute I stepped inside her front door, Allie gave me a big hug, squeezing my arms to my sides. "It's so awful, isn't it?"

"It is."

She let go and closed the door.

Being inside her house makes me feel like a loser. I shouldn't feel that way. I chose my life. I have a meaningful career. It's incredibly satisfying when I touch people, when my hands pull the aches and tension out of each muscle. I feel the calm spreading from one place to the next until my clients are literally putty in my hands. I like giving them a peaceful experience, with soft instrumental music and a touch of aromatherapy. Leeching the toxins out of their systems makes me feel powerful and good and necessary. It's a more worthwhile job than most. Anything in the healing profession is so much more rewarding than a large or even a steady paycheck. What's the point if you're bored, or worse, not adding anything to the world, not affecting any lives but those in your immediate circle? My life has meaning.

But it still stings a little that Allie and I graduated from high school together and she's way ahead of me with her gorgeous, devoted husband and a huge house of her own. She doesn't act like she's all that, she makes me feel welcome like she really wants to see me. But how can I not feel like a loser when she's a real adult, and I'm still in some kind of limbo land, wondering if I'll ever escape my childhood bedroom, wondering if anyone will ever love me?

"Do you want anything to drink?" Allie said.

I adjusted the strap of my bag where it had slipped down as a result of her vigorous hug. "What do you have?" I didn't remember her ever hugging me before, and now she'd done it three times in two days — once when we saw each other at Kimberly's memorial, once when we all left the golf course, knowing Tiffany was gone, and now.

"Lemonade. Sparkling water. Iced tea. OJ . . ."

"Lemonade sounds good." I followed her into the kitchen.

She put two tall, narrow glasses on the counter. She opened the fridge and lifted out a pitcher of lemonade in one hand and orange juice in the other. "It's fresh."

"Nice."

"I have enough lemons back there to keep everyone on the block supplied with lemonade for the entire summer." She filled the glasses, handed the pale yellow one to me, and put the pitchers back in the fridge.

I followed her again, through the living room and out to the back patio. She sat in one of the chaise lounges, and I took the other, dropping my bag on the ground. She raised her glass, and we clinked the edges. They made a satisfying, slightly hollow, clunking sound, much different from the ting of wine glasses. I kind of liked that we were drinking a healthy beverage instead of clogging our brains with alcohol like we usually do when my friends and I get together.

"Did that detective call you?" she said.

"Yes."

"When is he talking to you?"

"At five today. I don't know what else he wants to ask. When the cops talked to us after Kimberly's memorial, I told them everything I knew, which was nothing."

She sipped her juice and nodded. "Me too. He's coming over this evening. At first, he was going to wait until Marcus gets back, then he changed his mind. What's there to say? None of us saw her leave."

"I know. It's scary."

Allie nodded.

"She has everything. Why would she walk away from Byron, her adorable kids, all her friends?"

"Maybe she didn't walk away," Allie said.

"I guess that's why they want to talk to us." I took a sip of lemonade. It was kind of watery, but I licked my lips and smiled. Every so often, you have to be fake to keep your friends happy. You have to lie and be nice and act like you're not jealous. That you care about someone's stupid problems when yours are far more upsetting.

"It's a nice golf course. It's not like some creep could be

walking in the middle of the fairway." Allie closed her eyes and leaned her head back on the chaise lounge.

"Creeps are everywhere. Even in nice places."

"I guess. Did you see the page I made for her?"

I nodded, then realized she still had her eyes closed. "I did."

She squeezed her eyes so tightly her brow wrinkled like a piece of waxed paper, and her lips shaped themselves into a sharp frown. She still managed to look nice, her skin so unblemished, not like mine. It seemed like she wanted to say more. I took a few sips of lemonade.

She opened her eyes. "That was an adorable picture of you and your mom that you posted the day before the memorial."

"Thanks."

"You both looked so happy. Where was it?"

"Shadowbrook in Capitola. She took me there for lunch on my birthday."

"Awww. How nice."

"It was okay."

"I'd give anything to have lunch with my mom."

I didn't know what to say.

I know it was hard, having her mother die so young, and in such an ugly way. But I think she glamorizes her mother, doesn't remember the criticizing and the judgment and all that stuff. Or maybe her mom wasn't like mine. Maybe that's why she thinks it's so great having your mother around. Not that I wish mine were dead, not at all, just different. That she would be supportive instead of always telling me what I'm doing wrong, always trying to fix me.

By the time I'd finished eating a crab cake and drinking my first glass of Pinot Grigio at my birthday lunch, I felt like there wasn't one good thing about me — not my hair, my shape, my job, my finances. And she didn't even know the worst about the size of my credit card balance. She acted like she was doing me a favor, taking me to lunch. It was all, *Sit up straight, Megan,* and *Don't take such big bites, you look desperate,* and *Are you sure you need another glass of wine?* And *When do you think you'll earn enough to support yourself with this massage thing? Are you sure that's a valid career? Do people really think getting a massage is "therapy"?* She actually put down her fork to pantomime quote marks over her plate.

"It must be hard, having your mom gone," I said.

Allie opened her eyes and looked at the pool, blinking a bit, even though we were in the shade and there wasn't any glare to make her bat her eyes and squint like that. "You have no idea." She pointed her toes and leaned her head back again, stretching like a long, thin cat. The light glittered on her gold toe ring, it was loose on her second toe, making her toes seem even thinner than they were.

It had been a long time since her mother was killed. Was she still upset about it? I should have felt bad, but I didn't. *She* had no idea.

After we finished our drinks, we peed, and then went in the pool. We played Jai Alai for a while. We did some diving, and then I said I had to get going because I needed to shower and dry my hair before the detective came over.

It wouldn't look good to have wet hair and a swimsuit under my clothes, pressing wet spots into my t-shirt when the detective was asking me about a missing friend. Like I shouldn't be having any fun in such terrible circumstances. As if it would make me look guilty. Although guilty of what, I can't imagine. So I don't know why I thought that, but I had to get home and dry my hair.

THE DETECTIVE WAS a middle-aged guy with a shaved head. His neck and head looked as if they'd been carved out of a single block of wood.

He introduced himself as Detective Archer and ushered me into my mom's living room. He asked how long I'd lived there. I felt my face turn red. It wasn't as if he was a candidate for a date that I had to impress, he was at least forty-five, but still, I felt like he was looking down on me.

"I'm building a massage therapy practice, so I moved home to save money."

He nodded and wrote it down.

"How long have you known Tiffany Jones?"

"Since her and Byron got engaged. Five years, I think. I knew him in high school."

"Are you close?"

"I'm not sure what you mean by *close*."

He stared at me. I stared back. His eyes were hazel with

flecks of blue. They reminded me of agates. After another few seconds, he said, "However you define it."

"We all hang out together a lot. I know Byron better than her."

"And do you think he knows where she is?"

"No."

"Why not?"

"Because he doesn't. He was freaked out when he realized she'd been gone so long and she wasn't answering his texts."

"People can make you believe anything."

"He's not like that."

The detective wrote something in his notebook. "What's he like?"

"Very straight-forward. He has his own business."

"The deli."

"Yes. And he's devoted to Tiffany, and their kids."

"How do you know that?"

"I just do."

He continued on, asking me questions that all seemed equally pointless — about whether Byron ever got angry and if he lied and if he seemed depressed or felt tied down with two kids at such a young age. I said no to all of that. He asked about their church and said it seemed to lean a bit toward the extreme and I told him I didn't know much about it, that they quoted the Bible a lot. He wanted to know if anything either one of them ever posted on AboutFace was alarming. I said I couldn't possibly remember everything they posted, but no, nothing came to mind.

After about forty-five minutes, he said, "Do you know anyone who would want to hurt her?"

"No."

"And you were at the memorial for a friend who drowned, correct?"

It bugged me that he asked that as a question because he already knew the answer. I gave a single nod of my head, and he had the self-awareness to look a little embarrassed.

"Do you think there's a connection?" he said.

I hadn't until right that minute. Now, I wondered. But was I only wondering because he suggested it? And he had no idea, or at least that's how he acted. "No."

He stood, shook my hand, and turned and walked to the door without waiting for me. He called back from the front hall, "I'm leaving my card on the table here. Call me if you think of anything."

It was a strange way to leave. He seemed satisfied with my answers. I told the truth. Although, there was something about the questions and the order in which he asked them that made me feel I hadn't told the truth, that there was something more to say, a little bit of information that got left out.

Dave

DAVE EDDINGTON *THERE'S something about a detective saying he wants to talk to you that makes you feel like the principal is calling you into the office. Or your father saying, "Sit down, I want to talk to you."*

12 favorites — 4 comments

   Allie Sinclair *Did the principal interrogate you when you were a kid? LOL.*

   Megan Miller *I don't know why he's asking us all these random questions.*

   Adam Jamison *They should be looking for her, not asking questions.*

   Allie Sinclair *Be sure to check out the FindOurTiffany page!*

WHEN DETECTIVE ARCHER rang my doorbell at twenty minutes after six, I felt like it was a psychological game on his part. He'd said he'd be there at six, so he wanted me to sweat by showing up late. And it was dinnertime. He wanted me hungry, my stomach growling, agitated because my blood sugar was dropping.

Or it was all paranoia. Being questioned by a police detective would make anyone paranoid. He didn't say whether he was homicide or a missing persons guy. But do they have detectives devoted to missing persons in the suburbs? I don't know, and I wasn't about to ask. It was his show, and I planned to go along with whatever he wanted, including not complaining about his lack of consideration.

He was a burly guy, bigger in the neck and shoulders and arms than I am, and that's saying a lot. I wanted to ask if he worked out but it wasn't a social call, so I kept my trap closed. My dad would have been proud. Not that I gave a shit what he thought.

"Nice place," Detective Archer said. "Very authentic restoration." He sat on the couch facing the window seat that looks out on the peach tree and grassy area of my backyard.

"Thanks. You're familiar with Victorian design?"

"Not a lot, but my ex-wife was crazy about Victorian houses. Always wanted to buy one. Not really my thing, but I appreciate the craftsmanship."

I grimaced, which wasn't what I meant to do. I intended to look pleasant, to be pleasant. "I did it myself."

"Is that right?" He looked up at the ceiling as if he was looking for cracks or flaws in the molding. He looked back at me. "Nice job."

"Thanks."

"So, Tiffany Jones."

"Yes?"

"How long have you known her?"

"Five years, maybe a bit less."

"Do you think she wandered off on her own?"

"I don't know."

"What's your gut feeling?"

"I don't think she'd leave her kids."

"Okay. Do you have any thoughts on who might have taken her?"

"Not really. I mean, I hope she's not dead. Do you think she's dead?"

"I can't answer that. The more time passes, that's a more likely outcome."

"That's what I've heard. But not always, right?"

"Right. But usually. So the more you can provide honest answers to my questions, the better our chances."

I didn't appreciate his comment about being honest, but I kept my poker face steady. "I don't really know what I can tell you."

"We're painting a picture from everyone we talk to, composing a collage if you will."

I smirked at his pompous description and hoped he didn't notice.

"Let's get started. How well do you know Byron Jones?"

"I've known him since we were ten."

"And has he changed much over the years?"

"Doesn't everyone?"

"How about in the past two years?"

"Are you thinking it's him? I guess you always do, think about the husband first."

"Has he changed?"

"No, he's a pretty simple guy. All guys are, right?" I laughed.

"Is he an angry person?"

"No. He's very religious."

"Religious people can be angry."

"He's not. He's quite genuine, to be honest."

"Would you call him a fanatic?"

"Their church is kind of hardcore, takes the Bible word for word, but he doesn't have crazy ideas if that's what you're asking. No anti-government or snake charming or any of that."

"That's an odd choice of concepts."

"Fanatical."

"Is anyone in your circle of friends fanatical? About the government? Or snakes?"

"Seth's kind of right-wing, but he's not going off the grid or anything like that."

"Any extreme leftists?"

"Kristen Thomas, maybe. She's focused on human trafficking, animal rights, environmental rights, gay rights, women's rights, children's rights, that kind of thing. She goes over the top, in my opinion."

"Okay." He wrote in his notebook. What I wouldn't give to see that notebook. It made me crazy, watching him jot things down, wondering if he was writing what I'd just said, or going back to an earlier comment. Or only recording his own thoughts. It must be a gold mine of secrets in there. Although I don't know why I thought that. So far, he hadn't extracted any so-called secrets from me. I wondered if people used detectives as father confessors. I could see the temptation. His questions had a way of making me consider things I'd never looked at before — such as what qualifies a person as a fanatic.

"Back to Mr. Jones. Did he ever make negative comments about his wife?"

"No."

"Did he express any feelings of being trapped or tied down?"

"Not to me. Why would that make him hurt her if that's what you're getting at? Wouldn't he be the one to take off?"

"Negative emotions erupt in a variety of ways."

I didn't know what to say to that. "Do you want some water or anything?"

"No thank you. Are you aware of either of them being involved with anyone else?"

"They're super religious."

"Are you aware of any extramarital affairs?"

I guess he wasn't going to explain that religious people can cheat too. I guess I should have known that. I glanced at the window seat. As I turned, a peach fell off the tree. It made me anxious to end the questioning. Peaches will rot fast, flies get on them if they split open, and before you know it there's all kinds of rotten gunk eating into the grass. And it stinks.

Something so good turning so bad, so fast.

"Mr. Eddington?"

I looked back at him.

"Are you aware of either of them being involved with another person?"

"Nope."

"You hesitated."

"I was distracted."

"You're sure you don't have any suspicions on that front?"

"I don't know about anything like that."

"Even if it's just a thought, something nagging at the back of your mind."

"No. Nothing."

He looked disappointed. I'm sure it's hard to keep asking questions, leaping all over the place, fishing for information, and coming up empty-handed. I imagined it could get frustrating.

"Are you attracted to Ms. Jones?"

"She's cute."

"Did you ever flirt with her?"

"No."

"Did your friends?"

"I don't know. I don't think so."

"Are any of your friends drawn to her?"

"They're all very happy with their wives."

"What about your female friends?"

"Are they attracted to Tiffany? No way."

After that, he changed directions. He asked a bunch of tedious questions about what time I got to the memorial service, who I sat next to, who was there, whether I talked to Tiffany, what we talked about — which was nothing. Most conversations are. And then someone dies, and you realize the last thing you said was, *This wine isn't very good*, or *There's celery stuck in my tooth*. Not that I would say something that lame to Tiffany, but I said it to Byron. He looked at me like I was the most boring guy on the planet. Maybe I am. But the celery was bugging me, and everyone else talks about stupid bullshit like that — as if it's funny. I don't think it makes me any more boring than he is.

Detective Archer stood. "Thanks for your time." He shoved his notebook into his shirt pocket. "Really, it's very impressive what you've done here. You did all of it yourself?"

"Pretty much. You're interviewing all her friends?"

"Yes."

"I hope you figure out what happened. I hope you find her."

This time, he grimaced. "Me too."

I followed him to the doorway. Just inside the opening to the living room was a small rag-tied rug that my mom made. His foot skidded slightly. He grabbed the doorframe and grunted softly. That thing was really slippery on the hardwood floor. I should have gotten rid of it, but it would have hurt my mom's feelings.

At the front door, he handed me a card, shook my hand,

and stepped out onto the porch. "You have a lot of talent," he said.

"Thanks." I closed the door.

It was gratifying to hear my work praised. I got a lot of compliments while I was remodeling, posting the progress pictures on AboutFace, but then it seemed when it was done, there were no more admiring eyes. It wasn't completely done, the third floor was torn up, waiting for me to get around to it. After Sarah, I lost my enthusiasm.

I went into the kitchen and grabbed my wallet. I was starving. The detective had kind of motivated me. It was time to get back to work on finishing the third floor. There are only two rooms up there, and I should never have let it go for so long. I got derailed, but now, his compliments made me anxious to get back to work.

Jake

JAKE ASH *THINKING of saying goodbye to AboutFace.*
0 favorites — 83 comments

Allie Sinclair *What does that mean?*
Megan Miller *Are you deleting your account?*
Adam Jamison *It is a time sink.*
Jake Ash *It takes a lot of courage to delete your life.*
Megan Miller *Are you deleting your account?*
Allie Sinclair *What does that mean? You're scaring us.*
[See 77 more comments]

AMELIA WOULD NOT fucking shut up about how I needed to forget Kimberly, that it wasn't anyone's fault. But if she couldn't comprehend why I was questioning my life, then maybe we weren't meant for each other. There might be something to what Tiffany had said about each of us having one person. I was still drawn to Amelia, I couldn't take my eyes off her face or my hands off her body. She was intriguing, if heartless. She was so damn sure of herself it was like an aphrodisiac.

One night, when I was halfway through my fourth martini, I couldn't say what night it was, she turned and pounded her fist on my thigh.

"She twisted things around!"

"Twisted what?" I sucked the last olive out of my drink. I hadn't balanced them correctly. There was more gin, but I was out of olives.

"Nothing."

"What are you talking about?"

"We're responsible for our own choices."

"Did you tell her to strip and jump in the pool?"

"No. She was jealous and bitter."

"How do you know this?"

She stood and moved away from the couch. She picked up the wine bottle off the coffee table and topped off her nearly full glass.

I swallowed the rest of my drink.

"We make our own choices. We decide how much we want to drink, how needy we're going to be, where we want our careers to go."

"I thought people were inter-dependent. We're all one. That's what the philosophers say."

She picked up her glass and the wine bottle and walked out of the room. A few minutes later, the lights surrounding the pool came on, the glow filling the window. I went into the kitchen and mixed another drink. After that, everything is blank. I think I passed out before I ate the last olive out of that drink.

Amelia can be quite vicious, and I kept wondering what she

and Kimberly had talked about, but I couldn't seem to make any real effort to pursue it. I wanted to drift through my own thoughts without Amelia's interference. No matter what she'd said to Kimberly, I knew what I'd said — *we're all doing a striptease.*

Call it brooding, I needed to figure out where the hell I was going.

ONCE AGAIN, I was not going to be left alone. Amelia had gone shopping, and I still wouldn't be alone. As if I hadn't talked to enough cops after Kimberly drowned, now I had to answer more questions about Tiffany.

It felt as if girls were dropping out of my life left and right. Amelia hates it when I call women girls. "Girls. Girls. Girls!" I said it out loud several times just to piss off any piece of her aura that lingered in the house.

The bell rang. I walked across the entertainment room and into the hallway. My feet were bare, but even so, they echoed softly on the tile, the quiet lapping, like waves, washing up the walls, past the second floor to the ceiling so far away it seemed like the sky. I had an image of myself walking down the length of a throne room to meet the king, or the executioner.

Detective Archer showed me his badge and stepped inside without waiting for an invite. Fair enough. He had the authority, but it irked me. I felt a sudden reappearance of my old self, but I wasn't sure whether that old self or the new, contemplative, guilt-infused self would play better under the scrutiny of the detective. He had eyes like gold nuggets and a clean-shaven face that flowed seamlessly across his shaved skull — the persona of a tough guy. Maybe my former, wicked, got-the-world-by-the-balls self was required to win.

I led the way to the living room and offered the couch facing the window so I wouldn't have to feel the pool staring up at me. The minute I sat down, I knew it was a mistake because I sensed it behind me. A swimming pool is such a lie. The pale blue water, the pristine white over concrete, everything visible, no weeds or flesh-eating fish lurking in dark waters. No currents or rapids or rip tides. The personification of suburban tranquility, and yet, more than a hundred people a year take their last breath in a swimming pool. And that's just in the US. It seems so safe and playful, it's easy to forget the danger, to get sucked into its inviting arms. I never saw it coming. It felt like my brain had been ripped open and left to rot.

Detective Archer started in on the same line of questions, trite inquiries that I'd already heard once for Kimberly and once for Tiffany while we were still at the golf course. I'd become a pro providing trivial details about my limited knowledge of a woman's life as if any of those things mattered — *how long had I known her, did I think she was depressed, did she use drugs or alcohol.*

"How long have you known Mr. Jones?" he said.

"Byron? Since grade school."

"And how many years is that?"

"Probably about twenty years."

"What was your impression of their marriage?"

"Inspired." The word leaped out of me before I even thought. I guess that meant it was the truth. A belief I'd been considering and hadn't realized I'd adopted.

"Why do you say that?"

"I'm not sure. They don't seem to want things like everyone else does. They're content."

"I see. Because of their religion?" He made a note without waiting for my answer.

"Yes, I think so. I've never asked, but I should."

"Well, you can't very well ask Ms. Jones right now."

He didn't seem to expect an answer, so I said nothing.

"Do you think Mr. Jones feels confined?"

"He never mentioned it."

"What's your impression?"

"Is this really about impressions? I thought you needed verifiable facts."

"Gut feelings can provide leads."

"Is that right. Well, my gut feeling is the guy adores his wife."

"Okay."

He went on from there about other people who didn't like her, back to her mental state — whether I thought she had postpartum depression.

"I don't know anything about it."

"It's caused by massive hormone fluctuations, often not obvious as depression. A woman might seem detached from her child. She might do things out of character."

"What kind of things? Like wandering off and abandoning her kids and husband?"

"Yes."

"I don't know. She seems pretty devoted to her kids, from my perspective, but I don't spend a lot of time with them. I see them at parties."

He wrote in his notebook while I waited. He looked up, past my shoulder, presumably out the window. "Nice place."

"Thanks."

"Looks new."

"It is."

He studied his notebook. "Your fiancé is Amelia Loc."

"Yes."

"She lives here?"

"Yes."

"Is she home now?"

"No."

"I'll want to talk to her."

"Okay."

"Is she close to Ms. Jones?"

"No. They don't have much in common."

The detective nodded.

I wasn't sure what that meant, if he was agreeing that someone who was with me couldn't possibly have much in common with Tiffany, or if he was just acknowledging my opinion.

"What is your relationship with Ms. Jones like?"

The word was jarring. I didn't think of Tiffany and I having a relationship. "Average," I said.

"Average?"

"She's the wife of a guy I've known since I was a kid."

"Did you flirt?"

"Hell no."

"Why such a strong reaction?"

"I don't flirt with my friends' wives."

"People your age often have a flirtatious element to most relationships."

"Not me." I had no idea where he got that bullshit opinion, but it wasn't worth debating.

"I'd argue that point," he said.

"You don't even know me." I stood. "I don't flirt with other guys' wives."

"Okay. Please sit down."

"What's the point of all this? Shouldn't you be out looking for Tiffany?"

"Please sit down. This is how it works. She was either taken without her consent, or she wandered off. She either left willingly or had some kind of episode that left her incapacitated. We need to get a sense of who she is and her relationships in order to know how we should proceed."

I sat on the edge of the chair. He'd won, but not entirely.

Call it a draw. And I think he knew that.

"Did you flirt?"

"No, sir."

"Did she flirt with other men? Or they with her?"

"Not that I noticed. She's really into her kids. And Byron. And she's super-religious."

"Did her religion cause any conflicts?"

"Not that I know of. I think people on social media got annoyed with her, maybe blocked her updates. She can be overbearing."

"In what way?"

"She posts very intense comments. Bible verses, praise the Lord, stuff like that."

"I see. Is there anyone you know who would want to kill her?"

"No."

"Did she ever express fear about anyone following her, harassing her?"

"No. Nothing like that. She's sweet. I can't imagine anyone wanting to kill her."

"You said she's intense, that she posts controversial topics. You consider that sweet?"

"You have to know her. How she smiles. You've seen her pictures. She looks very innocent. She's devoted to her beliefs. It's just that she left this impression . . ." I laughed.

"What impression?"

"Of innocence. But not."

The detective gave me half a smile. His head crinkled into folds like the skin of pug, or a pit bull, like shaved heads usually do. He stood and put his notebook, too small to hold all the stuff he must be writing down, into his pocket.

I wondered why he didn't use a smartphone. Much more efficient, and he could copy it right into whatever reports or files he had to fill out. "Do you think someone killed her?" My voice was quiet as if I was scared, and maybe I was.

"We're looking at every angle."

"Wouldn't someone have found her body?"

"Not necessarily. Thanks for cooperating, Mr. Ash."

"Sure."

He handed me his card, shook my hand, of all things, and walked down the hall quickly, so I had to hurry to catch up before he went out the front door.

"I can't believe someone would kill her. It's a nice golf course. It was the middle of the day. It's a . . . a very high-end community."

The detective opened the front door and stepped outside. I closed the door.

When I went back to the living room, I wanted to throw something through the window.

Allie

FINDOURTIFFANY

ALLIE SINCLAIR *This page is to help us gather together as if we're holding a 24x7 candlelight vigil for Tiffany. That's why I posted that beautiful picture of all those candles at the top. You'll see pictures of Tiffany throughout her whole life. Please post other pictures and write your thoughts and messages to her. Ask people who don't even know Tiffany Jones to mark it as a favorite. The more people we have looking for her, the faster we'll find her. WE WILL FIND HER!!!*

432 favorites

AFTER MEGAN LEFT, I watched some brain-dead TV. I tried not to think about my mom. It didn't seem fair that Megan had her mom, but didn't seem all that appreciative. I gobbled half of a party-sized bag of potato chips and drank two glasses of orange juice. Then I felt sick to my stomach.

I turned off the TV and launched another useless search for my phone. I was sure Marcus had taken it with him, but I couldn't stop myself from looking. The hope that he wasn't being totally awful and had stuck it someplace where I'd eventually find it, kept me opening drawers and running my hand over shelves above my line of sight. I was chained to the desktop computer, chained to the house.

I went into the garage and opened his metal tool case. The top tray was filled with small screwdrivers and nuts and bolts and a roll of painter's tape that was almost used up. I lifted out the tray. The bottom of the case was empty except for a huge tape measure and a hammer. After I finished searching the garage, I went out to the backyard shed and took all the gardening tools off the shelves, even though I knew my phone wasn't there.

When the doorbell rang, I was sitting on the edge of our bed. The sun was almost ready to set, the backyard filled with shadows that darkened the bedroom. The cream-colored spread, the pale oak furniture, and the light beige carpet did nothing to diminish the darkness. I stood and walked down the stairs. I didn't have to look through the small window at the top of the door to see if it was the detective. He'd said eight o'clock, and that was the time, precisely.

He came inside, and I closed the door. He shook his head when I offered iced tea or OJ or lemonade. In the living room, he picked a chair with its back to the sliding glass doors. He told me to relax, the questions were just routine. I wished I'd poured myself some orange juice. He'd thrown me off by declining the offer, and my first instinct said it was rude to get my own beverage, but I was really thirsty. I swallowed.

He asked a bunch of questions about how long I'd known Tiffany and Byron and where I'd met them and stuff like that. He asked what I knew about their marriage and what I thought of her religious views. He asked about postpartum depression, how much Tiffany drank, if she used drugs, if she knew any people that made me uncomfortable. I said no to almost every question. I assumed he'd asked our friends and her family the same questions, that he'd repeat them to Marcus. "If I don't know anything and have no ideas, and none of our other friends do, how are you going to find her?"

"Sometimes, the questions trigger memories later."

"I don't think so."

"It happens more than you'd think. Memory is a funny thing. An incident or a conversation, even a gesture you'd completely forgotten comes to the forefront, stirred up by an unrelated question."

"Do you think she just left?"

"We're considering all possibilities."

I pulled my feet up onto the couch and bent my legs to the side. It probably wasn't the right position for being interviewed by the police, but I needed to curl up. Marcus seemed so far away, and everything between us seemed so wrong. I tried to keep my voice from shaking. "Do you think she's dead?"

"It's possible."

"But if she was depressed, she might have just run away, right?" I leaned forward as if knowing how much I wanted him to say *yes, that's the most likely possibility*, would make him say it, would make it true.

"Do you believe she was depressed?" he said.

"I'm not sure. She did post something weird on AboutFace the other day that made me think she was a little, I don't know . . . unbalanced?"

"What was that?" He held his pen high in the air, waiting.

"A Bible verse about taking what belongs to you, or that god was giving you something you wanted. I don't remember exactly."

"Can you look it up?"

"I don't have my phone. I have to look on the computer."

"I'll wait." He lowered his pen and leaned back in the chair. He crossed his legs.

"She posts Bible verses all the time. Do you want me to look up all of them?"

"No, we're reviewing her social media pages. Just this one, since you thought it was significant."

I stood. "I don't think it means anything, not more than the other stuff she puts up."

"You mentioned this one, so that's the posting I'm interested in."

I went upstairs and wrote the verse on a piece of paper. When I handed it to him, he glanced at it, folded it, and stuck it between the pages of his notebook. The edges protruded like wings.

"Why did you think this suggested she was unbalanced?"

"I don't understand what she's talking about. It sounds like she wants to take over something, or that she thinks she's supposed to. I don't know. I'm making too much of it."

"Is she affectionate to her children?"

"She's all over them, kissing the baby all the time. She's so patient with her son."

"Does she seem overwhelmed?"

"Not really. Tired, I guess."

"When is your husband expected home?"

"Tomorrow."

"And where is he?"

"He's in Atlanta now."

"Do Mr. and Ms. Jones have a good relationship?"

"I think so."

It was making me feel queasy again, the way he was jumping from one subject to something entirely different.

"Any conflict between them that you're aware of?"

"No."

"Were you there when she wandered away from the table?"

"Yes."

"Was anything said that might have upset her?"

"I don't think so. She argued a little with Amelia Loc about religion, but it wasn't anything big."

"Did you know everyone at the memorial?"

"A lot of them, but not all of Kimberly's family, and not her co-workers."

"So, about half the attendees."

"I guess so, yes."

"Anyone who seemed out of place? Who aroused your suspicion?"

"No."

He closed his notebook. "Tell your husband I'll be here at five tomorrow."

"What if his flight's delayed?"

"Does that happen often?"

"No, but it happens."

He stood and handed me a card. "Give me a call if it gets delayed."

I uncurled my legs, stood up, and put the card on the table.

"Was Ms. Jones flirtatious with any of your friends?"

"No, not at all."

"With your husband?"

"No!"

"Did he ever flirt with *her*?"

My eyes filled with tears, making it hard to see his smug face, his eyes hard and cold, not caring if he was talking shit about Marcus. I wasn't going to answer. He had no right to ask something like that.

"Did he?"

"Never."

He nodded and walked into the front hall. He thanked me again and went out. I said good-bye, hating myself for even talking to him.

As soon as he got in his car, I locked the door, went upstairs, and changed into my black bathing suit. I braided my hair and went outside. I dove into the pool. The water was as warm as a bathtub. It's funny how when bath water cools down to your body temperature, you can't wait to get out because you feel sort of clammy and cold, but when the swimming pool is the same temperature, it's soothing.

I glided to the surface and began kicking hard, keeping my head low enough that my ears were under the water so I couldn't hear the splashing. In the silent world, broken every few strokes by sound as I lifted my head for a breath, I remembered the last time I'd taken a bath.

It was late March, but the weather was really cold. I only like baths when it's cold. I avoid them all summer, and it seems like greeting an old friend when I start up again in the late autumn.

The bathroom door was locked.

I don't mind Marcus coming in sometimes, but other times, I just want to relax and not think about him suddenly appearing in the doorway.

He knocked on the door. "What are you doing?"

"Taking a bath."

"Why is the door locked?"

"I don't know. Because."

"I hope you don't have your phone with you. I'm not buying you a new one if you drop it in the water."

"I know."

"You do have it, don't you."

"Yes."

"You can't take a bath without checking social media? I thought the point of a bath was to relax by yourself."

"I'm relaxed."

"It's weird."

"No it's not."

"Saying things to your friends when you're in the bath? It's weird."

"Everyone does it."

"No they don't." He knocked again.

I'm not sure why he was still knocking, maybe he thought I'd immediately close AboutFace, get out and open the door. "How would you know? You don't know anything about it, because you treat it like a disease."

He was silent. I wasn't sure if he was still there or maybe flopped down on the bed, sulking like a little kid, burying his face in the pillow.

There was nothing weird about it. I didn't post that I was taking a bath. I was just checking updates and making comments about things I'd done that day. I'd posted about one of my students who suddenly transitioned from moving his lips while he was reading to following the words silently. I shouldn't post about my students since some of them are my friends on AboutFace, but this guy wasn't, and I said it in a vague and flattering way, so I think it was okay.

Allie Sinclair *Best day ever when a student gets lost in a book and forgets he's reading.*

A hundred and five people marked it favorite.

If Marcus thinks posting in the tub is weird, I wonder what he'd think if he knew I'd thought about what I might post while we were making love.

I turned at the end of the pool and rolled onto my back. I did the backstroke, staring up at the evening sky, still navy blue but punctured by sharp marks where the stars had come out. I can't help myself. I'm so used to thinking of posts, of composing what I'm going to say, it's part of my brain. He'll be playing with my breasts or getting on top of me, and the words just come to mind, wondering how I'd describe it — *Every one of my nerve endings is humming. Who else had an orgasm today??* I never would. I'm not crazy. But I think about it.

The water cradled my head, and I closed my eyes. I wondered where he was right at that moment. I used to know his itinerary by heart, but the past year or so, I didn't memorize every detail. I knew what city he was in, but not the exact times of his flights.

Then, I wondered where Tiffany was, if she was thinking of all the things happening on AboutFace, thinking of more Bible verses to post.

Seth

SETH PORTER *PEOPLE are conspiring to destroy this country. Trying to rip apart the fabric of the family, wipe out religion, get rid of our right to bear arms so the terrorists can take us lying down. It would kill my grandfather. It makes me glad he's dead sometimes, he was so proud, so patriotic. He would be horrified by the state of America. We used to be a force for good and now we're overrun with freeloaders and immorality and people who feel entitled and break the law without any consequences!*

25 favorites — 7 comments

Allie Sinclair *What does that have to do with anything? Kimberly is dead and Tiff is missing.*
Seth Porter *If Tiffany had a weapon, she would have been safe.*
Adam Jamison *Chill.*
Allie Sinclair *You're just upsetting everyone.*
Dave Eddington *You make it sound worse than it is.*
Seth Porter *Do I? Get informed.*
Lori Porter *Smile, babe. It's not all bad :)*

I HAD NO idea why the cops wanted to talk to me.

I hardly know Tiffany. Neither does Lori. We see her at barbecues and weddings and Christmas parties, but that's about it. I'm not sure I ever talk to her beyond *kids are getting big*, that sort of thing.

That's the government for you though, it's a great excuse for them to get inside your house, take a look around your living room without a warrant, pry into your thoughts with questions you're obligated to answer, poke around your stuff online if they're really ballsy. You're simply not safe from their spying, but I'm not going to let that betrayal of my privacy shut me up. I'm not afraid of anyone knowing what I think, because I'm right, and maybe if they'd shut up and listen for two minutes, they'd realize that.

Lori had taken Michael out, and we were going to swap after the detective was done talking to me so he could grill her. She didn't even know Byron when she was in high school, so it really bugged me that they wanted to talk to her. It bugged me even more that they insisted on talking to us separately. More of their control — letting us know who's really in charge.

The cop sat on the best chair in the room. I think he'd sniffed it out like the bulldog-looking character he was — typical cop. Big, bulky, shaved head. It's not like cops are liberals, but still, they have that entitled, governmental, *we own you* attitude.

I picked the rocking chair, a frail thing that Lori got from her grandmother. I thought I'd highlight to him that there wasn't a good place for me to sit since he'd squatted on my chair. I don't think he got the hint though. Too subtle.

He launched right in with a bunch of irrelevant questions about Kimberly's memorial. Because of the way he rattled them off, I knew he'd asked the same questions to every single person. I smiled in what I hoped was a friendly way. No sense antagonizing him right out of the gate. In each case, I answered with the simplest answer, mostly *no*. Then he got ugly, really fast.

"Is Mr. Jones the kind of guy who thinks he should keep his woman in line?"

"What kind of guy is that?"

"The kind who thinks it's okay to hit a woman or intimidate her."

"I don't think I should comment on their marriage."

"Why not?"

"It's private. Between a man and his wife."

"I'm just looking for your impression."

"My impression is, Byron's a good guy, and they're a great couple, a good family."

"Something's not right when your wife wanders off during a funeral."

"She was kidnapped."

"You know that for a fact?" He put his notepad on his thigh and folded his arms across his barrel chest.

"No, but she's a good mother. She wouldn't leave her children. Or her husband."

"And what's your overall impression of her husband? Tightly wound? Money problems?"

"What's her disappearing got to do with him?"

"I'd like to understand their relationship."

"Shouldn't you be looking for perverts and drug addicts and all the other creeps we know are living right down the street?"

"I'm asking about her husband, trying to understand any issues in their marriage. We haven't ruled out that she simply walked away."

"What kind of woman walks away from her kids?"

"A deeply unhappy woman."

"Tiffany smiles more than anyone I know. She's always smiling. She wasn't unhappy. Look at her AboutFace page, grinning like an idiot, most of the time."

"Not everyone that's unhappy exhibits their emotions in photographs."

"True."

"So what is your impression of their relationship?"

"Tiffany's a great mom, Byron does well with the deli, works hard, treats her like a queen."

"And what does that mean?"

"Are you kidding?"

"Just curious."

"Provides for her."

"Having two small children is overwhelming for a lot of women."

"Overwhelming? Not if they're full-time mothers."

"Yes, it is."

I laughed. "It's not like she has six or seven kids. That would be overwhelming. My mom had four kids, and she acted like it was a cakewalk."

The guy had the nerve to jot that down in his notebook. I wanted this to be done. It was a waste of time, but if I mentioned my wish, I'm sure he'd write that down too, and assume my eagerness meant I was hiding something. They always think you're hiding something. Maybe most people are.

"So they have a great marriage. No conflict."

"Everyone has conflict, but it's not like you parade that in front of the world."

"I'm not talking about the world, I'm talking about a group of close friends."

"We aren't *that* close, sticking our noses in each other's business."

"I've had the impression from others that the group is quite close."

"Well some of them are, but not everyone. It's been ten years since high school. And there are all these spouses now, so that changes things. People having kids. You start to focus on your own family, and a few friends."

"So the Joneses are not part of your inner circle?"

"I don't have an *inner circle*. I have friends."

"Do you think her religious views antagonized any of your friends?" He leaned back and put the notebook on his thigh again. It stayed there.

I couldn't help staring at his leg, thinking the notebook

would slide off any minute. "Everyone's views antagonize someone."

"Are you aware of anyone who was offended by her views?"

"No."

"There wasn't someone who might want to punish her for being so dogmatic?"

"Punish?"

"Just a thought."

"You have no idea what happened to her, do you? You're firing out random questions hoping something hits the target."

He glared at me.

It was politically incorrect, I know, telling a cop he didn't know what he was doing. Suggesting that he was incompetent. I rocked the chair back and forth. He picked up the notebook and flipped through it. Probably looking for something to trip me up, shock me, maybe by revealing a confidence from someone else. Well, I wasn't worried.

Being politically correct has never been one of my goals. Look what happened with college. Every single person I hung out with in high school was a programmed robot when it came to college. Even though Dave didn't stick with it, he went to a community college for a few years. Like four more years sitting at a desk was the only path in life. If you didn't go to college, you were nothing. I called bullshit on that. I knew if I had to spend four more years tied to a chair with my nose in a book, listening to some liberal idiot drone on, trying to brainwash me with their point of view under the pretense of giving me a higher education, I'd shoot myself. Literally. I didn't need that. When I was sixteen, I knew it was more important to work hard, to be satisfied with what you contribute to the world. Construction doesn't pay as much as some of my college-sputum friends' jobs, but I do okay. And I'm a lot happier than some of them. I'm not working on a computer all night and all weekend. I have a good wife, a great kid. Sure things are tight, sure we're worried we can't really afford more kids, but I didn't let society railroad me into thinking there was only one way to survive in this world.

"Anything strike you as odd at the memorial service?"

"No."

"Anyone you noticed who didn't look like they belonged?"

"How does someone look like they don't belong?"

"A person crashing the funeral."

"No. I didn't see anyone like that."

He studied his notebook again, flipping all the way back to the first page. Maybe someone else mentioned a person who didn't belong. I waited.

Nope, never been PC-minded. When I was fourteen, I kissed a girl at church camp. She was all smiley, giggling and putting her face close to mine, opening her lips a little bit. I kissed her, quite intensely, and rather well, I thought, considering I was fourteen. Then I slid my hand up her shirt, and she freaked. She reported me for assaulting her. They came down on me like the National Guard. This big guy, six-four, with muscles like Arnold Schwarzenegger, sat me down in a room with no windows, started talking to me about repenting, and not taking advantage of sweet, innocent girls. He said if I wanted to stay at camp, I had to come forward at the altar call and confess my sins. I told him to contact my dad. I was out of there.

That guy didn't scare me, and I wasn't afraid of this guy, no matter how big, no matter how he glared at me or flashed around his authority.

"Did you?"

"Huh?"

"I asked you a question."

"Didn't catch it."

"Did you see Ms. Jones leave the area?"

"No."

"Who were you seated with?"

"Lori . . . my wife. The Kenyons who I know from high school and Megan Miller and three guys I didn't know — people from Kimberly's work. For a while, Kristen Thomas was there too."

"And you didn't observe Ms. Jones walking down the patio stairs?"

"Nope."

"Do you find Ms. Jones attractive?"

"What the hell is that supposed to mean?"

"Just a question."

"You think I did something to her?"

"Not necessarily."

I wanted to punch the guy. If he asked Lori a question like that, I would definitely punch him. Just because he had no clue what happened to Tiffany didn't mean he got to go around accusing decent guys like me of checking out other guys' wives. "I don't look at other women. I love my wife."

"Surely, you notice whether or not a woman is attractive."

Of course, I thought she was good-looking, had a nice body, even after having kids. But that was none of his damn business. Another example of them wanting to get inside your life and snoop around. Private things should stay private. "I don't think in those terms."

"What terms do you think in?"

"I keep my attention on my wife."

"So you don't find Ms. Jones attractive?"

"I don't think about it."

He made me repeat the names of everyone sitting at my table so he could write them down, which I think was just filler on his part since obviously I shut him up on that last question. He stood and gave me a card, thanked me for my time. Like I had a choice.

Marcus

THE FRONT DOOR was locked. I inserted my key and opened the door. Allie wasn't in the entryway, ready to greet me like she usually was. I lifted my suitcase across the threshold and closed the door. The house was completely silent. I left the suitcase standing there and went into the living room. She was in the pool. The glass doors were closed, so I couldn't hear the water splashing, which made it seem like she was out in the center of a lake, a speck on the horizon. I went outside. She swam three laps before she looked in my direction, then swam a few more strokes before acknowledging my existence by stopping.

I wanted to kiss her, but she remained dead center in the shallow end.

"How are things?" I said.

The water came up to her ribs. She was wearing her bikini, which she does only occasionally when she swims laps. I wondered if that was for my benefit. The top was pulled off-center, and most of her left breast was showing. If she moved at all, her nipple was going to pop out. Not that it would do me any good. Swimming obviously hadn't calmed her, and I guess I deserved her being pissed. But so was I.

Pissed was the wrong word, the wrong feeling. It broke my heart that she believed she had real relationships on

AboutFace, that she thought it meant she had a lot of friends. Why couldn't she see how disconnected she was, always thinking in terms of stating what was on her mind or what she was doing, without ever engaging in a real conversation? The world treats me like the freak, while they're absolutely blind to how the digital dictator is destroying the social fabric.

"The police want to talk to you," she said. "I told the detective he can come by at five."

"What for?"

"They're talking to everyone. About Tiffany."

"So, no news?"

She shook her head.

"Are you getting out?"

"I have ten more laps."

"I just got home." I don't know why I was pushing it. I didn't want to fight with her. I'd be lost without her. I didn't know why I was making such an issue out of social media, and I didn't completely understand why her addiction had suddenly become intolerable. I suppose because she refused to choose me over it. Almost every night when I was in town, she'd cook a kick-ass dinner, but then she'd slip her phone out of her pocket while I was eating. I caught her taking it with her when she took baths, and if it were waterproof, she'd take it in the pool.

She gave me a look that I couldn't decipher, then took a little leap, dove under the water, and started swimming. She never swam on a team, but she's amazingly fast the way she zips up and down that pool. Even when her movements are graceful, and each stroke seems careful and slow, it's mesmerizing to watch her reach the end before I complete a breath. Her turns are perfect, and the pace remains so uniform. She's a mechanical toy on a track. Right then, her motions were not smooth and graceful — arms slamming into the water, feet kicking so hard that drops of water landed on the front of my shirt. I stepped away from the edge. There was no way to fix this without giving back the phone. I'd think about that after the detective interviewed me. Not what I wanted to do the first thing in the door after a grueling trip, but I knew the cops wouldn't accept a request to reschedule. Best to suck it up and get it over with.

When the doorbell chimed at three minutes after the hour, I was watching CNN and mindlessly throwing a handful of dice on the coffee table. Allie had gone upstairs to shower. The kitchen counters were empty, and the sink had the polished look she gives it after the dinner dishes are cleaned up. There was no sign she'd eaten lunch there. None of her cookbooks were out, and there wasn't a single suggestion she'd started dinner preparations. Maybe she was going to freeze me out, and starve me as well.

I answered the door, and the detective and I went into the living room. He sat with his back to the sliding glass doors. Even though there was no direct sunlight, it forced me to squint slightly when I looked him in the eye. I wondered if it was deliberate.

He started off with mundane questions about my career, followed by how long I'd been married, how long I'd known Byron, how well I knew Tiffany, the events at the memorial service, and where I sat during the lunch. I wondered if he got bored asking informational questions like that — question after question, not getting anything useful ninety-eight percent of the time. All jobs have their dull aspects, even mine, which seems glamorous to most people, but that's because it's shrouded in mystery. They don't know anything about flying a plane, and they don't know there's a volatile mix of adrenaline and boredom when you're cruising at thirty thousand feet.

The detective launched into the cliché that when a woman is missing, or worse, all roads lead to the husband or boyfriend.

"Did you ever observe Mr. Jones being physically aggressive with his wife?"

"No."

"Verbally abusive?"

"No."

"Is their marriage a good one?"

"I have no idea. It seems good. He helps her with the kids."

"Is that unusual?"

"I know guys who don't."

"Seth Porter?" He grimaced.

"Not really, Seth is into his kid. Although I suppose his wife does all the grunt work."

He nodded.

It seemed a bit gossipy for a detective to be talking about someone I knew, but maybe he was trying to leverage Seth's attitude into getting me to cough up dirt on Byron. He didn't seem to believe that there wasn't any dirt on Byron.

"Does Mr. Jones seem happy in his work? His home life?"

"Yes."

"To both?"

If he wanted separate answers, he should have posed the questions more carefully. I took a slow breath. "Yes, to both."

"Any financial problems?"

"Not that I know of."

"Any affairs?"

"No."

"You know that for certain?"

"They're very religious." I looked away from his face, trying to readjust my eyes to the varying types of light in the room. They ached after all that time in the cockpit, the dry air, the intense concentration.

"That doesn't mean a damn thing."

I jerked my head back and looked at his face. His expression didn't match the force of what he'd said.

"They don't just give lip service. They really believe it," I said.

"Still doesn't preclude fooling around. Sometimes it's worse."

"Well, he doesn't cheat."

"Has Ms. Jones seemed unhappy recently? Overwhelmed by her children?"

"She only has two."

"Do you have children?"

Surely he already knew the answer from talking to Allie. "No. Not yet."

"Then you don't know how demanding they can be."

"No, I guess not. Only from what I see. Do you have kids?"

"Four. So no problems you're aware of in the marriage. No drug use, no alcohol abuse, no sexual dysfunction?"

"How would I know about that?"

"You might have observed something. Do you find Ms. Jones attractive?"

I didn't like where he was going, but he was obviously shooting in the dark. I'm sure it was a standard question. There was no reason to get offended. "She's cute enough."

"Are you attracted to her?"

"I love my wife."

"I've heard that before."

I had no doubt he had heard it before, a million times, but still, uncalled for. "I'm not attracted to her."

"Are any of your friends attracted to her?"

"Not that I know of."

"Any of the women?"

"No. I don't think so."

"But you don't know?"

"No, I don't know. I would think I'd be aware of anything like that. With the guys or the women."

He nodded. "What do you know about postpartum depression?"

"I know what it is."

"The symptoms?"

"Not specifically."

"Failure to bond, withdrawal from family and friends . . ."

"Okay."

"Has Ms. Jones exhibited any of those symptoms?"

"No."

"Did you observe her leaving the area after the memorial service?"

"I noticed that she didn't finish her lunch."

"But you didn't see her leave the patio area?"

"No."

"When were you aware she was missing?"

"I don't remember. I guess when Byron asked if we'd seen her."

"Any thoughts on anyone who might have wanted to hurt her?"

"No."

"Do you think she left on her own?"

"I don't know. I don't know what happened. It's . . . disturbing."

"Yes, it is," he looked at me and waited as if the roles were reversed and it was now my turn to ask questions.

"Do you have any ideas? Any leads? Any suspects?" I said.

"I can't really talk about that." He seemed genuinely disappointed.

Suddenly I saw him in a different light — a guy trying to do his job. A job that probably was very gratifying when you got answers, but extremely frustrating when you had nothing. I had the feeling he had nothing. His questions were all over the map, but then, the first and only time I was questioned by the police was when Kimberly drowned, and that was pretty quick since they didn't really think anyone else was involved. So what did I know about standard police questioning techniques?

He stood and handed me a card that I hadn't noticed he was holding. "If you think of anything that might be useful, let me know." He walked to the entryway and went out before I could say good-bye.

The front door closed with a loud click. I locked it and started up the stairs.

Allie was lying on our bed, her hands folded over her belly, her bare toes pointed forward, stiffened as if she were a corpse. I moved closer. Her eyes were shut, her lids pale and so delicate they seemed almost transparent. She must have heard me enter the room, but she didn't move, not even a twitch of that tender skin or a shifting of one of her toes.

I walked to the side of the bed and folded my hand over her foot. She remained motionless. I wanted to ask what was for dinner, but I wasn't stupid. Although the room, the entire house, was wrapped in silence, I got the message as if she were screaming in my ear.

"Is this how it's going to be?" I said.

She lowered her chin in a half nod.

I let go of her foot. I could return the mobile phone and end this right now. Allie charms and flirts and persuades her way into everything she wants and I didn't know what to do with this person. "It's not like you're completely cut off," I said. "You have the computer. You just don't need AboutFace fused to your hand twenty-four-seven."

"Go away. I'm resting."

I went downstairs and got some sliced turkey out of the fridge to make a sandwich. She was scaring me more than I wanted to think about, but I was still somewhat confident she'd turn around.

Tiffany

MY EYES WERE covered by a piece of dark flannel wrapped around the upper part of my head. My wrists and ankles were strapped with duct tape. A piece of duct tape was pasted over my lips. The room was hot, and my dress and underwear were gross.

He hadn't spoken to me. I knew it was a *he* because his hands were heavier and stronger than a woman's. He'd been very gentle with me, which was confusing. What did he want?

My breasts ached like nothing I'd ever felt. It was worse than childbirth. At least with that, the contractions came in waves, giving me a chance to catch my breath. My breasts were as hard as granite, tugging on my bra straps, so they dug into my shoulders when he sat me up to eat. No matter how I tried to position myself, the pain was too much. Milk had leaked out, and the top of my dress was alternately wet, then stiff with dried milk. I could smell it, along with the rest of my body, unwashed for however many days it had been. I was no longer sure how many days. I'd eaten nine or ten meals, but at one point I ate mac and cheese for three meals in a row. At least I think it was three meals — time was blurred at the edges.

I cried until the cloth over my face was soaked with tears and snot. Not being able to blow my nose was horrible.

Finally, he came in, placed a blanket over my upper body so I couldn't see him, removed the fabric, and replaced it with a clean piece, a shirt, I think. He told me to stop crying as if that were simple and something I could control.

Each time he came into the room and removed the tape from my lips, I shouted at him. I refused to eat the mac and cheese the third time he offered it. I refused to sip water through the straw. The moment he left, I regretted it. Nothing changed, and after a few more hours, my stomach growled with rage and my throat was dry, forcing me into coughing fits that wouldn't stop. Every so often, he helped me to the bathroom.

Since I hadn't been raped or beat up, and I was still alive, I wasn't as scared as I'd been at first. Before this happened, all I wanted to do was sleep. Now, I was sick of sleeping. And I was getting scared on another level — that I would live the rest of my life blindfolded, alone in this room, fading from the memories of my children and my husband and friends. Paul and Ruth would grow up without a mother.

I'd spent so many hours thinking, remembering different parts of my life.

My thoughts had raced back to when I was seven years old. Almost as if it had happened an hour ago, I felt myself sitting on the living room floor, my newborn baby sister sleeping in her carrier. My mother was in the kitchen, calling out every five minutes — *How is she doing? Keep your eye on her.* Then my mother went out to the laundry room. I looked at Jill's fat, soft thigh. I reached over poked my hand between her thighs and pinched as hard as I could. As if I'd pushed a button, her eyes opened, her face turned red, and she screamed so loud I had to put my hands over my ears.

I heard the laundry room door slam. I took my hands away from my ears and leaned over the carrier. "There, there," I said, just like my mother. "It's okay." I kissed her scrunched up face just as my mother came into the room.

"What happened?"

"I don't know. Maybe a scary dream. She won't stop."

My mother lifted her out of the carrier. "It's okay, you did the best you could."

It was fun pinching my baby sister, so I did it more. Sometimes I did it when my mother was right there but not paying attention to Jill. I liked knowing that I could make her do things and she couldn't do anything back to me. We aren't very close now, so even though she doesn't remember, I'm sure it's buried in there somewhere. And in that secret place, she probably hates me. Or is afraid of me. It was fun to squeeze her soft baby flesh, being careful not to poke my nails or leave a mark that my mother would notice.

Now, I was as helpless as a baby who can't talk or move, strapped into a carrier. Maybe this was my punishment all these years later.

I wondered what was happening on AboutFace. Were they talking about me? Writing on my page? Was Allie feeling bad that she told me I was too preachy? I hoped she was, and

then I felt bad for thinking that. But I did. It made me angry
when people laughed at me for posting about Jesus.

They act like they have a right to say all kinds of nasty
things, but if someone talks about Jesus, it's offensive. They
think their views are right and everyone else has to shut up. I
have the Secret to *Life* — the Ruler and Creator of the
Universe. I was serious when I posted it — I really do wish
Jesus would get his own AboutFace page and shut them all
up.

Every time I moved, trying to get comfortable on the bed,
my thoughts slipped away from all those other things and
crept toward Byron. I'd wanted so badly to escape from him
and his sickening nickname. And now, I tried to imagine the
sound of his voice, speaking that word, lying next to me and
whispering, his face so close that his breath tickled the inside
of my ear.

It wasn't just the *Mommy* thing that used to make me upset.
There were other things. Once, right after Ruth was born, I
was nursing her in the chair in the corner of the living room.
Byron was watching the 49er game. I asked him if he would
hold Ruth when I was done nursing. He didn't answer, so I
asked him again. I said I was really tired and just wanted a
quick nap. He told me to shut up. He actually said that — *shut
up*. I said I was trying to tell him that I was feeling a little
exhausted and he said, *Women should remain silent.* I whimpered
softly. I said *That verse is talking about church services, we aren't in
church!* He said I sounded like a woman in a commercial who

squeaked and turned into a bird because all he heard out of my mouth was tweet tweet tweet. *You sound like a Mommy bird,* he said.

I cried, remembering every word. Now I wanted to hold him and tell him I forgave him.

At first, for a few hours, I wondered if it was Byron keeping me in this place. The hands were so gentle, the food generous, the water plentiful. I even had coffee with my eggs, although the eggs weren't cooked the way Byron likes them, so that argued against it being him. And surely I'd know if it was my own husband, tying me up, feeding me, giving sips of water from a plastic bottle. And of course, there was no way I could come up with any possible reason why he might do something like this. Besides, wouldn't I recognize his smell, his touch? But I wasn't sure. Nothing was recognizable.

Then who? And why was he doing this? I started to cry. My thoughts veered back in the opposite direction. I hurt so badly. What if he was a freak, fattening me up and then planning to cut off a foot, or both feet, or my hands? One appendage a day. What if he decided to take off all my clothes and force me to lie naked and cold while he stared at me or did other nasty things? The thoughts wouldn't stop — all the ways I could experience pain — pain that would make the ache in my breasts seem like nothing but a paper cut. Yet so far, for three days, maybe more, he hadn't done anything to hurt me. My clothes were in place, and my teeth were brushed.

The door opened. I twisted on the bed, turning my face toward where I thought the door was. My arm caught under me and I wriggled around. It was hard to move with my wrists and ankles taped so tightly. My feet were bare, and sometimes they got cold, but at night, he pulled a clean-smelling sheet and soft blanket over me.

He removed the tape from my mouth. He put his hands under my shoulders and pulled me up to a sitting position. He shoved two pillows between my back and the headboard. They were soft, filled with down, but there was no comfort. My breasts ached more than ever. Another bucket of tears rushed across my eyes. My head felt heavy on my body, a boulder that my neck couldn't support.

"What do you want?" My voice was hoarse from not talking. Hours of moaning had rubbed it raw. "Why are you doing this?" I cried harder. "It hurts."

His hand was suddenly there, cradling the back of my head, gently pulling it forward. He pushed the fabric up to my nose. A plastic bottle touched my bottom lip, and I felt the angle change as he lifted it and the liquid splashed my mouth and the skin above my lips. I swallowed slowly, then the water came too fast. I choked and coughed. He pulled the bottle away.

Not a word the entire time I'd been shut in this room. How could he not speak? Had he asked Byron to hand over cash if he wanted me back? Was Byron refusing? I couldn't imagine that, but maybe it was too much money. Maybe he knew I was friends with Jake, had seen news of Jake's windfall and made the connection, somehow, and was waiting for Jake to cough up millions. I wasn't sure he would.

During some of the long hours alone, I'd talked to the Lord, cried to Him. I filled my thoughts with self-pity, then worked for hours trying to get my heart to accept the test He'd handed to me. I worked hard to stifle the other voice, complaining that I'd had enough tests. Learning to love my husband was a big enough test. I know that makes me sound weak. Many people are tested beyond imagination — with disease and death, and disabilities and violence and grief, with poverty and cruelty. And lives lived in war zones. I know that. But when you're in the situation, even though in comparison it's much easier, it's still hard.

If he would just speak to me. "What's your name?" I'd asked this twenty or thirty times already, but I couldn't stop. Eventually, he'd answer, wouldn't he?

The water bottle was gone, and the tines of a fork pushed my upper lip away from the bottom one. It clinked against my teeth. I parted them and allowed the fork to enter my mouth. Macaroni salad. Very good macaroni salad. I chewed. The soft pasta and the creamy saltiness of mayonnaise and crunch of celery filled me as if I'd been waiting my entire life for macaroni salad. I wanted to chew forever. I hated myself for taking such pleasure in something when my daughter was fussing, screaming, for all I knew, refusing the unfamiliar rubber nipple and the unfamiliar tasting formula that Byron was feeding her. Unless my parents were there . . . driving up to help with the kids while Byron . . . what? What was he doing? Telling the police all about my life, trying to figure out where I'd gone, still searching the golf course?

I'd been standing at the edge of the water, watching five ducks paddle in circles. A blue heron stood near the opposite side of the lake, also watching the ducks. Then I walked along the soupy mud at the shore, wondering if I should wade into the water. Despite the mud dotted with bird droppings, the water looked clean and refreshing. Instead, I turned away and headed toward a tight growth of trees. The ground beneath them was dirt and rocks. It wasn't a good place to go barefoot, but I really didn't care. I was trying to keep my thoughts numb, refusing to let the smirk on Amelia's dark red lips slither across my heart.

All my thoughts, twisting in on themselves, must have made me oblivious to the person following me. Suddenly, there was a shirt wrapped tightly around my face, and I was on my knees. I screamed, but the thick fabric pressed against my mouth trapped the sound. I tried to kick and swung my arms around, but my movements felt limp. All I could think of was Byron telling me I fought like a girl, which was not fighting at all. I didn't recall him ever actually saying those words to me, but it seemed like he might say them.

As more macaroni salad came into my mouth, I stopped thinking for a moment. I chewed and swallowed. I was starving, and I hadn't realized it. The macaroni was sweet and satisfying. It tasted homemade, although Byron's salads at the deli taste homemade too.

After I'd fallen to my knees and helplessly tried to fight, I was pushed flat on my face, and then I think I got dizzy, so I'm not sure if he hit me on the head, or maybe injected me with something I didn't notice, because I was too scared and my knees hurt so badly from slamming into the ground.

The water bottle touched my mouth again. "Please talk to me," I said. I licked my lips. "I don't understand what's happening. What are you going to do with me?"

"Don't be scared." His voice was a deep whisper. And of course, I couldn't tell anything from a whisper.

"I'll take care of you." The whisper was the voice of a monster, hissing spittle at my skin, unable to speak like a normal human being.

I started to cry again. "I don't want to be taken care of. I want to go home."

The bed collapsed slightly as he sat on the edge. His hip touched mine. I tried to inch to the left, but the depression in the mattress and the lack of support from my hands and legs made it impossible to move. He placed his hand on my thigh. "Don't cry," he whispered. The sound was barely a breath. Was there something wrong with his voice, or was this someone I knew, disguising himself?

"I don't know why you're doing this." Without thinking about it, I whispered also, as if it was now required. "I want to go home."

"This is home," he whispered. "I'll make you a nice home." His hand tightened on my leg. I felt the bed shift as he moved toward me, leaning, and then his head was resting on my breasts. It hurt so badly, I cried out, but he didn't move.

FindOurTiffany

Allie Sinclair *Come home, Tiffany, everyone misses you.*

74 favorites

Dave Eddington *Tiffany's a strong woman. She'll be okay. Nice page, Allie.*

17 favorites

Allie Sinclair *Thanks. I had to do something. Marcus sort of gave me the idea.*

63 favorites

Megan Miller *I just know she's still alive.*

12 favorites

Allie Sinclair *Scared.*

52 favorites

[107 more comments]

Dave

DAVE EDDINGTON [*CHECKED in at Home Depot*] *My home away from home.*

7 favorites — 2 comments

Seth Porter *A good way to spend a Saturday. I need to get some things done around here, too.*
Allie Sinclair *So do we, probably.*

I TRY TO AVOID the hardware store on Saturdays because it's a zoo of weekend warriors, convinced they can re-tile a floor, or do some fancy faux paint project to spiff up the living room. I laugh when I see these losers buying faucets and showerheads, thinking they're going to just swap out the old ones before the game comes on. I wish I could be there to watch.

Talking to the detective and seeing how much he admired my work on the house fired me up to finish the project. After all that work — ripping out wood and insulation and laying new floors, replacing doors, scraping paint, upgrading bathrooms and the kitchen, I'd let the two rooms on the third floor remain in their stripped-down condition. It wasn't just because Sarah gave up on me. There was a practical reason.

I'd lost the additional hands that made the work go more smoothly. Everyone has his limits.

But the house was my masterpiece, my life's work. I'd made it a showcase of craftsmanship. Sara and I had done a lot of research on the Victorian period to make sure it retained its authenticity. Everyone had been impressed with the pictures I'd posted while the house was taking shape. All those great shots have disappeared under a sea of other stuff — cat pictures and baby pictures, dog videos and clever quotes. Photographs of food and sports and hot cars. The great work of my life lost in a never-ending flow — the river of life, I guess. And then Jake got his IPO millions and threw up that concrete and glass monstrosity. It was like his giant white eraser of a house rubbed out mine.

The parking lot at Home Depot wasn't too bad. I pulled the truck into a spot only five spaces from the main doors.

I hadn't walked more than ten feet inside the building when I saw Adam Jamison. A person can eat at the same restaurants and go to the same hardware store and supermarket as a bunch of people they know and never see them, and then, there they are. He was tan, a dark tan that was sure to whither and peel off. Adam, with his long, thin ponytail that he treats like a lucky rabbit's foot, and those hands — not a nick or a blister or a broken nail, ever. It was strange he'd gotten a tan in the desert. I didn't think of it as a place where a person would deliberately sun himself. Maybe they did a lot of hiking.

It's not that I notice guys and their tans. I don't notice guys at all. I hated that I was still worried about that after all those years. No one knows what I'm thinking, but I worry about it anyway, trying to censor the thoughts when they pop up. I guess that's what bullying does to a kid. And I'm not being dramatic. I was definitely bullied. There just wasn't such a focus on it back when I was in middle school. It was considered normal kid behavior. Now, if you're bullied, you can sue someone's ass.

I made a sharp right turn and headed toward the outdoor garden section, not that I needed any plants or yard decorations, I just needed to get out of there and get my head on straight.

I was a fat kid. I'm bulked up now, or at least what they call stocky. But I won't pull punches. I was fat. I blame my dad for it. I shouldn't, but I do. I blame him for a lot of things. He was the king of ice cream and cookies. He whined like a little kid if the cookie jar wasn't constantly full of chocolate chip or oatmeal or any one of the ten or fifteen stunning cookie types my mom baked. She always had her hands in the oven, pulling out sheets of round, beige circles, perfectly textured, so they were solid yet chewy. Kids called me balloon boy and pig-face. Not the girls. I'm sure they said things behind my back, but never to my face. Girls are nicer that way. Although they can be a lot meaner when you really find out what they're whispering about.

By the time I hit seventh grade, I didn't feel so great about myself. Looking into my father's blue eyes, I saw the reflection of a round kid who slept in his own urine until he was eight years old because he couldn't seem to wake up in time. Like a pack of wild dogs, the bullies picked up on the scent of weakness. A kid that only went to our school for five months started it. After that, it ran like a rash through the boys' locker room at Millbrook Middle School.

Eddington is always at the back shower so he can get a good view of everyone's ass.

It never occurred to the moron that the back of the showers was the best place for a fat kid.

Queer.

Homo.

He runs like a girl.

What are you looking at, faggot?

It more or less died out by ninth grade, but I still felt it. Their words, those faces with their big, shit-eating grins had lined themselves up inside my skull and hovered there, always ready to start eating at me when I least expected it.

Some people might say I wasn't really bullied. No one hurt me. No one drove me to consider suicide. Social media didn't exist, and no one had phones where they could snap a picture and blast it all over the school. But it was enough that I hated getting out of bed every single day of my life until sophomore year in high school.

That was the year I took advanced woodshop and really started to think I had something in my hands, my patience, my logical approach to projects.

The hardware store is home to me. It sounds kind of nuts, but the hardware store is like a father figure. I'd never say that out loud, but that's what I feel.

I cruised through the outdoor pots, the shrubs, and small trees and rose bushes, and looped around the tables of cactus. By the time I re-entered the store near the screen doors and windows, I was back in control. If odds were against me and my path crossed Adam's again, I wouldn't give his too-dark tan a second thought.

I headed toward the wallpaper aisle. I needed a fresh scraper and some wallpaper stripper to remove the paper and glue that was pushing sixty years old. It wasn't original to the house, obviously, but still had that antique feel. It was a shame to get rid of it, but like other parts of the house, some of the sheetrock needed replacing. Besides, I wanted the rooms completely re-done, and if I did re-paper, instead of paint, I'd be able to find something else with a vintage look.

I grabbed an abandoned cart, turned down the aisle, and there was Adam, staring right at me as if he'd been waiting for me.

"Hey." He stepped to his right, just far enough that I couldn't go around him.

"What's up?" I said.

"Lots of bad stuff going on."

For a writer, he wasn't very clever when he opened his mouth. "Yeah, there is. How was your vacation?"

"Great. It was great. I put up a bunch of . . ."

"I know. I saw them." Of course, I saw them. He put up thirty pictures a day, four or five every hour. I couldn't open up my newsfeed without a running stream of happy-lucky-spunky Jamison family photos. His wife's outfits and his kids' adorableness overshadowed the Grand Canyon.

"So what's the deal with Tiffany? They have no idea where she is?"

"Nope."

"Some detective called and wants to talk to me."

"He's talking to everyone."

"But I wasn't even there."

"Yeah, I don't know." I pulled my cart toward me, angling it to go around him.

"Well, why would he want to talk to me when I wasn't there?"

"How should I know? I guess he's thorough." I tugged the cart back a few more inches.

"What do you think happened?"

"No idea."

"What does everyone else think?"

"No idea. Everyone's in shock."

"I didn't know what to write on that page Allie set up," he said.

"Just put anything, it's not going to help them find her."

"What you wrote was good."

"Thanks." The minutes were ticking. I'd already gotten a

late start leaving the house. At the rate I was going, I wouldn't be able to start work until after lunch, but he was determined to keep blocking my way. I wanted to shove past him, but I hadn't seen the guy in ages. We're supposedly friends, although I'm beginning to wonder what that word means.

"I agree, the page won't help them find her. But I guess it made Allie feel like she was doing something," he said.

"I guess so."

"What kind of stuff did the detective ask you?"

"Are we in high school, you want the answers to the quiz?"

I didn't laugh. He smiled like he wasn't sure if I was serious or trying to be funny and failed. Which I usually do. I don't quite know how to joke around like other people do.

"Usually, you're the guy with all the information," he said.

"My mind's on finishing my remodeling."

"Well, can you give me a hint?"

"It's probably better if you don't know. Just answer and don't sound rehearsed."

"I wasn't even there. It doesn't matter how I sound."

"It's just a bunch of BS, what do you think of her husband, was he a wife beater, was she depressed. That kind of thing."

"He really said that? About being a wife beater?"

"No, but that's what he meant."

"What are you up to?" he said.

"Working on the third-floor rooms for the last part of my remodel."

"Oh, yeah. I remember that shot of your master bedroom. Nice."

"Thanks."

"Okay." He moved to the side. "Okay, then. Well, good seeing you."

I felt like he was giving me permission to pass.

While I was getting my supplies, I couldn't stop thinking about Kimberly's memorial and the lunch and Tiffany. She hadn't looked very happy, but she still had nice things to say to everyone. I spent a lot of my time talking to Megan. I should say, listening to Megan. God, that girl can talk. And people say I'm a talker. All I did was stand there and grin, but not too much. You don't want to look like a fool at a funeral.

Megan had taken such a big gulp of wine, I saw her neck muscles contract as she opened her throat to swallow. Her hair was piled on top of her head, held in place by her sunglasses, all these crazy curls falling around her face. "I'm so tired of AboutFace," she said. She took another sip of wine. "People don't think about how it feels when you're single, and they post all these things about their anniversary and how amazing their spouse is and how in love they are."

"Yeah, sometimes. I . . ."

"They never consider when they complain about their kids, and put these long things about how hard it is to be a parent, that some of us would give every last egg in our bodies to have a kid before it's too late." Her eyes were watery, but she didn't put on her sunglasses. She took two sips of wine.

"It's . . ."

"I'm thinking of giving up my account," she said. "What's the point, really? Does it make you any closer to people? Bragging rights to five hundred friends? Who cares?" She took a longer sip of wine.

"I actually totally agree with you," I said. "People hide all the bad stuff. They think they're being "real" and "honest" when they bitch about work, but they're just doing it in a fake way, trying to make it funny, not really saying how pissed off they are. They act like marriage is perfect and so easy, and feeling totally pissed off is toned down and turned into *haha, LOL.* It's all one big fucking lie. A billion people lying through their teeth every minute of every day."

She laughed and finished the rest of her wine. She shoved the glass at me. "Want to get me another?"

I took the glass and refilled one for each of us. When I came back, she went off about people forcing their views down everyone's throat and how she was sick of Tiffany and Byron's Bible-spouting. *"Take everything your foot touches. Really?"* She laughed. "No one even knows what it means, but I'm sure it's some kind of threat about hell."

"I thought it was sort of inspiring," I said.

She laughed like it was the funniest thing she'd heard all week.

Allie

ALLIE SINCLAIR *TODAY is the first day of the rest of my life. I think that's something Tiffany might say, or maybe not. But I hope she's okay. Good thoughts to you, Tiffany.*

56 favorites — 8 comments

Kristen Thomas *I don't understand why they don't have any leads!*

Megan Miller *I agree. All these questions, no answers.*

Adam Jamison *NO ONE saw her walk off?*

Allie Sinclair *Not that we've heard.*

Amelia Loc *Maybe she just wants to be left alone. I guess some people are like that, no matter how social they seem.*

Allie Sinclair *Without her purse? Or her phone? And she'd never leave her kids. Never.*

Megan Miller *The detective doesn't say what he knows, so maybe they have some evidence they're not telling us.*

Seth Porter *Wouldn't surprise me at all.*

THE WHITE STUCCO of Jake's house glistened in the afternoon light. The windows that ran from the first to the second floor glowed deep green. Despite its beauty and the tiny prick of jealousy as I walked beside the creek bordering the path to his front door, I felt sad at the suggestion of unrelenting cold. I couldn't help thinking the greenish glass looked as if it reflected an algae-filled lake.

Usually, it's old houses that seem to give off an atmosphere of secrets. Houses that have been around for sixty or seventy years, houses that have seen several families come and go, watched relationships fall apart and people die. Jake's house had only seen one death, but there was something very tight-lipped about it. A black ceramic pot as high as my waist, holding a single stalk of dried Manzanita, stood a few feet to the left of the doublewide doors.

The silence was profound, and when I pushed the bell, no sound was audible outside. It was a building that had been constructed and never fully inhabited. A woman died at that house, but before her flesh could tarnish it, her body was whisked away as if it had never happened.

For the first time in our married life, I'd left the house without telling Marcus where I was going, or even letting him know I was leaving. It felt good to walk out the door, no one in the world knowing where I was. Until now.

A few minutes after I pressed the bell, Amelia opened the door. "Allie! What's wrong?"

"I just wanted some company. I thought I'd see how you two are doing."

She stepped forward and pulled the door partially closed behind her. "I'm fine, but you saw how Jake was the other night. Nothing's changed. It seems like he wants to do penance for the rest of his life. He's obsessed with death and guilt. He won't stop saying it's our fault that Kimberly drowned, or killed herself, or whatever it was."

I'd never heard her speak so many words so quickly. Her breath was steamy, laced with a hint of cigarette smoke and alcohol. She pushed her hair back from her face. Even without make-up, she looked like a porcelain doll, her skin so white and her lips so perfectly formed. There wasn't a single blemish or stray hair or discolored spot on her skin anywhere that I could see. Her pupils were almost completely dilated.

"Do you think something happened that he's not saying?"

"Come on in." She opened the door and waited for me to follow.

I walked behind her down the hallway. Her bare feet slapped the tile like dead fish, shattering the porcelain doll image. She led the way out to the back patio and turned. "I don't have to worry about him overhearing us out here. He hasn't been anywhere near the pool since that night. He won't even look at it."

"Oh."

"You've known him a long time. Has he ever done anything like this before?"

"What's he done, exactly?"

We went down to the pool area. I kicked off my sandals, and we sat in lounge chairs with a large red canvas umbrella between us, our toes pointed toward the water. It was hot with a barely noticeable breeze. Even with the chair's mesh fabric that allowed air to flow through, my back already felt sticky. I wished I'd brought a swimsuit, although I suppose Jake wouldn't have liked hearing us use the pool.

"His whole personality's changed." She looked angry as if his personality change was a deliberate effort to spoil her happiness.

"How?"

"All he talks about is the meaning of life. And dying. And guilt."

"He's always been philosophical."

"He doesn't just think it's his fault she's dead, he hints around that it's mine!" She flipped her hair up over the back of the chair, so it hung there like a black bathing suit set out to dry.

I spread my toes and looked at the water through the spaces between them.

"If that girl got so upset she had to kill herself, that is not my fault."

"What are you talking about?"

Amelia closed her eyes. After a few minutes, I thought she was sleeping. Her face was smooth, no movement of her lips or any real expression.

A few doves, hidden somewhere in the trees behind the barbecue area, cooed. The sounds of their cries made the air seem softer. The automatic cleaner crawled silently across the surface of the water. "Amelia?"

She kept her eyes closed. "Yes?"

"Why do you think she killed herself? Why do you think it's your fault?"

"It's not my fault. I didn't say it was."

Her eyes remained closed as if she hoped that by not looking at me, the conversation would shift in another direction, as the pool sweeper did when it reached a concrete edge.

"Did you have a fight with her?"

"It wasn't a fight. She was whining. I suggested trying a different approach to life. To let go a little."

"And you think that's why she took off her clothes and dove into the pool?"

"Not at all."

"Jake thinks that?"

"He doesn't know what I said."

"Then why would he think you had anything to do with it?"

"I didn't have anything to do with it. She asked my advice, and I gave it like I always do. He's lathering himself in guilt and wants to spread it around to anyone who gets too close."

She stood and walked to the edge of the pool. Her hair swung across her back with the same rhythm as her skirt brushing against her legs.

I wasn't really that close to Amelia. She's standoffish. It's easy to make friends, I think. You just start asking questions, tell the other person a few things about yourself, but mostly listen to their stories, and before you know it — *voila!* A friend. But Amelia hadn't been that way. She looked somewhat blank, staring as if she hadn't heard you when you told your own stories. And she didn't talk that much about herself.

She stuck her left foot into the water, gasped softly, and pulled it out.

I thought about Tiffany's Bible verse post. It lodged in my brain. It was something I would have written off, and eventually forgotten all about, like her hundreds of other Bible verses. Meaningless words you hadn't thought much about turned into something important and lasting when the person died. They burrowed into your mind forever, as if they meant more than any other words dribbled out over a lifetime.

"We have this amazing place." Amelia swept her arm toward the pool and out beyond to the covered barbecue area, and the lawn beyond that. "He loved his new job, until this happened. We were supposed to start planning our wedding . . ."

"Are you worried he wants to postpone it?"

She walked back to the lounge chair and sat sideways, facing me. "I'm afraid he's going to cancel it. I don't know if we're going to stay together."

I sat up. "That won't happen. Jake loves you."

"He says he doesn't know what love is, that he doesn't know the purpose of life. He isn't sure why he wanted this house or what's so great about his career. He's floating around like he has no idea where to go."

I wanted to pat her leg, but she's not the sort of person you touch without permission. "Maybe you should give him some space. Let him work it out."

"I did."

"It's only been a few weeks. And now Tiffany . . . I was thinking we should all get together, talk about what we told that detective. He's digging all this information out of us. He sees the big picture, but we're in the dark."

"What good will that do?"

"We know her better than he does."

"She's probably dead. Some mentally ill guy wandered onto the golf course and killed her, and they just haven't found her body."

"Don't say that." I wanted to slap her. At the same time, I wanted to cry, because part of me was scared she was right. But she couldn't be right.

The sun was getting lower, reaching under the umbrella and touching our feet. Amelia had three toe rings, all gold, and they shimmered in the light as if tendrils of sunshine were wrapping themselves around her toes.

"Do you want something to drink? I should have asked you earlier," she said.

"Orange juice?"

She stood, her toe rings continued to glint under the intense sunlight.

"Is Jake home?"

"Yeah, but he won't want to come out."

"Can you at least tell him I'm here?"

She looked at me like I wasn't very bright, turned, and went into the house. A few minutes later, she was back with a champagne glass filled with orange juice and a glass of champagne for herself. "He said he's not up to it right now. You see what I mean?" She handed me the glass and sat down.

I took a sip and felt less dragged out, more hopeful. "I don't believe she's dead."

"Aren't you the little optimist."

"It's too awful — two of our friends, dead?"

"Lots of awful, inexplicable things happen," she said.

"I wonder if they have any suspects."

"Byron."

"That's crazy."

"Something like eighty percent of the time, it's the husband or boyfriend."

"I don't believe that."

"You believe whatever you want hun, that doesn't make it true."

I swallowed most of my juice. It burned so much in my throat, I wondered for half a second if she'd put something in it. "Crazy people don't just wander into a country club and see a woman and murder her in the middle of the day. That just doesn't happen. I think she either ran away or . . ."

"Exactly. You don't have any other ideas. And where would

she go without her purse, her phone, her shoes? Someone took her."

"I guess. Are you sure Jake doesn't want to come out and say hi?"

"I'm sure."

Watching her face, wondering what was happening behind the smooth skin, I realized that we all get interpreted through our spouse. A spouse or a partner can tell you anything about the other person, and how would you know any different? The person living with them knows the truth. A few days earlier, I'd seen for myself how Jake was, but how did I know that now? He might not even be there.

In fact, for all I knew, Tiffany was locked in a room at the far reaches of the house, and Amelia knew it. I squeezed my eyes shut. Crazy thoughts weren't going to help anything.

I put my legs over the side of the chair and looked at the lines the cushion had pressed into my skin. I stood up. I handed the glass to Amelia. "Tell Jake I'm thinking about him."

She took the glass. She stayed seated and sipped her champagne, then leaned over and put my empty glass on the ground. It clinked and made a scratching sound on the concrete.

"Do you mind finding your way out? I'd like to enjoy my champagne since I just poured it and it's nice and cold." She lifted the glass toward me, either toasting me or reminding me she hadn't finished her drink.

"Okay. What do you think of my idea of everyone getting together?"

"I don't see the point. I'll ask Jake, but he won't want to."

"He'll feel better once he works his way through it," I said.

"If you say so."

I went into the house and walked down the long hall to the front door. I stopped near the door and listened to see if I could hear Jake anywhere nearby, maybe noticing I was there. For all I knew, Amelia hadn't even told him. The house was silent. I opened the door and went out.

Megan

MEGAN MILLER *I'M tired of the heat.*
  5 favorites — 2 comments

  Kristen Thomas *People caught up in human trafficking are kept in horrible, unventilated rooms.*
  Seth Porter *Agree, Megan, too damn hot.*

ONCE I SHUT the front door behind me, the air was slightly cooler than outside, but not much. My mother is diligent about keeping all the doors and windows, drapes and blinds closed on hot days to trap the cool air inside. The problem is, by five or so, the house feels like a three-foot closet, and I can hardly breathe. After being inside for more than five minutes, the cooler temperature isn't noticeable. Her strategy is good for early afternoon, but by evening, she really needs to get some air circulating. Unless she's trying to suffocate all of us.

I eased the strap for my massage table off one shoulder and my duffel bag of supplies off the other. Every crevice and indentation of my body was bathed in a thick oil of sweat. I could smell myself, and I hoped it hadn't been obvious when I was giving a ninety-minute session to Greg Orson, a fifty-year-old guy who gets two massages a week. He gives me three bucks as a tip, but he's my most regular client, so I try to focus on his loyalty rather than his stinginess.

My mother appeared in the hallway at the point where it joins the living room. It was difficult to see her face because I still had my sunglasses on.

"How was your date?"

Even though I was oozing sweat and I wanted nothing but a glass of cool water and a comfortable chair, I lifted my table and bag back onto my shoulders and shoved my way past her, hissing inside my head — *Don't bite, don't bite, don't bite.*

"Do you want some water?"

I went into my room and closed the door. I leaned the table against the wall to the left of the window, dropped the duffel in front of it, yanked open the drapes, and slid the window along the track as far as it would go. I collapsed on the bed and closed my eyes. Outside, a crow cawed. Another answered, and I laughed. That's what I would have sounded like if I'd responded to her demeaning question.

Sometimes I think she hopes to get me out of her house by making me feel like such a loser I'll just give up and get an office job. Not that I'm qualified for an office job. But she has a firm conviction that every college-educated woman in the country is qualified for an *entry-level* office job.

My throat was so dry I could hardly swallow, but I was not going out into the kitchen. I sat up, took off my sandals, and dropped them on the floor. I eased my phone out of my back pocket and opened AboutFace. I'd had two clients that afternoon and hadn't checked since lunchtime. I read the updates on the FindOurTiffany page. The title was stupid, but I admired Allie's devotion. She's a good person. She's very sweet. No one disagrees with that. There were lots of comments from people I didn't know, probably Tiffany and Byron's church friends. Byron hadn't posted anything. Part of me thought he should be more grateful, and at least thank everyone for their comments, but another part of me decided to cut him some slack. Besides, he was buried in kid and baby care, which doesn't allow much time for checking social media.

There was a knock on the door. I tapped back to my news feed. "Come in."

My mother opened the door. "I brought you a glass of water." She stepped into the room and put the glass on my nightstand. "You should close the window and drapes. It'll stay cooler."

I scrolled through my updates.

"I'm sorry I made that rude comment."

I grimaced and picked up the glass. I took a sip. "This is good, thanks."

"I said I'm sorry."

"I heard you."

"You didn't acknowledge my apology."

"I'm not going to say it's okay, Mom. Because it's not."

"Your job is just . . ."

"I know what you think."

I swept my finger over the screen.

"Any news on Byron's wife?"

"Tiffany."

"Right, Tiffany." She sat on the foot of my bed. I wanted to tell her I hadn't invited her to stay, but I was too hot to stand my ground.

She stood again. "I'm going to close that window." She crossed the room.

"Please don't. I need some air."

She returned to the bed and sat down, but kept her head turned, staring at the window as if she thought she could close it by telekinesis.

I read the latest in my feed.

Allie Sinclair *Feeling blessed. Missing our friend Tiffany, but feeling contented grilling chicken for Marcus.*

I wanted to gag. Her post was a cruel blend of thoughtlessness and bragging. How did she think that status update made Byron feel? I'm used to having my face rubbed in *happy-couple-love* and *baby-love* and *we-don't-have-to-think-about-money* cluelessness. Sometimes I wonder if people ever think before they blab on social media, if they ever wonder how their friends might feel regarding their insanely good luck. She set up a page for Tiffany and then made Byron feel miserable because he doesn't have his wife to cook him dinner.

I feel that emptiness every day, but I didn't have someone ripped out of my arms. It made me want to go immediately to his page and write something comforting, and not on her ridiculous FindOurTiffany.

"What are you reading?" my mother said.

"Updates from my friends."

"Do any of them have any news about Tiffany? It's very frightening, don't you think?"

"It's weird, that's for sure."

"To think someone could just vanish like that."

"It happens every day."

"But not to people we know. It seems unreal enough when it's in the news, but this is so . . . so . . . I don't know what to say."

That was a switch. I wanted to point out that she always knows what to say, but I could tell she was trying. So even though her mean question really did hurt me, I decided to take the high road. "The detective is asking everyone questions, but he doesn't give any information."

"I wish I'd been here when he talked to you."

"Why? I don't need my mommy to support me." Of course, actually I suppose I did, or I wouldn't be so angry at her comments about my career.

"What did he ask you?"

"Random questions. At the end, I almost felt like I hadn't told the truth, because he skipped over things and just asked about what he was thinking."

"Did you tell him everything?"

"Everything he asked. That's my point. What if he didn't ask the right questions?"

"Is there something you think you should have told him?"

"I don't know. All he asked about was Byron. Anyone who knows him knows he's crazy about Tiffany. He'd never hurt her."

"I guess they have to ask."

"But then he asked if I knew anyone who would want to hurt her. And of course not. If I knew someone like that, I wouldn't know they wanted to hurt her. But he didn't ask any specific questions about other people she knows. Shouldn't he have other possible suspects?"

"I guess her husband is the most obvious."

"But there are other guys who are more crazy than Byron. Seth and all his guns and government stuff . . ." I scrolled through more status updates. "People post the dumbest things," I said.

"Like what?"

I read the rest of the posts out loud to her.

Amelia Loc *Day drunk — not good.*

Adam Jamison *At the Giants game but feeling we shouldn't be.*

Along with Adam's comment was a picture of the playing field from high up in the stands. All you could see was the grass and the lines. I didn't show it to my mother.

Seth Porter *Cops ask a lot of questions but don't have any answers.*

Kristen Thomas *We're all thinking of you, Tiffany. I hope you can find a way to read this.*

Dave Eddington *Feeling motivated for the first time in two years.*

"That's out of place," my mother said.

"No worse than what Allie wrote."

"It's different. Her comment is thoughtless. That one is, I don't know, kind of arrogant or something."

"Well, Dave can be clueless."

"It's just so . . ."

"So disconnected from reality?"

"I wonder what he's motivated about."

I stared at his comment, at his profile picture — a shot of the back of his head looking out his newly finished living room window. The panorama picture at the top showed the front of his house. He'd had the same pictures up for over two years. "Two years ago is when his wife left him." I continued studying the picture. He was so proud of that house, but to me, it looked like something out of the Adams Family. It even had the iron fence around a raised front lawn contained by stone blocks about a foot tall. The house was three stories. I remembered it was out of place with its neighbors — a yellow and white fourplex converted from a more pleasant looking Victorian on one side, and smaller homes from the 1920s on the other side.

"Maybe he has a new girlfriend," I said. "Maybe he met someone at the memorial."

"That doesn't sound like a promising start to a relationship."

"Better than hooking up at a bar."

"I hate it when people post things you can't understand," I said.

"Why don't you call him?"

"That would be weird."

She nodded. I could tell she wanted to say something but decided it was better to keep things on this vague, emotionless plane where we could talk without really saying anything, putting words out there so both of us had a sense we were connecting, even if, on a much deeper level, we were both lying. If not lying, at least avoiding the truth. The truth that she didn't respect and support me, and the truth that I felt like there wasn't one single person on the face of the earth I was truly connected to, and maybe that was her fault. I didn't even feel connected to the two guys I had massaged that afternoon. I had touched almost every part of their bodies that it's appropriate to touch.

She stood up, admitting defeat in her face and posture. I scrolled to Dave's page and posted a comment.

Megan Miller *Motivated to do what?*

I fell asleep with my phone in my hand, tucked under my pillow. Giving a massage is hard work. People have no idea.

When I woke, I checked to see if Dave had answered. I'd had a dream that he was sitting on the edge of my bed telling me some long, boring story that I couldn't follow. There were four favorites on my comment. And Dave had answered, telling me absolutely nothing.

Dave Eddington *Finally doing what I should have done two years ago.*

I wasn't sure if he was working on his house, changing jobs, starting a new workout plan, or getting back together with Sara. The last possibility seemed unlikely, but who knows. Kimberly's death was having more impact than her life, and I think each of us was examining our status, no pun intended.

Kristen

KRISTEN THOMAS *IF you want to make a difference on the planet, check out this Kickstarter devoted to stemming the tide of human trafficking.*

9 favorites — 5 comments

Allie Sinclair *I admire your hard work.*
Kristen Thomas *Thanks. Did you look at Kickstarter?*
Allie Sinclair *Not yet.*
Seth Porter *That whole issue is blown out of proportion.*
Kristen Thomas *You have no idea what you're talking about, Seth. Get informed.*

THERE'S NOTHING LIKE a tragedy, and in this case, a double tragedy, to turn people inward and make them forget that the whole planet is a tragic place. After Kimberly died and Tiffany disappeared, AboutFace was littered with worries. Littered! All over the globe, people are dying. Disease and starvation blanket half the earth. Young girls and boys are kidnapped into slavery every single day, and no one notices, much less bothers to speak up or do anything to try to slow the tide of human suffering. But let a young, successful, college-educated white American girl die, or have a little

Christian baby doll go missing and they act like god himself is smiting our entitled group of "friends". Singling us out for particularly vicious treatment.

I post important, eye-opening information and it's virtually ignored. A cat video? — Well, that gets thousands, tens of thousands of favorites and comments. The human race has an incredible aptitude for feeling guilty about minutia and ignoring a person lying in the gutter in front of them.

At least most do. Amelia Loc seems to be missing the guilt gene entirely. Of course, there's always been something inhuman about her with that unearthly white skin and black hair and those pale, crystalline blue eyes. If you look at her for too long, you can get queasy. It feels like she's looking inside you, reading your thoughts. I'm not a person who imagines the supernatural hovering unseen around us, but the woman gives me the chills. The first time Jake introduced her to us, a shiver ran through my body. My first thought was that she'd put some sort of spell on him.

Ridiculous, I know.

But after overhearing what she said to Kimberly at the party, then seeing Kimberly floating in the swimming pool, my blood froze.

Running into Amelia at the mall was the last thing I wanted to happen. I would have expected her to shop further up the peninsula, at high-end stores, but there she was, in the center of Silicon Valley. She was rubbing elbows with middle-class teenagers, moms pushing overloaded strollers, and the unemployed, who cruise the mall in lieu of looking for work when they've pretty much given up on finding anything, because, let's face it — technology is draining the planet of jobs.

I was walking along, thinking about being late to the table I was helping to staff, handing out literature on human trafficking. It was set up in front of *Anthropologie*, which attracts the sort of shoppers who care about things like that. A shopper who cares about something besides the height of her heels or the name stamped in gold on her leather bag.

I blinked, glanced to my left at a little boy throwing a royal tantrum, and when I looked up, there was a woman with long dark hair walking ahead of me. The way she managed to take small steps but still move quickly told me it was either Amelia or her twin. I'd seen her walk across rooms and patios and restaurants enough to recognize her eerie gait. She hadn't come out of a store — I would have noticed. I suppose other shoppers had drifted into stores or down escalators, opening up the space between us. It wasn't as if she simply materialized, but it unsettled me, all the same.

Normally I would not go out of my way to say *hi*, she's just that odd and unapproachable. She makes it clear that she's more attractive, smarter, and basically more deserving than anyone. Except maybe Jake. But knowing what she'd said to Kimberly, I couldn't stop myself. All my friends, selfish as they are, were in knots over her suicide or accident or whatever it was, and Amelia bore some responsibility for that.

All of us say terrible things to each other at one time or another, but Amelia basically trashed Kimberly and rubbed her face in Jake's success, like he was some career and money-making guru and because of his affected, don't-give-a-shit attitude, he had the effing secret to life. Underneath it all was a tone that suggested Amelia was part of that inside track and the money was equally hers, and therefore, she had the right, the duty, to tell people how to live their lives. As if she, too, knew the *secret*, and anyone who listened to her, would duplicate the results.

I walked faster. I'm sure I looked like a rodent, scurrying up to a giraffe. I scooted around, turned, and stopped a few feet in front of her. "Amelia!"

She stopped and squinted as if she wasn't quite sure who I was. I've known the girl since before she and Jake were engaged, and she pretended I was the rodent I'd imagined. She towered over me. Her four-inch heels weren't all of it — she's at least five-eight, and I'm five-five. I tilted my head up a few inches. "Are you doing okay?"

"Oh, Kristen. Hi."

The crowd flowed around us, talking, the scent of the cookies clutched in their hands leaving a thick residue of sugar inside my nostrils.

"How are you?" she said.

"I'm fine. Are you doing okay?"

"Absolutely." She pulled her phone out of her bag and glanced at the screen.

"Don't feel bad about what you said to Kimberly. I'm sure there were other reasons she dove into the pool."

"What?" She squinted at me again, then back at her phone.

"The things you said to her, making Jake out to be a guru of some kind. That she wouldn't measure up unless she did something wild. I heard you talking to her."

"I didn't say any of that." She slid her phone back into the depths of her bag, but kept her hand on it, making it appear as if the purse had swallowed her forearm.

"Yes you did."

Her pale lips, dusted with a hint of nude gloss, curved slowly. "We were having a private conversation. She asked why Jake is so successful and I told her." She took a small step to her right.

A guy bumped into me, then circled around, brushing my arm. He didn't speak or glance back just continued his forward push. "You're remembering wrong. I was looking for tea, and you were standing right there in the dining room, so there was nothing private."

"I really need to get going."

I pulled a leaflet out of my bag and held it out to her. "I'm here to staff a booth building awareness for human trafficking."

"That's not something I can influence at all. I try to keep my resources focused. But thanks for your vote of confidence."

"No one can influence it if everyone ignores it."

"What are you, a little guilt farmer? Trying to make me feel bad about some chick that got drunk and jumped in the pool? And now this?"

"I'm not trying to make anyone feel guilty. If you feel guilt, it's because we're all connected, and you know we have a responsibility to care for others on the planet."

"I really need to get going." She pulled her hand out of her purse, still holding her phone. She held it up and studied the screen. She took a few steps back.

It was impossible to rattle her. I felt mean and fed up with callous people. I tried to think of something that would break through that smooth, hard shell. Everything cracks, if you hit hard enough.

"Does Jake know you helped cause her death?"

She shoved the phone in the front pocket of her glued-on jeans and glared at me, her lips curled, her eyes like granite. "I had nothing to do with her dying. We make our own choices. I do, she did. Jake does." Her voice lowered and turned into something thin and whispery and furious as if I'd torn through the screen she was hiding behind. "Not that I agree with his choices lately."

"Oh?"

"Never mind."

"Is he okay? Are things okay between you?"

"Those are incredibly personal questions and none of your damn business. I don't really know you, Kristen."

"We've known each other for over two years."

"But not well."

"Is there anything I can do to help?"

"No."

I expected her to start walking. Her body language suggested she wanted to, yet she remained.

"The best way to get past bad things is to get outside of yourself. You could come sit at the trafficking booth with me."

She laughed. "I don't need to get past anything. You jumped in front of me like some whack-job with a religious message. And now I'm late."

I stepped back. "You're free to go. Any time."

Those pale eyes bored into my forehead, looking for something, maybe for a way to pour her guilt back on me. Or maybe I'd been right the first time and she truly didn't have any awareness of her guilt.

As I studied her eyes, I began to feel as if she wasn't looking at me at all. If I was so annoying, why didn't she just walk away? She was right, we didn't know each other well at all. We'd been to lots of parties and dinners and Friday night pizza and beer gatherings, but we never talked about anything important.

"What do you think happened to Tiffany?" she said.

"I don't know."

"I think she took off and they should stop asking us questions."

"She wouldn't do that. She's devoted to her kids."

"Too devoted. It's phony. Women who drown themselves in their kids burn out."

"That's not true."

"You think she was kidnapped? Murdered?"

"Kidnapped, maybe. I hope . . ."

"Everyone wants it to be something they can accept — the Madonna, taken against her will, but still alive. We can't imagine her dead. And she certainly didn't *do* anything *bad.* Like run off with someone else."

"Did the detective talk to you?" We'd been standing there too long, I needed to get to my spot at the table, but now that she was talking, I couldn't bring myself to walk away. Shoppers surged around us, and I had the feeling we were standing waist-deep in water, waves crashing around our bodies, about to be dragged under any minute, but for now, managing to keep our feet planted in wet, eroding sand.

"Yes."

"What kinds of questions did he ask?"

"Trying to get inside Byron's head. Wanting to find out if he was abusive, perverted, angry, overwhelmed. He was almost salivating, hoping I'd give him some dirt."

I nodded. It must be so hard for Byron — scared, grieving, whatever he was feeling, and then accused of doing something unspeakable to the woman he loved. And yet, so many times, that's exactly what happened. "Do you have any dirt?"

She smiled. "Wouldn't you like to know."

I felt sick to my stomach, mostly for asking the question, but also at her triumphant smile. And it was triumphant. It's funny how you feel things like that. I couldn't even tell you what made it give off that message, but it did. Although that smile could also mean she felt my discomfort and just liked watching me feel miserable.

"It could have been someone else we know," she said. "Seventy-eight percent of the time, it's someone you know. I looked it up."

My body turned cold. Her white skin like snow and her eyes like a pale wintery sky, her words, and that smile still dancing across her lips, filled the mall, up to the cavernous ceiling, with an icy cold. I didn't believe it was Byron for a single second, no matter what the detective tried to imply when he asked me all those nasty questions. But this was something else.

"Do you think it is someone we know?"

"A guy who needs a woman he can control. Or a guy with a young girl fetish. She talks in that baby voice, and she has that little girl face. I could see all kinds of weird, insecure guys being drawn to a girl like that."

I moved the leaflet to my other hand. "I should get going."

"Not liking what I'm saying? It's the truth."

"I told them I'd be there at eleven."

"Go do your good deeds. And I bet you'll be thinking about all the men you know from a different perspective." She stepped around me. I didn't turn to watch her go.

AboutChat

**KRISTEN THOMAS: GROUP chat to Megan Miller
and Allie Sinclair** *I saw Amelia at the mall. She is so cold.*

Megan Miller *She never fit in with our group.*

Allie Sinclair *She's nice enough. I saw her the other day when I
went to check on Jake.*

Kristen Thomas *Well she gave me the chills. Literally. She
thinks someone we know took Tiffany.*

Allie Sinclair *Why does she think that?*

Kristen Thomas *That's usually how it is, statistically. But still,
no one we know is that weird. Or crazy. He'd have to be a lunatic, don't
you think?*

Allie Sinclair *Definitely.*

Megan Miller *We know lots of mildly creepy people. Amelia for
one, LOL. Adam is a little weird.*

Allie Sinclair *No comment!*

Kristen Thomas *LOL.*

Megan Miller *Dave can be a little strange sometimes. He posted
something creepy on my page.*

Kristen Thomas *What?*

Megan Miller *Not sure I should say. I made him delete it.*

Allie Sinclair *Don't do that! You brought it up . . .*

Kristen Thomas *Yeah.*

Megan Miller *He said Kimberly looked like a sleeping angel when her body was floating in Jake's pool.*

Kristen Thomas *Ewww.*

Allie Sinclair *Yuck. That's icky, but also sad.*

Kristen Thomas *Besides, what does an angel look like? That's nonsensical.*

Allie Sinclair *He can be a little off, but I'm sure he meant it nicely. Wanting to say she was in a better place.*

Kristen Thomas *You always look at the good side. I guess it could mean that, if she wasn't almost naked!*

Megan Miller *Word.*

Allie Sinclair *Well it's not like that makes him a complete psychopath.*

Megan Miller *Just a partial one, LOL.*

Kristen Thomas *Not sure that's funny, but I can't help laughing.*

Megan Miller *;)*

Byron

BYRON JONES *THANKS to all of you for your prayers, support, and faith.*

250 favorites — 113 comments

Allie Sinclair *Find Our Tiffany.*

Byron Jones *Thanks, Allie.*

Allie Sinclair *It would be great if you could post some comments on the page I set up. No pressure.*

Adam Jamison *Keeping the faith.*

Kristen Thomas *Hugs.*

Megan Miller *She'll be okay. I can feel it.*

Seth Porter *The cops are hard on it. They'll find her.*

Dave Eddington *She's an amazing woman — like an angel.*

Byron Jones *Hi everyone, thanks again.*

[See 104 more comments]

THE DOORBELL RANG. Both kids were asleep. Even though I wanted them to sleep, knowing they were calm because they were starting to adjust to life without their Mommy was a knife in my gut. They hadn't been asleep at the same time since Tiffany disappeared, and I did not need a doorbell waking them up.

I stepped over three trucks and a pile of Legos and other useless toys that entertained Paul for about twelve minutes at a time. All that stuff, and he was still bored. I guess we're all ungrateful like that. God keeps giving us more and more, and we still get bored and want the thing we can't have. For all these years I'd had everything, and all I'd wanted was more — more sex, a bigger house, a break from the kids and the mess. Now I wanted the mess. I wanted Tiffany in her robe and her sweats, putting a reheated casserole on the table. If I could close my eyes in bed and hear her breathing next to me, it would be enough. All those nights I hadn't even noticed how precious she was, how I couldn't complete a single thought without her in my life, and I'd hardly noticed because of wanting what I didn't have.

Through the front window, I saw Allie standing on the porch holding a casserole dish. It was great that everyone had been bringing food, but I was overloaded. We hadn't finished the lasagna or the cold cuts and bread and potato salad or the huge container of stew. I didn't want to toss it because I didn't know when the food train would stop. I didn't want to wash the pans and go through the effort of returning them. At the same time, I didn't like looking at all that foil-wrapped glass in the fridge, reminding me Tiffany was gone. Would the food spoil before they found her?

I unlocked the front door and opened it.

"Hi." Allie held out the casserole as if she was offering it instead of a hug, which was what I really needed. Not from her. I mean, I wasn't feeling something for her, I missed my wife. Every cell in my body missed my wife. I felt like my arms had been ripped out of their sockets. Nothing seemed real, even the heavy casserole dish I was now holding.

"It's tuna. Tiffany posted once that Paul loves it."

"He does." I walked to the kitchen and stood in front of the fridge. I hate tuna.

She followed me and opened the fridge. "It has seashell pasta, which I thought would be fun for him."

"It will."

"Shells. To go with the fish."

"Ha. Sure. Very clever." I bent over to put the casserole on the last empty shelf. It wasn't going to help him at all. He'd cry for Mommy after every single bite, if he even wanted to eat. Most likely he'd demand cereal, and I'd cave, and we'd eat Lucky Charms — two bowls for him, three for me. Ruth had adapted to the bottle. I wondered if Tiffany was uncomfortable with all that milk backed up . . . if she was feeling anything. For half a second, I couldn't breathe, as if my lungs were filled with cement. I straightened my back, still holding the pan.

"Is it too heavy?"

"No." I gasped for air. "I got it." I shoved it in. The glass scraped the plastic shelf in a way that didn't sound good. I slammed the door.

"Are you okay?" she said.

I stared at her.

"I mean, you . . . I thought you . . ."

"I'm fine."

"I can't imagine how you're feeling." She stepped toward me, then turned toward the living room.

"I'm numb." To tell the truth, I envied Paul and Ruth who could scream and cry, but if I was given the chance to do the same, I'm not sure I could.

"Did you eat tonight?" She leaned her hip against the sink. "I could heat something up for you. Some tuna."

"That's okay. Now that both kids are sleeping, I just want to sit down."

"What can I do?"

I walked into the living room. I collapsed on the recliner and kicked it back. She sat on the edge of the couch, artfully arranging her feet around the ocean of Legos.

"Nothing, really. The casserole is great. Thank you. Tiffany's parents are coming up this evening. They kept putting it off because getting in the car and making the drive meant she hadn't been found, and being here will mean she hasn't been found, helping with the kids means she's still missing. And she might . . ." Allie looked like she was going to cry. "Sorry," I said.

"No, no. Don't say you're sorry. It's okay, it's okay."

"Anyway, they'll stay with the kids so I can go into the deli. My night manager has been covering everything for me."

"Does the detective have any ideas? Anyone they suspect, anything?"

"If he does, I'm not in on it. At least they've sort of stopped thinking I killed her and chopped her up and put her in the deep freeze at the deli. Sort of."

"Don't!"

"That's how they make it sound."

"They don't think that at all."

"You haven't heard the questions they asked me."

She stood. "Are you sure I can't heat up some food? You look so tired."

"I am, but it's not from lack of food."

"You need to eat."

"I'm fine. I can't eat right now, okay. I'll eat when Tiff's parents get here."

"I know they'll find her."

"They have nothing."

She sat down. "It would be great if you would post more on the Find Tiffany page. I think it would inspire people. It might help."

"Inspire them to do what?"

"I don't know. Maybe she said something to one of us that we've forgotten because it meant nothing at the time, but it might give a hint . . ."

"Allie. There aren't any *hints*." I thought about the last time we'd made love. I'd felt her body shake, crying without making a sound. How does that make a guy feel, knowing your wife is sobbing when you're trying to get her excited? Maybe I really did make her sick. I shouldn't have ignored her. I thought she was just over-tired, that if I hurried, she'd be happy. Maybe I made her so sick, she didn't care if she walked away with nothing, not even her shoes. She just wanted out.

"I don't know what you're thinking," Allie said. "But stop."

I folded my arms and stared her down. "What am I thinking, Ms. Clairvoyant?"

"You have to be positive. The answer might be right in front of us. I just feel it."

I laughed again. "You feel it? How does that work?"

"We can't give up."

"I know God has a plan. For me, for the kids. For Tiffany. I just wish He'd let me in on it."

"Have you read everything on the Find Tiffany page? Lots of people are with you. All that energy, all that love. All these people praying. They'll find her."

"I wish I could believe that. But it's been five days! And there's nothing. Not even a hair. All they have is their disgusting suspicions about what an evil person I am."

"The detective is talking to everyone we know. It could be anyone. Who knows what people are really like. You think you know them . . ." She got up and knelt on the floor. She scooped up a handful of Legos and dropped them in the blue tub where Paul is supposed to put them, but never does. Tiffany has to sit on the floor with him and pick one up and then he picks one up. It takes forever. And right now, I wasn't in the mood for cheering him on by gathering Legos like shells on the beach. Allie crept toward the couch, plucking them off the carpet as she went. When she had a bulging handful of blue and yellow and red and white bricks, she leaned toward the tub and dropped them in. They clattered against the hard plastic sides. She continued to make her way around the carpet. I should have helped her or thanked her, but I didn't care. Not really. Let her pick up, maybe it made her feel useful. She seemed to need to feel needed, even if setting up an AboutFace page was completely useless.

"Did you see what Dave wrote on your page? About Tiffany being an angel?"

"Yeah. He thinks she's dead."

"No he doesn't."

"That's what he meant. Why else would he use that word? Angel."

"Megan said he posted something kind of weird."

"What's that?"

"He said that Kimberly looked like a sleeping angel in the pool."

"That's effed up."

"Megan called him on it, and he deleted it." She sat back and reached into the Lego tub. She fished through and pulled out a handful of rectangular red bricks. She lined six of them up on the coffee table and pressed on a second row, overlapping them like a real brick wall. "I don't know why these things are so appealing," she said. "You can't help wanting to build something. I guess because it's easy."

"Those are, but some of the pre-set configurations, airplanes and spaceships, you need an engineering degree to figure them out. I don't know why they make them for little kids."

"I should get some. For my students."

"Kids outgrow them by the time they're ten."

"I haven't outgrown them." She dug in the bucket for more reds and extended her wall about six inches, then started building it up. "It might help them relax when they get frustrated with a concept they can't understand."

Although I didn't necessarily want to talk about Tiffany, I wanted even less to talk nonsense about Legos and her tutoring students. The attempt to distract me was insulting. Like I was an easily misled toddler.

I thought about Dave's recently revealed angel fetish and his chili. The pot was still on the counter. Tiffany had washed it but never returned it. It kind of bugged me that he'd brought us dinner. His dinner implied I should have been doing more to help out around the house. Or at least that's what it seemed like. Maybe the guy was creepier than I realized. He was so obsessed with re-modeling that house. It had been two years since Sara took off. Why did she leave, anyway? He said the remodeling broke them up — *Ha ha* — *just like they say, if your marriage can withstand a remodel, it can withstand anything. And mine didn't. Ha ha.* Or something like that. I remembered it still, after all this time, because it seemed like he was laughing that his wife left him.

Maybe I'd take the bean pot back and have a chat with him. It would give me something to do. Like Allie said, we had to do something. The detective thought I was scum, and I guess he thought I was so dumb I didn't notice the scruffy-looking cop watching my house, rotating with another cop every four hours, one phony disguise to another.

Dave

AS I LISTENED to my mom describe her hospital stay for the third time, now enhanced with news from the post-surgery check-up, I looked out the front window and thought about opening a beer. As she talked on, my mind took a quick departure to Kimberly in the swimming pool.

I think I'd dreamt about her, more than once. I didn't remember any of the dreams in detail, but when I woke up, the image was clouding my head. Throughout the day, that last view of her body appeared out of nowhere. Always at the wrong time. Like while I was supposed to be listening to my mom. I tried to stop the thoughts, but that made them more vivid. I had this thing on the back of my neck, stretching its fingers into my brain. It was bad enough fantasizing about a woman who was a friend, but remembering the appearance of a corpse and feeling my body take notice disgusted me. Every time the memory of how she looked floated through my mind, unwanted and unwelcome, I loathed myself more. Twice, I'd come close to vomiting. But I couldn't seem to make it stop.

If I could get naked with the love of my life, feel that soft skin, then, the memory of Kimberly's body would go away. But it wasn't possible, yet. Luring a woman in until she's entranced with you takes time and a lot of effort. I know that. Dinners, music, time outside doing things like hiking, or whatever. Talking. And listening. I had to remember to listen. That's how I blew it the last time.

"What do you think I should do?"

"What? Sorry, Mom. I think I walked into a dead zone. Can you say that again?"

She sighed and seemed to change subjects, forgetting she had a question.

Sara had always said I talked too much. Even when I wasn't talking, she could tell I was talking in my head, not listening to her. I don't know how she knew that. The ability to read my mind, I guess, but she was wrong. Sure, I thought about whether I agreed or disagreed with what she was saying, and I noted the points she'd left out of a particular explanation. Of course my mind wandered sometimes, like it was wandering while my mom talked, but I listened. I looked Sara right in the eye, faced her head on like women prefer, and I listened.

Yes, sometimes I talk a lot, but I have a lot to say.

Most of the time, people don't listen to *me*. I'm a pretty smart guy with a lot of experience, and I could help them out if they would quit complaining and listen to solid advice. People like to complain. I wonder if they really want to fix their problems or they just like whining. Take bitching about your boss, for example. If the guy's an asshole, get a new boss. Find another job, don't sit there day in and day out griping as if it's your favorite pastime, grinning with how much you enjoy pointing out his stupidity. Complaining over and over about the same thing is stupid in itself. Get a fucking grip and look for another job. It's not that hard. But they won't listen to me. They talk over me, they revert back as if they're salmon and they gotta swim up that stream again, no matter how tough it is, because it's programmed into their DNA. They gotta fight and struggle, and they can't even hear you telling them to Shut. The. Fuck. Up.

After my mom finished telling all her recent stories, we said good-bye.

I made two turkey sandwiches and filled two glasses with red wine. It wasn't quite dinner time, but close enough. I figured the wine would help loosen the conversational flow. It usually does. Although it can make me a motor mouth, so I planned to limit myself to a few sips, and make sure she had plenty. With a little wine in her blood, she'd talk, and she'd know I was listening.

I put everything on a cookie sheet. I didn't have any trays.

Climbing the stairs, stopping at the door that leads to the second staircase, opening it, walking up the next flight that turns at a right angle, is a bitch when you're carrying a cookie sheet with two glasses of wine.

I put the tray on the exposed plywood floor and took the key out of my pocket. I unlocked the door and pushed it open. I carried the tray inside and set it on the dresser. I removed the duct tape from Tiffany's mouth, and she turned on me like a mountain lion, screaming so fiercely I flinched.

"Get me out of here!"

I glanced at the window. It was nailed shut, taped with thick plastic, but my knee-jerk reaction was to quadruple check.

"Let me go! My baby is starving without her Mommy. My little boy . . . My husband needs me! What's he going to do without me?"

She had that last part right — Byron was not a guy who was built to hold it together. The guy knew about football and baseball — he was a self-appointed expert on the subjects — but that was about it. Everything else out of his mouth was one meaningless statement after another. Ninety percent of the time, he parroted someone else. He didn't deserve her. Deep down, she knew that. I saw it in the sweet, hungry look on her face, and I read it in her status updates. She only stayed with him because she thought that's what God required, until recently. Once she posted that command to take what was ours, I knew she was looking at the world differently. I knew she realized that God had a much more lenient view than most of his followers believed. She and I were perfect for each other. I could be the father to those kids. We'd have kids of our own. We'd fill my three-story Victorian house with little kids. I could see them already.

"What do you want?" Her voice was almost a howl.

I worried it would carry through the glass and plastic and drift to the street below, catching the attention of someone who was far too interested in the neighbors' business.

"God punishes those with evil plans!" She punctured the words with an inhuman wailing.

It was time to stop the whispering. I don't know why I'd been hiding my identity from her. It was a mistake. I saw that now. She had to get to know me as a different person — as her lover. She had to recognize me as her closest friend and her soul mate. Besides, she wouldn't hear my whisper above that awful sound.

"Tiffany." Her name sounded like a beautiful crystal bowl on my lips. Without warning, the image of Kimberly's naked body flickered past my eyes. I shook my head. I staggered into the hall and took a deep breath. I went back into the room and shut the door.

"I know your voice," she said. "Who are you? What's wrong with you?"

I hurried out of the room and thumped down the stairs. A full bottle of wine might be necessary to calm her down, to help her gain some perspective. I thought about rolling a joint, that always helped me when I was stressed out, but I was pretty sure that wasn't on her list of approved substances.

Back inside the third-floor room, I set the bottle on the dresser. It was the only other piece of furniture besides the bed and a wooden chair where I sat when I watched her sleep. It felt like I was at the gates of heaven, seeing all that beautiful milk seep out of her breasts. It made me want to go rescue the kids immediately, but it was too soon. I needed Tiffany on my side first.

While I'd been downstairs getting the wine bottle, all the rage had leaked out of her. Now she whimpered. She'd twisted her body sideways, turning her back toward me. The shirt over her head kept her from seeing me, yet still, she didn't want to face me. That hurt. I didn't know why I'd blindfolded her. It had seemed the right thing to do at the time, but now I wondered whether it had turned her against me.

The bed creaked as she wriggled around, working to get comfortable, which was impossible with her wrists and ankles taped. That part was necessary. Until she let go of the false obligation she felt toward Byron, I had to keep her contained.

I stepped closer to the bed and touched the back of her neck with my fingertips. She shivered. Her skin was damp. Stroking the soft part of her neck, feeling her sweat, excited me. All the thoughts of Kimberly's white skin and even whiter thong slipped out of my head like a piece of fabric sinking beneath the surface of a lake. I opened my hand and placed it over her neck. The warmth charged through me. I untied the shirt covering her face and pulled it away.

She didn't turn toward me.

I couldn't see if her eyes were open. "It's me," I said.

"I know."

I hadn't realized my voice was that distinctive. Or was she lying? Trying to get the upper hand? I'd forgotten that about women. It was easy to assume they were being straight with you, but in reality, it's impossible to know what they're thinking. Ever. Even when they're talking, they might be thinking something else entirely. At least that's how it was with Sara, and I had no reason to think Tiffany was any different.

Sara had been standing right next to me, choosing tile for the first-floor bathroom — an icy white that would be split with a narrow royal blue tile for contrast. The next day, she was standing in the middle of the living room, telling me she was leaving. At first, I didn't believe her. Then my lunch came out all over the new hardwood floor that I'd handcrafted myself, with her by my side.

Despite Tiffany lying in bed for several days without combing or washing her hair, it was still soft. I stroked it. Her neck stiffened as she tried to move her head closer to the wall. I put my hand on her shoulder and tugged gently to pull her onto her back. I wanted her to look at me. After all these hours of not wanting her to see, I wanted her eyes on me, looking at my face and understanding how much I loved her. "I have some food for you."

"I'm not hungry."

"And a glass of wine."

"No. Thanks."

I took my hand away and sat in the chair. "You said God promised that wherever we stepped, it would belong to us."

"You're completely misinterpreting it. Besides, that message is for His children."

"I'm His child."

"You're not."

"I thought He accepted everyone."

"You have to repent."

"I haven't done anything I need to repent for."

She flopped onto her back and twisted her neck to face me. "Are you out of your mind?"

"Why did you post that verse?"

"I don't even remember. But you don't get to take another human being. I have children. And a husband."

"You don't seem very happy with your husband."

"I adore my husband. No marriage is perfect. Although I suppose I can thank you for that. God did have a purpose here. I've had time to think about how much I love my husband. And now God will rescue me from your evil plans."

"You make me sound like a monster."

She closed her eyes.

"Please eat something. It's been hours." I stood and picked up half of her sandwich. I held the corner near her lips, but she refused to open her mouth. I touched the bread to her bottom lip. It was so soft, so creamy. I wanted to kiss her, but she needed to eat.

"I don't want it."

I put it back on the plate. I leaned down and brushed my lips across hers. Again, I felt her neck stiffen, but she didn't turn her head.

I picked up my glass of wine and took several long swallows. "Should we talk?"

"No."

"I want to know how you're feeling."

"I'm angry. And scared, if you really want to know."

This was good. I took another sip of wine. It was like magic, asking a woman how she felt. The whole atmosphere of the room began to soften as she opened up to me.

"What are you scared of?"

"You."

"There's no reason to be scared. I love you."

Tears spilled out of her eyes and slithered across her round, firm cheeks. They were bright red, whether from rubbing on the flannel shirt or crying, I wasn't sure.

"I'm not scary at all." Her sweet mouth and her huge, questioning eyes made me feel I could tell her about every dark thing inside of me. Or maybe it was the wine. I swallowed the rest and refilled my glass. "We should get to know each other more intimately," I said.

"I know all I need to."

"There are a lot of things you don't know about me."

"I don't want to hear your ugly secrets."

"A couple should share everything. That's how you get closer, and stay close. That, and making love."

"We're not a couple. Not now, not ever."

"You'll see."

Her stomach growled. She twisted on the bed, an ungraceful move, making her appear like a large fish flopping on the pier, helpless to return to its habitat. The same impression I had of Kimberly when her soaking wet body was lying on the concrete.

I moved the chair right up next to the bed. I touched one of her toenails. It had snagged on the sheets. I'd file it for her, and tell her how I knew all about her bohemian side. She couldn't hide that from me. She wasn't even trying to hide it, with those toenails. "I'm not as tough as I come across," I said.

She closed her eyes. I took that as a signal to keep talking, that she wanted to hear the sound of my voice without looking at me, without noticing that I was unbound and she was still immobilized. Not for long. Once she heard more about me, her heart would grow tender. Once she understood the need I had for her, for love, for a family, she'd welcome me into her arms.

Tiffany

DAVE WOULD NOT shut up, which made it impossible for me to think through how I could convince him to let me go. There was one thing I didn't have to think about — he'd lost his sanity. He was rambling and drinking wine, hardly taking a breath between words. He was going to finish the entire bottle himself.

I really was hungry, but not about to admit it to him.

I remembered the day he brought the chili over. Something hadn't felt right, and of course, I'd ignored it. He'd stood in my kitchen and wouldn't leave. He was very intense, his eyes jittering in their sockets. I felt he'd wanted me to invite him to stay.

I had no idea why the Lord was subjecting me to this. So far, one good thing that had come out of it was realizing how very much I loved Byron. I saw how silly my objections to him were. I feared my realization had come too late and I started to cry. What he called me didn't matter! It was his pet name. It didn't mean *anything*. Right then, I would have died to hear his voice calling me *Mommy*, feeling him touch me. But I'd learned my lesson. Wasn't it time for the Lord to rescue me? Maybe Dave had put something stupid on AboutFace and someone would figure it out. The Lord would lead them to me, I had to keep having faith. I had to. Dave didn't notice I was crying. He was going on about his redecorating plans for the room where I was his prisoner.

He actually thought we were going to be a couple! He kept saying he loved me, kept touching me, trying to kiss me. I'd thought a stranger taking me was scary. This was worse.

The plaster walls were pockmarked, and the floor was nothing but rough, bare wood. The window was framed in splintered, semi-rotted wood and the glass was cloudy behind a sheet of thick clear plastic, duct-taped to the wall. I'd never seen this part of his house, and now I understood why. Lying there, listening to him drone on, looking at the plastic and the gutted room, I wondered about Sara. He told all of us she left without any warning. But what if . . . I started to cry harder. My lips shook, and for a moment, I couldn't breathe.

Even though I didn't want to say one word to him, thinking he'd be more likely to let me go without hurting me as soon as he realized his insane, delusional plan wasn't going to work, I couldn't help myself. "Why did you stop remodeling?"

"She left. Sara. It was our project together, building our life together and she walked out before it was done. I was doing it for her. What's the point of a nice home without a family to fill the rooms?"

"Where did she go?"

"You have no idea what it's like to have the one person you love treat you like you don't even matter, like you're so uninteresting and so repulsive she can't look at you for another minute."

"That doesn't give you the right to kidnap me. Stealing me like I'm a used car."

"Everyone leaves me. At least they want to. But you won't. You're a godly woman, a devoted woman. You also have your wild side, and that's why I knew you didn't belong with him."

"What are you talking about?"

"Your toenails. They're very sexy, all long and pointy like that."

"That's gross."

"Not at all. They turn me on."

I felt sick to my stomach. "Were you married to someone else before Sara?"

"No."

"You said everyone wants to leave you."

"I meant my father. He didn't walk out, but he didn't want anything to do with me."

"I'm sorry."

He took a long gulp of wine.

"Maybe his father didn't teach him how to be a good Daddy," I said.

"Ha. He was disgusted with me. My mother had to go and blab to him that I wet the bed a few times. He doesn't like weak boys. Bedwetters."

"Well, I . . ."

"If his son were gay, he'd kill him on the spot. If he even had the suggestion of being a pansy."

"Is that what's wrong? Byron wondered if you might be

gay. He . . ."

"I'm not! I proved I'm not. How can you even think that? I'm not."

"Don't yell."

"I beat up a gay kid once. Well, not really beat up, but pushed him in a garbage can after school where everyone threw the food they didn't eat. It was hot, and it stunk like sour milk. Why would I do that if I was gay? Don't ever say that. Byron doesn't know shit about me. Maybe he's gay!"

"Okay. Calm down."

"I feel bad about it now, but after that, they knew I wasn't gay."

"God can help you if you have those urges."

He stood and grabbed the wine bottle. He waved it in front of him. I shut my eyes as he swung it close to my face.

After a minute, I peeked. He'd moved away. His body swayed, then steadied. He poured some wine into his glass even though it wasn't empty. He took a drink and sat down again.

"I don't have *urges*! I adore women. Not women . . . you. I adore you. I want you. But my dad, I think he thought I was. Although he didn't kill me, so maybe not. But he felt it, he felt I wasn't right. He . . . and Byron, he doesn't know what the hell he's talking about. He's a moron."

"Why are you telling me this? Just let me go. Can't you see this isn't how you find love?"

"You belong to me. You might not know it yet, but you'll

see. You're not disgusted with me."

I wanted to say I was. He absolutely disgusted me, far beyond, worlds beyond how I'd felt when Byron said those things to me. I stayed quiet.

"I deserve happiness too. Every day, every fucking *hour,* I have to look at pictures of your kids, of everyone's kids, comments on AboutFace telling me how happy everyone is, how wonderful their spouse is, how crazy in love they are. Every fucking day."

"Don't use that language."

"I know you're pure, I'll try to work on that. But do you know how that is? It's like the whole world is happy, shouting in my face how happy they are. There's an endless parade, a flood of pictures and love and good times running past my eyes. They never even think about how it feels to be me. It's like social media was invented to make people feel like shit about their lives. It's high school digitized and preserved forever — *I'm with the jocks, I have more friends than you. I get the inside jokes, I have fans, I have so many favorites I can't keep track of them. I'm a success* — *Loser.* I make comments and try to be happy for my friends, and they don't even acknowledge the effort that requires. They joke back and forth with each other and ignore my input completely. It's like I'm standing in a room, surrounded by beautiful women, and adorable kids, and successful guys, and everyone is talking over me, and I keep trying to say something, tell my story, and they interrupt and plow right over. I don't even exist. The other day I posted a picture of the inlaid wood I did on my living room floor. No one said a word and no one clicked favorite. No one!"

"Did you put a comment so they'd know what it was?"

"That's not the point."

He rambled on about other examples of how he'd been ignored on AboutFace. Jealousy was making his bones rot, exactly as the Bible says.

When he took a breath, I said, "You shouldn't be jealous. The Bible says we should shun envy and strife."

"Fuck the Bible!"

"Don't say that!"

"Sorry. I get upset."

He didn't seem to notice I could hardly move, that my wrists hurt and I felt dirty and so scared. Talk about being ignored at a party. I felt like I'd been cornered by the crazy uncle and I was going to be stuck there all night with him spewing sewage breath and spittle all over me.

"No one pays attention to me, no one thinks about whether they're hurting my feelings or making me feel bad. They act like they're all better friends with each other and if I disappeared, they wouldn't even notice. Since you disappeared, there's all this stuff about you, they go on and on about how much they miss you, how scared they are, they even have a special page for you."

He didn't pause, so I didn't have a chance to interrupt. Not that I necessarily wanted to. I was afraid of making him angrier. One part of me felt a little sorry for him, but mostly

I wanted him to wake up from whatever crazy world he was living in and let me go home. I'd never complain about Byron again. Never.

The blue comforter underneath me was making me hot. I twisted to my side. The bed creaked as if there were ten people moving around.

"What are you doing?"

"I'm hot. My arms hurt. I can't move. When are you going to untie me?"

"Don't you understand? I deserve a loving wife. I deserve a family like everyone else."

"I'm sure you'll find someone."

"I have." He slurped the wine. "You." His lips were stained dark by the wine. It looked as if he had blood in his mouth.

"I'm married," I said. Inside my head, I was screaming — *I don't love you. I liked you okay before, but now I hate you. I know God still wants me to love you as one of His creatures, but I hate your guts. You're a pig, and you make me want to barf.*

Little dribbles of milk trickled from my nipples. Just like it always comes out when I'm upset. Even though it had pretty much been leaking out constantly, there was less seeping through my clothes, and I was going to start drying up. When he let me go, if he let me go . . . I might never be able to nurse Ruth again. I started crying again.

"Don't cry. I hate that."

"I can't help it."

"Women cry to manipulate men."

"I'm crying because I'm upset. I miss my baby. Maybe if you cried a little, you wouldn't have all these bad feelings locked inside of you."

"Crying wouldn't make my feelings go away."

"It would give you a new perspective."

"Men don't cry."

"Yes they do."

"You're telling me Byron cries when life isn't going the way he wants?"

"He's cried before." That wasn't true, but I knew that he would cry. He was probably crying now, alone in our bed. I got it, that men don't want to show their weak side, but I was sure he was crying, scared that I was dead. So I didn't feel like I was lying.

"What for? Why did he cry?"

"That's personal."

"Easy way out. I don't believe you. Men, real men, don't cry. We're logical, and we know that bad things happen."

"You just told me you get upset about what people put on AboutFace. That's emotional. It never made you feel like crying?"

"Never. It pisses me off." He stood. "I don't want to talk about this. It's all going to change now. I'll have fun on AboutFace like everyone else. I'll have a family to post pictures of, I'll put new updates about my remodeling. I already bought supplies. I'm ready to get started. You can help, and I'll teach Paul how to use a hammer."

He sat on the edge of the bed and put his hand on my leg. The hair had grown a lot while I was lying on the bed for all this time. I didn't like his hand feeling the rough hair on my leg, but it made me sick, thinking that I cared one bit about his reaction. I didn't. But I still didn't like it. I wanted to tell him to get his hand off me. I wanted to thrash around and hit his back with my knees or elbows, but it was too hard. If I moved too much, my dress would slide up my thighs. He might get excited and try to have sex with me. What if he said I'd be a good Mommy for his kids? I bit down on my tongue for a few seconds so I wouldn't scream, or worse. "I can't help with your remodeling if I'm all taped up."

"I know. And when I see that you've accepted my love, I'll take off the straps."

"How long is that going to be? And how will you know?"

"I'll know."

"What are you going to do to me if I never love you?"

"You will."

The particles of dust in the air seemed to draw closer together, thickening around me. At the same time, my breasts were softer, and I realized the milk was starting to retreat back into my body, waiting for my next child. If there ever was one.

Jake

MY LEAVE OF ABSENCE from AboutFace had resulted in a human assault. First, Allie came over and spent nearly an hour conferring with Amelia. A day or two later, Megan stopped by to ask whether I wanted a freebie massage, to relax me, to make me *feel whole again*. It didn't occur to her that my world-class, so-called nest egg meant I didn't need freebies. For anything. Still, I appreciated her offer. Since she was already there, I let her give me a ten-minute shoulder rub. I had to admit it did take my mind out of the pit where it had been spinning. She lifted it gently to a different plane as if her hands actually shoved cells back up to my brain, cells that had slipped out of place and lodged themselves in my neck and shoulders.

When the bell rang a second time that same day, I thought about staying put and letting Amelia deal with it. But if the aftermath of Allie's visit was any indication, all that would accomplish was opening me up to more berating about how depressing I was, how I'd turned into someone she didn't recognize, how she was getting tired of it. Fine. She knew the location of the front door.

I pulled on a t-shirt and shoved my feet into flip-flops. I started down the stairs. Light spilled through the back windows, across the main hallway, causing the whole thing to glow like a mystical palace. Maybe I was about to be given the secrets of the universe. But I'd already learned the prime secret of the universe — death. Nothing matters like we think it does because all paths lead to death. As I put my foot on the floor, the glowing room filled me with a strange and startling hope. The benches that lined the hallway glistened and the white tile floor, streaked with grayish blue, pulsed with life.

I opened the door. Byron stood on the front patio. I clenched the door, wanting to close it before he spoke. But his unwashed hair and his red eyelids told me he was in worse shape than I was.

"I think Dave has Tiffany," he said.

"Why would you think that?" I opened the door wider so he could step inside.

He walked across the threshold, which is flush with the patio, nothing but a strip of polished wood that's seamlessly fitted between the patio and hall tile.

I turned and walked to the entertainment room. At least we could sit there without that damn pool staring at me like a big grinning mouth sloshing water around, ready to spit at me. I offered him the gray leather chair, the twin of one next to it facing the TV screen. I sat on the couch.

"Do you want a drink?"

He shook his head.

"What makes you think Eddington has anything to do with it? And a more pertinent question, why are you telling me?"

"I wanted to bounce it off someone."

"Shouldn't that someone be the detective who's investigating?"

"Someone I know."

"The cops should . . ."

"I'm not going to talk to him right now."

"Why not?"

"He acts like they've already decided it's me. They asked me things that are so bad, I couldn't imagine them. I'm missing my wife, I'm scared for her, and instead, I get this?"

"That sucks."

"I thought I'd have a chat with Dave myself."

"If he did something like that, if he actually took her, and I find that extremely hard to believe, he could be dangerous."

Byron laughed. "He's a wuss. I don't think he did something to hurt her or anything. He's just playing games. Trying to torment me."

"Why the hell would he do that?"

"I started thinking about stuff he's done. Comments he's made online. He brought us dinner a while back."

"So?"

"He came over when I wasn't home, showed up at seven-thirty in the morning when she wasn't even dressed."

"That doesn't mean anything."

"I just started thinking about how he looks at her. Allie said he posted something about Kimberly looking like an angel when she was dead! He called Tiffany an angel."

"No shit. Well . . . are you . . ."

"Don't go there."

"You think he just walked off with her and he has her in his house? You don't think he killed her, do you?"

He started crying. Tears ran down his face. He started gasping. "I said don't go there."

I'd never seen a guy cry. It was awful — his face contorted, his lips quivering. I wanted to punch him to make him stop. But if I did that, he might cry harder. What was crying going to accomplish? He should get a grip, keep that shit to himself. I looked away. I really wanted a drink. I stood. "Hey, dude. Stop."

"I can't help it."

"You can. I know you can. Get pissed or something. I'm sure she's okay. Especially if Eddington has her. He might say weird shit, but like you said, he's a wuss. She's fine. It's just hard to think about a guy you know doing something that fucked up."

"The more I think about Sara leaving . . . that would make any guy go a little nuts, don't you think? To have his wife walk out on him? And I started thinking back about how he was in school, even fatter than now. That probably didn't help him grow up feeling great about himself. And I remembered how he always kind of smelled like urine. And he thought no one noticed."

I sat down again. "You should tell the detective. Really."

"Not gonna happen. If you go with me. We could just get

her back."

"How does that work? Like a rescue mission? We're Batman and Robin?"

"It won't be that hard. He might even give her up. He won't have the guts to stand up to both of us."

I folded my arms across my chest. They felt soft. The muscle had grown mushy since I hadn't been working out. I did not want to be involved in this. And even with all that he said, he didn't know for sure. It was a wild guess based on a few weird comments. It did look odd, putting all those things next to each other. I could partially see why he was thinking the way he was. But it was a job for the detective. Byron should give all those stories over to him. If Dave really did have Tiffany, he was out of his mind. And no matter how much you think a guy is weak or easy to intimidate, a madman is something different altogether. "Yeah, I really don't think we should do that," I said.

"I need your help! She . . . who knows what he's done to her."

"Exactly. If it's true, and that's an enormous *IF*, you don't know what you're dealing with. The detective . . ."

He leaped out of the chair and came toward me. "I'm not talking to that fucking detective." His breath reeked, and I could feel the heat of his skin. Talk about a madman. I'd never heard him use a cuss word in the entire twenty years I'd known him. And then he hauls out the big guns. It made me wonder if he cursed all the time in his head and just bit his tongue. The word sure was right there, ready to roll. Or maybe when you get in a state like he was in, you finally realize the inadequacy of normal language. Cursing is more readily available, more helpful than pleading with an invisible god. "Hey. Calm down." I put my hand up.

He knocked my hand out of the way, turned, and walked around the chair. He grabbed the back like he wanted to pick it up and hurl it at the TV.

"Steady," I said.

"Don't patronize me."

"Okay, okay. Just get a grip. If you want to go over there, that's cool. Just be careful. Okay? Be careful. Maybe sleep on it. He could be dangerous."

He laughed. "Not as dangerous as me."

He had a point, but he scared me. I wondered if I should call the detective. I really didn't want to get involved.

A few minutes later, he left. I went into the kitchen and mixed a martini. By the time Amelia came home, I was pleasantly numb and not concerned about Byron at all. She immediately started in on me. I really sort of hoped she'd just leave for good, but she seemed to be hunkering down — she had four shopping bags with her.

Dave

DAVE EDDINGTON *THINGS are coming along more slowly than I thought, but making progress.*
    10 favorites — 3 comments

Allie Sinclair *What things?*
Megan Miller *I hate it when people make cryptic comments.*
Adam Jamison *It's a mystery. He wants us to think.*

WHEN IT WAS dark enough for the stars to start popping out, I turned off the light in Tiffany's room. I could just make out her body, curled like a large fetus. I took off my clothes and left them on the floor. I slid beneath the sheet, pressing myself close to her on the narrow bed. The minute my body touched hers, she began crying her little heart out.

The stiffness of her muscles, her back like a steel rod, told me to go away. She wasn't yielding to me at all. How long was it going to take? I stroked her arm, but she cried harder. I propped myself on my elbow and leaned down to pull the blanket over us. The air was thick and heavy from the warm weather. The room smelled of dirty clothes and sour milk and greasy hair. I didn't mind. It was like those uncut toenails, sexy in their lack of effort to be sexy. As I ran my fingers through her hair, grease coated my skin. I needed to bathe her, but I was pretty sure she would thrash around and resist me every step of the way, so I'd been holding off on that.

I put my hand on her stomach, trying to soothe her with my steadiness and the strength of my touch, but she sobbed harder.

"I want my babies. They need me. How can they live without their Mommy?!"

I moved my hand to her forehead, and she settled down a bit, gasping for air, so maybe she only settled because she was having trouble breathing. She was stubborn and willful, and I knew the Bible told her to submit. "Tiffany, honey. Once you calm down, the babies will join us. There's no reason to cry."

She started up again, moaning this time.

I slithered down until I was curled near the lower part of her legs. I put my finger on the nail of her big toe and felt the sharp point and thought about that jerk she was currently married to. How dare he accuse me of being gay. He knew nothing about me. I was so attracted to Tiffany, it was difficult to restrain myself. He was making wild accusations because he wanted to make me look bad in her eyes. He wanted to belittle my effort to help out with dinner. Did he ever help around the house? I was sure he did not. He didn't deserve her. Eventually, she'd recognize that.

I thought she'd wear herself out and fall asleep so I could get a few hours of rest, but she had endless stores of energy available for berating me and crying and feeling sorry for herself. Then, she turned her back on God.

"Why are You doing this to me? I was a good mother. I *am* a good mother. I love Byron, I showed him that in so many ways! Why Lord? Why are You punishing me? Are You even there? Can You hear me? None of Your promises are true! You've abandoned me. Oh, why? Why? Please help me." Her body shook, and I felt as if the sound of her despair escaped from her lungs, through the spaces between her ribs, and flooded my body.

It amazed me that she could get so angry at a Being she couldn't see, who didn't speak back or make Himself known in any tangible way. She bragged to God again that she'd been a devoted wife. She admitted she wasn't perfect, although she didn't go into detail. I was curious about that, but also angry. How dare Byron ever say one word against her. She was showing him to be more and more undeserving with each thing she said.

"I adore my children. They're my whole heart. I'm teaching them your Word, don't you want that?" She went on about how she told people about His love for them and their need to repent and trust Him. Then, she screamed over and over — *Why are You doing this to me?*

There was no answer of course. I didn't think God was doing anything at all to her. I'd rescued her from that clueless creep. It was taking her longer than I'd expected to recognize how much better her life was going to be with my love and attention and care. She'd grow to adore my beautiful home, designed for a family, so much better than that shack they crammed themselves into.

BEFORE THE SUN rose, before it got too hot to work, I was out in the front yard mowing the grass. It was a risky move because a neighbor might complain about the use of power tools before eight. But since it was a weekday, I figured they were all up getting ready for work and probably wouldn't notice.

There was a limit to how many days of work I could miss, but I didn't want to leave Tiffany alone in the house all day. I'd been considering going to the doctor and telling him I couldn't sleep so I could get something to help her rest. I hadn't gotten much sleep either, although I'll admit, having her in the house with me had given me a lot more energy and a passion for my life, for wanting to drink the joy out of every minute. Because of that, I wasn't as tired as I should have been. Once she recognized how much I loved her, that I was her soul mate, we would spend hours cuddled up together, sleeping the night away.

When I turned off the mower, it was so quiet I could hear my heart beating inside my chest. The birds weren't even awake. I hadn't looked at the clock when I went out, so maybe it was earlier than I'd realized and my neighbors were not getting ready for work after all.

I turned. A white SUV was parked near the edge of the driveway. I knew immediately who it belonged to. The door opened, and Byron climbed out. Every organ in my body developed an instant layer of frost as if someone had injected dry ice into my veins. I gripped the handle of the mower and waited. I didn't want to assume anything and accidentally show my cards. He might be visiting everyone, conducting his own little investigation. The timing was odd though. The sky was completely dark except for the stars and a sliver of a moon. It had the same heavy blackness you'd expect at one o'clock in the morning, and maybe it wasn't much after that.

"Convenient that you're awake," he said.

"What's up?"

He walked up the driveway and opened the iron gate into the yard. He stepped onto the lawn. A snail crunched under his boot. It sounded like a warning. I wasn't feeling as confident as I had when I'd first recognized who it was. The mower ticked as the engine settled down. I let go of the mower, turned away from him, and walked to the edge of the porch.

"Where's Tiffany?" He spoke loudly, loud enough that he might be overheard if a neighbor was awake.

I laughed softly "Tough deal, isn't it? It's a bitch having your wife decide she wants out. But you adjust."

"My wife didn't decide anything."

"It's looking like she did. The detective didn't seem to have any likely suspects for abducting her. Except you, I guess." I laughed.

It was impossible to read his expression in the dark. He

started along the stepping-stones toward the porch. Then, he bent his head and rushed at me. I dodged him. I'm quicker than I look, despite my bulk. I guess football paid off after all. Even though I was nothing but a benchwarmer. I did more drills than any human being should have to. I knew how to feint and dodge and block and tackle, and that's what I did.

I lunged, angling my shoulder toward him, crouching slightly. I plowed forward and shoved my shoulder right into his solar plexus. He grunted and stumbled back. I planted my feet and battered into him again. He skidded and fell on his ass, and I laughed. The grass was wet and extremely slippery, which I knew from trying to mow the damn thing, but he hadn't thought that through. Stepping on the snail should have been a clue — they only come out when it's damp.

He heaved himself up, and I backed up closer to the house. The pruning shears were propped against the porch rail a foot or so to my right. He didn't see those, blinded by the pre-dawn darkness, and his certainty. I was curious as to how he'd figured out she was with me, but I didn't have time for a conversation. I heard a car turn down the street.

I reached out and grabbed one of the handles of the sheers. I hid them behind my leg and backed up the steps onto the porch. I turned slightly, opened the door, and stepped inside. I knew what I wanted, and I hoped he was crazy enough to come after me. We'd see who was the real man here. The one who deserved Tiffany. I was sure he hadn't noticed the pruning shears, but I didn't want to underestimate him.

Predictable as always, he charged up the steps, flung open the door, and stumbled into the foyer. He kicked the door closed behind him. The only light came from the kitchen. I backed toward the living room. I ducked around the doorframe and caught my breath. He yelled and raced into the living room. His feet hit that rag-tied rug, and he flew across the room like he was snowboarding. He lost his balance and fell hard on his back. The sound of his head on the wood floor was like a chunk of concrete. He cried out.

I dropped to my knees and straddled his pelvis. He thrashed and twisted, heels thumping the floor. He yelled, but the sound was weak because the air was still squeezed out of him from my first hit. "You bastard. Get off of me. You're nuts. You sick, weak bastard."

He was the one who sounded sick and weak. I raised the shears. The room was dark, so I don't think he saw what was coming. I plunged the long, sharp blades, snugly fitted over each other — like a man and a woman — into his chest. Blood sprayed out with such force I felt like I was taking a shower. A sharp, tinny voice at the back of my head whispered, how the hell are you going to clean up this mess? But it was too late, I'd have to figure that out later, so I turned my thoughts back to the task at hand. I pulled out the shears and stabbed him again, three times, just to be sure.

After a few minutes, the shower of blood stopped. There were some sounds coming from his throat, but he wasn't moving much. I sat back and waited and when the sounds stopped, and all movement had come to an end, I slid the shears out of his body. I had the urge to clip off his fingers and maybe remove his boots and socks and cut the toes as well, a sort of tribute to Tiffany's very sexy toes that were now all mine, forever.

There was still an hour or more before dawn. I had quite a bit of cleaning to do, and some packaging of his corpse, but like I said, I was filled with this new energy and enthusiasm. Having Tiffany by my side, living in my house, filling it with the kind of love it was always meant to have, had changed everything.

For some twisted reason, my mind flashed to posting a status update — *All in a day's work* — *killed my nemesis and now Tiffany is free to love me.* That sounded a bit dramatic and corny, so I'd have to work on it. And of course I wouldn't really post it, but my brain kept chewing on the idea, massaging the words, trying to find the perfectly clever comment that would make everyone excited for my new life. They'd be on my side, for once.

Then, it came to me. I pulled my phone out of my back pocket and started typing.

I heard a voice calling out in the front yard, followed by heavy footsteps up the stairs and across the porch. A fist pounded on the door.

Allie

ALLIE SINCLAIR *I can't find my damn phone, and it's making it hard to stay up to date. Chained to my computer.*
28 favorites — 5 comments

> **Kristen Thomas** *What about find my phone?*
> **Allie Sinclair** *Never activated it :(*
> **Megan Miller** *That sucks.*
> **Seth Porter** *Maybe it's time for an upgrade.*
> **Megan Miller** *If you have money to burn.*

I SCROLLED THROUGH the updates on FindOurTiffany. There were over twenty new comments, lots of memories of her, but still nothing from Byron. He posted a limp-sounding thank you on his own page but completely ignored FindOurTiffany. I was trying to understand how he must be feeling, but it was a little upsetting. I was trying to help him! He didn't realize that a few comments from him would rally people. Sure, everyone was behind him already, but hearing that he appreciated their support would be helpful. There's something about everyone acting together that has positive energy. Wasn't that what his church believed? All his friends were trying to be supportive, and he was ignoring them.

Commenting would have made him feel better too, taken him out of his own head.

I heard Marcus moving around downstairs, but I couldn't tell what he was up to. The sound of his footsteps going from room to room echoed through the house. It seemed as if he was looking for something or pacing. Maybe he'd forgotten where he hid my phone.

Two status updates appeared. One was from Dave. It sounded slightly deranged . . .

Dave Eddington *Started the day by wiping out the competition.*
1 favorites — 0 comments

His brother marked it a favorite. A private message popped up. I opened it.

Jake Ash *Bad shit going on. Why aren't you answering your phone?*
Allie Sinclair *What's wrong?*
Jake Ash *Pick up your phone.*
Allie Sinclair *I can't find it. What's going on?*
Jake Ash *Call me on your landline.*

I turned to the desk phone and realized I didn't know his number, it was programmed into my cell phone. I messaged back, and he sent his number. I called. "What's wrong?"

"Eddington killed Byron. Stabbed him with hedge trimmers."

"Oh my god! That's so awful. When?" I started to cry. "Why?"

"He had Tiffany. They found her in this tiny, unfinished room on the third floor. She was filthy but okay. Not beat up, or . . . anything . . ."

"Oh my god!"

"Byron went over there early this morning. I told him to sleep on it. Shit. I should have gone with him when he asked!"

"Oh my god. Oh my god. Where did you hear all this?"

"His brother called me. A cop had been watching Byron. He followed, but stayed too far back, or something, and didn't realize what was going on until it was too late."

The computer went to sleep. I moved the mouse and clicked over to Byron's page.

Byron Jones *Thanks everyone for your prayers, support, and faith. 371 favorites — 128 comments*

Then, my eyes filled up, and I couldn't see the screen. I wanted Marcus there, wanted him to hold me, but we were so far away from each other. All I had was the sound of his footsteps, thumping across my heart.

Jake's voice hummed in my ear. I half-listened to how Byron had tried to get Jake to go with him to talk to Dave, how Byron had been dead sure it was Dave who took her, how Dave was a sick guy, and he'd always been that way — an easy thing to say, after the fact. Mostly he went on about how he'd failed so many of his friends.

"Byron was a mess," Jake said. "He practically begged me to go with him, but I didn't want to be involved."

My hand was so tired I could hardly hold the phone. The screen was a blur, and my stomach was churning orange juice and yogurt up into my esophagus, pushing against the back of my throat, making waves through my whole body. I needed Marcus so bad. I wanted Jake to shut up. He couldn't stop blabbering on and on, explaining details and talking about death, and how meaningless life was, and now he had even more blood on his hands. Every other sentence he said — *It's my fault, my fault.* Finally, he said, "I need to make some serious changes in my life. Before it's too late."

"What does that mean?"

"I'm selling the house. I'm thinking of joining the Peace Corps."

"Where did *that* come from?"

"I don't want to be such a total waste of space. I mean, PR? What the hell kind of life is that? What does that do for the human race?"

"You don't have to do anything for the human race."

"See, that's the problem. We're so locked in our own bubble of getting what we want and keeping what we have and making sure we're happier than everyone else. Recording it all on social media with our self-effacing wit. What does that even mean?"

"You don't act like you're better than anyone."

While Jake berated himself, I scrolled through Dave's page. It was hard to concentrate on Jake's self-created crisis when I hadn't even absorbed what had happened. Dave had killed a human being! He'd murdered one of our friends! Although Dave was a friend too. A friend I hadn't known at all. It was too awful and too hard to believe. I kept expecting Jake to tell me he'd got it wrong, like in a dream when it's one thing and then the scene and all the stuff that's going on flips to something completely different, and you're not sure if the first thing even happened.

"Are you there?" he said.

"I should go tell Marcus."

"You're lucky. Marcus is a good guy, and you're a good woman."

"Oh barf," I said. Jake had no idea what a total jerk Marcus was being. "You and Amelia are good together too."

"I think we're done."

"No."

"Yeah. It took me a while to face it, but yeah."

I searched for Amelia's page. It was full of posts about the house and shopping, even after Kimberly drowned. I clicked to Jake's page. Nothing since July 18th. "You shouldn't make such a serious decision right now when you're so upset. You love her. You two are perfect together."

"Love. What does that mean?"

"I've seen how you look at her."

"Because she's exotic? Because she's hot? That's not love."

"No, but . . . does she know how you're feeling?"

"Don't care."

"Come on, Jake. Don't be like this."

"You sound like her."

"You're upset, and I can see why. But nothing is your fault. I mean, Kimberly was an accident, and Byron . . . how were you supposed to know Dave is messed up?" I heard a tapping sound. I looked up. Marcus stood in the doorway, holding the doorframe as if he needed it to keep from falling over. "I should go," I said. "Are you okay? Please don't do anything. Wait until you have time to think."

"Thinking is all I've done. My head has turned into a very scary place."

"You know if you join the Peace Corps or break up with Amelia or do anything . . . sell your house. All that stuff. Your head will still be there. You can't get rid of your head."

"I can put my head in a different environment though."

"You're rushing into major decisions." I clicked back to my news feed to figure out what had just happened. Megan had posted something dramatic about Byron, but the words blurred into each other like they were underwater. It was hard to read and hear Jake in my ear at the same time.

"I'm not rushing," he said.

"Please don't do anything crazy." Marcus stepped into the room. He folded his arms. I could feel him glaring at me. I had no idea what I'd done wrong now, but I didn't like his angry face. He should be loving me, showing me tenderness. He didn't even know about Byron yet. And Dave. That would wake him up, make him forget about all his social media prejudice.

"It's not crazy."

"When can we get together?" I said.

"I don't know. I guess at the memorial service."

Tears dribbled out the sides of my eyes. Now I definitely wouldn't be reading what Megan posted. Jake said goodbye, and as I pulled the receiver away from my ear, Marcus dropped to his knees. He reached under the desk and yanked the computer cord out of the electrical strip. The screen went dark.

I put the receiver down as gently as a baby in its cradle. "What are you doing?"

"Are you talking to your friend or surfing the web?"

"I wasn't surfing the web, I was checking . . ."

"I know what you were doing. What's wrong with you? Someone was murdered! You have to check it out on AboutFace? Are people actually writing comments? You're sick. You're all sick." He turned and walked out.

"Who told you?" I know he heard me, but all that echoed back were his heels thumping on the stairs. I pushed back the chair and hurried out of the room. He was on the bottom step. "Marcus. Don't be like this! I'm upset. It's terrible. More than terrible. How did you find out?"

Without turning he said, quite loudly, almost shouting,

which he never does, "I sure didn't find out on AboutFace. I actually talked to a human being."

"So did I! I was talking to Jake."

Any minute he'd turn around and look at me, and his face would change, and he'd be transformed back into my Marcus — my best friend, my lover, my husband. He'd realize he was being so stupid.

"Megan called my cell because you didn't answer your phone. She wanted to make sure we knew, and wanted to see if you were okay."

"Oh."

Marcus stepped onto the floor and walked around the staircase. All I saw was the back of his head, and his ears — red, as if he'd been sitting in the sun all afternoon.

I called after him. "Where are you going?"

He didn't answer. I couldn't hear where he'd gone. I ran down the stairs and around the corner into the living room. He wasn't there. I crossed the room and looked in the family room. The shutters were closed, and the light was dim, but I could see he wasn't there. I went back to the living room and glanced out at the patio. I didn't understand how he could have moved so fast. The sound of his car starting in the garage drifted into the house. I ran back to the hall and opened the garage door. He was already backing out.

"Wait! Where are you going?"

He didn't even look at me. He hit the remote, and the garage door closed between us.

Marcus

MY CAR FOUND its own way to the end of the street. I felt as if I'd watched myself leave Allie, observed myself as I heard her cry out.

Running away was immature, but I couldn't stop myself. She gave the impression she couldn't live without her social network, but she could do just fine without me. I was starting to think I didn't know her at all. I saw only a small part of her life. I had no idea what she did with herself when I was out of the house for days at a time. Tutoring took only twenty or thirty hours a week, sometimes less. She couldn't possibly swim all day long. Did she sit in the house typing status updates and comments for all those hours?

I turned the corner and headed toward downtown where all the cool restaurants and bars were waiting for me. What else was there to do?

It's the solution to mankind's pain — have a drink. I try to limit myself to a glass of wine or an occasional cocktail, but mostly wine, because Allie freaks out when I drink. She's not all that thrilled when I have wine either. But I like wine. Was I supposed to go the rest of my life, never enjoying nice wines, never joining our friends' celebrations because she was so angry with people drinking and driving? She carried it too far. People die in a lot of ways. They die in swimming pools, for example. Does that mean we should fill our pool with cement? I should ask her that, if I went back.

At that moment, I didn't feel like ever seeing her again. I felt like I was in a relationship with a high school girl. And maybe that was the problem. She never matured past high school. All this giggling over social media, status updates, pictures of food and girls all grinning with their arms around each other, hamming it up. We're adults. Was the four-year difference in our ages more significant than I'd realized?

I turned onto El Camino Real and headed toward a Tapas place where Allie and I ate once a month or so. They had an awesome wine list and a spectacular bar, but of course I'd never tried any of their nicer wines because I was only allowed one glass when I was driving, and even the single glass changed Allie's smile to something brittle. I couldn't drink a bottle all by myself, and Allie would never share it with me. She'd be upset if I even suggested it. I guess she planned to spend her life drinking orange juice.

Now, I'd have a nice meal by myself, read a book or some articles on my phone, and enjoy an entire bottle of wine. I'd earned it.

It took three loops around the block to find a parking spot, but finally, karma was with me — an SUV pulled away from a curbside spot that allowed three hours of free parking. I snuck right in behind him and turned off the engine.

Most of the tables at Federico's Tapas were surprisingly empty for a Friday afternoon. I found a place near the window, ordered a plate of Ceviche with shrimp and octopus, and a bottle of Stag's Leap Petite Sirah.

The room was filled with watery light. From the second story, an open eating area looked down on the first floor. The bar was at the center, a circular arrangement with liquor stacked up ten or twelve feet. I studied it for a while, as I always do, wondering how they reached the stuff at the top.

When the wine arrived, I settled back to enjoy the dramatic art of displaying the name and vintner, the sexy removal of the foil top, the slow extraction of the cork, sliding out like a tongue sliding out of a woman's mouth, and the silky liquid flowing into a gorgeous, long-stemmed glass with a magnificent bowl. I swirled the wine around the sides of the glass. I held the glass under my nostrils, not sniffing like some pompous ass trying to show his expertise, but just a gentle inhalation, again making me think of a woman, drinking in the scent of her skin and hair. I took a larger tasting sip than was expected but didn't give a shit if the server thought I was a Neanderthal. I needed that wine, and I needed more poured ASAP.

The food came, and the server refilled my glass. I ate slowly and deliberately, putting my phone aside so I could enjoy each bite.

When the plate was removed, I pushed my chair a few inches back from the table and looked out the window at the flow of people walking past. I took a sip of wine. When I looked up again, Allie's high school friend was standing right outside the window, as if he'd been watching me. Adam Jamison — the mysteriously self-supporting writer. The guy wrote fantastical novels, but I had the impression it was his wife's senior position at a networking company that secured their 3000-square foot house and their two luxury cars.

He opened the door and stepped inside. He blinked. He turned and saw me, seemingly for the first time. He allowed a partial smile to flit across his lips.

There were three other occupied tables along the window where I was seated, two groups of friends in booths along the adjacent wall, and four or five people at the bar. He obviously couldn't walk past me with a simple hello. The situation required a longer greeting. Especially with all that had happened since I'd last seen him.

He stepped closer to the table. "Hey, man." He had a small laptop bag slung over his shoulder, and it bumped the back of the chair across from me. "How're things?"

"Want to join me?" The unexpected and unusual consumption of wine must have disconnected my mouth from my brain.

He looked around. "Uh, sure." He made no move to pull out the chair.

"Are you meeting someone?" I said.

"No. I'm here to write. It's hard with three little kids in the house." He lifted his laptop bag as if to prove the point. "But I can have a glass of wine. If that's what you're offering." He stared at me with those dark, probing eyes.

"Absolutely."

He pulled out the chair and sat down with extreme care, as if he wanted to protect the laptop from any sudden, rough encounter with the table or the metal beam running along the window, dividing the large panes of glass. He put the bag on the table, then moved it to his lap.

I looked around for the server. It took him a few minutes to show up, and while we waited, Adam moved his laptop three more times. I guess he was feeling the pressure of so quickly abandoning his purpose.

We talked about Byron and Dave, and Tiffany and Kimberly. He mentioned his trip to the Grand Canyon. The server returned with another glass. In a crazed moment of excitement over a real human conversation, I ordered a second bottle of wine.

"I probably shouldn't drink too much when I'm trying to write."

"Then why did you come to a bar?"

"True." He laughed. "One or two drinks is fine, but I don't want to end up like Hemingway, so plastered I can't see the point in continuing my life."

"He did okay."

"Yeah, but it's a dangerous path."

I sipped my wine. Adam did the same.

"What are you working on?" I said.

"A novel."

"Well, no shit. What's it about?"

"Uh, it's always hard to explain. I mean, when it's still taking shape. I uh, it's about this guy who . . ."

"That's unique."

He laughed and took a rather large gulp of wine. It was a wine to be swallowed luxuriously, but maybe he didn't know that. He probably spent most of his time at the bar with a beer or a whiskey, giving his due to Hemingway, as he said.

I was being a prick, but the wine was making my tongue slack. Besides, this guy used to go out with Allie. A long time ago, sure, when they were kids, but still. All our conversations over the years had been superficial — sports or the latest manufactured crisis in the US economy. Of course, maybe most conversations are superficial. I lifted my glass and stared through the glowing red liquid at Adam's wavering image.

If ninety-nine percent of conversation is trite and meaningless, it isn't really that different from social media. I suppose putting it all in recorded form is what makes it so abhorrent.

"Okay. Okay." Adam took another quick sip of wine. "A guy who stalks this woman that he used to be in a relationship with."

I saw where that was going. Now, his hesitation was understandable, but it made the situation worse. If he'd plowed ahead, I might not have picked up so quickly on the obvious parallel. I smiled.

"Yeah, he stalks this woman, and they end up helping each other put the past to rest."

"Interesting. It doesn't sound like much of a plot."

"I don't explain it very well. My agent writes the synopsis. I can never describe my own work."

I poured a small amount of wine into both our glasses. I felt my head moving beyond the tongue-loosening phase. I was now experiencing the hyper-awareness of every thought, as though each word was typed on a screen, alongside the numb sense that I didn't really know what I was saying until the sounds appeared in the air around me. The wine was hitting me harder because I'd been such a light drinker since Allie and I got together. Three years of marriage plus one year engaged plus three years seeing each other before that. Quite a pattern, I'd never noticed that before. It could mean we were at a crossroads.

I forced my attention back to Adam's bony face. "How do you get your ideas?"

"My life, what I observe, but writing about them turns them into something different. So it's not as if it's autobiographical."

"Don't you think stalking's been overdone?"

"Maybe. But I think the idea is intriguing. It's obsession taken to the extreme. And obsession is universal, don't you think?"

"Definitely." I poured more wine, no longer caring how much I drank, no longer caring about Adam's poorly described novel. "So. Why'd you and Allie break up, anyway?"

"I'm sure she's told you."

"She hasn't. Not to disabuse you of your importance in her life, but we've never really talked about you. I knew you were together in high school and a few months during college, but that's about it."

He took another long swallow of wine. "It was after her mom was killed. Allie got kind of weird, or I couldn't make her happy, or something. Or maybe it was too much for me. The grief, and how she reacted. No matter what I did, or said, it was the wrong thing, I guess." He put his glass on the table and stared past me. "I don't really know why we broke up. We didn't really break up, it just . . . stopped."

"You aren't still into her, are you?"

"Oh, hell no. I look at her stuff on AboutFace, but we don't interact, even virtually, which is what gave me the stalking idea."

"AboutFace. The entity that will finally wipe out the human race. It won't be a nuclear explosion after all."

"The human race is more resilient than that."

"Is it?"

He didn't answer.

"So what was Allie like, after her mom died?"

"Obsessed. She was convinced the drunk driver would get a harsh sentence."

"Sometimes, I wonder if she ever got over it," I said, surprising myself. "She has different obsessions now — not drinking, for one." I wondered if I was betraying her, mentioning her flaws. Especially with Adam. But it wasn't as if I gave away a secret. Everyone knew she didn't drink. And right on its heels was that pettiness again — she betrayed me first, posting my anniversary note.

"It's understandable." Adam took a long swallow of wine, picked up the bottle, and topped off his glass. Quite bold of him. There wasn't a glimpse of awareness over the irony of saying it was understandable Allie didn't drink, yet drinking faster than he should. Especially if he planned to move to the bar and whip that story to life when he was finished drinking with me. Certainly, a drink was the price to be paid for the public work area. Maybe he'd abandoned his writing plans for the day.

"Nice that she's thinking of going back to school." He took another sip of wine. "Maybe it takes a long time to get past things, and now that it's been almost ten years, she's finally there."

"School?"

"Culinary school. You know. Those links she posted. And the food pictures. It was sad how she gave up on her dream after her mom died. Just kind of plodded through college as if it was something she was supposed to do. Like she was still in high school."

"Uh-huh." I felt sick. I poured more wine. What else was she posting that I knew nothing about? Every so often, I looked at her posts, but obviously, I'd missed some important ones.

"So why did you break up?"

"I told you."

"Details."

"It's ancient history. I feel kind of weird talking to you about it."

"Why? Are you sure you aren't still into her?"

"Not at all," he said.

Even though happy hour was approaching, the restaurant was emptying before the early evening crowd. I felt as if our voices and the clink of the glasses echoed off the huge windows, concrete floor, and exposed beamed ceiling, not much different from the interior of a warehouse. I felt as if our physical forms had shrunk, the space growing larger around us. The wine seemed darker, giving off a purplish tinge.

A desire to punch the guy rushed over me. It seemed he thought he owned my wife, that he could put her in his novel as if he had a right to mold her into what he wanted. It seemed that he owned a part of her from the past that I didn't. He'd known her mother, he'd seen Allie at that ugly, dark time. I was a stranger. I'd never know any of that. It began to feel, watching his face, as if she'd hidden most of her life from me. And she was still hiding it. There had to be a way to find out about this culinary school without exposing my utter ignorance.

"What do you think about her going to culinary school?" I said.

"I think it's great." He lifted his glass. "Cheers to the arts and all the artists."

"Is cooking art?"

"Hell yeah."

"I guess." Allie was certainly a master at it. Everything she fed me was indescribably good. Better than what I had in a lot of restaurants. Maybe she felt it was wasted on me. "She's already pretty good. I'm not sure why she needs to go to school."

"Well, if she wants to start her own catering company, she needs the credentials. And I'm sure, even if she's a great cook, there's a whole world of stuff to learn if you really want to turn it into a paying gig."

I pushed the wine bottle to the center of the table. I turned it so the label was facing Adam. Not that he'd get it, or figure out the price.

"Good wine," he said, taking a sip.

"Thanks. It's one of my favorites."

"I thought you didn't drink."

"Allie doesn't drink. And I support her, for the most part."

"Good guy. I remember that about her."

"What's that?"

"You have to be on her team. All or nothing."

He was right, and it pissed me off that he knew that about her. It pissed me off that he was a kid when they were together, and he acted like he also knew all about the adult version of her. *My* wife. Like he knew my wife as well as I did. Everything about him pissed me off. I hated that long stringy ponytail like he was some sort of *artiste*. He had no need to dress conventionally like the rest of us suckers who had real jobs with real pressures. He simply sat in bars and fabricated shit out of his imagination, turned his friends into stories, made money off his *obsessions*. I hated his tiny laptop that was like some sort of prop announcing he was a writer. I hated that he was happily drinking half of the hundred and forty bucks I spent on wine and not saying anything more appreciative than *good wine*.

"Don't you think? All or nothing?" He picked at the label on the bottle, although his fingernails were bitten so low, he couldn't really get it to peel away from the glass.

"She's not the same. You knew her ten years ago," I said.

"I still know her. I guess if you don't drink so that she can feel superior, that she won't ever do anything to ruin someone's life, she's made it clear you have to be on her team."

"Aren't all couples on each other's team?"

"Not like with Allie. That's probably why she kicked me out of her life. There was some secret rule about her mom dying that I was supposed to know about, some role I was supposed to play, and I didn't figure it out. So that was the end of it. She can be cold. Brrr." He wriggled his shoulders and shuddered as if he'd just opened a freezer door.

He was right about that, too. The rage seeped through my blood, knowing this character had more information about my wife than I did. He knew her personality, her rules, and her career plans. When was she planning to inform me? Was this some little game of hers to live two lives? If I refused to get on AboutFace, she was going to have a separate life there and completely cut me out of it? What was running through her head when she swam up and down the length of that pool, plowing through water, cutting herself off from me in a silent world where all she heard was her own breath and heartbeat? I swallowed more wine.

"But you have her figured out," Adam said.

"Is that right."

"You don't think you do?"

"Does anyone ever have another person figured out?"

"Methinks my mate is feeling a bit insecure." He grinned and opened his eyes wide, making his eyeballs bug out. He looked as whacked as he sounded.

"You keep talking like that, and I'll have to cut you off."

He took the wine bottle and poured a generous amount into his glass. He picked up the glass with one hand and pulled his rat tail over his shoulder with the other. He took a sip of wine. "Don't like hearing yourself called out?"

"No, I don't like hearing absurd language."

He laughed. "Just trying to keep things light."

"Well don't. And I don't feel insecure at all. I just don't presume to know every nuance of another human being."

"You don't know shit about her. You should try joining the rest of the human race and see what she's telling her friends."

"I was serious. Social media will destroy us." There was no

way I was going to ask Adam what she was posting. I wasn't sure if I didn't really know the guy before this or if he couldn't handle his alcohol. He sounded like he was trying to get under my skin. He sounded like he still had a thing for Allie.

"Oh, come on. Lighten up."

"What kind of statement is *friend me*?" I took a long swallow of wine. "It sounds like you're saying, fuck me."

Adam laughed, but he didn't really smile, sort of like he felt he was supposed to laugh, but his eyeballs quivered slightly as if I was scaring him. Well good. Maybe more people should be scared.

The wine was almost gone, and I wanted him out of there. I caught the server's eye and pulled out my wallet while he was walking toward the table. Before he could speak, I handed him my card. I picked up the bottle, poured the rest into my own glass, leaving Adam high and dry. I took a long swallow and waited for him to excuse himself.

He pushed back his chair. "Well, I don't feel like this conversation is quite over, but it looks like you've decided it is."

So he wasn't completely oblivious to social cues. "I think it's run its course. I'm really not going to sit here and gossip and analyze my wife with you."

"Even though you want to know what I know."

"You don't know shit."

"I know her life on social media, and you, dude, do not."

He slung the strap of his bag over his shoulder and sauntered over to the bar. He picked a chair with its back to me.

When I walked outside, the sun was too bright, hitting me like some kind of laser. I didn't know where to go. I was deeply unsettled about my marriage, and maybe about the whole world. I was outside of it, looking in, shouting, but no one could hear me through the thick glass.

ALLIE WAS GOING to be pissed that I was pissed. I laughed out loud as I pulled into the driveway. I knew I wasn't behaving normally, walking with a slight list, my tongue thick when I spoke out loud to myself, laughing with too much self-consciousness of what my laughter sounded like. I liked my double entendre — conceived spontaneously, which doesn't always happen. I wished I could have said it to someone else. Allie would not find it amusing. I wondered if Adam would have, but it was too late. Besides, I didn't want Adam knowing there was a brick wall between Allie and me. Coming home with too much wine pumping through my veins was not going to remove even a single brick in that ten-foot wall, but I had nowhere else to go.

She was swimming, of course. A glass of orange juice sat on the table near the chaise lounge. The outside of the glass was coated with moisture, so she'd been in the pool for a while. I watched her, gliding through the water like a seal undulates above and below the surface, barely a splash, her black one-piece suit adding to the seal effect, her hair like pale seaweed floating behind her. She hadn't braided it as she usually does. If it had been Amelia in my pool wearing a black suit, the seal image would have been complete.

How do we end up with one person or another? Why did Jake meet Amelia and I met Allie? Was it just timing? Not that I was wanting Amelia, I'd never even considered it, but suddenly, mating seemed so random. If I'd met someone else at that stage in my life, if Allie had gone to a different college, if her mother hadn't died and altered the timeline of her life, would I have fallen equally in love with another woman? What if Jake hadn't gone to high school with Allie and they'd met later when both of them were single, would they have hooked up? What if her mother hadn't died and she'd stayed with Adam. Would she have married her high school sweetheart?

Despite her graceful moves, I could feel the anger pursuing her through the water. She hated me for trying to keep her from her so-called friends, even though I hadn't done any such thing. She had the computer. As if her friends lived inside her smartphone and without it, all her relationships dissolved into nothing.

I glanced back at the sliding glass door. If I made it up to the shower before she saw me, and took a good long one, she might not notice I was somewhat drunk. Although maybe I wanted her to notice. Let her get pissed off. I felt good, and I really didn't want to get wet and lather it all away. Unlike her, I don't get off on being constantly soaked with water.

She reached the shallow end of the pool, and without warning, grabbed the lip of the concrete and pulled herself out of the water, flipping around so she was seated on the edge, her lower legs still submerged. She looked in my direction and squinted. She yanked her legs out of the water, stood, and walked toward me, her hair clinging to her shoulders and arms like a second skin.

"You look different," she said.

I shoved my hands in my pockets and glanced at my feet, buying a few seconds while I tried to decide if it was worth it, or even possible, to hide my inebriated state. I decided it was not, so I didn't try to move away from her. "I ran into Adam."

She wrinkled her nose. "Did you have a drink? You smell like alcohol."

"Not alcohol. Wine." I grinned foolishly, knowing it didn't fit the situation and didn't even really fit my mood. I don't know why I did it.

She glowered. "Wine is alcohol."

"Yeah, I know. Just wanted to be clear."

"Are you drunk?" She stepped closer. She sniffed at me, then reached out and shoved me with the palm of her hand.

I stumbled sideways and grinned more.

"What the hell is wrong with you?" She grabbed her towel off the chaise lounge, wrapped it around her middle like a strapless dress, and walked to the door. She flung it open and stepped inside.

"You'll get water on the floor," I said.

She slammed the door and disappeared from sight.

I wasn't sure what to do. Part of me wanted to strangle her. Seriously. I wanted to wrap my hands around her neck and shake her until she stopped being so self-righteous, so clueless, so . . . so herself.

I picked up the orange juice, pinching carefully to prevent the slick glass from sliding through my fingers. I went into the kitchen and poured it down the drain. I looked out at the deserted street in front of the house, the Prius parked not quite straight in the driveway. I don't know why I hadn't pulled into the garage. Maybe I was afraid I was so unsteady I'd scrape the side of her car.

I had no idea what to do. The desire to grab her neck had subsided when the juice went down the drain. I turned on the water and hosed away the bits of pulp and ran the water until there wasn't a trace of orange anywhere.

I looked up. She was standing in the doorway. She wore a loose, sleeveless black top that drifted around her like a small tent. She had on black leggings, and her hair was still wet, combed back from her face and tied tight at the back. It looked colorless as if she had no hair at all. Her eyes were red. "How could you do that to me?"

"I didn't do anything to you."

"You got drunk and drove a car."

"It happens every day."

"And people die every day."

"I didn't kill your mother, Allie."

"You could have." I expected her to cry. I expected her to rush across the kitchen floor and rake her fingernails across my face. But she stood there with her arms hanging limp, her face like a gargoyle, with all the tears and rage she was holding inside.

"I'm not responsible for her death. Every person who has a drink is not responsible for her death."

"Drunk drivers kill innocent people. They destroy lives. I can't live with a drunk driver."

"So, you're telling me it's over between us?"

"If that's what you want. You sure act like you don't care. You know how important it is to me. Not drinking and driving."

"I had a few glasses of wine."

"You're drunk."

"I have a good reason to be drunk. My wife tells the whole world what she's doing but doesn't bother to tell me."

"I thought it was sweet. I wanted everyone to know how much you love me."

"Why do they have to know that?" I leaned on the counter. The wine was forming a film over my brain. I felt lightheaded and not sure if I meant what I was saying. I'm not like her. Or her friends. I don't have quick wit and repartee that I can fling out without taking time to consider what I'm saying. It's not that I'm stupid. I'm deliberate, and maybe that's not very valuable to most of the world. Although they certainly value it in the guys who carry them around the globe at thirty-nine thousand feet above the surface of the earth.

"It's important to share your life with your friends. That's what relationships are. Sharing what's happening, cheering each other on."

"I don't think I need a cheerleader for my marriage."

"That's not what I meant."

"Well, the flowers aren't what I meant."

"What you wrote on the card?"

"No. I meant your plans. For school."

She stared at me. Her body swayed slightly. I expected her to grab onto the doorframe, but her arms continued to hang limply as if all that swimming had exhausted them and she no longer had the ability to lift them from her side.

"Culinary school?"

"Oh. That."

"Why didn't you tell me?"

"If you were on AboutFace, you'd know."

"So, I don't get to know anything about your life now? It's only available in a news feed?"

She shrugged. "Don't make it something big. You weren't there when I was thinking about it, I posted a link, and we never had a chance to talk about it."

"We don't have a chance to talk because you're never really in the room with me."

"Well, you're always flying somewhere."

"It's my job."

Her eyes were killing me. I hated her, but I loved her. I hated her social media and her rules about drinking and her utter lack of understanding for how stupid they all sounded with their status updates and their favorites. One long parade of people bragging about their lives. But I did love her, and I could feel, from her limp body and her watery, vacant eyes, that we weren't headed in a good direction. "I'm sorry I drank too much."

"And drove," she whispered.

"I know." I stepped around the counter. "I'm sorry. It won't happen again."

"It's important to me."

"I know that too, but I can't bring back your mother by not ever driving after a few glasses of wine."

"But you don't have to kill someone else. You don't have to kill yourself." She turned and disappeared from the doorway as if she'd evaporated.

Tiffany

TIFFANY JONES *IT'S the saddest day of my life. Paul touched one of my tears and then wiped it on his own cheek. That made me cry harder.*

275 favorites — 120 comments

Kristen Thomas *So sorry for your loss.*
Pam Jamison *We're thinking of you.*
Seth Porter *Stay strong.*
Adam Jamison *We're all hurting with you, thinking of you.*
Allie Sinclair *Let us know what we can do. Anything!*
[See 115 more comments]

EVERYTHING IN THE church looked pale. The dusty rose carpet, the pinewood railing around the raised platform at the front, and the twenty-foot cross. The hundreds of wooden chairs fanned out around the raised platform, mirrored the pine at the front. Even the eucalyptus trees standing outside the narrow windows on either side of the cross were beige, the leaves drained of color. I'm not sure why the paleness struck me. Every Sunday, I'd looked at those same things and never considered the lack of color.

I took my seat in the front row, facing Byron's coffin. It

was dark grained walnut, but so glossy it looked like plastic trying to pretend it was wood. My parents were to my left, my mother holding Ruth, who was sleeping with her head on my mother's shoulder. My mother would take Ruth outside if she got fussy. Paul was on my lap, but there was an empty chair between my mother and me, waiting for him if he managed to let go of me.

All of us looked as pale as the wood, our faces blanched, our eyes and noses drained of liquid after so many tears. Even my father cried once. Paul sobbed, not really understanding. Mostly I was numb and hoping I'd make it through.

The music started a minute or two after I sat down. Maybe it wasn't that fast, but I wasn't sure. My thoughts raced like pinballs at times and drifted like dandelion fluff at others, so I wasn't really sure how long it had been. It wasn't as if I had my phone out, checking the time, looking at status updates like I normally would while I waited for a church service to start.

As much as I hated Dave, some of the things he'd said wouldn't leave me alone. I'd never really thought about how people reacted to my status updates. I thought I was sharing my blessings, being grateful, telling my friends about the Lord, doing what I was put on earth to do — spread the good news. I'd also been put on the earth to love my husband, and I was a total failure at that. I resisted his needs. I didn't love him completely, and now it was too late. Forever too late. I started to cry. My mother reached across the empty chair and patted my arm. Her fingers were damp, the tips sticking to my skin like tentacles. I wanted to pry them off of me. Luckily Pastor Eric stood up and started talking.

After he finished thanking everyone for coming, and talking about the tragedy of losing Byron, two women from church sang a beautiful song. I forgot the words the minute they returned to their seats. The pastor stood up again and talked about Philippians 4:8, which was Byron's favorite Bible verse. He was always going on about how we should only think about the good things in life.

Pastor Eric praised Byron for being so godly, for being a wonderful father, and a devoted husband. When he said that, my thoughts spun back in a different direction — how he wouldn't listen to me. I asked him to change that one little thing, which would have made all the difference in the world. Instead, he called me *Mommy* in front of other people. I was so humiliated, I walked away from everyone. If I hadn't done that . . . and now it was too late. Why did he have to *be* like that?! Why couldn't he think about how I felt, why couldn't he understand that his words were like spiders crawling up my legs?

Of course Pastor Eric thought Byron was a devoted husband. What did he know? Then, I felt bad for having such terrible thoughts. I started to cry again. He was gone. Forever. Forever. Forever. I'd never see his face, never touch him again. He was inside that box, and he couldn't hear a word we were saying. He felt nothing. So what if he had one little flaw? We all have flaws, things we refuse to change.

A woman played Amazing Grace on the harp. Pastor Eric stood with his head turned, watching her. I had the feeling he wanted to be the strings of the harp. I wondered if anyone else noticed. I looked at my mother. She was staring at Ruth. I glanced to my right. Everyone had their heads turned toward the harpist, a thin woman with short blonde hair and no makeup — that paleness, again. I wanted Pastor Eric to stop whatever nasty thoughts he was having, to think about Byron. To stop gazing at those long, thin fingers with the short, perfectly oval nails, as pale as the dusty rose carpet.

Then our friends, Byron's friends, really, began to take turns speaking about him. So much perfection. I closed my eyes for a few minutes, then opened them to watch Jake. His eyes were surrounded by shadows so that it looked as if he'd been punched in both eyes.

"I know I'm here to talk about Byron, but he didn't live and die in a vacuum, and two soul-destroying things have happened these past few weeks. It started with Kimberly's death and ended with Byron's murder. What I want to say is simple." He reached into his pocket and pulled out something small that I couldn't see. He held it up — a box of matches. He slid it open and pulled out a match. He raked the matchstick along the side of the box, and a flame burst out from the tip. He blew on the flame, and the matchstick went dark. "That's life. Burning for a moment. Gone. Don't waste it. I did, and now I have a chance to change that. Kimberly didn't have that chance. Tiffany almost didn't. Byron didn't." He straightened his shoulders. "Do. Not. Waste it."

He walked down the three wide steps off the platform and passed in front of me. He didn't look at me, didn't pause to touch my hand or smile. It felt like I didn't matter. All that was important was his little show. He might think he was completely changed, no longer wasting his life, whatever that meant, but to me, he sounded exactly the same — commanding and full of drama and more important than everyone else. This was supposed to be about Byron! Not Kimberly, and surely not about Jake's act with the match. I was glad he was finished. What he said had nothing to do with Byron and sounded like one of his *I-know-the-secret-to-a-perfect-life-and-you-don't* status updates.

Megan walked to the podium next. She wore a white dress and dark brown sandals. Her crazy, curly hair was wrapped up in a fat bun, so she didn't look like herself at all. She tipped the microphone close to her face, blocking her mouth and nose from view. She talked about how long she'd known Byron, what a kind person he was, how she loved watching him with his children. She said he was a hero for confronting Dave and saving me. I'm not sure why, but somehow, she made me feel like it was my fault he was dead.

"There are a lot of us who have been friends since elementary school," she said. "Our whole lives, almost. It's hard to find out that someone you thought you knew was actually a total stranger. A monster."

I shifted Paul onto his own chair. I hoped she changed what she was talking about very soon. I did not want to hear Dave's name mentioned or one word about him, even though he kept inserting himself into my thoughts — that harsh, frog-like whisper when I didn't know who he was, and then the long, long explanations of how he felt and what he needed and how unfair everything was.

"Byron was an amazing man," Megan said. "He was kind and so devoted to his little family. And . . ." She moved her head away from the microphone so we could see her smile. "He made awesome potato salad."

There was a gentle wave of laughter. It sounded canned as if they knew she wanted to lighten the atmosphere but realized there was nothing that could accomplish that ridiculous goal. I was glad. I secretly thanked every person behind me, people I couldn't see and would never know who they were, who gave out those phony laughs, reminding Megan she didn't know him all that well if the only thing she could think of was potato salad. I knew I was being uncharitable, but another small part of me thought that was a good place to be because it was keeping me from collapsing in a lake of tears. My lips were firmly in place, not wobbling all over as they'd done for days, even when I wasn't crying, and was just trying to eat or talk.

A few people from church spoke, and most of his childhood friends. Even Adam Jamison talked about how he respected Byron. He was followed by Seth, Kristen, and then Marcus.

"We all stand here and talk about Byron's good points," Marcus said. "But no guy is perfect."

There was the suggestion of a sigh from the crowd, and I worried, for half a second, he was going to say something bad about Byron, but I shouldn't have worried.

"Despite all his imperfections, the ones we know about, and the ones only Tiffany knows about, because after all, it's your spouse who knows it all, and loves you anyway . . ."

My eyes filled with tears. I blinked hard.

"Like Jake reminded us, life is short. But it's also long, and it can be confusing and complicated and not what we'd hoped. But Byron made the most of his life, and that's why there are so many good things to say about him. I'm sure none of us can imagine how it is for Tiffany, and how it will be for Paul and Ruth."

I gulped when he said that, reminded for the millionth time that she would never know her Daddy and Paul would have only a vague memory.

"Above everything else, with his flawed and heroic humanness, he loved Tiffany, and he loved his kids. What we all saw in his devotion to the deli, was that he loved people. He knew people are what life's about." He closed his eyes. "Thank you, Byron, for reminding us."

I worried Pastor Eric would think it was blasphemous, what Marcus did, closing his eyes and saying thank you as if he were praying to Byron.

Even though he was the one who'd known Byron the shortest amount of time, Marcus sounded more genuine than the others. Maybe because he wasn't always spouting off on AboutFace, maybe because I don't talk to him all that much. In fact, I don't think I've ever talked to him without Allie standing there mostly controlling the conversation. He stayed behind the podium for several seconds longer than normal, looking at me and Paul and Ruth.

Allie spoke next. Her voice was a whisper. "I don't know what to say, except this: He was my friend."

That was all she said. Allie, who usually has plenty to say. She gave me a kind and tender smile as she walked back to her seat beside Marcus — something I would never do again. I'd never sit by my husband, never lean on him for comfort, never feel him squeeze my hand to let me know he was there. I gasped and swallowed, and then, thankfully, the numbness returned.

After Pastor Eric spoke some more and prayed, the music started up — a song by Britt Nicole. The eulogies echoed in my mind like a bunch of audio status updates. I looked away from the coffin. I stood, took Ruth from my mother, and walked down the side aisle. My parents and Paul followed. I kept my eyes on Ruth's face so I couldn't see the faces of Byron's parents and friends, my other relatives, and all our friends from church. There were hundreds.

The reception was a blur of people touching my shoulder,

hugging me, crying, saying things I can't remember, but were mostly about how they were so sorry for me and how great Byron was and they were sorry for the kids and they were praying for me and let them know if they could help and how unjust it was but they knew God had a plan. I hoped so. At that moment, His plan seemed really messed up.

I took one bite of a tiny tuna sandwich made with triangles of white bread. It tasted funny. I put the sandwich on a napkin, wrapped it up, squished it, and gave it to my mother to throw away. I drank two glasses of coke. The casseroles smelled greasy, and the trays of cold cuts nauseated me with their red and brown and white flesh flapping about on platters.

After a while, everyone was making me feel tired and bored. I handed both kids off to my mom, who was treating me like a queen.

I wandered outside and around to the garden between the worship building and the church offices. It wasn't much of a garden — just a rectangular patch of grass surrounded by agapanthus — but it was soothing and surprisingly deserted. I guess everyone was more attracted to food after death than they were to nature. There was a bench at each end. The benches were close enough to the covered walkways that one was in the shade. I went over and sat down. The concrete was cold through my rayon dress. It was so cold it felt wet, but I knew it wasn't — I'd looked at it before I sat, and the surface was whitish-gray without a drop of water.

I closed my eyes. The grass smelled clean. Beneath that, there was a hint of damp earth, the same things I smelled before Dave did whatever he did to make me unconscious.

"Do you want to be alone?"

I opened my eyes. Allie stood a few feet away. It scared me that she'd been able to walk up that close without me noticing.

"I didn't mean to scare you," she said.

"It's okay." I gave her the best smile I could manage until my lips began to tremble and I had to let the smile slide away.

She sat next to me. Thankfully, she didn't put her hand on me to try to soothe me. I'd had enough of that. There was no soothing available, and the constant touching was as bad as the kids, always pawing at me. It was funny how five days ago, I would have given my life to feel them grabbing at me, and now, already, I sometimes needed a break from all the touching. "Thanks for what you said."

She nodded.

"And Marcus. You two were the best. I shouldn't say that, shouldn't compare, but it's true. It's like you know how it feels to suffer."

I heard her breath catch in her throat. She straightened her shoulders. After a few minutes, she said, "You probably don't want to talk about Dave."

"It's okay." I was glad she asked. If she'd launched in, I would have been angry. And really, I had a lot of him on my mind, and there'd been enough talk of Byron. Besides, if I talked about Byron, I'd start crying, and then she'd touch me. So Dave was a fine topic of conversation.

"I never had a clue he was so messed up," Allie said.

"Me neither."

"I guess none of us did. Were you scared?"

"Before I knew who it was, yes. I was terrified. The hard part, the horrible part is, I spent the whole time worrying about me and how Byron and the kids were doing without me, I never once thought something like this would happen." My voice got softer as I spoke and with the last few words, I wondered if she'd heard me, but I suppose she didn't have to hear the specific words.

"I'm sure it was hard having Sara leave him, but oh my god!" Allie said.

I folded my hands in my lap and pressed them against my legs, making a little nest out of my skirt, looking at my wedding ring and my diamond. It was small compared to Allie's, but it was the one Byron picked out for me. I rubbed the stone.

"What was he thinking?" she said. "I guess he's sick."

"Yeah, he is that. He saw all these things on AboutFace and was completely obsessed with what everyone else had, instead of being grateful."

Allie nodded. "What was he obsessed with?"

"I guess it hurt his feelings that we posted pictures and talked about the good things in our lives."

"What does he expect? That's what friends do." Allie

turned her head so I couldn't see her face. I couldn't figure out what she was looking at. There was nothing but the covered corridor running alongside the building.

"I guess if you don't have what you want, and you're a jealous-type person, it might be hard seeing everyone else being happy," I said.

"You should be happy for your friends, not jealous," Allie said.

"I agree." Even as I said it, I could imagine how it would be for the rest of my life — looking at pictures of families together, couples holding each other, and seeing the great big hole in my family.

Allie

ALLIE SINCLAIR *MISSING my friends who are shining down from heaven, giving light to my life like stars in the sky.*
112 favorites — 64 comments

Kristen Thomas *Beautifully said.*
Pam Jamison *Life can be so senseless.*
Megan Miller *It makes you think.*
Seth Porter *You should be a poet, Allie.*
Adam Jamison *Her cooking is her poetry.*
[*See 59 more comments*]

THE HOUSE WAS shadowy and silent, the kind of silence given off when no one has been there for a while, everything is in order, and the drapes and shutters and blinds are all shut tight. There aren't any smells or a definitive air temperature because it's been unoccupied for so long, like a sealed box.

Marcus followed me inside and closed the door behind us. The click of the latch echoed through the hallway, bouncing off the tile, and rising up the stairs. The click made me think it might be the last sound I ever heard. A door closing, the lid on a coffin snapped shut to prevent anyone from seeing your body as it fell apart, limb by limb, the skin decomposing, revealing each rotted organ. My stomach heaved, and I hurried into the kitchen to distract myself.

My phone was in my purse. Without saying a word about it, Marcus had left it on the dining room table that morning. I saw it right before we left for Byron's funeral. I didn't take it out of my purse. I was pretty sure most of my friends had not made any status updates. Of course, my other friends — people from college, friends we'd met on vacations, extended family — they were all still making updates and posting pictures, but I decided a small break from the activities of their lives might not be a bad thing for me.

The night before, I'd deleted the FindOurTiffany page. That page seemed awful to me now, as if I'd focused on the wrong thing. She'd been *found*, but the page had nothing to do with it. I wondered if Dave had visited the page, scrolled through the posts, drooled over the photographs. I'm sure he did.

My purse sounded like a bag of wet cement as it thudded on the kitchen table. I went to the fridge and took out a bottle of OJ. "Do you want anything?" I had to raise my voice to ask because Marcus remained in the front hall as if he had no idea where to go. And I guess I didn't either.

He stepped into the doorway. "Sure." He smiled, but it looked planned and somewhat uncertain, as if he wasn't sure how to look at me, his own wife.

I filled two large glasses with juice, put the bottle in the fridge, and closed the door. I picked up the glasses and stood with one in each hand. Should we sit at the kitchen table? In the dining room? Living room? Walk through the living room and out to the back patio? "Where should we sit?"

He looked at me as if I'd asked him where he'd hidden a million dollars.

"Wherever."

I turned and went into the living room. Marcus followed. I stopped in front of the back door. "Will you open this?"

He hurried across the room and stepped around me. He unlocked the door and slid it open. We went outside, and he closed the screen door. I set the glasses on the table, and we each pulled out a chair. I felt we were performing an elaborate dance, like those birds that hop around madly, puffing themselves up. They bow and fan out their tail feathers, eyeing the other bird, waiting for a first move, wanting to have the most graceful dance, and not sure how it's being accepted by the other.

I took a sip of juice.

"I'm sorry I hid your phone," he said. "If you have to have your social media, I'm not going to stop you."

"Why don't you set up a page?"

"Because I like to talk to people face to face. Because I don't want to live my life in a series of virtual sticky notes that might not even get read by the people I care about the most. Because I don't want the events of my life to be reduced to a bunch of limp, obligatory comments, and little red stars. Because . . ."

"Okay, I get it." I drank some juice.

"I wish I could make you understand," he said softly.

"I understand." Thinking about Byron and Kimberly, Tiffany unlocking her door, going into a house that was far emptier than ours . . . I didn't want to fight with him. I wanted things to be good between us. But he wouldn't stop being stupid.

"I don't think you do understand. You don't see how it is when you're caught up in it. I look around the room at a party, and half the guests have their heads down over their phones. I sit in a restaurant and see couples dressed up with glasses of nice wine standing in front of them and a candle lighting their faces and they aren't even looking at each other. They're spending two hundred bucks to sit in public and do something they could do on the living room couch. They could live in a basement with nothing but a hide-a-bed and a fridge, and it wouldn't be any different."

"That's not true. You exaggerate everything."

"Everything?"

"Well, that."

"I don't think so."

"Maybe if you tried it," I said.

"I'm not going to keep having this conversation."

"I'm tired of it too," I said.

"It's upsetting that you posted about going to cooking school and you didn't tell me."

"Where did you hear that anyway?"

"Adam. I ran into him when I was . . ."

"When you were getting drunk."

"I didn't plan to. You make it sound like I did it on purpose."

"Didn't you?"

"I can't bring back your mother."

"I know that."

"It seems like I have to follow these rules because you haven't gotten over her dying."

"You don't get over someone dying."

"Sorry. That's not what I meant."

"And drinking and driving is illegal, in case you didn't know."

"Okay, I was wrong. I shouldn't have done that. But I can't ever have a glass of wine without getting judgmental looks and a lecture?"

"I don't make you follow rules."

"I like wine."

"Okay. I don't care if you have a glass of wine. I just don't like it. And I don't like drunk people."

"Actually, neither do I," he said.

I smiled.

"Anyway, about cooking school, what are you going to do? Live a separate life on AboutFace and completely cut me out of it?"

"No. Why would you think that?"

"Because you're thinking about school and I didn't know

anything about it . . . and other stuff you post. He made it sound like you post a lot of information about your life that you don't tell me."

"No I don't."

"Adam said . . ."

"Why would you believe him?"

"He used to know you, he was . . ."

"*Used* to."

After a few minutes, he said, "It seems like you wouldn't even notice if I was gone."

Something squeezed my heart, wringing it out like a sopping wet sponge. For half a second, I couldn't get my lungs to take in air. A high-pitched tone pierced my left ear. The plants and the trees and the swimming pool grew darker, and I couldn't clearly see his face. "You're gone a lot."

"I know."

"It's how I stay in touch."

"But do you have to stay in touch when I'm home? It really seems like it doesn't matter if I'm in the room, if I'm even in the house."

I took a sip of juice. "So, you don't want to be married to me because of social media?"

"That's not what I said."

"Then what is it?" Part of my heart softened, but it still hurt, as if I'd been bruised and it would take a very long time for the ache to subside, knowing he could even think something like that.

He reached across the table and touched the back of my hand. "I don't want to feel like there's a whole bunch of other people in the room every time I'm with you. I don't want to compete."

"It's not a competition. They're my friends! They're your friends, too. I thought."

"What if you just tried not connecting every single minute?"

"What, like schedule office hours?"

"Sure."

I stood up. I went inside the house and got my phone out of my purse. I walked back outside and handed it to him. "Fine. Take it back. I'll disconnect from the whole world just like you. And when you're flying, I'll curl up in the bedroom and cease to exist for three or four days."

"That's not what I want." He handed the phone back to me.

"Well, what do you want?" I put my phone on the table.

His eyelids fluttered. He looked away from me. "I want you to live in the real world."

"This," I tapped my phone, "Is the real world. Wake up."

"The human race is disintegrating into a bunch of isolated people who do nothing but advertise and promote themselves. It's sickening. And it's scary."

"Don't be dramatic."

"Look at Dave," he said.

"What about him?" I sat down and gulped the rest of my juice.

"AboutFace destroyed him. If he'd actually talked to his friends, maybe he wouldn't have lost his mind."

"We'll turn into killers if we use social media? You don't use it, and you could have killed someone — getting drunk and driving home like that."

He picked up my phone and pressed the home button. Our wedding picture, the same one that was on the mantle, appeared on the screen. He tipped the phone slightly. Sunlight hit the screen, and all I could see was the shimmering glass, the image wiped out. He studied it as if he was trying to figure out whether he knew the people in the picture. He pressed the phone against his chest and turned to look at me. Then he put it back on the table. "Did you post that I got drunk?"

"No."

"Why not?"

"What kind of person do you think I am?"

"Did you tell anyone?"

"I talked to Jake a little, at the funeral."

"Why didn't you post about it? Did you post that I took your phone? Unplugged the computer while you were looking at it?"

"Of course not."

"Why?"

"Isn't that obvious?"

He got up and came around the table and stood facing me. "Don't you see how fake that is?"

"I don't want the whole world to know we're fighting."

"Neither do I." He knelt and put his hands on my knees. "If you put something real on there, if Tiffany posts about her grief — what it's really like sleeping in her bed all alone — or Adam admits he sort of stalks you, hundreds of people see it."

"Not always."

"But they could. Everything you don't say is one more piece of not being real. You're constructing a fake life, and the life you do have doesn't have any boundaries. You blast the same information to your closest friends and to the people you haven't seen for three or four years."

I didn't want to admit that I saw his point. I couldn't live like him, with a phone that does nothing but send text messages and make calls. I couldn't live without knowing what was happening. It would be like cutting myself off from the news, the whole world, really. Like that guy in Maine who walked into the woods when he was nineteen and didn't talk to another human being for twenty-seven years.

Of course it's phony. All social life is filtered. If Tiffany wears a dress that makes her look like she's twelve, I'm not going to tell her that. And she's not going to walk into a party and tell everyone she sleeps on the couch because she can't bear the thought of getting into their bed that's still covered with Byron's skin cells.

"I feel like you want me to choose between you and my friends."

"No. But if you can't be with just me, then I don't see the point."

"Are you saying you'd leave me?"

"I don't know what I'm saying." He took his hands off my legs and stood. He sighed very quietly. "I love you."

I stood up and wrapped my arms around his waist. I put my mouth close to his ear. "You haven't said that in a long time."

We held each other loosely, not squeezing any tighter, for quite a long time. When he let go of me, I took my phone back inside the house and put it on the dining room table.

We went out to dinner and talked about the funeral and Dave and Jake. I had pan-fried sole with garlic mashed potatoes, and Marcus had a steak. When he cut it, the blood ran into his fries. Usually, when we go out, he has a glass of wine, but he ordered iced tea and drank two refills. After dinner, we walked around downtown, listening to torn pieces of conversation from the people walking by. There were a lot of people walking and looking at their phones. Suddenly, they seemed to be everywhere — teenagers and grandparents, people our age, even a few little kids.

Back at home, we went upstairs without speaking. We took off our clothes and got into bed. We made love very gently. I tried not to think about Tiffany being alone. I tried not to think about how suddenly Marcus could die in a plane crash.

We fell asleep wrapped around each other.

At one-forty a.m. I woke. Marcus had turned on his side, facing away from me. I listened to him breathe for a while, but my body and brain felt like they were swimming in the ocean, trying to find sleep, but every time I poked my head out of the water, it was just as far away. Finally, I got up. I put on my robe and went downstairs. I picked up my phone and went into the family room. I opened AboutFace. There were thirty-seven notifications of new posts.

Megan Miller *Feeling very mellow tonight — death is part of life. I'm happy that I can provide healing through the miracle of touch.*

52 favorites — 22 comments

Seth Porter *If anyone needs excellent childcare, I'm thinking of you, Tiffany, Lori's decided to start a home daycare. She can bring in a little cash and still be around for Michael and his future siblings. ;)*

27 favorites — 20 comments

Tiffany Jones *Sometimes real flesh and blood human beings help more than God. He seems so far away right now. I'm not sure what He wants from me anymore.*

275 favorites — 143 comments

Kristen Thomas *You can see the face of god in each member of the human race.*

94 favorites — 31 comments

Adam Jamison *Make peace with the past. Otherwise, we lose our minds.*

118 favorites — 37 comments

Pam Jamison *Adam is too shy to say this, but he has a book signing next Tuesday at Main Street Books. Hope you can come.*

47 favorites — 11 comments

Dave Eddington *Guess you won't be hearing from me for a while. My lawyer let me make a comment here, but this is goodbye.*

1 favorite — 0 comments

Amelia Loc *Spread the word — there's a beautiful custom home for sale in the foothills. Time for a new chapter.*

180 favorites — 52 comments

[29 new updates]

WHEN I WAS FINISHED reading everyone's updates, I posted my own status.

Allie Sinclair *To each and every one of my friends — you are my life. I'm honored to know you and call you my friend.*

I put the phone back in the exact same spot on the table and went upstairs. I took off my robe and slipped into bed. Marcus rolled onto his back, and I put my head on his chest and closed my eyes. For a few minutes, the posts and photographs scrolled behind my eyelids, but pretty soon, they were covered with the distorted, senseless, fantastical images that come before sleep.

About The Author

CATHRYN GRANT IS the author of Suburban Noir novels, ghost story novellas, and short fiction. Her writing has been described as "making the mundane menacing".

Cathryn's short fiction has appeared in Alfred Hitchcock and Ellery Queen Mystery Magazines, and anthologized in The Best of Every Day Fiction. Her short story, "I Was Young Once" received an honorable mention in the 2007 Zoetrope All-story Short Fiction contest.

When she's not writing, Cathryn reads fiction, eavesdrops, and plays very high handicap golf. She lives on the Central California coast with her husband and two cats. Contact Cathryn through her website at CathrynGrant.com or sign up for her quarterly newsletter to receive updates when new books are released at CathrynGrant.com/contact.

www.ingramcontent.com/pod-product-compliance
Lightning Source LLC
Chambersburg PA
CBHW022234020726
47496CB00004B/898